Rogue's Call
Book Three
The King's Riders Series

Rogue's Call

Book Three
of
The King's Riders

C. A. Szarek

Paper Dragon
Publishing

Rogue's Call
C.A. Szarek

Book Three of
The King's Riders

Paper Dragon Publishing
North Richland Hills, TX

eBook ISBN: 978-1-941151-10-5
Print book ISBN: 978-1-941151-11-2

Published in the United States of America

First eBook Edition: April, 2015
First Print Edition: September, 2015

DEDICATION

I can't believe this is book three! It seemed a long time in coming, and it was a hard book for me to write. It took forever, too.

I ended up loving Alasdair and Elissa, and I hope you do, too!

So, this one's for you. My readers! Love you all, and without you, I couldn't do this!

Other Books by C.A. Szarek

The North

Chapter One

"Over here, Majesty."

Nathal tried not to sigh as he dismounted his white stallion, Destroyer. Dust puffed into the air as he thumped to the ground. His heels smarted but he ignored the minor bother and handed the destrier's reins to his squire. He strode toward his lifelong friend and captain of his personal guard, Murdoch.

Not. Again.

But it *had* happened again, this time in his own Province of Terraquist.

He was well aware of what awaited him inside.

It was the only reason he was here. Normally, his men handled these types of situations and reported back to him.

This was the third time, and Nathal needed to respond himself.

As king, his people were *his* responsibility.

He had to dip his head to enter the low doorway of the crofter's cottage. The acrid smell of burned flesh and blood smacked him in the face and roiled his stomach. Bile rose; Nathal swallowed, clearing his throat and exchanging a glance with one of his men.

"Your Highness." Murdoch inclined his head. The large man was hunched over a female body.

Her pale blonde hair was stained deep red, matted at the back of her head. She lay face down on the wood-planked floor of the small home, both her arms bent at an odd angle. Her legs, too, were broken, facing opposite directions. Blood pooled beneath her.

"Dammit."

"I know it, sire." His captain's auburn brows were drawn tight. "The third lass." Murdoch was on a knee, careful to avoid the crimson coating the floor.

"I believe it confirms they're looking for her, if the second did not. It's not a coincidence."

"Aye. They're killing any lass who looks about the right age if they don't get the right answers to questions about magic, I'd wager to guess."

Nathal cursed long and hard, tightening his fist until his gauntlets creaked a protest.

"My king, in here!" one of his knights called, peeking his head out of what had to be the main sleeping quarters of the cottage.

The crofter home sat on its own parcel of land, well outside the City of Terraquist, his capital. Although small, it was independent. According to the official royal records, it was owned by Fergal Onsted.

Onsted was a farmer by trade, and made the appropriate tithes. An upstanding citizen.

No reports of any issues — of any kind. The provost in charge of the area had confirmed. He, too, was outside with his marshals.

"What is it, Tarmon?" Nathal asked, but his stomach dipped, and he just *knew*.

"Two laddies."

Nathal's heart plummeted. The look on his knight's face confirmed the children were dead, too. The woman face down in the main living space was probably their mother. He assumed she was Onsted's wife, Rohaine — according to the records.

He blew out a breath and went to the doorway, dread churning his gut.

Two small forms lay crumpled and broken on the woven rug.

Nathal closed his eyes and looked away. "Blessed Spirit." Blood covered the room, the walls, even the large bed.

"They probably tried to hide." Tarmon's low voice was

thick, the man obviously affected by the scene. Then again, who wouldn't be?

Like himself, the knight was a father, too.

Both lads were blond, and they couldn't be more than four or five turns old. Two small hands were entwined, despite their contorted bodies; the brothers were connected in death.

"Any sign of the husband?" Nathal called to no one in particular. "His name is Fergal Onsted."

"Aye, Majesty," someone answered from the third, and final room of the cottage. "Over here. He's burned badly."

"Shite."

This was the third family decimated in the last sevenday. Three young women, their husbands, and now the toll of children sat at five.

"Get Rory in here to sweep for magic," Murdoch ordered, catching Nathal's eye as he came back into the main living space.

Nathal nodded agreement and watched one of the lads dash outside.

"Your Highness?" The redheaded half-elfin mage bowed as he appeared in front of Nathal, but he didn't miss the lad's eyes resting on the dead lass before meeting his gaze. Rory brushed his bright hair out of his face, the movement drawing Nathal's attention to the magic user's long tapered ear.

"Where's your sister?" he asked. Unlike Rory, Edana was tiny, barely over four and a half feet. She resembled a full-blooded elf more than her six-foot-tall brother. Neither came close to Nathal's own six-foot-seven-inch-frame. Few men did.

"Probing outside, Majesty."

"Good. She doesn't need to see this carnage. Tell her to stay out there, mark the perimeter and note any magic."

Rory gave a curt nod. He was still and silent, and although Nathal couldn't hear the message being relayed, there was no doubt the mage was thought-sending to the other redhead. He and his twin were Nathal's two most powerful mages, and connected to each other much more so than his other mages, because of their twin-tie and elfin blood.

"Tell me what you find here, lad."

"Aye, Majesty." The mage's chest heaved as if he'd taken a deep breath, and he closed his vivid green eyes. Rory spread his arms wide, and Nathal watched as his skin started to glow.

"Nathal." Murdoch spoke too low to have been overheard, so Nathal didn't chide him for calling his given name. His captain rarely did so when they were in the company of their men—as it should be.

They'd been lads together, trained together, and fought together. Even married at the same time. Nathal had no closer friend.

"What is it?" He tore his gaze away from Rory, and knelt next to his captain.

"Look." Murdoch had flipped the lass's body over.

Nathal glanced away from her mangled face, and the burned flesh of her neck and collarbone. One of her ears was missing. He cursed again as his friend gently closed her sightless eyes. The lass's bodice and tunic were torn open, baring her breasts. He murmured a prayer that the Blessed Spirit keep her soul safe.

Anger and regret darted across Murdoch's face when Nathal met his teal eyes. "A waste of one so young."

"Aye. There is no greater waste. What did you find?"

The captain pointed to a scorch mark high on her ribs, on her right side. "I think they know about the birthmark."

"Enough to look for it, aye. But this lass has none."

"Aye, but this is new. Different from the other two deaths." Murdoch gave a nod and sighed.

Nathal chewed over that bit of information, but it was true. "Cover her up, Mur. She deserves dignity."

The captain worked quickly, straightening the damaged bodice as well as smoothing bloody skirts. The lass's expression was serene in death, despite the horrors that'd escorted her to the afterlife.

He had to look away from everything that'd been done to her. He'd seen many bloody battles in the time he'd been king, but the death of innocents never sat right in his gut. Especially when this lass and her family—as well as the other two—had no idea what they'd done to become targets of evil.

Nothing. They didn't do a damn thing to deserve this.

"The question is, if they'd thought they'd actually found her, would they've killed or captured?" Nathal mused, trying to assuage the guilt churning in his gut.

"Captured. They covet her magic, do they not?"

"Aye, so we've always assumed. But why?" He growled as he climbed to his feet. "They haven't established *where* they think she is. The first lass was from western Greenwald. The second, North Ascova. Why were these lasses targeted? Three small holdings, none of the women were noble, or married to noblemen. It's as if they do not know their real target at all."

"Questions we need to answer, but thank the Blessed Spirit for any ignorance that'll play to our advantage." Murdoch shook his head, whispering prayers over the lass.

Neither of them had ever been considered holy men, not really, but in the face of the tragedy—and the other two— Nathal needed guidance. *His* people had been slaughtered. They deserved better.

He would avenge them—and protect his own, as he always had.

"Why would they come after her now? After all these turns?" Murdoch asked when he'd straightened.

"How did they find out she's alive?"

"I know not, Sire. We've done what we could to protect her, to keep her hidden for almost twenty turns. But never did I fathom it'd be at the expense of three lasses and their families. *Innocents* murdered. We have to catch these bastards."

"Aye, Murdoch. Before anyone else is killed."

Nathal held himself responsible.

He knew who they were looking for. And where she resided.

☆   ☆   ☆   ☆

The little girl giggled and Elissa failed to hold back the smile curving her lips. "Sit still, princess, so I can finish quickly," she admonished her young cousin.

"I *am* sitting still, Issa," Mallyn complained.

"Hmm…" She gave a gentle tug of the tawny-colored braid she was weaving.

The newly ten-turn-old whined for good measure, but straightened her thin shoulders and sat taller.

"That's better, lovebug."

Mallyn flashed a grin in the mirror and Elissa kept her fingers moving, fixing her cousin an intricate nest of braids for the feast. The little princess had begged for a *grown-up* style, one like her mother often wore. It was her birthday supper; the child had been a ball of excitement all morning and well into the afternoon. She'd had trouble focusing on her lessons, too. Mallyn had asked if she could get dressed in her *special outfit* for supper even before midday meal.

"Elissa, may I have a word?"

"Of course, Your Highness." She released Mallyn's hair and bowed to Queen Morghyn as she entered the room.

"Mama." Mallyn's high pitched whine made the queen's pale brows knit tight. "Issa is doing my hair! She can't go with you right now." The princess leveled a frown to match her mother's.

"Sweeting, just because it's your birthing day doesn't mean you can speak to me like that." Queen Morghyn's admonition was on the gentle side, but her dark eyes flashed.

Mallyn hung her head. "Aye, Mother. I'm sorry."

The queen swept further into the room, her fine golden gown rustling with each graceful step. She cupped her only daughter's cheeks, caressing her with both thumbs and murmuring.

Elissa bit back a smile she watched them together. The queen was her blood kin, first cousin to her dead father, and the only mother she'd ever known.

She resembled the white-blonde beauty more than Mallyn, who looked more like King Nathal. Elissa's eyes were hazel instead of deep brown, but her facial structure was just like the queen's; high cheekbones and straight nose. They'd been mistaken as sisters many a time, though the queen was old enough to be her mother. She'd never remind the queen of such things. Her cousin held her age well, looking much younger than her forty or so turns.

"Lady Elissa shall return to finish your hair with plenty of time before your feast, my love." Queen Morghyn kissed Mallyn's forehead, like she'd done to Elissa so many times over the turns.

Elissa was—and always would be—grateful her cousin had taken her in when her parents had died, and raised her as a lady-in-waiting. Her father had been a minor lord, and Elissa's position at Castle Rowan was one of honor. Lady-in-waiting or not, Queen Morghyn had always shown her affection, hugs, and love—as well as discipline—during her childhood.

The king, her cousin's husband, had always treated her with respect and love. Elissa couldn't have had a better man to consider a father.

Mallyn's expression was solemn. "Can you hurry?"

"Mallyn." The queen's voice held warning, but the corners of her mouth twitched.

The little girl beamed, unrepentant as usual.

Elissa cleared her throat to cover her laugh. "I know what we can do, lovebug."

"What?" Her little cousin's pale blue eyes went wide.

"I'll call Ketrice, and she'll help you get dressed. By the time you're done, I'll be back to weave flowers into your hair."

"Oh, aye!" Mallyn clapped.

The other handmaiden quickly stepped into the room as if summoned, the princess's fancy blue birthday gown in her capable hands. Elissa thanked her friend.

"Oh, Mother?" the child called as she slipped to her feet from the chair. Her ivory dressing gown was crinkled, and Elissa leaned forward to tug it straight.

"Aye, love?"

"You can still hurry, right?"

Elissa laughed—she couldn't help it.

Queen Morghyn whirled away so her daughter wouldn't see her smile. "Impudent lass," she muttered as they left her child's rooms.

Elissa knew better than to point out her young cousin wasn't much different from her mother. "Is something wrong, Your Grace?"

"Nay, lass. Don't worry. The king has some news."

"For me?"

"Aye." The queen's expression was serene, but Elissa's gut churned with unease.

What could the king have to say to me?

The dreams—nightmares, really—that'd been haunting her all sevenday danced into her mind, though she'd told no one, not even her roommate.

Women screaming, running; fire everywhere. White-hot pain searing her arms and legs, and her face. Elissa had woken screaming, too. She'd frantically grabbed for her left ear. It'd been burning, the pain only fading after she'd panted her way through two couplets of a calming spell she'd learned as a child. It'd taken much longer than that for the shake in her limbs to dissipate.

It was a wonder Dara hadn't woken from all the fuss she'd made, but her friend had always said she slept like the dead.

There's no way it could have something to do with that. Right?

Unless one of the mages with empathic powers had picked something up.

Did her dreams mean something? She shook her head. Elissa would rather forget about the nightmares than disclose them.

The king and queen knew of her magic, of course. They'd helped her hone her powers with the best mages. She could control all the elements, but water drew her most. Controlling it, conjuring it, shaping it had always been her passion. Elissa could draw water from non-existence, and could make it rain—even thunderstorm—without effort.

As a child, directing her powers had been a constant challenge, since they were linked to her emotions, but she'd learned, mastering the elements. Much quicker than anyone had expected.

She'd never had the desire to become a King's Mage, though several of her teachers had tried to steer in her that direction.

Thank the Blessed Spirit King Nathal had disagreed.

'Elissa is a lady' was always the reply.

She had no regrets that she'd spent most of her time inside, learning to run a household, and in the last few turns, acting as a companion to both of her young cousins, Mallyn, and the crown prince, Roblin. Although the lad was recently four and ten, since twelve he'd been training to become a knight.

Tension rose in the silence, but was Elissa imagining it? Her cousin didn't look upset in the least—as a matter of fact, Queen Morghyn's expression was…pleased?

Elissa's heart skipped.

They continued down the wide corridor. Every servant they passed stopped and bowed deeply to their queen. Her cousin gave each a nod and smile of acknowledgment.

When they arrived at a wide, dark door, Elissa swallowed hard.

The king's personal ledger room.

She'd never been inside—then again, there'd been no need.

The door swung open, and a tall sandy-haired knight bowed. "Your Highness. Lady Elissa."

"Hello, Sir Willum." Queen Morghyn's smile was genuine for the man who was probably only a few turns older than Elissa.

Elissa had always thought him handsome. He was soft spoken for a knight—in her estimation, anyway. Most of the king's knights had a tendency toward rowdiness.

She smiled and bowed, and Sir Willum inclined his head.

"Come in, love. Issa." The king's call echoed, and Sir Willum slid out of the way so they could enter.

Elissa looked around, trying to take in overwhelming surroundings. A map of the continent filled the wall to her right. It detailed the Provinces down to the last tiny holding. She'd had to memorize each major city and all the families of nobility as a child. She'd never relished those lessons.

Below the map sat a large bookcase, full to the brim. Actually, all the walls of the room were lined with full bookcases.

Elissa had never seen King Nathal with a book in his large hands, but obviously he liked to read. She couldn't see titles on the spines, but there were volumes of all sizes. She'd love the opportunity to explore. She, too, loved to read. Loved the smell of the parchment, the weight of a good story in her hands.

Castle Rowan had a vast library. Elissa loved stories of handsome knights and beautiful lasses that ended with happily-ever-after the best.

The place smelled like the king—clean masculine spice with a touch of pine. The man had always reminded her of winter, in a way. Crisp. But she'd always preferred sandalwood.

Odd to think such things now.

She chided herself and bowed before the large man. King Nathal was seated at his oversized desk, a quill in hand, and well of ink next to the parchment he'd been writing on. He gestured them to take seats in the chairs across from his desk, and excused Sir Willum.

King Nathal smiled and set the writing utensil down, then rolled up the parchment and grabbed his seal.

Elissa and Queen Morghyn watched in silence as he used deep blue wax—the main color of Terraquist—to secure the letter until it reached appropriate hands.

"Ah, there." The king's deep voice was saturated in satisfaction, and even though the contents of the letter were none of her business, Elissa was curious.

Could it concern me somehow?

"Thank you for coming to see me, lass." His pale blue eyes were kind, as she always remembered them.

"Of-of-of course, Your Highness." Elissa cursed the stutter and her stomach somersaulted.

Queen Morghyn leaned over and patted her hand, as if she sensed her unease. Her cousin smiled softly and Elissa made herself relax.

Nothing's wrong.

There was no issue with having a private meeting with the king and queen—right? These people had taken her in, raised her, even loved her. She met the large man's gaze and forced a smile.

King Nathal's tawny locks were shaggy as always, framing his face like a lion's mane. The curve of his lips was pleasant, befitting his handsome face as much as his crystal blue eyes. His beard was trimmed neatly, outlining his strong jaw. He was a good man, a good king.

"Is something wrong?" Elissa took a breath, telling herself relax in the chair. The carved wood at her shoulders grounded her somehow.

"Nay, Issa," Queen Morghyn said.

"How old were you on your last birthing day, lass?"

Elissa jumped, and looked at the queen before she could meet the king's gaze again.

He knew her age, did he not? "Two and twenty, Your Majesty."

King Nathal nodded, and exchanged a glance with his wife.

The seal of Terraquist, a roaring lion with a royal blue shield and a flag caught her eye. It was on the wall to the left, above Queen Morghyn's head.

"It's time, Issa," her cousin whispered.

"Time for what?" Elissa blurted.

"For you to wed, lass."

She bit back the exclamation on the tip of her tongue. Shock aside, Elissa was with the king and queen, and she'd do well to remember that. She'd never show them with any sort of disrespect, not just because of their ranks.

"Who?" she croaked when she managed to break the silence—a good thirty seconds later. She was grateful they'd given her time for the declaration to sink in.

For some reason, the hero of her favorite story danced into her head. A handsome knight. In the book, he'd married the woman he loved.

Elissa didn't want to marry someone she didn't love.

King Nathal reclined in his ornately carved chair. "That, lass, will be up to you."

She released a breath she hadn't realized she'd been holding.

"There are several appropriate suitors, but the best candidate is Lord Camden Malloch. He's young, and a good man, a good leader to his people. As was his father before him. He's recently become Duke of Dalunas. He's looking for a strong wife."

"Dalunas?"

The Province of Dalunas was the farthest from Terraquist one could travel and stay on the continent. It was a three sevenday ride. As south as possible from where they were in the far north. Along the southeastern coast.

"Aye, lass."

"So far," Elissa whispered.

"Aye, Issa. I know it's farther than you've ever been—"

"Away from everything, *everyone*, I know." Elissa bowed her head when she realized she'd interrupted the queen, but her cousin's expression was soft when she managed to meet her dark gaze again.

"It'll be all right, love." Queen Morghyn caressed her cheek.

"Will you consider Lord Camden as your match, my lady?" King Nathal asked.

Consider? Do I really have a choice?

"I want you to marry, but aye, the final say of who you call husband will be yours. You've my word." The king offered a curt nod.

Heat kissed Elissa's neck before searing her cheeks. She'd not meant to speak aloud, but she had. She forced a nod and sucked in a calming breath. "You…you…said there were several suitors?"

"Aye."

"Who…who…are the others?"

"Lord Avery Lenore of Tarvis, though he's younger than you. With either Avery or Camden, you shall be a duchess, but there are two other sons of minor lords that please me. Lord Audon Croly, heir to a large holding in the southern part of Tarvis, and last but certainly not least, Lord Lakyn Gallard, nephew to the Duke of Ascova. He resides in South Ascova, heir to the castle there."

So far away.

All her suitors lived so far away from Terraquist.

Elissa wouldn't get to see Mallyn every day. Her heart seized. "I…"

"I realize it is a lot to take in, lass, but it's time." His tone brooked no argument—not that she'd argue with her king.

Tears stung her eyes. She'd always assumed she'd marry—eventually.

Not like this.

Not being given a list of four men she'd never met, and being ordered *choose.*

Not leaving the only family she'd ever known.

Elissa wanted to ask why it was suddenly *time* when no one had brought such things up before. Had these men asked for her hand? Did they know she was being considered to wed one of them?

"I don't want to leave Terraquist. I have Princess Mallyn to look after and—" She swallowed against the lump in her throat.

Her cousin squeezed her hand and whispered reassurances, but Elissa didn't process the statements or the sentiment.

King Nathal stood, but her eyes didn't track him as he came around to the front of his massive dark wood desk. She stared at the golden lion lying atop the back of his carved chair. It had jeweled blue eyes—probably real sapphires.

Her king planted himself on the edge of his desk in front of her. He reached, and one of his calloused hands swallowed hers. "You can take as much time as you need to decide, lass."

"Do I…" Elissa sucked back a sob, "…get to meet them?"

"Of course."

Short-lived relief washed over her. Selecting a husband shouldn't be like choosing a melon at market. "I don't want a marriage without love." Elissa cursed the words as they fell from her mouth.

The king and queen looked at each other before King Nathal drew her gaze again. He was widely known for loving his wife, so her confession wasn't unreasonable, was it?

"Aye, lass. I'd never have you marry without it."

"But what if I don't love any of them?"

The king smiled kindly. "I'm sure when you meet them, get to know them, that won't be the case."

What if it is the case?

Overwhelmed, she didn't know what to do, or say. Elissa blinked to clear her vision, but it didn't work.

"Will you give it a chance, my lady?" King Nathal asked.

She forced a nod. What else could she say? "What's next?" she whispered.

"After Mallyn's feast, pack your bags and be ready to depart in the morning."

"Where am I going?"

"*We* are going to Greenwald, Issa," Queen Morghyn answered.

"Greenwald?"

"Aye, lass, we've a wedding to attend."

Elissa gasped.

King Nathal laughed. "Worry not, it's not yours."

chapter Two

"Come now, is this all necessary?" Alasdair flashed a grin at Roduch's scowl. He ignored his friend and swept his arm over the inner bailey. "Do they really *need* to put flowers on *everything*?"

Lasses bustled, arms full of bright-colored blooms, not one of them paying him or Roduch any notice. They giggled and darted all over, excited voices carrying in the sunny morning. Unusually warm, too, for a fall day in Greenwald. Welcome, of course, for the wedding.

Rows of chairs were set up neatly before a dais that had been erected for the outside ceremony, and a bright red aisle runner of the finest fabric was already laid out for the bride to go to the groom upon.

Alasdair had already been chided by Morag — the head woman in charge of all the female staff — for walking on it with what she'd called *'filthy boots.'* The accusation was unfounded, but he'd not told her he'd shined his boots for the wedding. It was better — smarter — to stay quiet and out of Morag's way, on a day of normal duties, let alone a special occasion.

The big blond knight grunted. "Maybe I should fetch a lass to shove some flowers into your mouth. Roses. With thorns."

"Now now, are we touchy on our wedding day?" Alasdair arched an eyebrow.

"Alas." Roduch sighed. "Leave off."

He sobered. "Something wrong?"

"Nay." His friend shook his head, shifting his shaggy golden locks. However, Roduch's fair brows were drawn tight.

"Are you sure? You're supposed to be overjoyed. It's your wedding day and all, and since I've failed to talk you out of it, you might as well be happy." He quirked a corner of his mouth, trying to lighten the look on Roduch's face. His brother-in-arms was in love, and all jesting aside, Alasdair was happy for the big man.

His jibe missed its mark, if Roduch's expression was any indication.

Poor sap.

Alasdair couldn't imagine being tied down by *one* lass for the rest of his life. There were too many he adored. Granted, the tavern girls were always welcoming to his coin, but he liked to think he had some skill in the beds he joined them in. He'd never had any complaints, anyway.

"Nothing is *wrong.*"

"If you say so."

Roduch sighed and rammed his hand through his locks. "I just want her to be sure she's ready."

"Ah." Alasdair gripped his friend's forearm and squeezed. "She is. I'm sure of it. It's been over a turn since Avril came to us, after all."

"How is *one* turn enough time?"

His fellow knight's lass had been through hell. Over four turns of abuse and rape at the hands of her former husband, but Roduch had saved her—in every way possible.

"She'll never be what she was, Roduch," Alasdair whispered.

Roduch's brow knitted even tighter.

"Don't mistake what I mean, brother. She's *better.* She has *you.* Mistress Avril is a delight to be around. Full of easy smiles and giggles. Easy conversation, too. I haven't seen her shy in some time." He patted his friend's shoulder. "So no worries on this fine day. You're about to get hitched."

The big knight smiled—finally. "Thanks, Alas. I don't give you nearly enough credit for the wisdom you possess."

He flashed a grin. "Don't tell anyone."

Roduch chuckled.

"The king's party is coming down the road!" The yell had them collectively looking up at the outer wall across the main courtyard. One of the men-at-arms atop the battlement waved and repeated the shout to anyone in hearing distance.

Leargan, captain to the Duke of Aldern's personal guard, and their commander, jogged across the bailey. He was already clad in wedding finery, a mix of Greenwald colors — pale green and silver — along with his decorative armor, for he'd stand with Roduch when their brother pledged himself to his ebony-haired lass. "Roduch, Alas, we haven't much time. The groom has to get properly attired."

"I know it." Roduch nodded as Leargan skidded to a halt, kicking up dirt.

"I'll meet the king's party. Lord Aldern should be down in a moment. Alas, you're not dressed, either."

"My dear captain, you're starting to sound like our headwoman, nagging us." Alasdair mock-frowned.

Leargan scowled. "Don't make me get Morag to get you into motion. I saw her in the great hall, waving a wooden spoon like a sword. Some poor soul called her from the kitchens for an emergency."

Alasdair chuckled. He offered his palms in surrender. "I've already been fussed at for stepping on the aisle runner, so I'll be a good lad and get gussied up."

One corner of Roduch's mouth shot up. "I appreciate your effort. It's not every day I wed, my friend."

Alasdair glanced into his friend's pale blue eyes. He blinked, then laughed. If Roduch could tease, things were well indeed. "This is a fine day, after all."

Leargan gestured. "Just go. Remember, you're with Dallon for the salute."

"Aye, Captain. See you in a bit." Alasdair offered a wave and left his brothers to head to his quarters in the soldier wing of the vast Castle Aldern.

Another wedding.

He shook his head and tried not to count those of the personal guard left *unmarried*. The number danced into his head anyway.

Six and six...as of today.

Marriage.

And children.

Niall had one, Leargan had two, but of course, the captain's had come as a set. Lastly, Padraig and his wife were expecting. It was probably only a matter of time until Laith and Merrick — the other two newlyweds of the guard—were announcing that they, too, were going to be fathers.

His brothers were all younger than him, yet dropping like flies. Or, more accurately, dropping at the feet of a pretty lass they'd all decided to keep.

"Sheesh."

Alasdair ran his hand through his long hair. He wasn't envious. In the least. Would never give up his freedom for *a* lass. No matter how beautiful. He liked his life just the way it was.

So why was his chest a bit tight when he looked at any of his brothers and the women they loved?

He kept one boot marching in front of the other. Alasdair needed to dress and get back to the great hall. He'd always looked best in blue, but the colors of Greenwald weren't even close to the deep royal blue of the Province he'd grown up in, Terraquist.

The king had raised him. First a page, then squire, and finally the knighted warrior he was today.

Alasdair opened the door to his room and managed a grin. One of the servants had set out his decorative armor, as well as the fancy dark blue breeches and under tunic he'd wear.

Of course, his pledged Province was represented in the seal etched into his chest plate. A howling white wolf, like the duchess, Lady Cera's, bondmate. He'd wear thick silver braided cording on his right shoulder denoting his place in the guard, like all the rest of his brothers, except Leargan. The captain had an epaulet pinned to his armor to signify his rank.

He dressed quickly, donning his armor last. Alasdair had long learned to put on his own armor, for he'd never taken a squire. With his position within the personal guard, there wasn't really need of one, although his commander's second, Niall, had a lad, as did their captain.

Alasdair was content without one. It wasn't as if he was ambitious enough to want to rise in the ranks performing heroic acts and gain his own lands from the king. He enjoyed working with the men he'd been raised with, had trained with. Being a part of the Aldern personal guard was an honor he had no desire to forfeit.

The knights that made up the guard—himself included— had only been living and working in Greenwald three turns, but he'd never been happier.

Now if his brothers would quit getting married…it'd be like the old days.

Who was he kidding? Knights were a good catch, especially his brothers.

Alasdair was too old to still consider himself a troublesome lad. Marriage was *normal*. A part of acceptable society, of being a grown man. Just not for him.

Melancholy wasn't like him, especially on such a happy occasion. His brother was pledging himself to the woman he loved.

So what's your issue?

He shook out his arms and legs, chiding himself to snap out of it. Alasdair plastered on a smile — as if he needed the practice — and wandered to the window that overlooked the inner bailey. He watched the organized chaos of the lasses still preparing the area.

His eyes scanned what he could see of the main courtyard. The nobles of the castle — the duke, his second, and their wives — stood in a receiving line, along with Leargan and his wife.

King Nathal's vast entourage wasn't even through the outer gates as of yet, but his gaze shot that way, assessing their procession. The king wasn't difficult to spot, a large, fair-haired giant on a massive white destrier. Next to him rode Sir Murdoch Fraser, the king's captain and one of the few men Alasdair knew that was close to the king in size.

He'd trained most of the Aldern guard, and practically all of King Nathal's knights. Alasdair considered them equal parts a father to him. It'd be good to see them both.

This procession was larger than the usual fair, but as he studied each rider, he understood why. The queen rode with the men, despite the fact there was also a large carriage.

"Why would Queen Morghyn be here for Roduch's wedding?" he mused. It was true Roduch was a distant cousin of King Nathal's, so perhaps she'd wanted to see a man considered blood wed.

The queen didn't often leave Terraquist, and for good reason. Having both rulers away — together — could be dangerous. Everyone would have to be on extra guard — as Alasdair and his brothers, as well as the king's men, would no doubt be.

A knock on the door made him jump. "Enter."

"I'm sorry, sir. I don't mean to disturb." A dark-haired lass with a basket of linens and cleaning supplies bowed deeply as she came to stand before him.

"Nay, you're not. I was just leaving. The wedding is to start soon."

"Aye, I'm to freshen the wing while the men are away."

"Ah." Alasdair caught her eye and winked.

She was a cute little thing, especially when her cheeks brightened as their eyes met.

He flashed a grin. "Lasses are scarce in this wing." Most of the servants Morag sent to clean the soldiers' and knights' rooms were male. The headwoman's greatest fear was impropriety—or even the appearance of it.

The lass looked embarrassed and shifted on her feet. "The headwoman said—"

"Lass, I was teasing. I apologize." Alasdair bowed.

When their eyes met, her big brown eyes were as wide as saucers. "Sir—"

"No worries. I've not seen you around before."

"I'm new. My name's Elena." She smiled. Her pride in her duties was obvious. Her white apron was crisp, as was the white kerchief pinned to her dark hair between her pigtails. She looked young, happy, and innocent. "My husband, Henger, is a castle man-at-arms."

Husband? The lass looks no more than six and ten.

"I know him. Good man." The lad wasn't much older than his wife. Henger was new to the castle's soldier roster, and one of the men he'd been training in swordplay over the last few months.

She beamed and Alasdair couldn't help but smile back. "Thank you, sir."

"Any time, lass." He nodded and inclined his head. "Good day, Mistress Elena."

"Are you in need of bathing sheets?"

They shared a few words about his room and supplies before Alasdair bid her farewell. He had no desire to be caught in his quarters with the lass by Morag, even though she was married. The headwoman knew him to be a rake, yet he'd never tupped a castle maid—no matter the lasses that'd offered. And he'd never touch a married woman—maid or not.

Married.

Was everyone married?

☆   ☆   ☆   ☆

Elissa looked around as she followed Sir Murdoch into the courtyard of Castle Aldern. The castle wasn't as large as Castle Rowan, but she loved the raised turrets on each corner of the front of the structure. The wide double doors of the main entrance were thrown open — probably due to the wedding celebration.

"Are you well, lass?" Sir Murdoch smiled as he approached her gray mare.

"Very much so, Captain."

"Not sore from the ride? You didn't complain once."

"Who could complain with such competent leaders?"

"Who indeed?" The captain winked and Elissa found herself grinning. He grabbed her waist and lifted her off the horse as if she weighed nothing.

She stared up into blue-green eyes regarding her fondly. "Thank you, Sir Murdoch."

"Aye, my lady. Don't mention it."

"Your daughter lives here, doesn't she?" Elissa asked.

"Aye. My lass, Ansley, is married to Sir Leargan Tegran, captain of the Aldern personal guard."

"A captain like you."

He chuckled. "I wouldn't go that far, but aye, the lad's a captain."

One of the men within earshot coughed as if he was covering a laugh.

Elissa smiled; she'd heard the tease in Sir Murdoch's voice, even if the older man was trying to hold on to a stern expression. "I'm glad you'll get to see her, Sir Murdoch."

"Aye, me too. They've a wee lassie and laddie. Twins." The captain's tone was soaked in pride and her heart gave a pang.

Was she jealous?

She'd barely been able to digest that she was to marry, let alone contemplate children. Elissa swallowed and tried not to fidget.

The king and queen had their heads bent together — or rather, King Nathal was leaning down and speaking lowly, so she waited by her horse. She'd not want to intrude on any private royal exchange.

Soon, the king's men were calling orders at each other, and started unpacking numerous trunks from the carriage they'd brought—the one she and the queen hadn't ridden in. Servants from the castle met them and started hauling their things inside.

She felt out of place and in the way, especially when lads from the stable came and took her mare.

Sir Murdoch winked and Elissa almost jumped. Then he was gone, bustling around the area with his men.

Her gaze scanned the inner bailey. The semi-private area opened under a thick brick archway. She wandered that way, throwing a glance at the queen, but her cousin was still conversing with her husband.

A thick woven garland of flowers hung from the arch, and when Elissa stopped before it, she rested her palm against the stone. It was warm from the sun, though the day was not overly hot.

The inner courtyard was decorated for the wedding, complete with a dais, rows of chairs, and every flower variety she'd ever seen, maybe even some she hadn't. Magic tingled over the place, even some of the flowers. They'd been conjured, she realized, especially the unnaturally large roses of every possible color. Elissa smiled.

Serving lasses were still decorating and organizing the area. No one paid her any mind as they worked. They were excited as they bustled, grinning and giggling.

It looked beautiful. Flowers and woven garlands draped everywhere, and a red aisle runner that made the area appear regal.

The bride would no doubt be overjoyed when she saw what'd been arranged for her. She didn't know Mistress Avril, but she was acquainted with the groom, Sir Roduch Grantham. He was a former King's Knight.

For some reason, Elissa's heart sped up. She shook her head and loosened her cloak. It was warmer in Greenwald than Terraquist, but the day was pleasant for a fall day. The sunniness just made the whole place more welcoming. She ignored the sweat on her brow and the tightness of her chest.

This is not my wedding. I have time.

She didn't want to think about it anymore.

Elissa had been born in Greenwald, but she didn't remember the Province at all. Her father's holding, which had been sizable, complete with a castle—dubbed with her surname—Castle Durroc, was not too far from Greenwald Main, or so she'd been told.

No one lived there, but as heir, the property was hers.

Or her husband's when she married.

She tried not to cringe.

Why the king had left the castle untended was a mystery. The lands were cared for, she'd been told, but no family had ever moved into her former home. She'd never asked what state the property was in, either.

Why?

The question reverberated in her mind. Elissa had never been curious about it. Terraquist and Castle Rowan had always been her reality. She didn't remember her parents or her older brother, who'd been four turns old and killed in the same accident that'd taken her parents from her.

She knew about the coin the crops from her property yielded. The king's stewards reported her earnings to her every season, and King Nathal kept her money for her.

Queen Morghyn had told her about her parents — particularly her father — whenever she'd asked, but it was no more than information that left her heart aching.

Elissa couldn't bring them back, and felt guilty she couldn't even recall their faces now. Logically, she knew she'd been too small, not yet having started her second turn, but not even the small painting of the four of them had ever triggered anything in her mind. The faces of three strangers stared at her when she gazed at it. She recognized her own small face, chubby cheeks and pale hair.

That only made her even sadder.

Elissa was grateful she had the painting. Held it dear, and carried it with her even though it triggered no memories. She'd brought it to Greenwald and hoped to hold it later, when she unpacked her trunk and dressed for the wedding.

Her cousin had told her it'd only been done a fortnight before they'd died, and somehow saved from the fire that had started in the kitchens. Elissa didn't know how much of her former home had burned.

She supposed she'd never gone out of her way to wonder about a holding she would be entitled to *someday*.

But now…she was going to marry.

Castle Durroc and the lands were a part of her dowry. Perhaps she could see them again.

Butterflies were born and flitted about her stomach. Elissa's grip on the brick beside her tightened until her fingertips throbbed. Suddenly, she wanted to know *everything* about the place she'd been born.

"Elissa!"

She jumped; heat singed her cheeks. Automatically, Elissa turned toward Queen Morghyn's call and bowed at the waist.

"Majesty."

"Come, lass, I want you to meet the duke and duchess."

Her heart in her throat, she rushed to her cousin's side.

Chapter Three

Charis cursed as he entered the dark cave. The protection barrier gleamed at him, as if taunting. He didn't want to go through the damn 'wall.' It wasn't a *real* wall, only a thickly woven spell, but it didn't matter. The unpleasantness of his employer's magical signature made his stomach roil.

Dark. Thick. *Evil.*

Moist, dank air skirted over his skin, and he fought a shiver as magic slid down his spine. The hair on the back of his neck stood on end. He flexed his hands and chided himself to leave his sword sheathed at his waist. Even if he drew it and brandished it like a madman, there wasn't anything to kill.

Spiders.

The magical *keep out* felt like spiders creeping all over his skin; clothing gave no protection. He fought through the discomfort, breathing a sigh of relief as the spell faded, kicking him to the other side of the imaginary barrier.

He frowned and planted one boot in front of the other, glancing over his shoulder. The spell had shoved him, as if placing hands on his back.

Charis scowled.

Damn old bastard. And damn Bracken and Nason, too.

His cowardly men had all too eagerly obeyed his order to guard the vast cavern's entrance while he went to check in with the old codger pulling his strings.

Nothing like eating humiliation for breakfast and being called a failure.

All the worse, because it's true.

Despite his magic, he'd failed in his quest so far.

"Half-breed, is that you?"

Charis swallowed a growl. He didn't allow anyone but Drayton to refer to him as such, and that was only for the time being. He'd get revenge as soon as he was done *working* for the controlling idiot. "Aye, 'tis me."

"Come forward."

He nodded even though his wretched boss couldn't see him yet. On principle, Charis had bound his long hair in a leather strap at the back of his neck and left his wide-brimmed hat with his men. Making sure Drayton would be able to see his tapered ears—a "gift" from his elfin father.

The old man squinted as he came into what Drayton liked to call his *throne room*.

Charis snorted.

Throne room, my arse.

The cave was high ceilinged, he had to give the mage that, but other than a huge ornate chair on a dais at the center of the natural room and a few blankets on a pallet off to one side, the wide cavern had a whole lot of *dark* and *wet* and not much else. Oh, and *stinky*.

Or is that just the old man?

He didn't know how the mage could live there.

Drayton frowned when he noticed Charis' bare ears. His milky eyes flashed, suddenly lucid; light brown with an odd black ring around the color. It didn't fix the hanging flesh on his ugly face, from age as well as too much magic use. His black robes swallowed his too-slender frame, covering his hands and feet.

He was perched on his chair; the only place Charis had ever seen him. But despite the elderly mage's diminutive appearance, he was powerful. His aura was radiant around his small form, belying his age. It was the aura of a young person, soaked in power. Strength and magic. Magic that superseded his own. But it was also tainted with an onyx ring that screamed evil.

Charis didn't fool himself. Drayton could kill him with little effort. Had he been able to handle the physical requirements of the task Charis and his men had been charged with, the mage would never have sought help.

The old man had probed his magic when he and his lads had answered the call for hire. Drayton had scowled at his ears from the moment he'd recognized Charis wasn't *all* human. His magic had saved his life. Had he not been useful to him, Drayton would've killed him as soon as look at him, and all because of Charis' mixed blood.

Persecution from humans wasn't something he was unfamiliar with, except for the humans of Aramour, where he'd grown up in a diverse community of elves and humans alike. There were many of dual parentage in the mountain community. It was only when Charis had set foot into the Provinces he'd started to hide his father's contribution to his physical appearance.

Made a man want to hie home to his mama at times, although he'd never admit it out loud. However, for the last several turns he'd spent most of his time in the Provinces. More gold on this side of the border, for sure. On principle, he refused to be ashamed of himself or where he'd come from, but sometimes it was smarter to disguise himself under a cloak and hat—Charis hated to admit that.

His reputation as a ruthless mercenary was the only thing that forgave his heritage in Drayton's eyes. And had the bastard not had deep purses and a great deal of magic himself, Charis would've run him through for being a bigot the day they'd met. He'd killed men for less.

"Was it she?"

Good. No reason to beat around the bush. Indeed, he had no use for small talk with the fellow mage. "Nay, my lord." Charis could've choked on the forced honorific. Drayton was no more a lord than Charis' boot.

Drayton cursed in Aramourian, the language of the elves.

Charis swallowed a guffaw. The wizard's accent was horrific. He'd claimed to have been trained in the Mountains of Aramour, but Charis didn't believe him. Even humans from Aramour could usually speak the elfin language with proper inflection. His mother was one, even though she hadn't been born of Aramour.

"Did you take care of the lass?" Red anger bathed the old mage's aura. His wrinkled hands made an appearance from under the sleeves of his robing. Drayton clutched the arms of his chair with white knuckles.

"Aye, her family, too." He'd never had the stomach for killing children, so Bracken had had to handle the laddies, same as the other three little ones from the previous failures, in the neighboring Provinces of North Ascova and Greenwald. Too bad guilt was eating at him, even though Charis hadn't delivered the death blows. He understood the need to wipe out witnesses — they couldn't risk word getting out that Drayton was on the hunt for the elemental lass. But still, dead babes didn't sit right in his gut. "She didn't bear the mark."

"Keep looking."

"Aye, my lord. None of the lasses so far were the one you seek."

Drayton snarled from his throne. "I need the lass." He leaned forward but made no move to exit the carved dark-wood chair.

"I'll find her."

"Your magic is useless." The accusation was a bark, backed by magic intended to intimidate him. "I located those lasses. You've done naught for me."

You failed, too. But he couldn't say it.

Power rushed at him and Charis planted his boots in the dirt so his arse wouldn't meet the cave floor. He didn't argue. Justification, no matter how true, didn't work for Drayton. His magic wasn't useless. The lass Drayton sought wasn't in Terraquist, so this last stop had been a waste of time as well as life. Not that he'd bring his opinion to light.

Charis' seeking spells *never* failed. Tracking was what he did best, even without magic.

Drayton had been the one to insist he'd located the lasses as possible matches for the one he wanted. The old mage had insisted Charis and his men confirm and capture, or destroy the *mistake*. Drayton's mistake. Plural, now.

Death had never bothered Charis much, but the blood was on his employer's hands, not him and his lads. They were simply the means to Drayton's ends.

"I'm almost out of time."

Charis straightened his spine at Drayton's obvious desperation. The first sign of weakness he'd ever seen from the old man.

Why? hung in the air, but he wouldn't ask, even if he thought Drayton would shed light on the reasons for his task.

He never asked questions, so long as the coins were presented as promised.

★   ★   ★   ★

Drayton stifled a cry as soon as the half-breed's back was turned and the mercenary wretch was well on his way through the protective spell-wall that kept Drayton's home concealed. Putting up the required airs for his hireling took it out of him.

It was only getting worse, too.

Agony was what he was made of these days.

Pain crumpled his form, but he couldn't use another healing spell. The more magic he used, the more his body suffered. He couldn't call the water to him and bathe himself in blessed heat, either. He hadn't the energy after the blast spell he'd thrown at Charis. He'd missed, or the magic had failed him. Again.

There was no relief for his pain, for his plight. At least *not yet*. Even a true healer couldn't stop the disintegration of his form.

He raised both hands, wincing as white-hot bolts of negative energy shot up into his shoulders. Drayton turned his palms over. His skin was nearly transparent, his veins glowing blue and purple; they, too, ached. His body was showing his ancient age, as it always did when he got this close.

Wrinkled. Hanging flesh. *Weak*.

Looking in the mirror wrenched his stomach.

Bile rose and Drayton swallowed. Twice. His head spun, temples aching. He needed to seek his pallet. Sleep hung as a heavy demand, even his eyelids offering bite and sting.

Fighting back a moan, he tried to lift his legs, planting booted feet to the wooden dais. He needed to stand, but when he pushed himself up, his knees buckled and he landed hard on the padded seat of his throne. His tailbone smarted and Drayton closed his eyes, trying to breathe through the burning in his arms and legs.

His fingers shook but he held his hands still on the chair's frame as fire raked him, burning slowly down his spine and into his hips.

He hadn't much time left.

Hadn't gotten this close to death since the first time he'd taken someone's magic to prolong his life, over two hundred and fifty turns ago. When he'd been an old man not so different from his current situation.

Drayton needed the lass.

Now.

His stolen turns were catching up with him, and the only thing that would save his life was an elemental mage, a powerful one.

Like he used to be.

Once he absorbed her powers, he would be whole again. *Young* again.

The lass he sought was indeed powerful, so it'd give him another sixty or seventy turns, maybe more.

Until he'd have to find another.

And he would. He always did.

Drayton's magic could seek like powers, but his health prevented him from handling his affairs. Forced him to seek the services of the dirty-blooded half-breed. Promised the bastards more coin than he possessed, a trick of magic to make Charis see what he wanted—needed—to get the task done. Served the half-breed right for demanding evidence of his wealth.

When he had his powers back, Drayton would kill the half-elf and his two cronies. Rid the world of their like.

He cursed and shook his head. Anger didn't assist his pain; his gut churned and his chest throbbed.

Where was the blasted lass?

He'd been searching for her for five turns.

Five whole turns, from the first signs that his magic was starting to fizzle out. His spells had lacked the power they had in turns past.

Drayton had been unable to locate her, despite his powers' natural ability to call to like. She was strongest in water, but she, like him, had master over earth, wind, and fire as well. He'd known what she could do from the moment he'd hovered over her cradle at the hearth in the small castle over twenty turns before.

Even then, a babe of barely two, she'd protected herself from him on instinct when he'd killed her people—servants and nobles alike.

Drayton hadn't been able to touch her. He'd intended to pluck her from her mother's breast and raise her as his own—to have her with him when he needed her powers.

The lass was the most powerful elemental he'd ever encountered.

Even at the tender age of the cradle.

She'd called the waters to her, her eyes glowing blue, and just about drowned him. She'd ordered water to engulf him before he could counter with his own magic. All without words, because she'd been so young.

He'd been surrounded by a bubble with no breath or control. Drayton had woken in the woods surrounding the home's lands, where he'd always assumed the tidal wave had washed him.

The lass had been gone.

His powers had failed to locate her even then.

When he'd made his way to the market, people had been whispering about the whole castle being murdered *days* before.

The tiny child had knocked him out for two days.

Everyone thought she'd perished with all the castle residents in a fire. He didn't remember a blaze, or know if she'd started one. Or perhaps he had, but he couldn't confirm. But Drayton had known she'd lived. Never was able to ascertain what'd happened to her, though.

He didn't think she was dead. He would've just *known*.

No, *someone* had rescued her. Taken her away, and covered her in magic he was somehow unable to sense.

She was out there, somewhere.

He needed to know where now.

His life depended on it.

Chapter Four

Nathal saw to his wife's needs as they reached the bailey of Castle Aldern. He helped her dismount and held onto her for a moment. She'd insisted on riding her own mount instead of inside the carriage he'd brought.

As king, he traveled extensively, and even though he was surrounded by men and mages he never left his home without, a part of him was leery that Morghyn was with him.

They'd not been pursued—he'd checked with his half-elfin twin mages what could've been considered obsessively—during their two-day journey, but one could never be too careful.

Had Lady Elissa not accompanied them, Nathal wouldn't have allowed Morghyn's presence—no matter how much his feisty wife of twenty-five turns would've made him pay later.

He understood her desire. Elissa was her blood, so she wanted to make sure the lass was safely ensconced in Greenwald. Morghyn needed to see it with her own eyes before they departed. But he didn't have to like it.

Although Nathal hadn't explained to the lass, they were leaving her in Greenwald because Lucan—the lone official Mage of the Province—was the most powerful magical being he'd ever encountered. His mages had told him—and he readily agreed— if Lucan couldn't protect the lass, *no one* could.

He wanted her married — that part was true. It was also true that Elissa could select her husband. The four men he'd made inquiries with had agreed to come to Greenwald to present their suits. All were interested. Camden was the only one truly searching for a wife, but the other three young men hadn't refused.

Jorrin had agreed to handle the negotiations. Nathal had already transferred her dowry to the Duke of Greenwald's custody. He hoped the lass could find happiness. He'd known all four suitors since they were children. The lads were good, stable, and could provide for her.

Avery Lenore was the youngest of Elissa's choices, and Nathal didn't think she'd pick the shy lad, but he was of marrying age, and the son of one of his closest friends.

His wish was that she select Lord Camden Malloch. Dalunas was far, and there was — hopefully — little chance that the men after her would put it together that she'd be so far from Terraquist. Besides, Cam was the best of the bunch. He was the eldest, at seven and twenty. Already a duke, established in the responsibilities of running a Province and caring for his people. He'd be good for his wife's cousin.

Nathal didn't push marriage on anyone. His wife was his world. As were his children. They'd waited a long time for the Blessed Spirit to give them children — they'd had trouble conceiving for turns.

His eyes swept the bailey for danger, but there was none. He called himself a fool, but...

Greenwald or not, men and magic or not, Nathal preferred Morghyn at Castle Rowan, with their son and daughter.

Roblin had begged to come on the journey, since he was already a squire, but Nathal couldn't allow it. His son had taken the news like a man. When they'd left, he'd been sparring with his mentor, Sir Willum Maron. Roblin had also told Nathal he'd keep his sister safe. He couldn't have been prouder of the lad.

"Nathal, is something wrong?" Morghyn's concern was evident.

He looked into his wife's dark eyes. "Nay, love."

Doubt flashed in the midnight orbs he loved so much. "Are you sure?"

"Aye." Nathal dipped low and kissed her. Much too quickly, but now wasn't the time.

Morghyn smiled and patted his chest. "Let us go inside. I'm eager to greet Cera and see the babe."

He let out a breath and nodded, easing into a smile. "The laddie is walking and talking a bit now, according to Jorrin's last missive."

Fallon, little lordling and heir to Greenwald, was eighteen months old, if Nathal remembered correctly.

His wife gave an un-lady-like snort. "Why are men discussing children via long distance letters?"

Nathal chuckled. "I've a secret to impart, my queen."

"What's that?"

He leaned down, hovering above her ear. "Men are no different than women at times."

She laughed and the sound made him grin. "I'm sure I cannot spread this revelation over the realm, can I, my king?"

Nathal shook his head, loving the twinkle in her eyes when their gazes met. He tried to maintain a serious expression. "Nay. T'wouldn't do well to get out."

"Especially from a warrior king, my love?"

He slipped off a gauntlet and caressed her cheek. "Exactly."

Morghyn's smile flipped his heart again, and he wanted to gather her up and take her mouth. Nathal squared his shoulders.

Later.

She'd be with him for the duration of this trip, there was no worry. He'd have her in his arms, in one of the many guestrooms of Castle Aldern.

Even after all their turns of marriage, he couldn't get enough of his wife. Wanted her *always*. The ease of pleasing her only made him burn more. They knew each other so well, how they both liked to be touched, caressed. He could still make her squirm and scream, and that was all that mattered.

Nathal grinned to himself as he released her.

Later wouldn't come fast enough.

He offered his wife his arm so they could greet the Duke and Duchess of Greenwald. The captain of the Aldern personal guard, Sir Leargan Tegran and his wife, Ansley, stood arm and arm next to their lord and lady. The lass flashed a grin when their gazes brushed, looking so much like her father, Murdoch, Nathal had to smile.

Lord Tristan Dagget—Jorrin's second—and his wife, Aimil, stood with them as well, and Nathal's smile was one of pride. He'd known each of the young people before him—save the duke, half-elfin Jorrin—since they were wee laddies and lassies. They'd all grown up strong and married well, for *love*, and were starting their own families.

The tragedy of Cera losing her parents and younger sister almost three turns before at the hands of an evil man was nowhere in sight. They'd moved on. Healed. Running a strong Province. Together.

Nathal still missed Cera's father every damn day. Like Murdoch, Falor had been one of his closest friends, but the daughter was doing the fallen duke proud. No doubt he watched from the heavens with a smile on his face.

Lord Jorrin Aldern stepped away from his wife and bowed deeply. "It's good to see you, Majesties."

"You as well, my lord." Morghyn spoke first, a smile in her voice. She inclined her head.

Polite conversation commenced, and the women broke off, huddling together. Morghyn introduced her cousin and soon their speech consisted of babies and marriage.

Nathal smirked.

"They'll start complaining about us in mere moments." Jorrin's words were wrapped in amusement. The wind shifted his dark hair past a long tapered ear, and he shoved it out of the way.

Leargan caught Nathal's eye and winked before looking back at Jorrin. "Not Ansley. I happen to be the perfect husband."

Jorrin snorted and Tristan laughed out loud.

Nathal shook his head and chuckled. "I see you lads haven't changed at all. Damn good to see you."

The duke nodded. "You too, Your Highness. Thanks for coming. I'm sure Roduch appreciates it."

"Aye. All you lads are like my own. I couldn't miss his wedding. We come from the same people." The knight was Nathal's distant cousin, and like Leargan—as well as most of the Aldern personal guard—he'd raised him at Castle Rowan. Shaped them all. Ensured they were strong knights and warriors—and fought for what was right.

For a number of turns, Nathal wasn't sure he'd be a father, so he'd gathered the lads to him, no matter where they'd come from. He loved them as much as he did his children.

"You brought the lass to us, Majesty." Leargan nodded toward Elissa.

"Aye, lad." Nathal met the captain's dark eyes.

"We'll keep her safe, Highness," Tristan whispered.

It didn't surprise Nathal that Jorrin had already briefed his second and captain. *Good.* It'd save him time explaining what he needed the duke to handle.

"What does she know?" Jorrin asked.

Nathal met the duke's deep blue eyes. "Not much. For the time being, I'd like to keep it that way."

"Of course." Jorrin nodded, crossing his arms over his broad chest.

"Let's have a word before the ceremony, if you don't mind. I'll also require Lucan; I have some questions for the lad, but I'd prefer to converse with you lads first."

"Aye, Majesty," Leargan said. "I'll call him when it's time."

He followed the lads into Castle Aldern—dubbed so after the duke just two short turns ago. Although Jorrin wasn't noble by birth, Nathal had never used rank to judge the value of a man. The lad had proved himself when he'd helped Cera defeat a former archduke, Varthan, who'd betrayed Nathal and tried to assassinate him.

Jorrin had fallen in love with Cera, at the time heir to Greenwald. So Nathal had made the lad a duke and the couple had married.

Well, after some prodding. The duchess was fond of the term *meddling*, but Nathal would never acquiesce that it was such. She'd loved the lad already, no matter her stubbornness at his "forcing" her hand. He was king, after all, and could do what he wanted.

Though he'd never mentioned it, Nathal suspected their firstborn was well on his way before the marriage, so it'd saved them all from public impropriety that would've had to be explained, anyway. Demanding they marry right away had provided a way out—even though the necessity hadn't been known at the time.

Jorrin was proving to be a hell of a duke, so it was validation for Nathal that Cera couldn't argue with anyway. He was fair to his people, yet wasn't afraid to make tough decisions, and had no qualms about assistance from his wife—who'd been raised for running a Province.

The duke was perfect to oversee Elissa's marriage plans.

Nathal thanked him when Jorrin gestured for him to take the seat behind the dark wood desk in the ledger room.

The duke and Tristan both took seats across from the desk. Leargan stood between them.

"I'm going to be frank. Lady Elissa Durroc is in serious danger. I need you to keep her safe."

"What's changed since our last missive?" Jorrin asked, his sapphire eyes keen. He leaned forward in the chair, shooting glances to his two men.

"Another lass and her family were murdered. This time in my own Province. Not three hours' ride from Terraquist Main."

Leargan cursed, his dark eyes flashing.

"Same situation?" Tristan whispered. His face was tight, pained. As a healer, he had an especially low tolerance for senseless death.

Pain darted across the duke's face and Nathal cleared his throat—and tried to push his emotions away. Jorrin was an empath, and the more strong emotion in the room, the more the lad would be affected.

He could obviously feel the healer's pain. Nathal didn't want to add to it. "Aye. Husband and two laddies also slain."

Leargan made a fist. "Baby killers. We need to get these bastards."

"Aye, lad, that we do." He nodded and swallowed a sigh. "Murdoch and I agree they haven't a clue where to look next. I want her to stay here. I want Lucan to cover her in magic. Safer than my own mages can make her. Whatever he has to do so she can remain concealed here and still meet her suitors."

"It'll be done, Your Highness." Jorrin made a tight fist.

"The Terraquist death was different from the others."

"How so?" Tristan's posture mimicked the duke's, but his forearms were tight to the wooden arms.

He informed them of her birthmark, and that the last lass had her clothing ripped open.

Nathal was glad there was no protest to what he needed from young Lucan. Elissa would be safe in Greenwald. And welcome.

"I hated to do it, because he can be sensitive, and he's so young, but I had Lucan go over the cottage of the girl killed in Greenwald. The holding isn't far from Terraquist borders. He didn't sense much as far as magic, which alarmed me, because as you know, the boy is *good*." The duke's expression was tight, pained.

Nathal cursed and shook his head. He'd been hoping for more information. "Nothing?"

"He sensed residual spells, but nothing he could name specifically. Nothing that could lead us directly to the killers. I want to take Avery there, since he's coming to meet Lady Elissa, anyway. He has a keen sense of his own, even if his magic isn't as strong as Lucan's."

"Good idea. I want Rory and Edana to go, too. Perhaps they should converse with Lucan, as well."

"Of course." Jorrin nodded.

"Where on my borders, lads?" Nathal asked.

"About an hour northwest of the Durroc holding." Leargan's dark brow tightened even more when Nathal cursed.

"That close to her former home? That close to Terraquist?" Damn, he'd been hoping there wasn't a rhyme or reason to the locations they'd selected. What if they were following a mapped pattern?

Could they know where she'd gone?

Nay. Magic still protects her.

Nathal couldn't afford to doubt. Not now. He had a plan. Needed to stick to it.

"Aye," Tristan said. "We spoke to the caretaker, Master Uncel, but he'd seen no one, and Lucan reinforced the spells on the castle itself. It should keep people out, as designed."

"Good."

"The property will be deeded to her husband, will it not?" Jorrin asked, head cocked to one side.

"As a part of her dowry, aye. I was hoping whoever she chooses will make no changes, and continue to pay the salary of the caretakers. I won't order such, but I'll encourage it." Nathal quirked one corner of his mouth. His *order* may have to come disguised. "The crops have proven profitable for Elissa, as well as the farmers."

"Aye, unless they cared to live in it."

Nathal nodded. "I'd considered that. I'll still discourage it, at least until we apprehend the killers. However, I could see Lakyn Gallard making that choice. He could start his own horse breeding farm; there is adequate land. I wouldn't complain about that kind of stock closer to home." He smiled when Jorrin and Leargan nodded. The finest horses were bred in South Ascova, by the young lord's father, Roald. "The others have their own lands and castles, especially Avery and Camden. What Audon Croly stands to inherit is much larger than the Durroc holding. I hope it matters not. I hope she chooses Dalunas."

The duke smirked. "Then why give her a choice, Your Highness?"

"I cannot force marriage on her."

Leargan snorted and muttered something that sounded like, *"Meddling."*

Nathal let it go, but arched an eyebrow when his gaze collided with the captain's. Leargan squared his shoulders and schooled his expression. Nathal bit back a smile.

"Do you know who we're dealing with?" the duke asked.

"Unfortunately, nay. We've tried for turns to ascertain a *name*. All I know is when my mages went over the holding they sensed something of another elemental mage. Strong, almost as much as Elissa."

"Elementals who can control all four are rare," Tristan mused.

"Aye, that they are lad. Whoever it is, Elissa bested him at barely two turns old."

"Her instinct saved her life?" Jorrin asked.

"Aye, that's what we've always assumed. There's no turning back time, but I wish Rory and Edana had been there, in the aftermath. I might know more now." The half-elfin twins weren't but two turns older than his wife's cousin, and hadn't come to him until about ten turns before. They'd been street children he'd rescued. Thank the Blessed Spirit they'd chosen to stay as two of his Mages.

"Perhaps if they put their heads together with Lucan, we'll discover *who* we need to kill." Leargan's expression darkened. "Five children murdered, not to mention their parents. It's unconscionable." The captain flexed his hand on the hilt of his sword.

Nathal nodded. Now that Leargan was a father, it probably hit home harder than before. "I ensured they all had proper burials and had the home cleansed. I placed a good man to hold the farm until kin arrives to take over. Paxton Gallard similarly handled the murders in his Province." He steepled his hands on top of the duke's desk and sighed. "How is the family of the Greenwald lass?"

Jorrin scowled. "Troublesome."

He frowned. "How so?"

Tristan shook his head as he answered. "Two of the lass' uncles are squabbling over the land. It's a sizable parcel, and the husband had no blood kin. They demanded an audience. Jorrin complied. While they were here, someone torched the stables and killed several horses. The uncles are blaming each other."

"Naturally." Nathal sighed.

"We've sent men to help rebuild, as well as half a dozen soldiers to post there. Two of the guard, Dallon and Kale, spent several days there, but I've no time to play nursemaid, any more than you do, Majesty," Leargan said. "I refuse to spare knights for a squabble."

"This is all my fault," Nathal said. He didn't miss the look Jorrin and Tristan exchanged.

"Nay, Your Highness," Leargan said.

Nathal cast his eyes to the ceiling and took a fortifying breath. "It is. If I would've caught whoever was after Elissa when she was still a child, I could've prevented the death of three young families, as well as the aftermath of a fight over lands." He made eye contact with the young duke. "Quash it, Jorrin. Now. I won't order the how, but small problems can get out of hand."

He didn't mention the battle of North and South Ascova from more than twenty turns before, but from the looks on their faces, he didn't have to. They were too young to remember living the rebellion, of course, but they were all well-read young men. Leargan was one of the victims of the war that split one Province into two. He'd been orphaned, like so many other lads.

"Yes, Your Majesty. I placed a man to hold the property for the time being, and I've told the uncles they must prove to me they can make the land prosper. They were given two sevendays to present their plans," Jorrin said.

"Good start. If there's backlash by whoever doesn't succeed and you need assistance, let me know."

"I will. Thank you. I've told them I'll auction the lands off if neither of them prove adequate."

Nathal smiled. "Good. Perhaps fearing it'll go out of the family will be the correct motivator."

"I hope so. Aside from the horses, no one has been killed, but fighting has left injuries and more tension. I told them I won't have it. Even threatened Dread Valley."

"Ah. I trust that received the appropriate reaction?"

Leargan grinned. "Pale as ghosts."

"Good."

The penal colony on Nathal's continent was far away, on the southeastern tip of the Province of Dalunas, and it was far from pleasant. People worked through their sentences if they were lucky—and died if they weren't. He trusted the provost he'd placed to oversee it, but allowed the rumors of despair to spread as a deterrent if nothing else. "She'll need a guard. Someone to watch over her, despite the magic I need Lucan to work."

Leargan nodded. "One of the personal guard would be best."

"Aye." Nathal nodded.

"Alasdair will do well. He's been training men-at-arms for the last several months, and I'm sure a change in duties could benefit him."

Nathal arched an eyebrow. "Alas? Training? He's got to be bored out of his mind." The man had always been the front-of-the-line type knight. Draw his sword, rush in, and ask questions later. Reckless, but damn good.

Alasdair loved the opposite sex, and they adored him just as much, but the lad had the appropriate decorum to look after a noble lass. He was charming, too. Probably had more than his fair amount, but Alasdair Kearney was a good man.

Leargan laughed. "I think he enjoys working with the lads and Roduch on the sword, but aye, bored. However, he does his duty, well and without question."

"As it should be."

"Will Alasdair be adequate to guard Lady Elissa?" Leargan asked.

"Aye, 'tis fine with me. What say you, Lord Aldern?"

The duke shrugged. "He'll keep her safe, but I don't think he'll enjoy playing chaperon with the suitors."

"Well, he won't be jealous." Nathal laughed.

Leargan grinned. "Not at all. He was trying to talk Roduch out of the permanence of marriage when I found them in the bailey."

He chuckled. "Poor Alas. He doesn't know what he's missing."

"Don't ask him. If you do, you probably won't like the answer." Jorrin winked.

"Ah, my dear lad. I've known Sir Alasdair Kearney since he was a wee sapling of eleven. I know he's got a list of lasses as long as I am tall."

They all laughed and Jorrin shook his head.

The king stood, and the lords followed suit. "Well, lads, we've a wedding to get to. Leargan, you'll brief Alasdair?"

"Aye, Majesty."

"Well, let's do our best to enjoy this day, for the sake of Roduch and his lass. Just don't lose sight of the danger to Elissa. I'll speak with Lucan, and we can plan to ride out to Castle Durroc tomorrow."

The duke and his men nodded as they left the ledger room.

Nathal sighed and prayed to the Blessed Spirit everything went as planned.

Chapter Five

F
"ine day for a wedding, is it not?"

The rich feminine voice washed over him. Alasdair could hear the smile in her words. He bowed with extra flourish for his queen. "I was just saying that, not ten minutes before, to the groom himself."

Queen Morghyn beamed, a twinkle in her dark eyes. "It is good to see you, Sir Kearney."

"You as well, Your Majesty. You look radiant beyond words, as usual."

She laughed. "Still a charmer, I see."

Alasdair flashed a cheeky grin and allowed the queen to take his hands. Never would he have reached for her. She was royal, and despite his scamp tendencies — even at his age of one and thirty — he respected her. Liked her. He had decorum. And a healthy dose of fear of her husband, too. He'd seen his king on many a battlefield. The man was fiercely protective of women in general, but especially those he cared about.

She squeezed his hands with great affection that had him returning the gesture.

Her burnished gold gown was a complement to her fair complexion as well as one of the colors of the king's Province, Terraquist.

Queen Morghyn wore a royal blue sash from shoulder to slender waist, denoting the other color of Terraquist, as well as her rank. No crown graced her head at the moment, but the queen's hair was ornately braided and arranged up. It only enhanced her beauty. She'd always been a stunner with pale flaxen locks and dark *dark* brown eyes. Time wasn't touching her appeal.

"Are you well, my dear Alasdair? Happy in Greenwald?" The questions caught him off-guard, but shouldn't have.

She'd seen him as an orphaned lad of eleven, bastard of a minor lord dropped off at Castle Rowan's gates in Terraquist to be accepted as a page or left to fend for himself in the harsh streets of the city center—either would have been acceptable to his guardian. The first cousin who'd inherited his father's holding cared nothing for the lord's *unofficial* child.

Alasdair's mother had been a maid in the household and had died birthing him. His father had kept him, but was indifferent, if anything. He'd been a servant, like the woman who'd given her life for his. His father had had no other children—including bastards. He knew no one of his bloodline, and carried his mother's surname instead of his father's.

Still, he often thanked the Blessed Spirit for King Nathal seeing his value and raising him as a knight—and not giving a rat's arse about his parentage.

"I am, Your Majesty. I've come to love Greenwald as I do Terraquist. Lord Aldern is a good man to back, and as always, I have my brothers." The twelve knights of the personal guard, including himself, didn't share his blood, but they were his brothers. Always. "Are you well?"

She smiled and nodded. "I am. Thank you for asking." The queen released Alasdair's hands, and gestured to the lass standing next to her. "Do you remember my cousin, Lady Elissa Durroc?"

He'd seen the lass trailing the royal when they'd crossed the great hall, of course, but he'd assumed she was an attendant. Queen Morghyn didn't travel often, and it made sense she'd bring her ladies, even for the short trip of Roduch and Avril's wedding.

Alasdair's intended polite smile stalled and he had to swallow hard instead when he glanced at the lass. He blinked. He might've remembered the name—it triggered a tease in the back of his mind. But he couldn't recall the vision before him. He would've remembered *her*.

Gorgeous was too weak a word.

Her gown was blue. A few shades lighter than Terraquist-blue and low-cut, but not enough to do more than hint at cleavage. The bodice had red roses embroidered on it and was just the right amount of tight. The bottom of the dress billowed out to only hint at a perfect waist and rounded hips instinct told him would be just as perfect.

Unlike Queen Morghyn, the lass's fair hair was free from restraint, flowing around her body. It hung to her waist, and she a blue ribbon headband on that matched her dress.

"Hello, Sir Kearney." She inclined her head and met his eyes.

He had to clear his throat. Her sultry voice was like a caress and his thoughts scattered.

Just how she should sound.

A tremor shot down his spine and Alasdair chided himself.

Her coloring, as well as heart shaped face with high cheekbones, marked her as kin to Queen Morghyn even if he hadn't been told, but her eyes were hazel. The perfect mix of light brown, green and even — Blessed Spirit help him — gold flecks.

She was looking at him expectantly.

Why?

Ah…she'd greeted him, hadn't she?

Speak, idiot, lest she think you daft!

Alasdair cleared his throat — again — and bowed with just as much of a flourish he'd presented for his queen. "Nice to see you again, my lady."

Her face was stained an adorable shade of pink when their gazes met again, but he fought the urge to shift in his boots.

The traitor below his belt was interested in her suddenly — something he didn't need. Alasdair might be loose with his favors as his brothers teased — but he'd never touched a lass of nobility — let alone the queen's cousin.

Wasn't about to start, either.

She was no doubt innocent, which doubly crossed her off his list.

"Sir Alasdair Kearney!" King Nathal boomed from across the hall. *Saving* him. The king closed the distance to between him and the ladies with only a few long strides.

"Hello, Your Highness." Alasdair bowed.

King Nathal buffeted the back of his shoulder and beamed.

Alasdair grinned, rocking in his boots so he wouldn't

embarrass himself and keel over. Boisterous as always, the king was a big man, and the tap was more of a pounding.

"Good to see you, lad."

"You too, Majesty." He nodded, meeting his king's pale blue eyes.

"I see you've greeted my ladies. You better not have used your charms on my wife." King Nathal flashed a mock-stern glare along with his growl.

Queen Morghyn laughed and patted her husband's decorative Terraquist-blue doublet, right over his heart. "No one could steal me away from you, my love. Not in form or affection." She gazed up at her man.

The king looked down, softness in his expression that made Alasdair feel like an intruder.

Lady Elissa swayed in her pretty slippers, as if she felt it, too.

His eyes locked onto her hazel ones against his will. Looking at her wouldn't help his forbidden interest, especially since he couldn't help but notice the green and gold flecks in her gaze.

She smiled. It was just a slight curve of her lips, but it was all for him.

Alasdair's gut clenched. He needed to go. Maybe Roduch needed his help. Or Leargan. Was it time to line up?

But there he stood, locked onto the lass, and she on him.

The king spoke, breaking the spell. "Shall we go out to the bailey? The ceremony won't be long now. Seats are ours for the taking." He lifted his arm for his wife.

Queen Morghyn smiled and tucked herself close to her husband, but she looked at Alasdair. "Will you escort my cousin, Alas?"

Lady Elissa looked at him.

He forced a nod. "Aye, of course." Alasdair offered his arm, trying not to gawk at the delicate hand that slid into the crook of his elbow.

A bolt of energy shot into his biceps and he almost jumped. Through layers of fabric, he could feel her touch. He imagined how it would be to have her hands on his bare skin—then promptly banished the ludicrous idea.

"Thank you." Those hazel eyes bored into him, like before.

He lost the battle with trying not to fidget. His armor felt too small, as did his skin. Straightening his spine didn't help the constriction in his chest. Alasdair forced a nod and a smile.

"Shall we?" The queen's query was as bright as her smile. Alasdair jumped.

"Are you all right, Sir Kearney?" Lady Elissa whispered. Her pale brows were drawn tight.

She was concerned for him?

He cleared his throat, needing her to stop looking at him like that. "Aye, lass—my lady. I'm well, my lady. Thank you for asking." Widening his smile made her blush deepen, which pleased him—much more than it should. However, his sharp mental reprimand did no good.

Lady Elissa offered a demure nod, one corner of her delectable mouth up.

He hoped the slight smile wasn't because she'd sensed his discomfort.

The king and queen walked in front of them, but Alasdair didn't care to eavesdrop on their conversation. He was acutely aware of the lass trying to match his longer stride. She didn't plaster herself to his side like the queen to the king, but Lady Elissa wasn't far away, either.

Her hip brushed his, and he could feel every inch of her petite frame from that barely-there touch. Heat spread, flipping his stomach and making his cock twitch. Alasdair wanted to tug away, or warn her not to touch him again—because it made him want more—but what could he say?

Scream *'Don't touch me!'* like a scorned lass? Alasdair swallowed a groan of disgust.

What's wrong with you?

Not a question he was familiar with. He tried not to seem too eager to run away as soon as he'd seated her next to the queen on the front row of the linen-covered chairs before the dais.

Lady Elissa thanked him and he straightened, giving her a nod because his voice had evaporated.

Queen Morghyn smiled and patted his forearm. "I appreciate your kindness."

The lass blushed when Alasdair spared her a look. He fought the urge to swallow...again. She was so beautiful it hurt to look at her. Sweet, polite and...*innocent.*

Not. For. You.

He didn't want a lass of his own, so it mattered not, anyway.

"It was nothing, Your Grace." He thanked the Blessed Spirit when Dallon waved hello from the end of the aisle. Alasdair bowed deeply. "My lady, Majesties, I'm sure I'll see you later."

King Nathal smiled and gave a hasty nod. People were lining up to greet him.

Alasdair took the opportunity to dash away without a backward glance. He took his place beside his fellow guardsman behind the last row of chairs.

His partner for the day threw him a look. "You all right?"

"Right as rain." He flashed his signature grin and received an arched eyebrow as an answer.

"It'd better not," Dallon said.

"Better not what?"

"Rain. I hear it ruins weddings."

"Ah. Just a figure of speech."

Amusement danced in Dallon's brown eyes. "Are you sure you're well?" He crossed his arms over his broad chest, partially blocking the Seal of Greenwald etched into his decorative armor. His usually wild dark hair was brushed flat and neat—and shorter, not quite reaching the back of his neck. Dallon must've gotten a trim for the wedding.

"Aye, why?" Alasdair tried not to bristle at his brother.

"You seem…out of sorts."

"Me?" He glued his gaze to Dallon's, even though his instinct was to glance toward the first row of seats. If he did, his friend would know where his mind was—and tease him relentlessly, no doubt. "I'm great." Alasdair gave a dramatic sigh. "Well, if you must know, I'm in mourning."

His brother snorted. "Not that again."

"What?" He packed all the innocence he could managed into the word.

Dallon laughed. "I hope to the Blessed Spirit you didn't hound Roduch about choosing to wed. Again."

"Of course I did. What kind of big brother would I be if I hadn't?" He grinned.

Shaking his head, Dallon said a few curses, but he grinned, too. "I suppose you wouldn't be yourself then."

Alasdair chuckled and patted Dallon's shoulder. He felt normal—almost.

Kale and Teagan arrived then, catching his attention. He waved as they nodded and lined up next to him and Dallon, and the rest of their brothers weren't too far behind, most arriving in the pairs they'd approach the dais in.

They were to be posted behind the last row of chairs, as ceremonial guards until it was time to salute their brother-in-arms and his new wife after the exchange of vows.

Wedding guests were starting to file in as well, people taking seats and quietly chatting. Most took a moment to greet the king and queen before finding their seats.

Alasdair made his gaze stay away from the first row of chairs. He didn't need to look at the lass. Instead, he scanned the row of men standing beside him. All were dressed in their finest clothing, covered by matching decorative breastplates, swords belted at their waists. As the eldest, he stood farthest left, almost directly behind Lady Elissa.

He had a keen vantage point of the queen's cousin, although he wasn't going to use it.

At. All.

Music started softly—coming from a large magical sphere that hovered above the dais—as if to let the crowd know to quiet down so they could start. It got gradually louder, playing a soothing, welcoming tune as they waited for the wedding to begin.

The device was no doubt Lucan's design. Alasdair had never seen the like before, but true to all of the lad's ingenuity, the idea would likely spread.

He straightened his spine, and felt more than saw all his brothers stand at attention when Roduch and Leargan, along with a Priest of the Blessed Spirit, walked down the aisle and mounted the stairs to the dais.

Alasdair studied his friend. Gone was the worry from earlier. The big knight was radiant—if a man could be so. His face was shaved clean, his blond hair lying in more order than Alasdair had ever seen, and his wedding attire of embroidered pale blue doublet and matching breeches impeccable. The fine ivory tunic beneath was also embroidered with pale blue thread trimming the wide sleeves. It was detailed and delicate, yet not feminine.

Roduch exuded joy.

"Good for him," Dallon whispered.

The ceremony was nice as far as weddings went, he supposed, but his attention remained scattered. Against his will, Alasdair couldn't stop looking at the queen's cousin. Every once in a while, she'd glance over her shoulder, and once or twice her eyes found his. As if she sensed he was staring.

He couldn't stop fidgeting.

Dallon kept arching an eyebrow at him.

Niall, second-in-command of the personal guard, who stood on the far end from Alasdair, sent him a questioning look.

Blessed Spirit, stop being transparent. And stop looking at her.

He made sure to stand very still after that, but his gaze kept wandering to the front row, no matter how he cursed himself.

☆   ☆   ☆   ☆

She could feel his eyes on her.

The handsome knight her cousin had obvious affection for. Sir Alasdair Kearney.

Somehow Elissa wanted to look at him, too. Her heart skipped and she forced herself to focus on the couple pledging themselves to each other on the dais.

The girl was gorgeous, petite, and clad in a lavish pale blue gown. Her smile could've warmed any heart. Her hair was a mass of dark curls that hung loose to her waist. Pale blue buds were woven throughout with ribbons, and a woven crown of flowers, the same blue roses, sat atop her head, making her look like a wood nymph from one of the stories Elissa had read.

Mistress Avril only had eyes for the man who'd just been instructed to take both of her hands by the priest.

For the knight—Sir Roduch Grantham—it was the same. He towered above the lass, more than a foot taller than she, but their love for each other was plain.

He wore a doublet that matched her wedding dress, and his breeches were of the finest material, a slightly darker blue than the wedding gown. His handsome face was clean-shaven, and his smile for his bride was brilliant.

Elissa frowned.

Marriage.

That would be her—in what?

Days?

Mere sevendays?

Months?

Would she find love with one of her suitors as the king intended? So her husband would look at her the way Sir Roduch was looking at Mistress Avril?

Would Elissa have to marry anyway if she didn't?

King Nathal had said no. She'd always trusted him. But could she in this?

Could she love one of her suitors? What if *none* of the four men presented to her was *the one*?

Her stomach dipped and she fidgeted on her seat next to the queen. Her cousin sent her a sidelong glance; Elissa forced a smile.

Lightning flashed overhead, causing several of the guests to look up. People murmured about rain.

She sucked in a breath. Needed to calm down before her magic caused a storm and ruined Mistress Avril's wedding.

A rumble of thunder rolled in. Elissa winced. Her heart galloped and she clutched both hands in her lap. She urged her fingers to release the fabric of her gown, but they shook, tingling as magic greeted her. She half-expected the blue fabric to be permanently creased and stained from her sweaty palms.

Water in the clouds above called to her, but she denied the draw of magic and forced them back, commanding the white fluff to recede, so the sun would shine down uninhibited like it had all morning.

Go away.

Calm. Calm. Calm.

Sweat bathed her forehead.

"Issa, is that your doing?" Queen Morghyn whispered close to her ear.

Elissa cleared her throat. She couldn't deny it. She'd never lie to the queen. "Aye. Sorry. Seeing them on the dais has me... thinking of my own impending..."

Her cousin squeezed her hand. "Don't worry, lass. 'Twill be all right. Calm so the magic-blue clears from your eyes. People will notice."

She nodded and chided herself. Elissa hadn't lost control of her emotions in a fashion that affected her magic in longer than she could remember. She returned the queen's kind smile, ordered her heart to regulate, and her stomach to stop churning.

Her peripheral vision caught Sir Alasdair...again.

Elissa hazarded a look in his direction, over her shoulder. He was looking her way. Their gazes collided.

Her heart skipped and two bolts of lightning flashed above. It was heat lighting; the kind that proceeded a summer storm. Very out of place in the fall.

Embarrassment stung her neck and crept into her cheeks, searing her as it refused to disperse. Anyone with a whit of magic would know the impending storm wasn't natural.

Calm down. What's wrong with you?

She straightened her shoulders and intentionally bumped the back of her chair. Elissa needed...

Well, she didn't know *what* she needed.

Clapping took her attention and her eyes snapped back to the dais. She'd missed the pronouncement of man and wife.

The couple was kissing.

Catcalls from the surrounding knights caused the newlyweds to break apart. Elissa smiled at the bride's pink cheeks, but she was still only all-eyes for her new husband.

They stood hand and hand, and waited for the first two knights of the personal guard to make their way up the aisle to salute the couple.

Sir Roduch was a member of the duke's personal guard, so as an addition to the ceremony all his brother-in-arms would approach to let him know they accepted his new wife and she was now included in those they protected.

Her cousin had explained it was a common thing to see in weddings of knights, but Elissa was touched in a way that surprised her. It was a beautiful sentiment. They were *family*.

Sir Alasdair strode up the aisle alongside a tall knight with short dark hair. He didn't spare her a glance, but Elissa couldn't look away. As if captivated by his armor catching the sunlight. She'd never been able to easily read auras, but light surrounded the knight like it was his. His long brown locks shifted as he bowed in tandem with the other knight.

They recited their salute. Then Sir Alasdair said something to make the people on the dais laugh, but Elissa didn't catch it. The groom grinned and the captain, Sir Leargan, shook his head, but he was wearing a smile, too.

Her eyes continued to trail him as he split from his partner. The other knight went right, and Sir Alasdair went left, walking right past her seat.

He inclined his head to the king and queen. Then Sir Alasdair's eyes landed on Elissa. Heat kissed her neck all over again as his gaze didn't waver, as if it was stuck. He was studying her face, and it made her want to shift on the edge of her chair. Again.

His eyes are so blue.

She sat taller and smiled.

Sir Alasdair winked. Then he was gone, walking down the aisle in the direction he'd come.

"Elissa?"

She jumped. The concern in her cousin's tone made her think it wasn't the first time Queen Morghyn had called her name.

"A-aye, Your Majesty?"

"Are you well, lass?" The king leaned toward her from his seat.

"Aye. Of course."

Her cousin didn't look convinced. She reached for one of Elissa's hands and squeezed. "Let us go into the great hall. The feast will begin shortly."

Elissa looked around. She'd been so absorbed in watching Sir Alasdair that she'd missed the couple exiting the dais. Actually, she'd missed *everyone* leaving the raised platform. It was empty. "Of course." She scrambled to her feet.

The queen took King Nathal's arm, but the big man offered the other to Elissa.

She hastily thanked him and slid her hand in the crook of his elbow, chiding herself to focus on why she was here, instead of on a handsome knight.

Elissa forced a laugh to join her cousin's when the king made a jest about everyone being jealous that he had the privilege to escort the two most beautiful women there into the hall himself.

Chapter Six

The feast carried on well into the night, and Elissa couldn't remember the last time she'd enjoyed herself so much. Dancing, laughter and new friends almost made her forget *why* she'd made the journey from Terraquist—*almost.*

She collapsed into a chair after a vigorous group dance to a lively tune about young love.

Greenwald's bards were fantastic, led by a willowy female vocalist with pale blonde hair down to her hips—so blonde it was practically silver. The lass was as beautiful as her voice, too.

Each song was carried across the entire hall by hovering magic orbs that amplified the sound. There were two on the stage, and one more in each corner of the great hall.

She'd never seen anything like them before, but had been told they were the work of the young Mage of Greenwald, Sir Lucan.

Currently, the lovely head bard was singing a slow love song, her long locks swaying as a sweet chorus fairly floated from her mouth.

The bride and groom were at the center of the dancing space in the great hall, eyes only for each other, as if they heard nothing, saw nothing else. The world was only the two of them.

A dreamy sigh to her right had Elissa's eyes darting there, only to collide with the gray orbs of the Duchess of Greenwald, Lady Ceralda Aldern.

A former King's Rider, Lady Cera was renowned for her toughness. Hearing such a light feminine sound from her was a surprise—and had Elissa smiling. "Hello, my lady." She straightened, not wanting the duchess to realize she'd startled her. The table she'd picked wasn't on the dais—where the duke and duchess always sat. She hadn't heard Lady Cera join her, either.

"Hello, my lady," the duchess echoed, a cheeky grin curving her full mouth.

Elissa laughed and inclined her head before gesturing to the dance floor. "She's beautiful." The bride was plastered to her new husband's torso. His strong arms were protecting her as they danced. Even though he was so much taller than his new wife, they looked right. *Perfect.* So much love surrounded them, it was hard not to be envious.

"They're beautiful *together.*"

"They are."

Lady Cera nodded when Elissa looked back at her. The duchess's gown was dove gray and brought out the color of her eyes. The square-cut bodice was laced in the front and low-cut, coming together with straight sides that hinted at hips even as it hugged her slender waist. Her dark red hair was braided and piled on top of her head, but the ends were left free in a mess of dangling curls that surrounded her pretty face.

"With a love like that, you don't need much else." Elissa cursed the wistful sentiment as it left her mouth, but the smile the duchess flashed was agreement. Maybe she was thinking of her husband.

Elissa tried not to frown—or think about the four men from whom she was supposed to select her own. Knowledge of what was in store only caused more nerves, despite the happy evening around her.

Sir Alasdair's blue eyes flashed into her mind. He wasn't one of her choices, no matter how handsome he was, so she really shouldn't think of him. She swallowed against the sudden lump in her throat and her stomach somersaulted.

"You can call me Cera, you know."

"Nay. I could not. You're—"

"No lower in rank than you, really. Blood to the queen and all. And besides, since you're staying here for a while, I thought we could be friends."

"Staying here?"

Lady Cera frowned. "The king didn't tell you?"

"Nay, my lady." She shook her head.

The duchess cursed. "That meddling…" she continued, muttering some very un-duchess-like things. She even called *King Nathal* names.

Elissa blinked. She'd heard the duchess could be a little rough around the edges, but she'd never *seen* it. Or rather, heard it.

Chagrin crossed Lady Cera's face when their eyes met again. "I'm sorry, Elissa. I don't mean to offend. I can call you Elissa?"

"Aye, of course, my lady."

"Cera."

Heat burned her cheeks and she forced a nod. Elissa couldn't call the duchess by her given name, no matter the woman's urging.

Lady Cera grabbed her hand and squeezed. "I wish I could say I'm surprised he didn't tell you, but I'm hoping at the very least, it was in his plan for the evening. However, I'm not sorry I spoiled his *surprise.* You know why you're here, right?"

"If I'm staying, I suppose I don't. I was told it's time for me to marry. And the king has chosen four suitors."

She nodded, and looked as if she was about to say something else, but Lady Aimil Dagget, the wife of the duke's second, Lord Tristan, took the seat next to the duchess, flashing a smile.

"Aimil, glad you joined us. I was just speaking with Elissa, who didn't know King Nathal intended her to stay with us for a while."

The petite dark-haired beauty frowned. Her gown was dark blue, denoting her Province of birth, Ascova, where her father was the duke. "He didn't. *Again.*"

"He did." Lady Cera offered a curt nod.

"I don't understand," Elissa said.

"Our king *loves* to make decisions for the fairer sex and leave them in the dark under the guise of *protection.*" A scowl marred the duchess's pretty face.

"Oh."

"You don't have to worry, though." Lady Aimil smiled. "We'll take care of you."

Elissa didn't know what to say. "Why wouldn't he tell me I'm to stay? I assumed we'd travel to the homes of my suitors."

"They're coming here." Lady Cera said. "My cousin should arrive tomorrow or the next day."

"My cousin should be here soon, as well," Lady Aimil smiled.

"Both of you are blood kin to my suitors?" She swallowed a gulp. That could be good or bad. Did she want to know about the men *before* she met them? Perhaps Elissa could ask questions.

"Lakyn is actually my favorite cousin. Well, besides his sister Nyja, but don't tell I said that." Lady Aimil's dark eyes twinkled.

"Avery's my only cousin, but I adore him."

Elissa tried not to frown. Both ladies cared a great deal for the men she'd be presented. What if she didn't like either one?

"What's wrong, Elissa?"

"N-n-nothing."

"Your expression says otherwise, my lady," Lady Aimil whispered.

"This is…"

"Overwhelming." Lady Cera spoke the word at the same time it fell from Elissa's mouth.

She could only nod. "I…assumed I would marry. Someday. Not like this." She bit her bottom lip so it wouldn't tremble.

Sympathy bled from the eyes before her. "I know," Lady Cera said. "But it'll be all right. My cousin Avery is shy and sweet. He's young, but he's a good man. If you don't pick him, it's fine. Just meet him."

"My cousin Lakyn would rather breed horses than get married, but he's funny and kind."

"What if I don't pick either?" The blurt was out of her mouth before she could slap her hand over it, and her cheeks seared all over again.

Lady Cera laughed. "Then you don't. Lord Camden and Lord Audon are still on the list."

What if I don't want them, either? But she couldn't ask. "Do you know them?"

"I've only met Lord Audon a few times. I know his father better, since he's the lord of a holding under my uncle's purview in Tarvis, but I've only heard good things about him. And yes, I know Lord Cam quite well. I like him very much." Lady Cera winked. "He's certainly not a hardship to gaze upon."

Lady Aimil snorted.

"Blessed Spirit, it's like going to market for a man," Elissa said under her breath, but evidently not low enough. Both her companions laughed and heat threatened to consume her face.

"I think Elissa will get along just fine with us," Lady Cera declared.

"I agree," Lady Aimil echoed.

"I'm sorry." Elissa chided herself for her new talent of excited utterance. Her gut churned.

"Whatever for?" The duchess's gray eyes danced. "You can be yourself here, Elissa. I promise you that."

A striking redhead with hair in a long plait and wearing a red-orange gown that matched her fiery locks made her way to the table.

"Ans, where've you been?" Lady Cera exclaimed, wearing a frown.

As the duchess said the nickname, Elissa realized the pretty woman was Sir Murdoch's daughter, Ansley.

"Brynn was giving the nursemaid fits. She wouldn't be comforted, so I had to go see what was wrong before she woke her brother. Brogan was fussy all day and she'd just gotten him to sleep." She blew out a breath as she took the last open seat at the table.

"Oh…teeth coming in?"

"Aye. I got her fed and down, though. My father spoiling her is more the reason, I think. He held her most of the afternoon. When I hollered at him, he complained about me taking his grandchildren from him when he never gets to see them."

The duchess' grin was full of mischief. "Just wait. He'll be threatening to retire to Greenwald."

"Oh, Blessed Spirit, you hush. Leargan'd be in a tizzy."

The ladies laughed.

Elissa couldn't imagine any man *in a tizzy*, not to mention the captain of the Aldern guard. She'd known the knight when he'd still lived in Terraquist. Sir Leargan was strong and handsome. Before coming to Greenwald, he'd never been far from King Nathal's side. He was a king's favorite, not unlike Mistress Ansley's father, his own captain.

"Ans, have you met Lady Elissa, the queen's cousin? She's going to be staying with us for a while."

Sir Murdoch's daughter turned her attention to Elissa, her smile widening. "No, not officially, though my da speaks highly of you."

"He does?" she squeaked, and she chided herself.

Mistress Ansley nodded, her teal eyes kind. "Aye. Welcome to Greenwald. I hope you like it here."

Elissa took a breath. "I do very much already. I am enjoying myself tonight."

"I'm glad," Lady Cera said. The duchess reached over to squeeze Elissa's hand.

The ladies continued their chatter; she could tell they were great friends. They laughed and teased, discussing everything from horses and their wolf bondmates—evidently Lady Cera's wolf and Lady Aimil's had had a litter of cubs some months ago—to husbands and babies. They spoke about duties and trips to market, and plans for the upcoming fortnight. Of the feast attendees, the ladies speculated on whose gown was the finest, which man looked the most handsome—their husbands, of course, were the most perfect in their eyes.

They included Elissa in every facet of conversation. It was *normal*, yet different in a way that she'd never experienced before. Warmth and gratefulness washed over her. These ladies could be *real* friends to her, closer than even her roommate Dara. She wanted that.

Lady Aimil giggled at something Lady Cera said, and both looked around the great hall. Elissa's gaze followed theirs. The atmosphere was light; happiness and laughter enveloping the vast space.

The bards went right into another love ballad, and more couples drifted to the dancing space, swaying to the music and holding each other close, the king and queen included.

Elissa watched the rulers for a moment. They conversed as they danced, but her cousin's face was lit up for her husband—not unlike the newlyweds dancing near them—despite being married longer than she'd been alive. She couldn't help but envy that kind of devotion.

Could she expect it from one of her suitors?

Movement caught her eye and she glanced to her left. Her stomach somersaulted when she noticed who was approaching their table.

"My ladies." Sir Alasdair bowed deeply.

Her three companions greeted him warmly.

Elissa had to swallow for some reason. She wanted to fidget, but made herself remain still.

"How are you this fine evening, Alas?" the duchess asked.

"I'm well. Thank you for asking." He winked and even though it wasn't directed at her, Elissa felt telltale heat burn her cheeks.

Lady Cera laughed.

"I've come to steal Lady Elissa away, if she'll have me."

Elissa squirmed.

"Why of course. We're just chatting," Lady Cera said.

When Sir Alasdair turned his attention to her, Elissa's heart darted from canter to full gallop. "Would you care for a dance with me, my lady?"

"Aye." She was relieved the word came out steadily, because nerves had taken over her body. Elissa returned his warm smile and placed her hand in his outstretched one.

A bolt of energy shot up her arm and she almost jumped. She studied his face, but if the knight had felt anything, his expression betrayed nothing.

What was that?

She was torn between moving away and the desire to shift even closer to him. Her legs wobbled, and Elissa blamed it on all the dancing she'd already done, especially the last one. The lively tune that'd required more jumps and turns than not.

And perhaps two goblets of wine. Aye, that must be it.

Elissa rarely imbibed, and the sweet wine had tasted more like juice. She'd likely lost her head.

She ignored the voice that reminded her that she'd followed conversation with the ladies with no fear of lucidity.

"Are you well, lass—my lady?"

"Aye." Elissa widened her smile, but when her gaze collided with his, her heart stuttered all over again.

So handsome.

His dark hair was loose now, not tacked down as it had been for the wedding, and the thick locks played at his shoulders, their rich brown hue catching the light of the magic orbs in the great hall. His eyes were so blue. Stubble graced his jaw. It was light, new, as if he always went clean-shaven.

She caught herself imagining what it would feel like beneath her fingertips and banished the thought. Elissa would never reach for him like that. It was inappropriate—and much too intimate.

He led her to the dance floor and she couldn't help but stare at the way he moved. He was tall, probably eight or nine inches more than her five-foot-six, yet he moved with grace. Sir Alasdair smiled again when they found an open spot, and reached for her hand. He held it high in one of his, as the dance required, and it took all she was made of not to jump when he settled his other hand at her waist.

Sir Alasdair had shed the decorative chest plate he'd worn for the ceremony. His navy doublet looked soft and a part of her wanted to touch his chest to see if it was so.

Elissa settled her free hand on his shoulder. He was solid and warm, the heat seeping into her palm through the fabric.

Awkwardness made her eyes dart around the dancing area. They were one of the few couples not holding each other close.

Her belly fluttered and she didn't know whether to feel grateful or jealous.

She easily followed the dance, letting Sir Alasdair lead; he never missed a step. He was elegant in his movements, but the more they danced, the more Elissa wished she was against his chest.

His attire hinted at thick muscle. His shoulders were broad and she could see defined biceps even through the wide sleeves of his ivory under tunic.

Her eyes couldn't help but trail down. The knight's waist was tapered, and even that was…attractive.

I'm attracted to him.

Elissa jolted in his hold.

"Lass—my lady. Are you well?"

She met his eyes, scolding herself for studying his body in the first place—and forced a smile instead of giving in to her urge to swallow hard. "Aye. I'm enjoying our dance." True, but she wanted to move closer to him. Elissa didn't.

"I'm glad. You're a fine dancer."

"Thank you. As are you."

Sir Alasdair whirled her around. "Well, I have to be. To impress the lasses, you know." He winked.

Elissa giggled, she couldn't help it. "I can see why my cousin thinks you charming."

His chuckle was deep, endearing. "Aye. Airs I've to keep up. Especially if the queen thinks so."

She couldn't stop smiling. Or staring into his sapphire eyes.

The music melted into another song, this one livelier, requiring faster steps. People clapped with the beat and Elissa looked around the dancing space. Most couples, including the king and queen, didn't leave the floor, they just adapted to the change in song.

"Lass, shall we leave or dance once more?"

"Dance," Elissa said.

The knight gripped her waist, lifting and swinging her

around without missing a step. She laughed with delight, and tried not to focus on the fact Sir Alasdair was touching her body. Elissa kept up with him and the music, having the most fun she'd had all evening. She didn't have time to be embarrassed his large hands were all over her—appropriately, of course.

She laughed, he chuckled, and they moved with the other couples.

Elissa mourned when the music faded and the knight's hands fell away.

"Shall we get something to drink, my lady? You're flushed."

"I am?" Her hands flew to her cheeks.

The smile curving his lips was soft, and he offered a nod by way of answer. Sir Alasdair lifted his arm and her face burned even more, but she tucked her hand into his elbow.

He returned her to the table where the ladies were still sitting after they'd both gotten a drink from a passing servant.

She found herself mourning all over again when his captain called his name. The knight had been about to take a seat beside her.

"Alas, may I have a word?" Sir Leargan asked.

"Aye, of course." Sir Alasdair glanced at her. "Thank you for the dancing, my lady. I enjoyed myself."

Elissa didn't find it hard to smile. "I did as well. Thank you for asking me."

The captain went to his wife's side and planted a chaste kiss on her mouth. He whispered something that made Mistress Ansley smile.

She found herself staring as the two men weaved their way to the entrance of the great hall, and disappeared from sight.

Chapter Seven

"You want me to what?"

The wedding feast was in full swing, yet his commander had asked to see him in private, in Lord Aldern's personal leger room.

It's just as well.

Alasdair had needed to be pulled away from Lady Elissa. His captain had rescued him, as the king had that morning.

His captain arched a dark eyebrow and Alasdair slid to the edge of the chair across from the duke's desk. "Guard Lady Elissa Durroc." His longtime friend obviously didn't like repeating himself.

Alasdair stared, trying to gather his words, but his thoughts were dominated by a flaxen-haired pixie.

He shouldn't have danced with her. Especially the second song, which consisted of picking her up, swinging her around, holding her close. Touching her…everywhere.

It wasn't how he wanted to touch her, really, but still. Alasdair now knew what she felt like. Her slim waist, the small of her back, the curve of her hips.

Stop. Now.

Forbidden.

Even more so now that his captain had assigned her to him. As a duty.

Before he'd sucked down some ale and gathered the bollocks to approach her, his evening had consisted of him perched at the personal guard's table, watching Lady Elissa as if she was prey to his predator.

No matter what Alasdair tried, he couldn't keep his eyes off the lass. She laughed and danced, her face lighting up as she socialized with the ladies of Greenwald.

She was beauty personified, her long pale hair swaying with every graceful movement, either walking across the hall, or on the dance floor for a lively tune.

He hadn't been able to remain in his seat and not ask her to dance. Alasdair had needed to bask in some of the glow she was giving off. Her joy made him smile. Made him…want.

Want what? Her?

Aye.

The only thing he regretted was the *forbidden* part of the situation. Oh, the *suitors* part was considerably undesirable as well.

It matters not.

Too bad repetition of the idea wasn't doing shite for his want.

"She knows not why she's really here. Lucan has assured the duke and the king he can place a magical damper, if you will, on her powers without her knowledge. She can still use her magic as always, but it will make it so anyone seeking that kind of magic won't be able to sense her," Leargan continued.

"To protect her."

"Aye. Her suitors will arrive soon, starting with Lady Cera's cousin and the rest within the next two sevendays. Just act as her escort. Keep her safe, keep your eyes peeled, and use your sword if necessary."

"Escort?"

"Chaperone the visits as well, actually."

"Me?"

"Alas, is something wrong?"

"Nay. Just trying to take all this in."

One corner of Leargan's mouth shot up. "I'm not exactly used to you questioning my orders."

He straightened his back and met his captain's dark eyes. "I apologize, Captain. I'm not trying to question you, nor my duty. Only trying to fathom why *me*."

"Because I trust you."

"To be chaperone to a lady?" He would've laughed if he didn't think Leargan would be offended.

"Aye. Your sword is only matched by myself, and perhaps Lord Aldern."

Alasdair smirked. All the men of the guard had skills with a sword that not many could best. But his captain and the duke loved to spar. Who won their matches tended to shift back and forth, and involved a lot of teasing on both sides.

He'd presented them a small gold sword mounted on a plaque and they passed it back and forth, making a grand jest of who maintained custody and for how long. All the men bet well in advance as to who would remain the master.

Alasdair had been filling his purse with his brothers' and the castle men-at-arms' coin for months. The prize was the best idea he'd ever come up with. Especially since it'd been well received by his captain and the duke.

"Besides, she won't *tempt* you, considering she's a noble lady." Leargan said with a tease and a wink.

Wrong. You have no idea.

His heart thundered and he swallowed hard. His temples throbbed. Alasdair couldn't exactly blurt how wrong his captain was this time.

Oh, so wrong.

"Alas…" Leargan cocked his head to one side, studying him. Making him want to squirm.

Could his captain see through him? "Aye?" he croaked.

"I want you to do this because it'll be a nice change of pace for you."

"A change of pace?" Again, the query came out cracked, delayed.

"Aye. You seem discontent with your duties as of late."

His instinct was to protest, but his captain was right. Alasdair didn't have it in him to train men-at-arms to the sword, even though he did enjoy his time with the lads. Too bad everyone commented on his apparent skill as a teacher. "I don't mind lessons with Alaric, Brodic, and Lucan."

They'd been living in peace, and while it was more than acceptable, he'd been itching for some action. Some kind of change. A challenge. A fight that meant something. A battle, even.

Sparring kept his skills sharp, but was missing an edge of danger he thrived on.

"Aye, I know it. Those can remain the same, our young squires and Lucan are improving under yours and Roduch's tutelage," Leargan said.

He let the praise roll over him, and offered a slight smile. "I'm sorry I was transparent." Alasdair prayed Leargan had only spotted his unrest about his duties, and not about Lady Elissa Durroc.

His captain grinned. "We've known each other a long time, you and I."

Alasdair chuckled, forcing himself to relax. "Aye, so we have. I appreciate that you know me so well, is all." At least at the moment.

If his captain noticed his attraction to the lass that was now his charge, would it change his new duties? Leargan knew he valued his self-control as much as his sword, so probably not.

He had no intention of acting on his draw to Lady Elissa.

"You know me just as well." Affection shone in his captain's dark eyes. "So, other than your afternoon lessons with the lads, your day-to-day will be with Lady Elissa. She's staying in the guest wing, so you'll move to the room next to hers, to be at close hand."

The lass must be in grave danger if he needed to be at her side, at the ready all times of the day.

Alasdair arched an eyebrow. "Tell me what I need to know."

"I'm getting there."

He forced himself back in the chair, loosening his shoulders. "Why does she need a guard when she's safely within the castle walls?"

"The king will take no chances with her. She's not to venture out of the gates."

"Understood."

"Some very dangerous men are after her for her magic."

"And she doesn't know this?"

"Nay."

"Hasn't the king learned keeping information from smart lasses does no good?" Alasdair smirked.

Leargan looked as if he was fighting a smile. "I have a feeling Lady Elissa is a bit more placid than Lady Cera or my Ansley."

"But there is fire in her eyes."

His captain paused.

Alasdair swallowed a curse.

Leargan was really studying him now.

Why the hell did you say that? He tried not to fidget on the chair—an urge so foreign Alasdair froze and intentionally pushed his shoulders into the wooden back of his seat. He cleared his throat.

"Do you remember the lass murdered a few sevendays past? From that small holding on the northwestern border of Greenwald and Terraquist?"

"Of course." Relief washed over him that Leargan made no mention of his comment.

"She was the first of three. Whole families slaughtered."

Alasdair cursed. "How is it tied to our new lady?"

"They were all blonde, and of an age with Lady Elissa."

"Shite. They're looking for her."

"Aye, so the king and my father-by-marriage think. But they haven't a clue *where* she is." Leargan shook his head.

"And we need to keep it that way."

"Aye."

"Who's after her?"

Leargan's regret was palpable. "The king doesn't know. The second lass lived at a holding in North Ascova, within a day's ride of Terraquist. The last lived in Terraquist, a few hours from Terraquist Main. Tomorrow, the king wants to see the Greenwald site. He's taking his twin mages and Lucan. Maybe the three of them working together can find magical answers."

His captain launched into a story twenty turns past. One of murder and magic that'd left a wee lass an orphan.

Alasdair's gut ached. He might not have any magic to speak of, but his own childhood wasn't so different than the queen's beautiful cousin's, as far as missing parents went. "What *does* Lady Elissa know?"

"That she's here to meet her suitors. The king wants to keep it that way. He'd like to steer her toward Lord Camden Malloch, the Duke of Dalunas."

He swallowed again, trying not to wince at the fact he would see her with men—one of which she'd marry. He'd see them court her, make her smile. Make her laugh?

Like he had.

Alasdair frowned.

Lady Elissa is not for you.

Which was just how he wanted it.

She was noble—likely innocent—so he couldn't bed her

anyway. Which was all he was interested in. Perhaps he needed to go into the city. He'd not had a lass for almost a month, his longest period of celibacy in turns. Greenwald Main had some nice taverns. And he had a lass in every one.

"When do I move to the guest wing?" He cursed the shake in his voice, and the eyebrow his commander arched at him. Again.

"The king isn't leaving for a few days. So if not tonight, tomorrow is sufficient. Take your time to gather your things, if you need to."

"All right."

Leargan's eyes roved his face but his captain said nothing.

"I'll protect her."

"I know you will."

He needed to lighten the mood. He couldn't have Leargan looking at him like that. "Perhaps I'll advise her who to marry."

His captain laughed. "You?"

"I'll never marry, but I'm not so bad at helping one choose a mate." Alasdair arched an eyebrow of his own, giving his captain a long look. "Need I remind you I knew Mistress Ansley was your match before you did, my dear captain?"

Leargan laughed. "Right. And clouded her mind with reprobate stories. She is *still* hassling me to tell her what happened in the stables."

He chuckled and shook his head. "That, my friend was your doing. *You* brought it up. I only told her about you getting your hide tanned when we got caught watching the servant girls bathe."

His friend grumbled, but wore a smile as he shook his head. "Well, just warn me before you go sharing any more epiphanies. Or better yet, *never* share any more with my wife."

"Of course, Captain. Your secrets are safe with me." Alasdair grinned.

"I don't believe that for a second. She bats her eyes and smiles sweetly and you'll tell all."

"Well your lass is no hardship to look at, Captain."

Leargan mock-growled.

He laughed again. "You're lucky she's been busy with the twins."

His captain beamed, his pride as a father practically radiant. "They're getting so big, I can't believe they're nine months old. Brogan looks like me, despite the red hair. Of course, her father is overjoyed our son is a redhead like him, but Brynn already has the big man wrapped around her pinky, despite my dark locks, or so Captain Murdoch says."

Alasdair couldn't keep the smile off his face. He was happy for his friend, but had no desire for the same. Lady Elissa popped into his head and he fought a frown.

"Well, I'll not keep you any longer, unless you have questions?"

"Nay."

"As progress develops, we'll discuss it. The king and Lord Gallard are continuing to investigate."

"Lord Aldern and yourself as well, I would assume, since murders were in our Province."

"Aye, of course."

"I would rather assist you and the duke."

Leargan smiled. "You are. Keeping Lady Elissa safe is just as important as finding who's done this."

Alasdair tried not to grumble like a spoiled lad. "Very well."

"Anything else?"

"Nay."

The captain stood. "Good. I'd like to dance with my wife before the feast ends." Leargan clapped him on the shoulder. "Come, my friend. I'm sure there's a lass or two awaiting you, since I secreted you from the great hall."

Alasdair smirked.

Too bad the first thing to pop into his mind was a pair of hazel eyes.

chapter eight

Sleep had done him good. Although he hated to admit it, Drayton had no idea how much time had passed. He stood from his soft pallet and stretched. His back popped, but it felt good, as if he was letting go of built up tension.

He breathed deeply, *in-out, in-out,* for several minutes. The silence of his dank home enveloped him. Not even a drip of condensation could be heard. No air moved, since it couldn't pass through his spell-wall. It was neither hot nor cold in the large cavern.

Drayton closed his eyes and centered himself where he stood. For the first time in days…maybe *months*…he felt good. "Better than good."

His first two steps away from his bed told him his legs didn't ache.

There was no delay when he called to his magic. Warmth rushed his limbs, loosening him even more. Bathing him in light and contentment.

It won't last long.

It was always like this when he woke from restorative sleep. The false hope that everything was all right with his body…his powers.

The negative thoughts made him frown and he pushed them away.

Drayton wouldn't have to endure this…existence…for much longer. He'd have the lass soon, absorb her magic, then search for another like her.

A child he could raise.

The plan that'd been botched with the lass all those turns ago could finally see itself through.

He wished one of the dead lasses had been the one he sought. All three had had children already. Drayton could've probed them for elemental powers. Might've even gotten lucky to find one. Magic was passed through the generations, after all.

Too bad he couldn't wait to absorb the missing lass' powers. If he had a turn or two, he could sire a child with her. She was so powerful there was no doubt her own blood would be strong like her. He could live for more than a century with the lass *and* her child's powers.

It mattered not that he was thinking of killing his *own* child. Blood liked blood, and an elemental of his own line could make him even stronger.

Too bad there hadn't been any others like him in his family, though they were long gone by now, even his youngest sibling. He'd hunted down his descendants — the children of his siblings, as well as their children and theirs. Not one of more than one elemental power in the line. He'd killed them all in a rage, down to the last wee one.

Hindsight reveals all.

Drayton lifted his arm, said a few spellwords and smiled when the cavern lit up before him. The draw of power hadn't weakened him. He jogged up the steps of his dais. Whirling around the place still didn't wind him — body or magic.

The invigoration was odd, considering the degradation of his form as of late, but perhaps the trance he'd put himself into before he'd passed out had done its job. Hopefully it would last longer than the previous time. He was tired of feeling his three-hundred-and-twenty odd turns, even if it was only natural — even more so since his turns had been stolen.

Natural wasn't a word he was fond of.

Drayton refused to die.

He paced the length of his dais, his fingertips pressed into his bottom lip. The half-breed needed to work faster. This false energy wouldn't last long.

The lass was strong. The most powerful elemental he'd ever

encountered, even more so than himself with his natural powers at the peak of his turns — when he'd been in his mid-twenties.

Young. So young.

Their encounter had stunned him, considering she'd been under two turns old. It was a waste to just take her magic. He needed to make it last *longer* somehow.

Drayton's thoughts spun in chaos that made his temples ache. He closed his eyes and thought of his mother — the source of his magic. She'd been a powerful elemental like him. He'd been her favorite child — which said a great deal, considering she'd given birth to seven.

She'd passed by the time he'd absorbed the first mage to sustain his life. Most of his older siblings had as well. Most of his siblings' children had been grown and old by the second. No one from his bloodline had been alive for the third.

He could still see the surprise on his family's faces when he'd slaughtered them. But he should've kept the children alive. Bred them. There could've been an elemental eventually. Even one with mastery over only one power would sustain him for a period of time. Months. Perhaps a turn.

"That's it!" He froze as his voice echoed off the massive cavern ceiling.

Drayton would seek an elemental — any would do, though he could hope for a young water mage, since he was drawn to water most.

Then, when his lass was captured, he would get a child on her. Keep her alive until it was born. Test it for magic. Absorb the lass' powers and raise his child — or kill it.

He smiled and made a fist.

Always liked when he had a plan.

A foolproof plan it is.

★　★　★　★

Elissa took a breath and let her eyes sweep the guestroom. She smoothed her hands down the front of her silver gown. She'd chosen it as homage to the Province she was staying in. She preferred the glimmery silver fabric more to the pale green color of Greenwald.

The queen had gifted her with it, though her cousin had given her a dress of Greenwald green as well, and many others to meet her suitors. The delicate lace embellishments on the bodice of the silver gown made her feel feminine. It was even finer than the blue dress she'd worn to the wedding. One of the finest she'd ever worn.

"The color of your gown matters not." Her shakiness made her close her eyes.

Pull yourself together. Now.

She was supposed to meet Sir Alasdair so he could escort her to the great hall.

Where she would meet the first of her suitors, Lord Avery Lenore.

The last two days of relaxation and enjoyment had been divine. She'd had no duties. Now her true purpose for being in Greenwald came crashing down on her—with the arrival of her suitor.

Her first night in the Province had been...pleasant. Elissa liked the residents of Castle Aldern very much. She'd be sad to leave this place when the time came.

After all the dancing and chatting with the ladies—not to mention the ride in—she should've so been fatigued that she'd collapse in bed. However, a certain pair of blue eyes had haunted her every time Elissa had closed her own.

The second night hadn't been much different as far as the knight was concerned. As a matter of fact, after spending most of yesterday with her chaperone, her thoughts of him before sleep had probably fed her dreams. He'd been at the center of every one.

Elissa had walked in the gardens with Sir Alasdair. She'd taken her meals with him. Talked with him. Laughed with him.

It'd been nice. *More* than nice.

This morning—her third in Greenwald—Elissa needed to focus on meeting her suitor, not on the distraction of her knight. Although, he'd be with her the whole time.

Was she dreading that?

Or taking pleasure from it?

She sighed, her thoughts dancing back to the wedding feast, unbidden. Even after they'd danced, her eyes kept finding him. And most of the time he'd been looking her way.

Her heart skipped—then and now.

Why had the knight been watching her?

Well, of course *that* question had been answered, hadn't it?

Turned out it had nothing to do with them dancing, so enjoying his company yesterday had been foolish—as was looking forward to being with him again, in any capacity.

Fantasy dissipated a bit.

He hadn't been at her side of his own accord. Sir Alasdair was stuck with her.

She was an *assignment.*

Elissa frowned—and not for the first time. Didn't want to be *anyone's* charge. It rather ruined the day she'd spent with him, didn't it?

Besides, two and twenty was an *adult. She* was fully capable of making her own decisions; she didn't need someone to watch over her at Castle Aldern. The king wouldn't have left it up to *her* to choose her husband if she'd been too inept to make choices, right?

Scooting to the bed, she fluffed her pillows—it was as unnecessary as the earlier smoothing of her gown. Magic skittered down her spine. Elissa flexed her fingers and took a breath. She pushed her powers away—or tried to.

The bowl of washing water perched on a pedestal in the privy started swirling. She didn't have to see it to hear the sloshing as it whirled like a cyclone.

"Stop. Get a hold of yourself."

Desperate for a distraction, she made one more loop around the rooms she been given. The space was more than she'd shared with Dara in Terraquist, complete with a private privy, sizable hearth, as well as two sitting areas—one by the fireplace, and the other by the window. There was a desk and ornately carved wooden chair in one corner. It even had parchment and ink at-the-ready, in case she wanted to craft a missive.

The bedding was dark green and ivory, and the mattress was the most comfortable she'd ever had the pleasure to sleep on.

Much finer than home.

Home?

Elissa had no home. She knew not where she'd live.

Tarvis? Dalunas? South Ascova?

Emotion tightened her chest and she blinked away the urge to cry. Magic tingled her limbs again and she cursed in her head—using a word no lady of gentle breeding should know—let alone utter.

She hadn't dealt with this much loss of control of her powers since she'd been a wee lass. It was as unsettling as her forced task of choosing a husband.

Elissa shook her head and squared her shoulders. If even she didn't end up desiring to marry Lord Lenore, she owed him the courtesy of meeting the man.

Duty. She had one. Might as well get it over with.

"That's not fair to him, really." Despite the words, she suddenly had a hard time caring.

Gracious had always been a trait of hers, but *damn* it all. The harsh word didn't shock her. She wasn't like Lady Cera, she'd never say it aloud, but she could *damn well* say the words in her own *damn* head. Although *damn* was mild compared to her earlier thoughts.

Elissa wanted to stomp her foot like Mallyn still did from time to time.

Was this situation fair to *her*? Lady Cera didn't seem to think so.

Don't despair. Prove to the king — and yourself — you can do this.

"Aye. I'm stronger than this." Elissa made a fist and sucked in a breath.

She couldn't dally in her room any longer, no matter how she wanted to. Elissa forced one slippered foot in front of the other, but her stomach tightened more with every step that brought her closer to the door. Her hand shook as she reached for the handle, and she couldn't even hide it. Or stop it.

The corridor was empty.

She'd expected Sir Alasdair. He'd told her he'd be with her shortly. His room was right next to hers.

Should I knock on his door or wait?

When Elissa realized she was pacing, she planted her feet to the stone floor and swore — again. That made her smile. So far, she'd declared four very unladylike curses.

Perhaps the duchess had rubbed off on her.

Waiting on an errant knight had her twisted up in even more knots. Her palms were clammy, her forehead felt damp. She made a fist and knocked on the door next to hers.

Nothing.

With a final shake of her head, Elissa started off down the corridor. She'd just escort herself. The great hall wasn't far, after all. It was rude to keep a suitor waiting.

The word made her tummy somersault all over again.

She'd made the two required turns, and the corridor widened. One more hallway and she'd be standing outside the huge double doors that led into Castle Aldern's great hall.

Elissa heard male voices and her gaze shot to the right. A door was ajar, but only by a few inches. Whoever was inside the room probably didn't realize it wasn't sealed tight.

The king's northern accent—not so different than her own—caught her attention first. Then the duke's, as he responded. His voice was deep, though not as much as King Nathal's, and his accent was a mixture of the mountainous far north, and a slight lilt that had to be from his elfin side. Lord Aldern's mother was an elf, if she remembered correctly.

Though she couldn't speak it, she'd heard people—and elves—speaking Aramourian, the language of the elves. It was a beautiful, flowing dialect that sounded almost musical.

A third male she didn't recognize said something, then the king spoke again.

She stilled. *King Nathal said my name.*

Elissa scanned the corridor. She was alone, so she risked scooting closer, almost against the wall. She didn't touch the stone, but leaned in, straining her ears. Then she straightened. Didn't want to be obvious to any passerby that she was eavesdropping.

She heard three—no, four—male voices in what had to be Lord Jorrin's ledger room.

Guilt churned over her body, but she shut it down. If they were discussing *her,* she had every right to know. After all, the king hadn't been wholly forthcoming. He'd not told her she would be staying in Greenwald, and hadn't even apologized when Lady Cera had mentioned it to him in front of her.

Aye, Elissa had *every right* to know what the men were talking about.

"…is not to know."

She only caught the tail end of King Nathal's statement, so she hazarded one more step, suddenly thankful for her decorative lady's footwear. The soft sole masked her movements.

"What does she know?" the unfamiliar voice asked.

"That I want her to marry."

"Is this not true?"

"Aye, Everett, 'tis true. No worries. I want the lass good and wed. Safe. Far from Terraquist."

Safe? Far from Terraquist?

Why?

"Good."

Everett. The man had to be Lord Everett Lenore, the Duke of Tarvis. Her suitor, Lord Avery's, father.

"The lass is sweet, but stubborn. Lack of knowledge is to protect her, as it has always been."

Always been?

What does that mean?

"She knows not that her parents were murdered? That the fire never happened?"

"Nay."

A cold flush rolled over her form, and her heart plummeted to her toes. Magic made her spine tingle, then a slow burn that heated, not hurt. She needed to get control before she flooded the corridor with water.

Murdered? No fire at Castle Durroc?

Her parents didn't die in a fire which had also taken the life of her older brother? Her father's heir had been four turns to her almost two. She didn't remember Emery — or their parents.

Anger replaced her shock and hurt, creeping up from her gut. Elissa made tight fists at her sides and restrained herself from bursting into the duke's ledger room.

Not telling her she would remain in Greenwald was one thing. Keeping something as important as the death of her family secret was *betrayal*.

Her powers made her skin hum, but she pushed it all way, grasping for calm. Tears stung her eyes and she fought the shudders that racked her frame. She wouldn't cry.

Wouldn't let it affect her. Or her elemental magic. Elissa couldn't.

What was she supposed to do now?

Act like nothing had changed?

Like she hadn't heard the horrible word. The word that was currently floating around in her mind. Taunting. Causing crippling agony.

What else is he keeping from me?

Elissa swiped at her face, but her cheeks weren't damp. *Good.* She swallowed.

"There you are, lass."

She jumped, her heart skipping, her mouth dry. The distraction was what she need. Her magic receded, the pressure in her spine and shoulders loosening. Her thoughts scattered, but for this, she was grateful as well.

Elissa cleared her throat and scrambled to act normal for the knight. Hopefully the blue that glowed from her eyes when she called water had faded. "Sir Alasdair. I waited for you." The statement came out as accusation. She chided herself for it. Hadn't meant to be harsh.

The smile he wore faded a bit. Sir Alasdair bowed at the waist. "I apologize, my lady. I had to take care of something and was gone longer than anticipated. I knocked on your door."

"I knocked on yours." She wanted to demand what'd kept him, though it was none of her business.

Stop. You're acting like a haughty brat. Something she'd always despised in other females at court. Her eyes raked his tall frame as she chided herself and prayed for the beating of her heart to slow.

He was dressed in earth tones today, dark brown breeches and a matching doublet. His long-sleeved tunic beneath was olive green. Dark hair loose, like she'd seen it most often, and his blue eyes were bright, warm, despite her surliness.

The sword at his waist somehow made him look even stronger. *Perfect.* The knight was so handsome it took her breath away.

Sir Alasdair bowed again. "I won't make you wait on me again." He flashed a smile that made her belly tingle. He was teasing, something she was coming to know was a part of who he was.

"See that you don't." She'd meant to be light, to tease back, but Elissa's words came out breathy. She bit back the urge to wince.

He gave her a once-over and sobered. "Are you well?"

She nodded, forbidding her gaze to dart to the ajar door. The men were still talking, making no indication that they could hear her and Sir Alasdair conversing in the corridor. "I am. Eager to meet Lord Avery."

Something flashed in his eyes, but he offered a curt nod.

Elissa took a step toward her chaperone. "Shall we go?"

"Aye." Sir Alasdair offered his arm, like always.

She tucked her hand into his elbow and they were silent the rest of the way to the great hall. Elissa wanted to speak, but couldn't. Her nerves were back, making a mess of her stomach, and she wavered between worries about Lord Avery and what she'd overheard from the duke's ledger room.

What am I going to do?

It wasn't like she could barge into Lord Aldern's private space and petition the men — King Nathal in particular — to tell her what she wanted to hear.

What happened to my parents? What happened to Emery?

Why?

"Are you sure you're all right?" Sir Alasdair asked when they were right outside the huge double doors that lead into the great hall.

"I am, thank you." She forced a smile. "Perhaps my nerves are showing?"

"There's nothing to be nervous about. Lord Avery Lenore is a fine lad." The knight smiled.

Her heart tripped and it had nothing to do with the kind words Sir Alasdair had just said about her suitor. "Let us not keep him waiting then."

"Aye, my lady."

Chapter Nine

h e couldn't stop looking at her. And he really needed to.
Posthaste.
Alasdair was escorting her to meet a suitor. A possible match.

A possible *husband.*

His mouth was dry, and his tongue was plastered to the roof of it. He couldn't have spoken at the moment if ordered by swordpoint.

At least he'd managed not to compliment her when they'd found each other in the corridor. Lady Elissa looked lovely in the shiny silver gown. More than lovely.

Radiant, because *beautiful* was too weak a word.

The bodice hugged her forbidden body, with a low neckline that placed her breasts high for the visual taking. It was tight enough to make her slender waist look even more streamlined, yet still hinted at the hips he'd felt when they'd danced. The skirt was overlaid with intricate silver lace that drew the eye and flowed perfectly as she walked.

Young Lucan had snagged him while he'd waited for her. They'd stepped into the closest sitting room for privacy. The knighted mage had wanted to assure him his spell was cast, and every magical precaution taken—including the fact that Lady Elissa wouldn't be able to sense the protection enveloping her.

Too bad when he'd asked the lad about the ride out to the murdered Greenwald lass' holding the first expression in Lucan's eyes was regret. Even putting his head together with the king's twin mages hadn't shed any light on the killers—except the confirmation that the bastards had strong magic on their side and an inconvenient level of intelligence. They'd covered their tracks—magically and physically, leaving no clues to what direction they'd gone. Lucan had told him his gut said they were up against a tracker—one who was skilled in vast tracking and masking magic.

Alasdair hated to think they wouldn't know anything more unless—or *until*—another young blonde woman was killed. No more should die, especially because of mistaken identity.

The conversation had taken longer than Alasdair had expected, but he'd also not expected Lady Elissa to be so cross with him when he'd finally returned to her.

She'd snapped and demanded. Reminding him of her station. Yet…from what he knew about his charge over the past two days, that was unusual behavior.

A part of him liked the fire that rode beneath the surface. There was more to Lady Elissa Durroc than a pretty face and coveted magic, and Alasdair wanted to be the one to discover it.

He studied her profile as they walked. The same feeling of unease settled over him as before. Something was off about her, and he wasn't wholly convinced it was nerves regarding meeting Lord Lenore. Then again, he'd never been a lass meeting her possible mate for the first time.

He wanted to growl for some reason.

Her grip on his arm tightened when the lord came into view, jarring him from his thoughts—thank the Blessed Spirit.

Alasdair glanced down at her again, but Lady Elissa was looking at the tall, redheaded man with his back toward them, not at him.

Evidently, Lord Avery heard their footsteps, for the lad stopped studying the tapestry hanging above the dais. It depicted a battle, and was quite intricate in its display. Every time Alasdair took a long gander at it, he noticed something he'd missed before. No matter how many times he'd studied it.

They closed the distance and Alasdair released the lass so he could bow to the heir to the Province of Tarvis. "Lord Lenore, it's nice to see you again."

Lord Avery smiled. "You as well, Alas." He stepped forward and clasped Alasdair's forearm.

He returned the physical greeting, though they'd never been more than acquaintances. Alasdair had always liked the shy lad who knew more about magic than anyone he'd ever met—save Lucan.

Lord Avery was taller than the last time he'd seen him—just about equal to his own six-foot-three—but he was still lean. The muscles on his frame weren't those of a bulky knight.

"How was your journey, my lord?"

Gray eyes like his duchess cousin's met his gaze. "It was good, thank you. We made adequate time."

"Good to hear."

Lady Elissa hovered. She hadn't said anything yet, and part of Alasdair didn't want to introduce her.

Lord Avery glanced at her and the apple of his throat bobbed. No doubt the lad knew the *why* of the meeting, and also he'd noticed how lovely she was. He might be young, but the lordling was still a man.

Alasdair wanted to growl. Again.

Lady Elissa smiled and stepped forward. Her eyes were locked onto her suitor.

His face was clean-shaven, and now his cheeks were the same color as his hair. Ruddy and bright.

Alasdair tried not to smirk.

The lord bowed at the waist and smiled. "Hello." The word was a croak, and he cleared his throat as he straightened. He reached for her hand.

She inclined her head and set her fingertips against Lord Avery's palm. "Hello, Lord Avery."

His cheeks stained an even deeper red.

Alasdair tried not to blow out a breath. If the lad wasn't going to do anything but blush all morning, and the lass wasn't going to say much beyond polite conversation, this day was going to be more torturous than he could've imagined.

"It's nice to meet you. I'm Elissa. Lady Elissa Durroc." She spoke gently, as if she would to a child, and Alasdair wanted to roll his eyes.

But it worked.

Lord Avery seemed to regain his composure. "I'm very glad to meet you, too, my lady."

When she glanced his way, Alasdair didn't know what to make of her gaze. She looked him up and down, then did the same to her suitor. Their eyes locked. He arched an eyebrow and *her* cheeks pinkened.

She couldn't be...comparing him to the lad?

If it wouldn't have shamed Lord Avery—and if Alasdair didn't like him—he would've assured the lass there *was* no comparison.

Lady Elissa cleared her throat and put those hazel orbs of hers back where they belonged—on Lord Avery Lenore. "Shall we walk in the gardens, my lord? It's a nice day out. The sun is warm."

The lad jumped and nodded. "Of course. What a wonderful idea."

"Aye, a good plan." Alasdair made himself agree. He'd shown her the gardens in their vast entirety the afternoon before.

Satisfaction that *he'd* taken her there first washed over him before he screamed at himself for being ridiculous. First of all, she wasn't for him. Which was *exactly* how he wanted things.

Pin that to your brain.

Secondly, Lord Avery was a *lad* of twenty.

Alasdair hadn't been a lad for turns. He was all man, and when it came to pursing a lass, he always got what he wanted. They'd never complained, either.

Lord Avery couldn't compete.

He doubted the heir to Tarvis had ever had a woman in his bed. His bashfulness all but shouted his virtue.

Still, aggression raced down Alasdair's spine when the lord offered his arm to Lady Elissa and she slid her petite hand onto his sleeve.

They turned to leave without a word.

He groaned. Was he supposed to follow like some lost wolf cub?

It was going to be a *long* day.

★   ★   ★   ★

She tried to concentrate on the sweet, shy young man whose arm her hand was tucked into, she really did. Lord Avery's blush was charming, and he was handsome.

His face lit up when he talked, especially about magic tomes. Lord Avery's gray eyes were just like the duchess'. So much so, it was like looking into hers. His red hair was cropped short, and was also like his cousin's, yet his was a few shades lighter than Lady Cera's.

At least meeting him is out of the way.

It'd gone well, too. But Elissa's mind kept wandering back to what she'd overheard in the duke's ledger room.

How *dare* King Nathal keep the truth from her?

Her parents were *murdered*. Her brother, too, she assumed. The king hadn't mentioned Emery specifically, but nothing else made sense. They'd died together.

Murdered.

The word bounced around in her head, commanding all her attention.

I need to get out of here.

But she couldn't. Not right now, and maybe not even later. The holding of her birth wasn't far from the center of Greenwald. Perhaps an hour's ride. She wanted to go to it.

Elissa *needed* to see Castle Durroc with her own eyes.

Why? It wasn't like she could do anything about what'd happened so long ago.

Still…

Something felt like it was missing. Had for a long time. Maybe if she went there, the place where she'd lived at the start of her life, she could find it.

Maybe she could remember her parents and her brother.

She swallowed and made her stride match her suitor's. He was talking again. Elissa chided herself to pay attention to him, for the fifth or sixth time.

Castle Durroc can be for later.

It would be. She refused to accept defeat. She'd accepted too much already. Perhaps she should confront the king about what he'd told the Duke of Tarvis.

"My lady?" Lord Avery asked. He shifted in his boots, his discomfort palpable.

Elissa felt a pang in her chest. She didn't want him to be uneasy around her. "Aye, my lord?"

"Are you well?"

"I am, thank you." She made her lips curve upward.

Act natural.

Elissa needed to get through midday meal and the time she was required to spend with the young lord from Tarvis. She forced her eyes on his.

He inclined his head. Lord Avery was tall, several inches past six feet, and he was leanly muscled, more of a scholar than a warrior, but he'd been knighted a few turns ago, so the duchess had told her, as a result of helping defeat the evil former archduke, Lord Varthan. Although his physique was pleasant, he didn't have the muscle-mass of a certain knight that was trailing them.

They toured the gardens, looking at the fall flowers and discussing others that were asleep for the season. They didn't speak of anything of consequence really, and the lack of pressure Elissa felt was nice.

It *almost* took her mind off the king's conversation.

She'd never been meant to hear the words, but they swirled around in her head.

Lord Avery understood the purpose of their time together as well as Elissa, yet neither mentioned—nor seemed to be affected by it.

Well, except for his red face. He was twenty, he'd confessed, and the constant embarrassment made him seem even younger. She suspected this was the first time he'd been introduced to a potential bride, but if so, Lord Avery was doing well. He—and his awkwardness—was endearing, not irritating.

They strolled passed a small fountain, and the water called to her. She stared at the carved copper statues, which were shaped into two children appearing to play in the fountain base. Water shot up between the figures and flowed back down at the center of the piece. It was complex, detailed, but the water drew her eye, not the sculptures.

She lifted her hand and the water froze, forming a ball that floated above the fountain.

"Fascinating," Lord Avery whispered.

Heat bit her neck and her gaze flew to his. The water ball sloshed back into the fountain. "I'm sorry. Sometimes...water just draws me." It was more than that, but she couldn't tell her suitor she was distracted by what the king had told his father. Her magic had shot out on its own, the water demanding it's due.

"That is your main power?"

"Aye."

"Yet you can control earth, wind and fire as well?"

"Aye."

"Can I see?" His speech gained speed with every sentence. His gray eyes shone, and Elissa couldn't help but laugh.

This particular distraction from her chaotic thoughts was welcome.

Lady Cera had told her Lord Avery adored everything magic—as well as understanding *why* magic worked the way it did.

The young lord looked down. "I'm sorry, my lady." His cheeks were bright enough to match his hair again. "It's just... elementals of your strength are rare."

Sir Alasdair cleared his throat as if he was covering up a laugh as well, and Elissa's eyes were drawn to her chaperone. When their gazes met, he tipped his head, a smile playing at the corner of his mouth.

Awareness zinged down her spine and she forced her attention back to Tarvis' heir.

Nothing. Elissa felt nothing when Lord Avery looked at her. Not like when she looked at her knight—something she'd been consciously avoiding after the embarrassing moment in the great hall. His arched eyebrow had shouted he'd caught her sizing the two men up. Comparing.

There is no comparison, a voice whispered.

One was a lad, the other was all man.

Too bad Sir Alasdair wasn't one of her suitors.

Guilt churned her stomach. She swallowed and forced a smile. "It's quite all right, my lord. I understand the rarity of my gifts."

Lord Avery nodded. "I don't mean to be...pushy, my lady. I'm just curious."

She nodded. "You may ask me anything you would like, my lord."

"Call me Avery. '*My lord*' is not necessary—considering the circumstances." His blush reddened even more, if it were possible.

Elissa smiled—this time genuinely. Lord Avery was adorable, even if she didn't feel a spark with him. She already knew he wouldn't be the man she'd marry. But he was kind and sweet, and she would very much like to be his friend. She hoped he'd understand her decision. "You may call me Elissa, in that case. Considering the circumstances, as you say."

She felt Sir Alasdair's eyes on her and threw him a glance. The intensity in that blue gaze made her want to shift on her feet, but she didn't. Elissa ignored the sensation darting all over her body and made herself look at her suitor.

"Very well, Elissa." Lord Avery really did have a fantastic smile. It wasn't as distracting as when the knight smiled at her — blast him — but it wasn't hard to gaze at the lord's countenance.

Her mind darted back and forth.

Lord Avery. Sir Alasdair. The new information about her parents.

Elissa's gut twisted and her heart sped up. She needed distance from her young suitor, lest he sense — or worse, feel — her rapid pulse.

She drew her focus to magic. Needed to regain control of herself or risk something foolish like starting an accidental storm or flooding the fountain and drenching the three of them in the process.

Lord Avery fired questions rapidly, like loosing arrow after arrow, and she laughed when she couldn't keep up. It helped with her loss of control, because she had to concentrate to process all his sentences. He apologized again, but didn't protest when Elissa gently tugged her hand away from his arm.

"Here, let me show you," she whispered, telling herself centering on her powers would help. She could keep her mind off her parents and maybe even banish that *m-word* that refused to exit her mind.

She closed her eyes and called to the air. Her body warmed, her skin humming with magic. It felt good. Warm. When she opened back up, both men were watching her intently. Elissa smiled for them and swished her hand back and forth.

A tiny wind was born, kicking up until it threw her hair around. It made their clothing flap. She could keep it going, offer more power, but her suitor was adequately impressed, his gray eyes wide, his expression delighted.

"Air," Lord Avery said. "Your eyes glow almost white."

She nodded. "A different hue for each element, or so I'm told."

"Wow. Earth next?"

Sir Alasdair chuckled.

Lord Avery looked repentant, studying his boots for a moment. His chest heaved as if he'd taken a breath.

Elissa shot the knight a look. She wanted to scold him for making the lord uncomfortable. She could toss dirt in her chaperone's handsome face, but that wouldn't be the best demonstration of her powers. "Aye, my lord, whatever you desire."

Sir Alasdair's gaze was sharp now, and she threw a smirk at him. A muscle ticked in his cheek. She paused, her heart skipping. Elissa made herself look away—for the hundredth time that morning.

Her suitor flashed a lopsided grin that made him seem like a little lad.

She felt herself grinning back and called to her magic again. The scent of freshly churned earth tickled her nose, but Elissa had never found the scent unpleasant. She cupped her hands. Sparks rode under the surface of her skin as she shaped the dirt that came to her.

When she was done, she offered what she'd made to her suitor.

"Your eyes glowed green. Wow," Lord Avery breathed. "A rose? Made of dirt."

Elissa nodded. "I know it's not very manly, but it'll hold its shape. I sealed it."

"I adore it. May I?"

She transferred the flower to his hand. It was a rosebud caught in mid-bloom. She'd always loved roses. Elissa conjured it by just thinking about blooms she's seen in the queen's vast rose garden in Terraquist.

"It's hard. Feels like a wood carving. I cannot believe it's made of earth..." Lord Avery's concentrated completely on the item. "May I...keep it?"

"Of course, my lord."

"Thank you, my lady—Elissa."

She offered a nod. Elissa felt the knight's gaze, but she didn't spare Sir Alasdair a glance. A jolt that wasn't a result of her magic skittered down her spine, but she forbade her feet from shifting. "There's only one more element. Lord Avery, would you like to see it?"

"Fire," he breathed, gray eyes wide.

"Aye."

Elissa extended her palm, held it flat and concentrated. Heat kissed her body again and magic danced up and down her arms. She pinpointed her power on her hand.

Soon, a small flame was born. She urged it larger, until it burned bright and hot, the center bright blue.

"Impressive," Sir Alasdair whispered.

Delight washed over her. The knight liked what she could do as much as her suitor did.

"Red eyes. And it does not hurt you, despite your draw, your strength being water?" Lord Avery asked, clear, clinical, like a healer trying to diagnose a patient.

"Nay, it doesn't hurt me."

In her other hand, Elissa called water, making its shape imitate the flame. She held both palms up to her suitor.

"Fascinating," the lord said. "And do you not tire?"

She shook her head. "I would, with more exertion, like anyone. Magic can exhaust, but not from what I've shown you."

"You're so strong," he praised.

Warmth settled in her cheeks. She shook her hands and the water and fire faded away, along with the surge of her magic required to keep them around. Elissa rolled her shoulders. She felt good.

Until she remembered what she'd overheard.

She sighed—and hoped very much neither of her companions noticed.

After her suitor had had his fill of her magic—adding a dozen more questions about what she could do—Lord Avery offered his arm and they completed their turn of the gardens.

It was a lovely fall day, and Elissa enjoyed herself.

"My lord, my lady, are you ready for midday meal? The bell sounded."

She and her suitor exchanged a grin and nodded.

This morning hasn't been so bad, after all.

Elissa could only ask the Blessed Spirit to ensure meeting her other three suitors was easy, and that they were just as pleasant as Lord Avery Lenore.

Chapter Ten

"Lady Elissa, is something wrong?" Alasdair stopped short of putting his hands on her, though he wanted to. So he could banish all visions of Lord Avery Lenore's touch on her.

It had been innocent—first her hand in his, then her hand on the lad's forearm, and tucked into his elbow.

Then she'd said, '*Aye, my lord, whatever you desire.*'

He wanted to stab something—then and now.

She'd no idea what she'd said—or how he would've given his favorite sword for her to say it to *him*. Of course, Lady Elissa hadn't meant anything untoward. Certainly not the *forbidden* things Alasdair's mind had jumped to. What she'd said had been as innocent as Lord Avery's touch on her hand, her touch on his arm.

So why was it bothering him?

Midday meal had been surprisingly pleasant. The lad and Lady Elissa had included him in their discussions. They'd sat in a place of honor on the dais, and Alasdair also had a place, since he was their chaperone.

"Nay." She paused in the corridor, before they'd made the turn to go into the guest wing of Castle Aldern.

Was it his place to confess his observations? She'd seemed upset and fidgeting during her time with the young lord.

She hadn't been...normal. It'd worsened from what he'd thought he'd seen before they'd entered the great hall to meet the lad. She hadn't been the even-tempered Lady Elissa he'd been getting to know for the past few days.

The most relaxed he'd seen her was in the gardens when she'd been working her magic—that'd been something to behold. His admiration of her had shot up considerably. The glowing of her eyes had been fascinating, but he preferred her natural hazel to each magical hue.

Such power in her small frame.

Then she'd been tense all over again at the high table. Perhaps distracted? Oh, she'd smiled when appropriate and even laughed at Alasdair's teases and jests, as had the young lord and their other tablemates, but instinct told him something wasn't right with her.

When the king had entered the hall to join them for the meal, she'd thrown a glare at him—or so Alasdair had thought. The lass had schooled her expression so fast he'd discounted it as imagined.

Why would Lady Elissa be cross with King Nathal?

The meeting with Lord Lenore had gone well. And her smile was back in place as she'd met the Duke of Tarvis, Lord Avery's father.

She'd *seemed* normal.

Am I reading into something?

He cleared his throat.

"Sir Alasdair?"

Alasdair inclined his head. "Forgive me for overstepping, my lady, but you seem upset about something."

She flashed a smile, but he didn't buy it. Especially when she started to rub her arm, then plastered her hands at her sides as soon as she'd realized what she'd been doing. "I'm well. I enjoyed meeting Lord Avery very much. He's a kind lad...man. Sweet and funny."

Alasdair nodded, but he didn't stop studying her face. His gut said her suitor wasn't really what was on her mind. "If something is bothering you, you may tell me. Secrets are always safe with me." He patted his chest and winked, trying to make her give him a *genuine* smile.

Lady Elissa laughed, but it still had an edge he didn't like.

She squeezed his forearm and he had to swallow as a bolt of energy shot into his biceps. If she'd noticed—or felt it too—she didn't give any clues.

Not for you. She's not for you.

It's fine. That's what I want, anyway.

He needed to keep adding that caveat. If he didn't, he might…

Oh, hell. Stop.

He'd escorted her to meet a *suitor*—with three more to come—for Blessed Spirit's sake.

"Thank you, Sir Alasdair." She chewed on her bottom lip as if she wanted to say more, but didn't.

Her mouth was thick…luscious, and the last thing he needed was for Lady Elissa to draw attention to it. He tried not to groan. "Any time."

Finally she gave him a real smile. Her small hand gripped his arm again. Alasdair felt hot, although the touch had been light.

"Actually…"

"Aye, lass—my lady?" He couldn't keep the proper honorific on his tongue, and it made him want to kick himself. Even if he hadn't called her by her given name—he'd never, maybe not even if invited—he couldn't seem to stop calling her *lass*. It was too casual. Not proper.

Her breasts rose and fell as if she'd taken a big breath, and he tore his gaze from them.

"I'd like to go riding." Lady Elissa's beautiful eyes implored, and Alasdair's gut tightened.

He didn't want to tell her no, but he had to. "Unfortunately, that's not possible."

"Why?"

"You're not permitted to leave the castle walls."

"Even with an escort?"

Alasdair inclined his head. "Nay, my lady. I'm afraid not."

She opened and closed her fists at her sides. "I need to get out of here."

Concern constricted his chest. He took a step toward her. "We can go outside, walk in the gardens again. Or tour the bailey. Whatever you'd like."

"I'd like to go riding." Lady Elissa cleared her throat and shook her head. "Nay. I *need*…to go…riding."

"I'll request an audience with the king."

"I can't wait. I have to go." Now she wouldn't look at him.

"My lady, what's wrong?" Every fiber in his being wanted to reach for her, but Alasdair didn't.

"I need to go." She squared her shoulders and stood taller. "I'm sorry. I can't wait."

He reared back. Grabbed her wrist, but was careful not to hurt her. He tugged, until she looked at him. "You will obey. You'll stay here. With me." Alasdair kept his voice even, but gave her a hard edge, so she'd realize how serious he was.

So she'd stop arguing. She wouldn't win. Not in this. It was his duty to protect her. He'd do so, no matter what it took.

Hazel eyes flashed, almost glowing with green and gold flecks. Her loose hair surrounded her like an aura. Her delectable mouth was a hard line. Alasdair didn't miss her fists clenched tightly at the sides of the pretty silver gown, either, as if she was restraining herself from hitting him. Gone was the polite lass who'd met one of her suitors. "*You* have no power over me."

Alasdair growled and took another step, intentionally towering over her. He could feel her body heat—and her ire.

She tilted her chin up. Her posture was regal. *Angry.*

"*I* have every power over you. I'm supposed to protect you."

"I need no protecting."

"The king disagrees." He shoved away the urge to wince. Mentioning the king was akin to tattling like a lad, and Alasdair needed no justification for following orders. His *duties.*

"I refuse to be a prisoner here."

"No one said you're a prisoner."

"I won't be trapped. You're treating me worse than a captive. I've done nothing wrong."

"Nay, my lady. I'm following orders." He made an effort to soften his voice. "I'll keep you safe."

Her eyes narrowed, but it didn't diminish her beauty. "I am safe."

"Lass—"

"Aren't I?"

The question was a dare, and he wasn't permitted to tell her the information she was digging for.

"Aye. I'll keep you that way."

"As ordered."

"Aye." Alasdair offered a curt nod.

Lady Elissa said nothing, but unnamed emotion darted across her ethereal face. He couldn't begin to guess what she was feeling, but her stare was still pointed. "You will not command me about."

"When it comes to my duties, I shall do just that."

Lady Elissa perched her hands on both hips and glared. "I am not a child."

The lass before him sure as hell wasn't a child.

She was a temptress.

Alasdair wanted to taste every defiant line of her mouth. Make her lips soft and pliant under his demand; make her open for him so their tongues would meet, rub, dance. Make her clutch at his shoulders and beg for more.

A chill shot down his spine and his gut clenched.

The desire wasn't just *unwanted*.

It wasn't *him*.

Alasdair rarely kissed the women he bedded. Had no need for such intimacy.

A rule he didn't often break.

He swallowed hard and fought the urge to fidget. He was supposed to be angry at her for challenging him; threatening to disobey.

Not fantasizing about how she would taste.

Besides, he'd escorted her to meet the first of four possible men she would marry. Lady Elissa Durroc was more than *forbidden*.

Her fate had been decided by their king.

☆　☆　☆　☆

Elissa glared. Of course the knight—her *keeper*—wouldn't cooperate. "You have no right to address me as such."

His frown melted into a scowl, and she saw the tremor in his shoulders as he leaned over her. Trying to scare her. Sir Alasdair was controlling himself, but anger rolled off him in waves.

Well, Elissa had news for him. She wasn't scared. *She* was angry, too.

Just as much as him, if not more.

Magic pounded down her limbs. Elissa flexed her hands, kept them at her sides. She wasn't afraid of hitting him, she was more worried she'd drown him. Her powers were boiling beneath the surface of her skin. Rolling over her in waves, gaining speed and heat, tempting her to give into the sensations and the fury. Let the water free. Fling it at him. She couldn't give in. Didn't want to hurt him.

How can I get away?

Desperation clawed at her, like the magic.

She needed to go to Castle Durroc.

"I'm going to my room," she bit out. "There's no reason for you to escort me. You're dismissed."

"Dismissed?" He roared the word.

"Aye." She nodded, squared her shoulders and cursed the fact she had to look *up* at him. Elissa concentrated hard. To push her magic away, as well as mentally reach for an expression of disdain.

She wanted to maintain a countenance like she'd seen her cousin do when displeased. Even the fiercest warrior scrambled out of Queen Morghyn's way when she was upset. Including King Nathal.

"It seems you've made my head ache." Not a lie. Her powers were making her temples pound.

Sir Alasdair narrowed his eyes, but said nothing. Nor did he move away. His gaze traveled down her body before settling on her face again.

Heat crept into her cheeks. A burn that had little to do with magic.

He was looking at her as if he'd devour her. She didn't hate the idea, or the passion in his sapphire eyes. However, Elissa wouldn't give him the pleasure of breaking their eye contact. No matter how uncomfortable he was making her.

I am not weak.

"You will obey me," he rumbled. "And I *shall* take you to your rooms."

"Why? To ensure I enter? What'd you think I'm going to do? Run away?" That was *exactly* what she planned. Saying it out loud might not be smart, but he'd probably never consider she'd do such a thing.

He didn't answer her jibe.

"Alas, I need a word."

They both jumped.

King Nathal had a smile on his face as he approached. Sir Murdoch Fraser was on his heels. Both men looked at her, then at her knight. The king's face fell. "Is all well?"

"Aye," Elissa said, praying the word was even. Her heart leapt and she fought the urge to swallow.

The king was the *last* person she wanted to see, despite her ire with Sir Alasdair. Her anger at King Nathal trumped what she felt regarding her knight. Betrayal tightened her chest even as she met his pale blue eyes.

Sir Alasdair bowed to the king, but she didn't miss him clearing his throat. "Aye, all is well, Your Majesty. You need to speak with me?"

The king nodded. "Aye. Murdoch, please escort Lady Elissa wherever she wishes, and meet us in the duke's solar."

"Aye, Highness." The big redheaded man nodded and offered Elissa his arm.

She didn't want to argue, so she returned his smile and tucked her hand into his elbow, not bothering to look over her shoulder to watch King Nathal and her stubborn knight walk away.

"My lady?" the captain asked.

Elissa tried not to hedge at his side. "I was headed to my room to lie down."

His brow furrowed. "Is something wrong?"

"Oh, nay. Tired from the morning, is all."

Sir Murdoch gave her an indulgent smile, and seemed to accept her words.

They walked in silence and when they reached her guest suite, Elissa bowed deeply to the captain. "Thank you, Sir Murdoch."

"My lady..." He shifted in his boots, despite the smile he still wore.

The gesture was unnecessary because her rank was higher than his, but she needed him to hasten his getaway. Making him uncomfortable should do the trick.

She widened the curve of her mouth. "You're so kind, Captain. Shall I see you later?" Her heart thundered as Elissa set her hand on the doorknob.

His huge shoulders loosened a bit. "Of course, my lady." After a nod and another awkward pause, Sir Murdoch was gone.

"Thank the Blessed Spirit," she whispered. She paused, fingers slipping from the handle. Elissa sucked in a breath and scanned the corridor.

No one was in sight—a boon. She darted around the corner.

The repeated *click-clack* of something hard tapping the stone floor caught her attention and she threw a glance over her shoulder. Two wolves, one much larger than the other, were headed down the corridor away from her. It should be a shock seeing beasts inside the castle, but there were several bonded animals living at Castle Aldern.

Ladies Cera and Aimil, as well as Mistress Ansley, had all been members of the King's Riders—King Nathal's royal messengers—before they'd married. They were all magically bonded to a wolf, as was common amongst the Riders.

Duties often included long solo rides, so the beasts were for protection as well as companionship. She was told it wasn't limited to wolves. Any animal with intelligence and claws would work. Big cats were almost as common as wolves.

Bonding was a serious matter, though. Magic tied the parties together for life.

From the larger wolf's white coat, she knew him to be Trikser, the duchess' bondmate. Lady Cera had mentioned a litter of cubs had been birthed by Lady Aimil's she-wolf, sired by Trikser.

The smaller one must be one of them.

Elissa's heart kicked up when the smaller beast paused and sniffed the air, then glanced in her direction.

He was too far away to inspect, and she hoped the wolfling stayed far, but his fur was beautiful. Darker than his sire, he really couldn't be considered white or completely gray. Several shades of steel graced his coat, becoming darker as it lay down his spine. His tail was the darkest part of him, a definite gray hue. She would call him silver in color.

Trikser stopped at the end of the corridor and wuffed. A sound low in his throat, but not menacing. Rather like a question, although he didn't turn toward Elissa.

The cub looked at her again. His tail swished once. Then he faced his sire and darted to catch up. They quickly disappeared around the corner. Her breathing didn't return to normal until the wolves were out of sight.

What were they doing in the guest wing?

They probably had free reign of the castle. They were as much residents of Castle Aldern as the people who lived here.

Elissa reminded herself of her task, and snuck into what she knew to be a supply closet. She closed the door silently, blowing out the air she'd fortified herself with and leaning into the solid wood at her back.

A magic orb floated close to the ceiling. It brightened, lighting up the whole area.

She stared up at the circular bulb. It must've sensed her entry, as well as the room being shut off from the bright corridor. "Fascinating."

Elissa had never seen the like—aside from the similar ones at Sir Roduch's wedding—and sensed the young knighted mage, Lucan's magical signature all over it. She prayed he didn't have a connection to the magic he'd left to power the light. If he sensed her in a closet, he'd surely have questions about it.

She shivered and looked around. Shelves lined all the walls, filled with cleaning supplies, bed linens, bathing sheets and bedding materials, baskets with soaps in them, and even a shelf with nothing but decorations.

Elissa swallowed. She'd been hoping for some clothing. Couldn't go to the main stores of the castle. There'd be too many questions. If she'd needed something, surely a servant would've fetched it. She could hear them saying, *"My lady, you but only had to ask."* Then they'd shoo her away from an area she had no business being in.

Yet, she couldn't request breeches and a tunic—there'd be too many queries about that, as well.

Damn the king for confining her. Damn her knight for agreeing…and trapping her inside.

Of course, she could gather *why* from her eavesdropping excursion…couldn't she?

No.

What did her parents' murder have to do with *her*?

It'd been a long time ago….over twenty turns. The only home she remembered was Castle Rowan.

Had they been killed at Castle Durroc? Somewhere else?

Somehow she'd survived. Or had she not been there?

What else *hadn't* Elissa been able to discern?

"A whole hell of a lot." Her cheeks burned. She's spoken a curse word.

Her first. Ever.

She rolled her eyes at herself and pushed off the door. Again, Elissa scanned the racks before her. There was a small trunk on the bottom shelf to her far right. It was next to a fluffy folded sleeping fur that wasn't too different from the one on her bed.

Kneeling, she reached for the handle on the side of the small chest and pulled. It was heavier than expected. Her grip slipped and the trunk slid to the stone floor with a *smack* and *thud* that resounded in her ears.

Elissa froze. Her heart took off, stealing her breath as it bounced off her ribcage.

Why hadn't she thought to bar the door?

"Calm. Down." She tried to stave off a magical reaction. Her powers danced over her shoulders and down her arms. "No one heard. No one has come running. You're fine." Her whisper became more frantic with every word, but she repeated the phrases in her head, too, and it helped. A little.

Cursing herself — she was becoming a regular foul-mouthed lass — she straightened the fallen chest with shaky hands. Elissa failed to control the tremors even as she reached to open it.

The Blessed Spirit had answered her silent plea. Garments sat in two neat piles, covering the whole interior of the trunk and filling it to the brim.

It shouldn't be difficult to find something to fit me.

Guilt nudged her. She'd never stolen a thing in her life, let alone clothing that was poorer in quality than most of her gowns.

Stop. It's not stealing. It's borrowing.

The feeling didn't dissipate.

Sneaking out only made sense if she couldn't be easily recognized, right?

She needed to get away from Sir Alasdair especially. Time was of the essence.

Elissa had no idea how long the king would keep him. He wouldn't likely let her "sleep" — despite being the cause of her aching head. She had no desire to continue their *discussion.*

"That is, unless —"

Nay.

There was no way the king would change his mind if what Sir Alasdair had said was true. King Nathal wouldn't let her leave the castle grounds. He was a stubborn man, and when a decision was made, it was just that. *Firm.* Unchangeable.

Besides, her knight was angry with her. He probably wouldn't even appeal to King Nathal. Not with how they'd left things.

I have to go on my own.

Guilt gave a second bite when she contemplated Sir Alasdair.

Would he have consequences if she was able to sneak away from him and the castle?

I don't care.

Liar.

She sighed.

If I'm quick no one will know. That's it. Quick.

Elissa had to go and return before anyone could find her missing. It would work.

It has to.

She had every right to see her former home. It was *hers*, after all. Even a part of her dowry. The king had assured her of that.

Elissa received gold for her personal coffers annually from the produce that was still farmed on her land. Had her own money; would receive it in full upon her marriage.

"How will I get out of here?" She'd need her horse, but how could she get the gray mare without questions arising? Especially if she was minus her guard.

Am I foolish to try this?

"Nay."

Her *rights* were not a lost cause. She wouldn't allow them to be.

She'd figure out how to get to Castle Durroc. Elissa wasn't a prisoner here — as her knight had so aptly put it. She could move around freely — and she would.

"But, first things, first." She dug into the chest of clothing.

Chapter Eleven

Dismissed.

The word had boiled his blood as much as her regal expression. Her pretty face had shouted *'I'm better than you.'*

He'd wanted to shake her. Demand her justification for talking to him like that.

Alasdair stalked away from Lord Aldern's solar after his meeting with King Nathal, Leargan, an assortment of mages, Captain Murdoch, and the Dukes of Greenwald and Tarvis. The bright warm room had been packed to discomfort. The meeting had been a waste of time—Lucan and the twin mages' formal account of their visit to the Greenwald murder site. Information Alasdair had already known, and nothing new had been discovered.

He'd lost his temper with Lady Elissa. Something that didn't often happen, especially with a noble mistress. But…

Dismissed.

The offending word bounced around in his head.

Coming from her…it'd been…a shock. Since they'd met, the lass had treated him as an equal, even when she'd met her first suitor.

Rationally he knew why it'd bothered him. He didn't want to admit hurt—even to himself. But his chest felt heavy, carrying an ache he couldn't deny.

Alasdair had flashed back to being ten turns old. In his father's household.

He'd always been looked at with disdain, even by the man himself. An embarrassment. The regretful result of a tryst.

Unwanted memories of his father teased…the man barely looking up after he'd set down a trencher of food on his desk.

No *'Thank you, son.'* Maybe an order to get more wine, or shine his boots.

He'd been too small to manage armor or laundry, but in all other things, Alasdair had been his father's man—or lad—servant.

Lord Henrik Gerard had recognized their blood tie. Everyone in the household had known he'd sired Alasdair, but the position offered him nothing more. He'd not been legally acknowledged, nor did he have the man's surname.

The only benefit had been having his own room. It wasn't fancy—a converted closet that consisted of a small bed and a trunk.

It'd been to Alasdair's detriment at any rate, because the other servants treated him poorly—seeing him as the favored one when it couldn't have been further from the truth.

The housekeeper especially had made his young life a living hell. She'd dragged him around by his ears and beat him when his father was away. He'd always had to eat last, after all the adult servants and their children. Left with scraps—or worse. There'd been many a night he'd gone to bed with an empty, burning stomach. His father had trusted he'd been well cared for by the wench and had never once—at least that Alasdair had seen—ventured into his own kitchens.

When Lord Gerard had perished, it'd almost been a relief to Alasdair. He'd been kicked out. King Nathal had saved him. Given him a purpose. A *life*. He'd never looked back, and wasn't about to start, no matter what his little charge said.

Alasdair still shouldn't have spoken to Lady Elissa as he had. He sighed. He owed her an apology. Had used a tone he wouldn't even have implemented if scolding one of the lads he trained. It'd been uncalled for.

Rude.

Un-knight-like.

Guilt swirled in his stomach. He might as well make it up to her now, so the rest of the day would be pleasant.

If she was still in possession of her cross disposition, she'd likely question him about meeting with the king. Of course, all he could tell her was the king and his retinue would depart for Terraquist in the morning, leaving her in his capable hands.

He couldn't tell her that her family had been murdered, or that even now little was known of the evil responsible. He couldn't tell her about the other murders, the three lasses and their families. He couldn't tell her someone was after her, likely coveting her magic.

Alasdair couldn't tell her that the trip to the home of the murdered Greenwald family had failed to find anything they didn't already know, despite combined strong magic.

Now that he'd seen her use her powers with his own eyes, he was in awe of more than her beauty. Alasdair could understand why someone would risk horrible things to get at Lady Elissa.

He just wished they knew more.

Helplessness wasn't something he was fond of.

All he could do was fulfill his duties.

I will protect her.

But first...he'd grovel.

Say whatever she needed to hear so they could have an agreeable remainder of the day.

Lady Elissa would have to put up with him alone — unless she wanted to dine later with Lord Avery — for the next day or so, until the next suitor arrived to woo her. The Duke of Tarvis and his son were planning on leaving before that. Then...Duke of Dalunas, Lord Camden Malloch, would arrive.

For some reason, he wanted to growl. Lord Avery was a lad. Barely a man, truth be told, but Lord Cam...

Alasdair knew the duke. Liked him even.

The tall fair-haired man could be a real match for Lady Elissa, and rumor had it he was seeking a wife, not just meeting the lass at the behest of the king. Lord Camden was a good man, and a hell of a fighter.

Alasdair rubbed his chest and rounded the corner toward the guest room his charge had been assigned. Next to the one that was his new home.

Too close to her, really. Yet, not close enough.

He'd enjoyed their one-on-one time together the previous day or so. Talking with her. Laughing with her. She was sweet and charming.

She'd made *him* laugh. Something he was more used to doing for the others around him. He'd been called a jester-knight more times than he could count.

The lass was perfect.

Part of him, more than *a part*, hated the idea of sharing her.

Guarding her wasn't the chore he'd first dreaded when Leargan had charged him with it.

Therein lay the problem.

It was becoming difficult to resist tugging her in his arms and taking her mouth. Especially when she showed him the fire in those hazel eyes. Even when she was angry with him. Perhaps even more then.

"Stop. Just get this over with." Alasdair made a fist when he reached her door. He chided himself some more, and knocked twice.

Nothing.

Forcing himself to be polite, he knocked again, instead of barging in. She'd said she wanted to nap, that she'd had a headache after their argument.

Said I gave her a headache.

Alasdair scoffed and knocked a fourth time. Still nothing.

"Lass?" he called, pushing the door open.

Taking two steps into the room, Alasdair's eyes landed on the bed. It was made up neatly, the curtains tacked to the oversized carved bedposts. A dozen pillows of different shapes and sizes were arranged against the headboard, as if they hadn't been touched since the night before.

"Lady Elissa?"

He wandered to the private bathing room since the door was open. No lass yelped in fright for invading intimate space.

"Shite."

Her rooms were empty and Alasdair was the biggest fool in the world. Losing his temper had made him…fail.

Without having laid a finger on her.

"Headache, my arse." He barked every curse word he could think of and whirled. Should've never refused her request for a ride, even though his gut screamed she'd had other motives for wanting to leave the safety of Castle Aldern.

The lass had been shaken, something big had upset her, despite her denial and plastered-on polite smile.

He very much doubted it was nerves from meeting Lord Avery Lenore. "Run away," he whispered.

She'd said it herself. It'd been a dare.

The lass snuck out. Why?

Alasdair had to figure it the hell out.

He griped as he stomped down the corridor. Then he paused, squaring his shoulders and forcing a breath. Needed to calm. Definitely wouldn't want anyone to see him visibly angry. Wasn't about to announce that on day three he'd lost his charge.

Alasdair gripped his sword and squeezed the hilt until his fingers smarted and his knuckles whitened, instead of kicking himself.

Quick steps had him out of the castle, across the bailey, and at the stables. He encountered none of his brothers or his captain — thank the Blessed Spirit.

Something told him she wasn't within the castle walls — and he wasn't about to question the instinct.

Most of the personal guard were on the training grounds, and he could easily avoid the area. The king and Captain Murdoch — as well as both dukes and Leargan — had declared they were heading that way when their meeting was over.

Here's to hoping they're already out there.

How Alasdair would be able leave the castle gates unnoticed was another dilemma. He swore again.

People were after her and she had no idea. It made him want to tell someone, in case of real danger — almost. Alasdair needed to do this himself. Get her back. And resist ringing her neck.

He tried not to bark at the stable lads when they failed to meet him at-the-ready.

Since Niall had taken young Alaric to squire, there were only two youngsters under the stable master, Gean, his sons. The only other adult responsible for their horses was an older man named Elden, and he was as out-of-sight as Master Gean himself.

Two sets of big brown eyes regarded him.

"Sir Alasdair?" The elder, Brinson — no more than three and ten — spoke.

"Have you seen Lady Elissa?"

"She left with the ladies."

"Excuse me?"

When the younger lad, Idan, paled, Alasdair chided himself to watch his tone. He was only a turn or two behind his brother, but seemed so young — and scared. He'd not wanted to petrify the lads. He liked them both. They were good lads, well on their way to follow their father in his trade. They'd become skilled horse masters in a matter of turns.

Brinson stood taller. "Aye, Sir Alas. Wedding guest ladies, as well as some of our own, wanted to go to market. But not the duchess or Lady Aimil."

"Did they take an escort?"

"Aye, sir." This time, Idan answered. "A dozen men-at-arms."

"When?"

"Not long, sir."

He'd bet his favorite sword his little lass didn't leave with the group.

How'd she get away, though?

Lady Elissa must've timed things exactly; lucky Lady Cera was not among the group. There was no way the duchess would've allowed her to accompany the ladies, no matter who their guards were.

None of his brothers must be in the escort, either. Normally, if the ladies of the castle went to market, his captain escorted them himself — especially if his wife was with them. If Leargan didn't go, Niall did. Both his captain and the personal guard's second-in-command were sharp. They wouldn't have allowed the lass' presence.

They would've called for *him*. Perhaps even demanded to know why he wasn't at her side.

He ignored the sinking feeling in his gut. She had protection spells covering her. She had her own skillset. Powerful magic. Lady Elissa could protect herself, could she not?

If something happened to her, punishment from his captain and the king paled in comparison to what it would do to him.

Alasdair had let *emotion* get in the way of protecting her. He'd let her out of his sight.

Guilt crept up from the pit of his stomach, burning in his throat. His heart thundered and he swallowed hard. "Where's your da and Elden?"

"Elden went to market, too. First thing this morning, not with the ladies. Da's breaking a colt. He finally got him saddled and they went for a ride." The wind shuffled the older lad's sandy locks. "He left after the ladies did."

"We're supposed to be mucking stalls," Idan offered.

Alasdair sighed. "What horse did you give her?"

"Lady Elissa?" Brinson's voice cracked, like a lad about to become a man.

"Aye, lad. Quickly."

"The gray, sir. The mare she rode in on."

"Do you need your horse, Sir Alas?" Idan asked.

"Nay, lad. I'll do it myself."

The lads exchanged a look, but he didn't have time to wait on children.

"But, sir—"

"No worries, lads. I won't tell your da."

They followed him into the stable anyway.

His movements were stiff as he saddled Contessa. She could be finicky, and her whinny told Alasdair she could sense his mood. He calmed her with low nonsense, but his lass talked back, neighing and bumping his hands for a caress.

"Easy, lass. We'll run in a moment."

His horse was an elegant red roan from the finest Ascovan stock. He'd spent two months' salary on her—and that'd been a discount. He'd had to negotiate hard with the Duke of Ascova's brother, Roald, the finest horse breeder on the continent.

Tess was huge, as big as any warhorse and had an attitude to compete with the best destrier.

Alasdair didn't wait to pull her from the stall to mount. She didn't like that, shifting forward without command. "Just a moment, my lass." He patted her neck and hollered at the lads to move away.

Tess fidgeted, hoofing the dirt floor of her wide stall. She wanted free rein to rush from the stable, but he held her in tight, making her walk. She grunted and flared her nostrils, but complied. Alasdair would reward her with a good run. They hadn't dashed down an open road at top speed in months.

His gut told him his wandering charge had headed south. He didn't know where the knowledge had come from, but he learned long ago not to ignore his instinct. Many a time, Leargan had said his senses were innate magic.

Alasdair had never had the guts to ask Lucan to probe him, to confirm or deny he had skills he'd never known about. "Lads."

Both youngsters looked up at him.

"Muck your stalls, and mention to no one, not even your da, that I was here."

"Aye." Brinson nodded.

Guilt bit at him again. It wasn't fair to ask the lads to keep a secret. But he wasn't ready to admit to anyone he'd lost Lady Elissa.

She'd better be all right, because when he caught her, Alasdair was going to kill her.

☆   ☆   ☆   ☆

Chills raced down her spine when she heard the hooves pounding behind her. She slipped even further into the hood of her mantle and clenched her jaw. Elissa refused to look over her shoulder.

She'd ditched her gown for the breeches and a tunic she'd found in the trunk as soon as she'd made it outside of Greenwald Main. She couldn't in good conscience part with the gorgeous silver gown, so she'd stuffed it in the larger of the gray mare's saddle bags. Hopefully whoever had to clean and straighten it would forgive her. And that the wrinkles weren't permanent. Maybe she'd be better off handling the task herself. It'd mean less explaining.

Elissa had almost gotten her size right with the borrowed breeches, but the tunic was too big. It kept slipping off her shoulder, until she put her cape on over it.

Thank the Blessed Spirit the stable lads hadn't questioned her presence with the minor ladies and maids that had gone to market. The large group consisted of mostly wedding guests, and no one had recognized her as the queen's cousin. They'd been too busy tittering and chatting, planning what they'd buy at the large market in the Province's busy city-center.

She'd waited until they were all mounted up—as well as the guards who would accompany them. Luckily, none of the personal guard—all of them surely knew her—were included in the escort. There were only a few Castle Aldern men-at-arms. The rest consisted of men the guests had brought from their own households.

When the party had headed out into the courtyard, she'd rushed in as if late, apologized, and begged the two lads for her horse.

The sweet innocent lads had hurried Elissa's mount to her. Apologizing that they'd delayed her.

She'd told them not to worry—she'd catch up. Assured them she was in no danger of getting lost. Elissa had smiled and taken off—urging her mare after the sizable party. It wasn't until the ladies and their men-at-arms were out of sight that she'd turned off the main road, plunged into the woods and changed her clothes.

The hooves behind them pounded closer. Louder.

Fear rode under the surface, but she thrust the doubts all away.

I have to do this.

Damn the king and his secrets.

Tears threatened but she swallowed against the lump in her throat. Her whole *life* had been a lie. She shook her head and chided herself.

Elissa couldn't focus on her betrayal at the hands of a man she considered a father. She needed to focus on her ride, and being invisible to the rider on her heels.

I'm just a lad on my way home.

Dread at being stopped, questioned, and discovered as female—highborn, nonetheless—skittered down her spine, but she tightened her hold on the gray's reins and leaned closer to her mount's neck.

Travel was free, after all. There was no legal reason for her to be impeded.

Elissa prepared a story in her head anyway. She lived on a Greenwald holding within an hour's ride—due south. The hour's ride part was true. Her former home wasn't far; at least, she didn't think so.

She was grateful she'd taken the time to study the map of Greenwald on the wall of the great hall the night of the wedding feast. She thanked the Blessed Spirit the Alderns proudly displayed it there. All Greenwald holdings—whether large or small—were greatly detailed on the vast canvas.

Lady Cera had told her it was new, drawn by the most famous mapper on the continent.

"Lady Elissa!" The shout had her freezing in the saddle.

Sir Alasdair.

She concentrated on the road ahead, ignoring the knight. The rush of hooves came even closer.

"Come now, my lady. I know there's nothing wrong with your ears. And it's not windy enough to obscure the sound of my voice."

Still she said nothing. Refused to spare him a glance.

"You didn't think this through, lass. Your cloak and your

horse are too fine for your breeches. You stick out like a sore thumb. A lass on her own is never safe. It'll be dark soon. Rein in your mount," he said, as if his lips were right above her ear. His almost-gentle tone made her heart trip.

Elissa frowned. She refused to acknowledge the sense he made—especially his order for her to stop. She nudged her horse faster, banishing her physical reaction to him.

Sir Alasdair cursed.

His horse surged forward and he leaned in, pushing hard to reach for her mare's reins, but Elissa tugged them away and the horse shied before darting right, off the road and into the woods.

The reins flew from her grip and she clutched the horse's dark gray mane with shaky fingers. She screamed as her mare bucked over and over and careened past trees.

Elissa scrambled for the flying straps of leather. Her hand made purchase and she yanked as hard as she could, hollering at the gray to halt. The horse wouldn't stop, no matter how hard she tugged or shouted, "Whoa!"

Panic took over and her magic gushed out of control.

Thunder roared high above and lightning flashed across the sky. Elissa tried to shut the magic down. She tightened her hold on the mare, but the newly born storm only frightened her—them both—even more.

The sky opened up and rain poured. She closed her eyes and took a breath, but her heartbeat resounded in her ears as much as the noises above. Her temples throbbed as magic bit at her.

Sir Alasdair cursed again, but the beating of hooves behind her suggested he'd followed.

Stop the storm. Now.

Elissa's mare was breathing heavily, but she slid into an even harder run with the knight's horse so close. As if the gray couldn't stand to be chased. Or caught. "Stop. Please stop!" she beseeched of her magic, of her mount.

It did no good.

"Stop, lass!" her protector bellowed.

"I can't! She won't! I tried!" Elissa yanked the reins again, but her horse didn't respond.

She heard him yelling at his own mare, urging the red roan faster.

Her mare screamed again when Sir Alasdair attempted to come up next to her. The gray shot forward, but her knight kept his horse close, until they were running abreast.

Rain drenched the wooded area, hammering down on their heads, saturating her mantle.

Elissa yelped when his large hand enclosed her wrist, but she didn't yank away.

"I'm going to pull you to my horse. Jump when I say."

"Wha—? Nay!"

"Do it. I promise I won't let you fall." His voice was steady, sure. Sir Alasdair seemed *calm*. His long dark hair was loose and flying, despite the rain soaking him as they rode hard. His deep blue eyes were trained on her face.

She trusted him.

Without question.

The rain eased as suddenly as it was born.

With a final breath, it was completely gone. Elissa bit her lip and joined both hands with the knight's.

"Come. Now. Jump, lass!"

With a whimper, she crushed her eyes shut and pushed out of the stirrups hard. Sir Alasdair's hands landed around her waist, holding hard, but he wasn't hurting her. Elissa collided with his chest, and his grip around her tightened.

He righted her against him, tucking her shoulder under one of his arms, nestling her closer to his chest.

She bit back a gulp and glanced ahead.

The gray mare was still running from them, becoming smaller and smaller as she went and they slowed.

Elissa met the concerned sapphire gaze of her protector. She was lying across his lap, both her legs on one side of his horse. Despite his drenched clothing, she felt the heat of his body through her borrowed outfit. And the firmness of his thigh against her hip. She slid one arm around his waist for balance and wanted to gulp. He was solid there, too.

If Sir Alasdair minded her touch, he said nothing. His warmth surrounded her, staving off shivers from her magic storm.

"Are you all right?" His genuine concern made her heart skip.

"I am." Her words cracked. "Thank you."

"Was the storm your doing? Your eyes glowed blue."

Elissa nodded, because her voice wouldn't cooperate on the first try. "I…I…was terrified. I lost control of my magic."

His grip tightened, but was comforting. Sir Alasdair didn't comment and it took all she was made of to resist burrowing further into him.

"Are you better now?" he whispered.

She met his very blue gaze again. "As well as can be expected."

"Good."

Elissa paused, because his expression said he was far from done speaking.

His face darkened. Gone was concern for her wellbeing. He was angry. "Where the hell did you think you were going? You *lied* to me."

She averted her gaze. Heat burned the back of her neck as it crept up, all the way *up,* until even her ears stung—and it had nothing to do with the rushing wind or chill of being wet. Sir Alasdair had every right to be angry with her.

"You refused my request for a ride." Her protest was small, shouting even to her that the notion was subterfuge.

He was silent—too silent—but she didn't miss his growl as he urged his mare to a walk. The horse neighed and tossed her head.

"Shhh, lass. You ran hard, did me proud, my Tess." The knight moved his arm and Elissa shifted against him. She couldn't see, but she heard the patting noise as Sir Alasdair caressed the mare's neck, soothing her. "You, on the other hand, I couldn't be more disappointed with."

Elissa's stomach flip-flopped and she didn't have the guts to look at him again. She took comfort in his solid form against her. She was safe again, and even if she wouldn't be able to admit it out loud, she needed him. "I'm going to my childhood home."

He stilled.

Her heart kicked up again.

"What?" Sir Alasdair barked.

"Castle Durroc is not far from here, and I need to see it."

The knight shifted, then sat her up higher, but said nothing. He'd never been so silent with her, in the days she'd known him. The Sir Alasdair Elissa knew was charming, witty, and open. Very talkative. It was almost as though he was another person. Containing himself. From lashing out in anger?

Or…is it something else?

She narrowed her eyes and glared at him. "What do you know?"

"I should be asking the same of you, lass."

"The king betrayed me," she bit out.

Sir Alasdair's expression tightened, his brow furrowed. "How so?"

"My family was murdered."

He was too quiet again. Averted his gaze, too.

"You knew!" Betrayal washed over her again and she swallowed against the lump in her throat. She choked on another sob.

Her knight…her protector…had betrayed her, too?

Weight settled on her chest, making her lungs burn as she struggled for breath.

Why do I hurt so much?

She wanted to pummel his chest. Or yank away from him. She could do neither, since she had to cling to him so she wouldn't slip off his horse.

Elissa cursed the tears that stung her eyes. She wouldn't cry in front of the man who'd been assigned to trap her inside Castle Aldern. She sniffled.

His gaze swung back around. The knight's expression softened, and she cursed that, too.

Why did she care if Sir Alasdair hadn't told her? She didn't know him.

It doesn't matter.

But repeating the idea didn't lessen her pain.

Chapter Twelve

*D*ammit.

Angry he could handle. *Crushed* he could not.

She had tears in her eyes.

Alasdair's ire dissolved. He wanted to make her feel better. Banish that look from her pretty face. He wanted to cup her cheeks, wipe away the tear that'd crept its way down, but he didn't.

Lady Elissa broke eye contact and sniffled, but when she glanced back at him her expression was clearer, harder. She'd composed herself.

Good lass. Strong.

He still wanted to kiss her pert little nose. It was red with the effort to hold back her emotions, but he admired her strength.

And that storm…another damn.

She was powerful, without effort, more so than in the gardens. The winds had been at gale-strength and they were both soaked to the bone. Had he not held on to Tess with all his might, he wouldn't have managed to avoid falling on his arse.

"Lass—"

"I…" They spoke at the same time.

The pain in her hazel eyes undid him. It took all he was made of not to tell her what Leargan and the king had told him about her past.

He couldn't.

He shouldn't.

But as she looked at him after the scare that had taken five—no, ten—turns off his life, he couldn't refuse her. "Aye, I did know about your parents."

"And my brother," Lady Elissa snapped.

"Aye, and the laddie."

Her countenance tightened, her brows knitting, her mouth a hard line. Her nose was an even brighter red, but the sheen of tears in those beautiful eyes was what took his breath away. His chest tightened.

Why can't I breathe normally?

"You knew. You knew. You knew." She repeated the phrase over and over until he felt like a piece of hammered shite. Betrayal saturated her voice.

"It wasn't my place to tell you." Alasdair winced at his defensiveness.

She glared, which was better than her sobbing. He needed the solid ground mutual anger offered.

Lady Elissa grabbed his doublet with small tight fists and yanked. Her grip slipped on the wet leather and Alasdair tightened his hold on her torso.

He chuckled; he couldn't help it. She was rather adorable with that black look on her face, and her hazel eyes flashing.

Did she think she was going to strike him?

Alasdair stilled, instead of tugging away.

She glared harder.

"Easy, lass. I'll not let you fall."

"I want to get my horse and continue on my journey," she bit out.

"I'd reckon your mare will run until she's exhausted. We'll catch her one way or another. Worry not."

"And?" She arched a fair eyebrow.

"And?"

Lady Elissa glowered. "I will continue on my journey."

"Nay, we will return to the castle. Castle *Aldern*."

"Nay."

Alasdair sighed. He wasn't going to argue with her. "You could've been true to me about your desires to see your holding." The censure he'd packed into his voice made her wince, but he didn't regret it. He ignored how his stomach jumped, too.

Her expression lightened a touch. "So you would've taken me?"

It was Alasdair's turn to arch an eyebrow. "No."

The lass in his arms narrowed her eyes. "Then it matters not." She released his doublet and shifted, trying to sit up taller. The soft roundness of her breasts pressed into his chest.

He swallowed a groan and helped her straighten the rest of the way. It didn't help his discomfort at the intimate contact. Now she was fully in his arms, facing him.

Alasdair needed to turn her so her back was against him. Touching her was still a very bad idea, but her back was preferable to chest against—perfect—breasts.

She looped her arms around his neck and shifted closer, rubbing her hip against his crotch in the process. Sitting on the pommel of his saddle had to be uncomfortable, so he didn't tell her to stop moving, but soon the lass ended up with her bottom—also perfect—directly on his thighs.

Sucking in a breath he hoped to the Blessed Spirit she didn't sense, he threatened to lop his cock off when she adjusted again and ground into him. His manhood wanted to stiffen. To be used. Tingles hit him in waves, radiating out from his bollocks. He tried not to grunt or move at all. More friction would only result on heightened discomfort.

"I need to do this, Sir Alasdair. I need to see it for myself." The wobble of her bottom lip did him in.

He swore—savagely.

Those big eyes were wide—and misty again—when their gazes collided, but damned if he was going to apologize for her lady's ears.

She'd have to deal with his anger. It was her fault. "You put me in an uncomfortable position, lass." *In more than one way.* "The king—"

"Doesn't have to find out." Lady Elissa held her chin held high. "We're already far from the castle walls."

"And we should return before anyone can discover you're— we're—missing."

Her lip disappeared inside her mouth as she gnawed on it.

Alasdair's need to taste her was paramount. It warred with his sense of right and wrong. "If I consider taking you, you *will* vow you won't do anything foolish like this again." Statement. Not question. He wouldn't accept anything less than her word.

Shouldn't even accept that. He should take her back to Castle Aldern without delay.

Hope danced across Lady Elissa's countenance. It lit her up from the inside out. The lass in his arms glowed. Like he'd given her a gift.

His chest swelled. His heart stuttered. Alasdair swallowed. Hard. With her looking at him like that, he'd promise her anything.

That scared the shite out of him.

Her smile sealed the deal. He'd give her his soul if she but asked.

"Aye."

"Aye?" The word cracked and he cleared his throat.

Her nod was solemn. "Aye. I promise I'll not run away again. If you take me to Castle Durroc now."

Alasdair grunted. And bit back a few more curses.

"Is that an *'aye'?* Will you take me?" Expectation infused her tone as much as it did her gorgeous face.

He nodded, because he didn't have the bollocks to try to speak. If he did, he'd likely crack like a lad yet to become a man. Or worse…assure her he'd like to *take her* in an entirely different way.

Lady Elissa squealed and crushed even closer, hugging her arms around him and chanting, "Thank you, thank you, thank you."

Alasdair froze. Sucked back another groan as her supple flesh pressed into his chest. His arms rose of their own accord to return her embrace, no matter how he chided himself it was inappropriate. With her he had no decorum, and his honor teetered on the brink of misstep. A mistake he couldn't afford to make. What he wanted with her—physically—was something he could never take back. So he could never take *her.*

When she pulled away and looked at him, it took all he was made of not to kiss her. She was so beautiful, so honestly, openly grateful. And he was the wretch who wanted to take advantage of her body against his and sample her mouth.

"Is something wrong, Sir Alasdair? You look as if you're in pain. Did I hurt you when I landed in your lap?"

He wanted to snort. He was in pain, all right. "Everything is wrong." Technically not a lie. Self-disgust and guilt twirled in his stomach. *Wanting her is wrong.* "This isn't a good idea, lass," Alasdair said as gently as he could.

Anything to distract himself from the feel of her against him.

A tiny frown was born on her delectable mouth and widened, slowly taking over her lips. "I...I..."

He mourned the loss of her smile, especially since it'd been his fault. "I'll keep my word and take you to Castle Durroc. But we haven't much time. We need to be back at Castle Aldern before supper is served to avoid questions. You know that as well as I, my lady."

"You're right." She looked down as she whispered.

"Let's get your horse."

"Aye, as you wish."

He wished something a whole hell of a lot different...*more*... but Alasdair kicked Tess forward, praying to the Blessed Spirit this decision wouldn't bite him in the arse.

It was too bad King Nathal hadn't left that morning instead of tomorrow.

★   ★   ★   ★

Nothing.

Sorrow engulfed her and tears burned her eyes as Elissa took the fourth—or was it the fifth?—turn around the great room of the castle she'd been born in. She clutched the small painting of her family in a tight fist. She'd removed it from the frame to bring it with her, but she couldn't look at it.

"Why doesn't anyone live here?" she whispered, more to herself than to her knight. She sniffled and hoped he hadn't noticed. With a labored sigh, she buried the small canvas in her borrowed breeches' pocket.

"I know not, lass."

If she wasn't so angry at King Nathal, perhaps she would've asked him. When they'd ridden in, Elissa had seen the property as something she could be proud of, but the reminder of fire that'd been a lie bit at her like a rabid dog.

Trees lined the direct road to the castle gates, offering beauty and a natural shaded canopy. The fields lay in view, neatly farmed, even though they were past harvest now, and the weather was growing colder. They were still beautiful, a sight to behold.

The grounds were kept, groomed and farmed by a man named Thomad Uncel. He had a wife, and several grown sons, as well as a staff of farmers.

No one greeted their ride in, and the gates had been open. No one intercepted them, either. No one prevented them from entering the castle. The doors hadn't been barred, either.

There was only a small bailey, with no crofter cabins lining the walls like the much larger Castle Aldern, but there were stables inside the gate as well as two carriages that looked ready for horses at any moment.

Elissa had sensed magic, like a warding or protection spell over the whole area, but whatever the nature of the magic, it hadn't prevented their entrance.

She stepped closer to the wide hearth in the main great room. It was really too small to be called a hall, but she imagined the room lit, alive with laughter and love.

A small family sharing meals.

My family.

The small canvas burned a whole in her pocket, begging her to pull it out and look at it; hold it.

She couldn't.

There was no dais, but there was a head table, as well as four more long tables perpendicular to the one where her father and mother no doubt would've sat.

Had sat.

Would her brother have joined them? Or would he have taken meals in the nursery with a caretaker?

Because it wasn't proper for the children to eat with the adults of the castle.

King Nathal had never proscribed to that particular facet of decorum. The prince and princess, as well as Elissa—as their companion—had always taken meals in the great hall of Castle Rowan. Seated on the dais next to the king and queen.

She liked to think her parents would've been like that. Inclusive. Full of love for her and her brother.

Elissa forced her eyes away from the head table. All the chairs were covered in white sheets of fabric, as if shouting their opposition to disuse.

The room wasn't cold, but neither was it warm.

A welcoming fire should be burning in the central hearth. The space should be alight. People should be bustling, getting ready for the meal.

Her people.

Emptiness echoed, making her ears scald and her heart hurt. Pain threatened to double her over. Elissa struggled to breathe through the tightness in her chest. A single tear rolled down her cheek.

Magic tingled up and down her body, but she fought to control herself. Pushed her powers back so she could gather her composure.

"Lass?"

She didn't answer the knight. Just couldn't. Nor did she look at him. Couldn't do that, either.

Elissa extended her hand and called to her magic. Warmth raced over her arms, but it didn't heal the agony inside. She closed her eyes, only to sense the bright flame now dancing at the center of her palm.

Giving a small smile, she opened her eyes and stared at the blue center of the growing fire-bud. It burned brightly, and she shoved more magic into it. The fire gave off an inordinate amount of light for a spark its size.

Using magic—instead of fighting it—made her focus and made it easier to breathe…but only a little.

"Lass?" Sir Alasdair's concern bathed the repeated word.

"I couldn't see. Now I can." She gave him a small smile as she finally turned to him.

"Like in the gardens."

"Aye, like the flame I showed Lord Avery." She walked the length of the hearth again. "I want to see more. I want to see it all."

"All right."

She froze. Hadn't expected him to acquiesce. Elissa mentally banished her tears and threw him a glance. "Thank you." Even that whisper shook.

His blue eyes scorched but he said nothing. After a moment, her knight offered a curt nod.

"I know we haven't much time," she said.

Again, Sir Alasdair said nothing. He stepped closer, and she could feel his body heat at her back. She shivered and it had nothing to do with their wet clothing.

Elissa wanted him to reach for her. Hold her, like he had on the back of his horse.

He didn't.

Her cloak hung heavy over her body, and the too-big tunic drooped off one shoulder, despite the fabric covering it. Tremors took her over, chasing each other down her spine. Partly due to the chill in the air, she supposed. But mostly it was due to her shaky emotions and his closeness. For some reason, she wanted him closer. To feel safe in his arms, against his hard chest.

She'd never been so scared as when her mare had taken off. But he'd…saved her.

They'd caught up to her horse, too. The poor lass had finally stopped in a small copse of trees right inside Durroc property lines. At least she'd been fleeing in the right direction, and not away from Elissa's holding.

She favored her right front leg, but after Sir Alasdair examined her, he declared she'd be fine with rest. Nothing was broken. The gray horse's breathing was heavier than he liked, though, so even if she didn't have a small limp, Elissa would have to ride with the knight. He'd be stuck with her the same way when they headed back to Greenwald Main, too.

"My lady." Warm breath kissed the shell of her left ear.

Elissa ignored him and moved away, so she wouldn't turn and jump in his arms. "I should dry us. Especially since the storm was my fault."

Sir Alasdair cleared his throat. "Can you?"

She risked eye contact and her heart sped up. "I think so. I can use warm—or hot—wind."

"Aye?" He shifted on his feet. The sound of his boots echoed in the large, almost empty room. "Then…do so, if you wish."

Elissa nodded. Her chest ached and her throat was tight. She extinguished the flame on her palm with a thought, and took a breath. She'd never used her powers over the wind in such a manner, but it was worth a try.

She was glad for the renewed darkness, but she could still feel Sir Alasdair's eyes on her. "It'll get…windy, but I'll make it warm. As warm as I can. We'll see what happens."

"All right."

She stepped closer, but didn't reach for him. Their eyes locked and Elissa called her magic, which was already playing under the surface of her skin.

A warm gale kissed the air, gaining strength as she pushed heat and power into it.

Her hair started to dance at her shoulders, and her cape flapped against itself and the borrowed breeches. Warmth floated over her face and shoulders, moving down her limbs.

"Take my hand," she told the knight.

It took everything in her not to jump when his large calloused hand engulfed hers. Heat spiked, intensified, and her belly flipped. Elissa's magic stalled with the sudden distraction, but she concentrated and pushed it forward, to encompass Sir Alasdair too.

His long dark hair shifted, then lifted to prance his broad shoulders as each lock dried. The hot air danced over them both. He looked wild, beautiful.

She fought the urge to fidget or pull away as her cheeks seared.

"It's working," he whispered. "It's feels like a warm bath... of air." Sir Alasdair smiled. It lit up his face and made her heart skip. He didn't wear a mantle as she did, but his tunic sleeves caught the air, puffing out as the last of the moisture left them.

Elissa let the warm air swirl around them for several more seconds before she released the magic and it faded away.

Sir Alasdair didn't stop looking at her, nor did he drop her hand. "Thank you, lass. Your magic is powerful...impressive."

She looked down, tucking a lock of hair behind her ear. "Thank you."

His tug on her hand had her meeting those blue eyes again. "You really are extraordinary, my lady." His voice was thick, and the apple of his throat bobbed as he swallowed.

Elissa turned away, dropping his hand as if he'd burned her. She had to. Or she'd throw herself at him.

He shouldn't look at me like that.

Her heart skipped and she took a calming breath, calling the fire to her palm to light her way down the corridor as she all but fled the great room.

"Lass, wait!"

She didn't pause at her knight's shout, but she did shiver at the rush of his heavy boots behind her, as well as the *swoosh* when his sword cleared its scabbard.

"What's wrong?" she breathed when Sir Alasdair caught up.

"What lies here is unknown. Do not leave my side." The order was hard, and his sapphire eyes glinted in the light of her magic flame.

"I feel a protection spell over the castle," Elissa told him.

"Good, but I'll not take your safety lightly." The knight straightened, but didn't sheathe his sword. "Be quick about your exploration."

Elissa nodded and continued down the corridor. She didn't ask what he was supposed to keep her safe from, even though she wanted to.

He wouldn't tell me anyway.

A kiss of fear chilled her, but she did her best to ignore it.

Chapter Thirteen

1 don't remember any of this…" Desperation suffused her words, along with sadness so thick Alasdair's mouth went dry.

He regretted his bark to her when she'd left the great room of Castle Durroc, but abnormal panic had consumed his chest at the mere seconds she was out of his sight. The notion likely had more than to do with more than merely the fact he was charged with her protection, but he wouldn't—couldn't—explore it.

Alasdair focused on Lady Elissa's exploration of the lord and lady's chambers. Like the furniture in the great room, everything was covered in white linen sheets.

Although it was for preservation, grief was palpable in the air. It was as if Castle Durroc *felt* its abandonment. He crossed the room to the lass' side.

She didn't acknowledge his closeness, but ran her hand along the top of the thick mantle of the large hearth in the suite. There were no trinkets on the shelf, no paintings on the walls.

He slid his sword back into the scabbard, fighting his urge to comfort the lass.

The pain on her beautiful face made his lungs burn.

Alasdair cursed under his breath and commanded himself to ignore the urge to tug her to him. Rub her back and whisper sweet reassurances in her ear. Hold her and taste her lips until she felt better.

Wretch.

Only a rogue would see an upset lass as an opportunity to take advantage.

Steal a kiss.

He shook his head and watched her study the forgotten room.

The windows were boarded shut, which somehow upped the desolation. The sitting area was also covered in sheets, obscuring the exact amount of chairs that lie beneath the ocean of dusty white.

Alasdair avoided looking at the large bed. Blessed Spirit knew he didn't need his thoughts to traverse back to forbidden land. It'd been bad enough holding her in his arms on Contessa's wide back.

He had a damn good imagination, after all.

The lass crossed the room again, moving away from him. She stared at the wood panel covering the largest window in the chamber. "I…" Her broken appearance made his gut tighten even more.

Alasdair should direct they leave now. Explain she was in danger, though he'd been prohibited. Sweep her back to Castle Aldern and holler until she understood.

He couldn't.

She had a right to know where she'd come from.

They were already here, at the Durroc holding. There was no harm in her looking around — other than the pain it caused. He wanted to stomp that agony, snuff it out.

Keep her from it.

"It's all right, lass." His whisper was thick to his own ears, and his feet carried him to Lady Elissa's side of their own accord.

"It's not all right." Her hazel eyes were shiny in the light of her blue flame. The red they'd glowed from her initial magic call had faded. "It's *not*. I…don't remember this home. Or my family. Living here…anything…" She averted her gaze when a sob sounded.

Alasdair's chest stabbed at him with each breath. He couldn't abide it. He wanted to make her feel better.

Nay. I need to make her feel better.

He cupped her face, making her look up at him. The first

tear made its way down her pale cheek, followed by another illuminated by her magic fire.

Alasdair thumbed it away, caressing her soft skin, and leaning down without thought.

Lady Elissa yelped when his mouth took hers, but she didn't tug away.

The room went dark—he could sense it even though his eyes were closed. She must've released the flame from her palm like she had in the great room.

Her arms slid around his neck and the lass moved in to him instead of away. Moved her lips under his, pressing into his kiss. He pulled her closer still, until they were chest to breasts, hips to hips. Alasdair ran his tongue along her bottom lip, coaxing her to open for him. He didn't have to wait long. She let him in to the cavern of her mouth and Alasdair groaned, slanting for a deeper kiss.

Damn, she's sweet.

Just like he'd fantasized she would be. Like honey and summer berries he needed more of.

She held on tight, kissing him back tentatively at first, touching her tongue to his, then rubbing with more fervor as she tasted him, too.

Alasdair let her in, kissing her harder, deeper.

Lady Elissa made mewling and whimpering noises against his mouth that had him granite in his breeches.

Aching. Throbbing.

He wanted her with a fierceness he'd never experienced before. He caressed her shoulders, then dragged his hands down her slender back, to her waist, wishing her mantle and the oversized tunic were gone.

Squeezing and kneading the perfect globes of her bottom, Alasdair rocked against her. He needed to lift her, get her legs around him. She moaned and angled back, swaying with him until it wasn't enough. His cock threatened to blow its top in his tight breeches.

Lady Elissa was everything he'd imagined from the first time he'd seen her in the great hall with Queen Morghyn.

He wanted her.

Had to have her.

Alasdair walked her back to the nearest wall, slanting his lips over hers again and again, kissing her until they were both panting.

Small, high breasts flattened against his chest as soon as the wall was at her back, and he groaned as Lady Elissa fit her body even more perfectly against his, slipping her arms around his middle, holding him tighter.

He needed to get her breeches off. Alasdair shoved his hands down between them. Reached for the ties. His fingertips were unencumbered since she hadn't stolen a belt. Soon, he'd have his hands on her warm flesh.

Would she be wet for him?

She paused, stilling as he struggled with the knot. "Sir Alasdair…" Lady Elissa breathed.

Alasdair swallowed a moan when their gazes collided. Her eyelids were heavy with desire; her face was flushed pink, and her delectable mouth swollen from his. She was more gorgeous than he'd ever seen her. Thoroughly ravished.

Perfect.

But she looked…innocent.

Shite.

Lady Elissa probably *was* innocent.

She was the queen's blooded cousin, for Blessed Spirit's sake.

What am I doing?

He pulled out of her embrace so fast she wobbled against the wall.

Lady Elissa yelped and slapped her palms flat on either side of her so she wouldn't fall. Wide hazel eyes regarded him. "Sir Alasdair?"

"I'm sorry."

Confusion knitted her fair brow. But the hurt that darted across her pretty face was what made him look away. He wanted to reach for her, pull her away from the wall and make sure she could stand on her own, but touching her was too big a risk.

Alasdair turned his body from hers, making a mistake by focusing on the huge bed. Even in the dimness of the room he could make out the four carved posters of the frame. It was dark wood and elegant. The kind of bed Lady Elissa should be in when she gave herself to a man for the first time.

Not just *a* man, but her *husband.*

Alasdair would never be that man.

He didn't want to marry her; he just wanted to take her.

Which is why I can't.

Not to mention all the other reasons he needed to tick off

in his head. Obviously it'd been too long since he'd lain with a woman.

"Sir Alasdair?"

He still couldn't look at her. "I'm sorry," he repeated.

"Why?" A small hand slid onto his forearm, and he jumped. "I just wanted to help you to feel better."

"You did."

Somehow his gaze found hers, even though he cursed himself. "That wasn't the proper way to do it. I apologize. It won't happen again. I'm deeply sorry." *Liar.*

He didn't regret kissing her.

He regretted that he couldn't *have* her.

"Oh." Again, hurt dominated her expression. She gnawed on that full bottom lip.

Alasdair damned himself to hell and back. Or…maybe he didn't deserve to come back. "You're so damn innocent."

Her eyes widened as his unintended statement slipped out and she took a step back. Her hand fell from his arm. "I am not." Stubbornness reflected in her expression now. She set her jaw, and glared.

Is she saying she's not a virgin?

Alasdair cleared his throat. "You are. And I haven't the right to the liberties I took with you." He forced himself to bow to her. "I shall remember your station, my lady. Once again, I apologize."

"I don't want your apology." Lady Elissa's voice was as hard as her frown. "And *your* station is no different from my own."

"You're cousin to the queen."

"And I am a *minor* lady. Raised at Court. Hardly innocent."

His heart skipped.

Second time.

Perhaps she was saying she wasn't a virgin.

Dangerous thoughts.

He wouldn't read into what she'd said; it didn't matter if she wasn't a virgin. Rumors always abounded of noble ladies at Court who were loose with their favors, but Alasdair wouldn't break his personal rules.

Wouldn't lie with a highborn lady he had no intention of marrying.

Especially Lady Elissa Durroc.

Not just because she was Queen Morghyn's blood.

King Nathal has decided her fate.

"Let's go," he snapped. "We need to get back."

Her eyes widened and she touched her cheek. "I'm not done here."

"You are." Alasdair reached for upper arm. Even through her cape and tunic, the heat of her skin all but burned him, made him yearn for more.

To touch her bare skin. Kiss her entire body. Show her passion.

Had she really had a lover? More than one?

Alasdair tightened his grip. He didn't want to think about her writhing beneath another man. Kissing another man. Calling another man's name. Coming for another man.

Past *or* future.

She's not for you.

I don't care.

"Let me go," she ordered.

"Am I hurting you?"

She paused and tugged, but he didn't release her. "Nay."

"Let's go. You should be well rested before the morrow. You've another *suitor* to meet."

Lady Elissa reared back as if he'd slapped her, but Alasdair didn't censor his next statement. "Raised at Court or not. Innocent or not, you'd do well to remember your *purpose* in Greenwald."

☆   ☆   ☆   ☆

"You will go to your rooms, you'll change into a gown, fix your appearance, and I'll escort you to the great hall for evening meal. We will tell no one of what happened today." Sir Alasdair seethed, and his grip on her upper arm was iron as he practically dragged her across the bailey.

Is he referring to the kiss or me running away? Her heart skipped.

Elissa didn't utter a word even though he was hurting her. She moved her much shorter legs as fast as she could to keep up, her head spinning.

His orders were the first he'd spoken since they'd left Castle Durroc. He'd had her ride behind him on his red roan mare, and he'd been stiff against her, his back an immobile wall of granite, despite his body heat.

She'd held on to his waist tightly so she wouldn't slip off the back of his horse. Elissa hadn't relaxed against him, or rested her head on the back of his shoulder, despite the desire to do so. Her whole body ached from the tension she'd held in her muscles.

The knight had grumbled a great deal under his breath.

What did he have to be upset about?

He'd kissed *her.*

Then crushed her afterward.

Discarded her feelings…and her words.

"You're so damn innocent."

Sir Alasdair thought her naïve?

Damn him.

Unless…

Had he been referring to her virtue?

"Move faster."

"I can't." She sucked back a whimper. "I…am sore. From the rough ride. And you're hurting my arm."

Sir Alasdair startled, as if he hadn't considered that. He loosened his hold but didn't release her. Nor did he apologize.

The wretch.

"Sir Alasdair!" The shout had them locking eyes and freezing.

Her knight glanced over his shoulder and cursed. "Stay here."

Elissa swallowed, nodding and pulling her mantle's oversized hood further over her face, until it all but blocked her vision. She made sure her long hair was tucked inside, not even one strand visible. She hiked the strap of the hide bag containing her silver gown higher on her shoulder.

The stable master charged over to Sir Alasdair, the glare on his face deep and evident even at her distance and in the dimming light of the setting sun.

Elissa shivered.

"What is the meaning of this?" Master Gean demanded.

Sir Alasdair squared his shoulders and stood taller. The knight towered over the portly balding man, but anger rolled off the stable master in waves, and magic crinkled in the air.

She didn't know what kind of magic Master Gean possessed, but whatever it was made his aura glow red and pulsate. Elissa watched intently. She usually had to concentrate hard to read auras.

Will Master Gean strike Sir Alasdair?

"What's wrong, Master Gean?" Her knight's question was steady, even.

"What's wrong?" the stable master echoed, but he was anything but calm. He made a fist. "Do not play innocent with me, Sir Alasdair." He shook his fist in the knight's face.

Elissa winced.

"That mare is damaged. I thought I knew you well enough to be assured you would not harm a horse, but—"

"She got away from me, Master. I apologize. She wasn't harmed intentionally. I examined her, and couldn't find a break."

"You examined her?" Master Gean barked.

"Aye."

"She was mistreated. Run so hard she still hasn't caught her breath. She's frothing! Her whole body is covered in sweat!"

Sir Alasdair shook his head. "It wasn't intentional. She was startled from the thunderstorm and took off running."

"Storm?"

Elissa heard her knight's groan even from her distance. She wished she had the power to become invisible on the spot.

No one in Greenwald Main had been affected by her loss-of-control storm.

Her knight dropped his voice, and she missed his next statement, but it was clear whatever he said did nothing relieve the stable master. The man's body was still tight, and his fists were still pinned to his sides.

"Whatever were you doing with the gray, anyway? She is of the king's stock."

Wrong.

King Nathal had given the mare to Elissa before they'd left Terraquist, but it wasn't like she could remind Master Gean of that.

Sir Alasdair hadn't told her to conceal her identity, but he didn't have to. The stable master couldn't guess the knight hadn't been with a servant lad or squire when he'd rushed after them from the stables. Hopefully the distance she was standing would assist in the subterfuge.

Again, she couldn't hear the knight's answer to the man's inquiry. They spoke for a few more moments, then the stable master retreated.

Her knight stomped, as if his anger had been reignited by the exchange. Tremors shot down Elissa's spine. He gripped her arm, but this time he didn't hurt her. "Let's go."

"What did you say to him?"

He didn't answer, just tugged until she didn't have a choice but to accompany him. It was either that, or truly be dragged.

Sir Alasdair didn't say another word until they were in front of her guest suite's door. "Get inside and change. Clean yourself up as best you can." He crossed his arms over his impressive chest when she hesitated.

She tried not to think of how she'd felt in his arms, up against those hard muscles. Elissa failed. All she could remember was his heat, how he'd held her, and what his mouth felt like moving over hers. What his tongue tasted like. Her belly warmed. "I—"

"Just. Go."

"What about you?"

"I'm not foolish enough to let you out of my sight again. Get in there and put on an acceptable gown before I drag you inside and do it for you."

Anger shot her newborn desire away, churning her stomach. "Oh…you…" Magic awakened and burned to be let free. Elissa clenched her fists at her sides.

He arched a dark eyebrow. Daring her.

She narrowed her eyes. Wanted to throw curses in his face but couldn't muster the courage to say them aloud. *That* made her even angrier.

Elissa turned on her heel and wrenched open the door.

When she was on the other side, she slammed it shut. She only wished he'd been closer, so it would've been in his face.

Maybe she even could've hit him.

Chapter Fourteen

We're going to Terraquist Main; mount up."

"What the 'ell for?" Nason demanded, a frown marring his pocked face. The blond man's far northern accent wasn't much different than Charis' own. Although familiar, it was suddenly irritating.

He suppressed a shudder as the last of Drayton's magic skittered away from his spine. He stalked forward and towered over the little man. "Just do what I say. Get your arse up on that horse before I knock you out and drape you over it. I want to get the hell away from this cave." He took a breath and forced himself to calm. "*Then* I'll explain."

Bracken smirked when Charis met his midnight eyes. "Aye, aye, Cap'n." The big man gave a mock-salute and flashed a lopsided grin that looked wrong on the face of a baby-killer. The lasses liked the oversized oaf. Enough to make a man jealous. Of course, none of the tavern lasses knew of their…predilections, anyway. So, it mattered not as long as they got to swiv, right?

Charis growled and yanked his horse's reins from Nason. He didn't have time to buck up to a man twice his size, nor was he fond of the headache that usually followed a rumble with Bracken.

Nason said nothing aloud, but he was grumbling under his foul breath. Charis let it go, because if he didn't calm down, he'd give in to his desire to pound the man's flat nose even flatter. He could—and often did—inflict more damage to the smaller minion than the larger.

But right now, getting away from Drayton was paramount.

He swung himself into the saddle, but patted Barley's neck when his roan gelding neighed a protest of Charis' stiff, rough movements. "Sorry, lad." His horse was about the only being he'd apologize to. Ever.

Charis swung Barley around and put his knees to his sides. His horse jolted forward, well on his way through the woods and back to the public road.

Bracken and Nason followed, but said nothing—they rarely did when Charis was in such a foul mood. Well, Bracken knew better. Nason had sported many a black eye for running his mouth when it was less than desirable to hear him speak.

The stupid old mage had been invigorated for some reason. He'd kept rubbing his hands together, and his aura had glowed brighter than before. Drayton had been hyped about something, but what, the codger hadn't said.

He'd been less than pleased when Charis had admitted there'd been no progress since the last holding they'd visited in Terraquist. And Drayton hadn't earmarked any more blonde lasses for them to *visit*, either.

However, the mage had charged Charis and his lads with a new mission: find an elemental, *any* elemental. Drayton had used his magic to locate one, and ordered him to gather the water mage up; return him to the cave.

Being the fine mercenary he was, Charis hadn't asked questions, but he had demanded a separate fee for the new task. Drayton hadn't batted an eye at the exorbitant amount he'd named. That should've sent red flags up, but he'd bowed and backed through the wretched protection spell.

Tingles ran up and down his spine—then and now. Charis straightened in the saddle. He'd always hated spiders, and invisible ones were even worse.

"So, what's in Terraquist Main?" Bracken's deep voice made him jump.

He sucked back his curse. Didn't want his companion to sense any weakness. "We've a new task."

"Oh?"

Nason urged his mare closer to Charis and Bracken's mounts. He leaned in.

Good. They're both listening.

"Drayton needs an elemental mage."

Charis didn't miss his lads exchanging a glance.

"Aye," Nason said. "'Tis our task, isna'?"

"Aye. Not the lass. Another."

"Another?" Bracken asked.

"Aye. A lad that performs water tricks for coin in Terraquist Main. Should be quick. I know where he is." Charis hated to admit it, but Drayton's ability to pinpoint other elementals was handy.

Too bad it'd failed for the lass he sought. Hence the old mage seeking Charis' services. He'd long told Drayton if his tracking magic couldn't find something—or someone—they were dead.

Or cloaked in very powerful magic.

Questions he never asked swirled around in his mind. He'd always refrained from more than need-to-know, as long as he got paid.

What was the old codger *not* saying about the lass?

Three who were not her were dead—upon Drayton's insistence of no witnesses.

Who is this lass?

Supposedly, Drayton didn't even have a name. Just fair-haired, and in her early twenties. An elemental he'd encountered turns ago. A birth mark roughly half-moon shaped high on her right side. If the mage knew more, he wasn't saying.

"How much?" Bracken's bark tugged Charis from his head.

"One-eighty."

Nason whistled.

"One-eighty? All gold?" Bracken asked.

"Aye."

"The old fool agreed ta tha'?" The big man cocked his head to one side, a dark brow arched.

"Without hesitation."

Nason swore in Aramourian and snapped his fingers, delight written all over his countenance.

Charis smirked.

"'Tis too good ta be true," Bracken mused.

"So far, he's paid well."

Doubt crossed Bracken's broad face, despite Charis' truth. He grunted at his companion and kicked Barley.

He had nothing more to say; definitely wouldn't remind

them that Drayton was holding the majority of their prize hostage until they'd found the elemental lass.

"Let's go."

They had a task. Needed to get to it.

Hopefully this was one they'd see through quickly and without issue.

★   ★   ★   ★

Enduring evening meal was horrid.

It took all her self-control to avoid the duchess' searching gaze. From the moment she'd taken her seat of honor on the dais, her eyes had collided with Lady Cera's gray orbs. Over and over.

Elissa had barely eaten, since her stomach remained in knots.

She'd picked the simplest of the gowns she had, a light flowing rust-colored dress with embroidery on the bodice. She'd tried to put her hair in a simple bun at the base of her neck, since Sir Alasdair hadn't allowed her time for anything more, but Elissa never wore her long tresses in that style. Had always considered it messy, and unfortunately Lady Cera had noticed. The duchess had seemed to analyze her appearance for a full minute.

It only worsened when the lady spoke. "Is something wrong, Elissa?"

Sitting still was a challenge. Elissa reached for her goblet of wine and brought to her mouth. Sipping, she shook her head.

"Are you sure?" The duchess' auburn brows drew tight and Elissa wanted to squirm.

Now the duke, Lord Jorrin, was looking her way, too. As well as the healer, Lord Tristan, and his wife, Lady Aimil.

Staring.

They're all staring.

She tried not to gulp.

Sir Alasdair froze in the chair next to Elissa's; her suitor, Lord Avery, seated on her other side, seemed to notice. His red brows knitted, and he looked at her knight, then back at her. He didn't remark, though.

"I'm well. Thank you for asking." She didn't spare either man a glance as she plastered on a smile and nodded for her audience of nobles. "I've had a lovely day, meeting your cousin and walking in the gardens."

Lord Avery beamed—and blushed. "I've enjoyed today as well."

His father and Lady Cera looked pleased. As did King Nathal. He sat at the head of the table—several chairs away—but evidently could still hear their conversation.

Seated next to him, her cousin smiled.

Elissa reminded herself she could *not* openly glare at the king.

Sir Alasdair hadn't said a word the whole meal—and everyone had taken note of that, too. Although no one at the dais had inquired if all was well with the knight, he was getting some quizzical stares. The way he hunkered down in his chair and hovered over his plate told her *he* hadn't missed the silent observations, either, but he didn't remark. However, his normal jester-nature was nowhere to be found.

Not looking her chaperone's way wasn't proving too difficult, though. Elissa was still furious with him for the way he'd spoken to her in the corridor outside her rooms.

When she'd dressed and met him, the rogue hadn't said two words—and he hadn't escorted her properly into the great hall. He'd walked—or stalked—beside her. They hadn't touched at all and she was mad at the part of her that was hurt by his slight. She'd told herself she'd been upset about his lack of decorum, but had to ignore the voice that called her a liar.

Now he barely looked at her, and Blessed Spirit knew he wasn't talking to her. That hurt, too.

Elissa had done nothing wrong. Had she?

She pushed slices of meat around on her plate with her fork. Although she loved smoked venison, her appetite had vanished. She'd made efforts, stuffing food into her mouth to appease her growling stomach, but it didn't satisfy. Nor was she able to taste anything.

Eventually, their tablemates returned to normal chatter, and she breathed a sigh of relief the spotlight was no longer shining in her direction.

Lord Avery engaged her in light conversation she tried her best to return, but Elissa wanted to flee his company, the dais, and the great hall.

And Sir Alasdair.

After-meal music started playing. She didn't want to stay for any kind of dancing, and finally gained the courage to tell her suitor and her chaperone.

Sir Alasdair gave a curt nod and rose. He didn't look at her for more than a second.

Her chest ached.

"Oh, you intend to retire?" Lord Avery's countenance fell.

A pang of guilt bit at her and she tried not to react. Or care. That made her feel like a wretch for being selfish, but she didn't change her mind. Elissa nodded. "I'm sorry, my lord, I'm a bit tired. It's been an eventful day."

He nodded and stood, offering his arm.

She gave him a small smile and slid her hand in the crook of his elbow, despite the black look her knight flashed. Elissa ignored how her heart skipped, too. She wanted to snap at him.

Now he cares?

They'd gotten no further than the base of the dais when Sir Alasdair's captain, Sir Leargan Tegran, called his name.

Lord Avery spoke with her as they waited, but she couldn't stop her gaze from resting on her knight and Sir Leargan. She couldn't hear what they were saying, but she assumed the captain asked after her. He smiled in her direction, and she forced a curtsey.

"I've enjoyed meeting you very much, Elissa."

The heir to Tarvis gained her attention and she looked up into his gray eyes. "I have enjoyed meeting you, too, Avery."

He smiled and bowed deeply, kissing her knuckles even as it made his cheeks bright red. "Thank you again for showing me your magic, and for the gift."

Ah, the dirt rosebud.

"It was nothing, my lord." Elissa stood on tiptoe and pressed her lips to his cheek.

Lord Avery blushed three or four different shades of red.

She grinned; she couldn't help it. "I think we shall become great friends, Avery."

He regarded her silently for a moment, then nodded. As if resolved.

Elissa scanned his face for disappointment but saw none. She was relieved he'd not asked about a marriage contract—and hoped he continued to avoid the subject.

She'd tell Lord Jorrin when the time was appropriate that she wasn't accepting Lord Avery's suit. Her future was not as the Duchess of Tarvis. Elissa prayed Lord Avery wouldn't be upset.

Her first suitor and his father were leaving in the morning with the rest of their party.

The king also was leaving in the morning, but she ignored the panic that crept up at the thought of being left in Greenwald. She was angry at King Nathal—justifiably so. Besides, it wasn't like she was being abandoned.

I'm an adult.

Elissa had a task in Greenwald. She'd see it through.

When Sir Alasdair collected her, he didn't say what he'd spoken about with his captain. Then again, he'd not told her what he'd discussed with Master Gean, either. And she'd asked then.

"I'm sorry if I'm pulling you away from dancing," she said quietly as they strolled the nearly empty corridor.

"Don't worry about it."

She glanced at him, then regretted it. Her knight wore a dark expression like a shroud and he wouldn't look at her. Again.

"I…" Whatever she'd meant to say melted from her tongue before it was born. She didn't know what she wanted to say to him, anyway. Elissa couldn't stand this new awkwardness between them. Wanted to banish it, but she wouldn't beg him to talk to her, either.

She wanted to discuss the kiss they'd shared. Wanted to ask him to clarify what he'd meant when he'd called her innocent, but couldn't seem to form the words.

His expression didn't offer encouragement.

He still wasn't touching her, either. Walking beside her, not escorting her properly, with her hand tucked into his arm, their bodies in step, closer together than they were now. Elissa felt the distance between them more keenly. Her throat burned and her mouth was dry.

The silence was deafening as they made the last turn that would take them into the guest wing. A weight settled on her chest, making it hard to breathe well before they reached her door. Pain made her heart throb, but she couldn't put her finger on exactly what was wrong.

She wasn't supposed to be upset that Sir Alasdair Kearney had rejected her.

Had he actually rejected her?

Aye.

The painful—repeated—apology was a cast-off disguised as manners.

He's not one of my suitors.

Elissa wasn't supposed to be thinking about what it'd been like to be kissed by him. She should feel guilty that she hadn't pushed him away.

She *definitely* shouldn't be pondering if it would happen again. Or plan to kiss him back like she had the first time.

Sir Alasdair clearing his throat had her glancing into his face. *Oh, we're here. When did we stop walking?*

She looked up into his sapphire eyes.

He said nothing. The mouth she'd just been fantasizing about was a hard flat line.

"Why did you kiss me?" The words were out in a rush, and heat seared her neck on its way into her cheeks.

Sir Alasdair didn't just stiffen. He became a statue. "Go inside, my lady." His order was as hard as his posture.

"Why won't you talk about it with me?" Elissa frowned.

He averted his gaze. "Good night, lass."

Tears pricked her eyes. "Why?"

Her knight wouldn't even look at her when she tugged on his forearm. Sir Alasdair dropped her hand as if she'd burned him and turned on his heel. He practically fled into his own rooms and slammed the door.

Shock washed over Elissa. She stared at the door as if her eyesight could penetrate the thick panel. Or make him appear in the corridor. Surprise melted into something that stabbed. A lump formed in her throat and worked its way painfully downward, settling like a brick in her gut. Tight. Hard. Full of agony.

Unwanted moisture kissed her cheeks and she repeated those unladylike curses under her breath as she reached for her door handle.

Damn him.

Elissa should shout it, even though his door was sealed.

Damn you, Sir Alasdair Kearney.

A whine took her attention and she glanced over her shoulder. Her gaze locked onto the wolf cub she'd seen with Lady Cera's bondmate.

Blessed Spirit, was it just this afternoon?

During the horrific evening meal, she'd told Lady Cera about seeing the wolves in the wide hallway. The duchess had explained that the wolfling was the only one to remain unbonded from the litter of four wolves born. He was half a turn old now, and Lady Cera worried he'd never find a person to be bonded to.

The headwoman, Morag, had no love for the beasts in the castle, but this one had taken her dislike to new heights, from what Elissa had heard—and not just from the duchess.

Mistress Morag had dubbed him *Mischief* for his antics, and Lady Cera had half-laughed, half-winced when she'd told Elissa how much the name fit the cub.

He wouldn't mind any person, including Lady Cera. Only his sire had luck with him, and only because in the castle Trik—as the duchess called him—was alpha amongst the wolves, including Mistress Ansley's she-wolf, Ali. The three—now four—wolves made up a small pack.

The silver cub made no sound as he stared her down.

She didn't move.

Neither did he.

His eyes were ice blue; their beauty took her breath away. He sat about ten feet away, gazing back at her as if cataloguing everything about her. Or as if he could see through her. His eyes almost glowed in the dim light of the corridor.

Elissa's heart skipped for a reason other than her knight's rejection.

She wasn't afraid of the wolf—not really. What could he want with her?

Finally, the wolfling rose to all fours, swishing his tail once, much like he had when she'd seen him with his sire.

The movement broke the spell over her and Elissa pushed her door open with shaky fingers on the decorative handle.

He made no move to approach—or move away.

Do I want him to come closer?

Aye. Elissa wanted to find out if his fine silver coat was as soft as it looked. "Mischief?" she whispered.

The wolfling wagged his tail again, harder. Cocked his head to one side, his tongue lolling out of his open mouth.

She swallowed and took a step away from the open door. Toward the wolf.

Could she go to him?

Should I?

The wolfling scooted forward, and tossed his head back as if he was agreeing with her mental questions. As if he was saying, '*Aye. Come here.*'

Could he thought-send?

She'd learned how when she'd trained with the king's mages, but she'd always been under the impression that unbonded animals could not. She'd never heard of animals having magic on their own.

I must be imagining things.

A howl had Elissa stilling before she reached the cub's side. Then another sounded. Which soon became a series of howls — from more than one wolf.

It was eerie and beautiful. Like music, in a way. And coming closer.

Mischief made a sound in his throat and glanced over his shoulder. He looked back at her and wuffed, as if to say, *'I have to go, but I'll be back.'* Then he pivoted and bolted down the long hallway.

Away from her.

Sadness washed over Elissa as she stood, watching the corridor even after the wolfling had disappeared.

"What's wrong with you?" She didn't answer herself, but as she turned to go back to her guest suite, her eyes rested on Sir Alasdair's closed door.

Pain hit her chest full-force, ripping away her curiosity about the wolf.

Elissa darted into her room and shut the door hard, wincing at the resounding, unintended, slam. Leaning hard on the thick panel, she closed her eyes and tried to breathe, but counting and exhaling slowly did nothing.

All she could see behind her tight lids was her knight.

She scowled and shoved off the door. She'd just get ready for bed, read one of her favorite stories — she'd brought several books from Terraquist — and go to sleep.

Forget about a certain knight.

Forget about the kiss.

"My...first...kiss." She sobbed and cursed herself. "Just forget it. *All* of it."

Forget about how it'd felt to be in his arms, up against his hard body, how his mouth had moved over hers.

Elissa traced her bottom lip with her fingertip, as if she could still feel him there. Then she ran her tongue over the same spot, trying to savor him still.

All she could taste was the salt from her tears.

His words haunted her all over again. *"You're so damn innocent."*

"Naïve or virginal?" Did it matter to which he'd been referring?

He'd rejected her.

Wouldn't talk to her about the kiss. Wouldn't even tell her *why* he'd kissed her.

"It matters not."

She wasn't naïve. She *was* a virgin.

In either case, it wasn't any of her chaperone's *damn* business.

He'd ruined her first kiss by what he'd said afterward. Then he'd treated her to the roughest horseback ride she'd had in her life—her body still ached. *Then* he'd been angry at her in the bailey.

"So, why do I care? Why am I letting him hurt me?" Elissa pounded her thighs with tight fists. She wouldn't let him make her feel this way.

Her knight *wasn't* one of her suitors. What he did or didn't do *didn't* matter.

She wouldn't marry Lord Avery Lenore, but her other suitors would arrive soon, one by one, and she would give them as much of a genuine chance at her heart as she had the young heir from Tarvis.

"My heart?"

Aye. Her heart.

She wouldn't marry for any reason other than love, like she'd told King Nathal. The king had agreed, after all.

Resting her hand over her left breast, she pressed down and felt the organ in question jump against her palm. Her pulse sped up, echoing in her ears as she paced the room, her rust gown caressing her legs as her movements quickened.

Magic pushed back, the more agitated she got, but Elissa ignored her powers and refused to give in to the new tears that threatened.

I'm stronger than this.

She wouldn't let her chaperone do this to her.

Sucking in air, she pulled her magic around her like a cape and breathed in and out until the pressure, the temptation of the elements melded into the background.

Elissa lifted her trunk's lid, and the Durroc family seal caught her eye. She reached down and grabbed the brooch she never wore, tracing the embossed edges of the cold metal with her index finger.

She'd seen her home today. Walked the same halls as her parents and her brother. Touched their—her things. Yet she remembered nothing.

Despair enveloped her and she couldn't fight the sob that bubbled up. She dropped the brooch and shut her trunk.

Collapsing on her bed fully clothed, Elissa didn't bother wiping her face. More tears would just blind her.

Was she crying for her family? For the hurt Sir Alasdair had saddled her with? Or were her tears for the betrayal at the hands of King Nathal, since she'd never known the truth about her parents and Emery?

Does it matter?

Chapter Fifteen

*K*nock. *Knock.* Then a hammering noise that echoed.

"Who the—?" In his rushed irritation, he failed to grab his tunic, but when Alasdair wrenched the door to his temporary quarters open, he had a fleeting wish he'd grabbed his sword. He frowned. "You're going to wake the whole corridor pounding like that. What the hell is wrong?"

His heart skipped and he glanced at Lady Elissa's door, half-expecting her to be standing in the frame, scowling at him, hands on her perfect hips.

It was shut tight.

"Nothing." Bowen's shaggy sandy locks shifted as he cocked his head to one side. Amber eyes wide, he was looking at Alasdair as if he'd gone daft.

"Then why did you pound on my door?"

"You didn't answer fast enough." Dallon flashed a grin.

Bowen tipped his head, arching an eyebrow. "Aye, what he said."

Alasdair dragged a hand down his face. Stubble grazed his palm. He crossed his arms over his bare chest. "You two are pretty far from the soldier wing."

"Aye, because you are," Bowen said as if it made all the sense in the world.

"What do you want?"

Bowen and Dallon exchanged a glance.

"What?" Alasdair barked.

"Thought so," Bowen muttered.

"Looks like you *were* right." Dallon offered a curt nod.

Alasdair leaned into the doorframe in lieu of popping each of the younger men with one of the tight fists his hands had worked their way into. "What the hell nonsense are you two going on about?"

Bowen whistled, Dallon shook his head.

"It's a damn good thing we've come for you, brother." Dallon's dark eyes were serious.

"Come for me?"

"At supper I suspected, but now I'm sure," Bowen said.

Alasdair growled and grabbed Bowen by two handfuls of his shirt. His fellow guardsman wore no doublet, as it was evening. The knights were relieved of their duties until the morning, no doubt. Both wore soft breeches and loose tunics. Clothing to relax in. "Stop being obtuse."

"Obtuse?" Dallon echoed, chuckling.

Bowen grinned, despite the fact Alasdair had him in a tight grip. "You, my dear, older, usually wiser—"

"Spit it out." The mocking just irritated him more. Alasdair leaned into the knight, tempted to smash his forehead into Bowen's nose. Mess up his handsome face a bit.

"You're wound tight, Alas." It was Dallon who spoke.

Alasdair reared back, releasing his hold on Bowen. "What?" He couldn't deny the accusation, as much as he wanted to. He'd been as taut as a bowstring all night…well, closer to *all day*. Since that afternoon.

Since you kissed her.

Then acted like the biggest wretch in the world.

Hurt her.

"Proof positive." Bowen crossed his arms over his chest, not even bothering to tug his tunic straight or smooth the wrinkles.

"Get your shirt, brother. We're going to Greenwald Main."

Alasdair tried to sputter a response. A denial. *Anything.* But two sets of strong hands turned his shoulders—against his will—and shoved him into the borrowed rooms. They followed, Bowen uttering a command for Lucan's magic orbs to alight and brighten the suite as Dallon shut the door.

He liked the dark. Had been wallowing on his own just fine. Obsessing over every bit of conversation he'd had with Lady Elissa since the kiss.

On a loop of torture.

Fighting the embarrassment that'd come with his actions, as well what he'd said. He'd been worse than a wretch. He'd been rude. Hurtful. A total arse.

"I can't go anywhere," Alasdair said, although he snatched his olive green tunic from the back of the chair by the fireplace and shoved his arms into it.

"Your charge will be fine," Bowen said.

"We won't be gone long," Dallon added.

"I'm…not supposed to leave her." He yanked the shirt over his head and into place.

His brothers exchanged a look before glancing back at him. "You're going," they said in unison.

Alasdair stared.

Was he that transparent? Next they'd ask him what'd happened. Alasdair swallowed and scowled. "Are you two wretches going to explain to Leargan if he discovers I'm gone? We're not lads anymore. Dereliction of duty is serious."

"The captain has given his blessing."

He narrowed his eyes. "Aye?"

"You're as *off-duty* as we are." Dallon nodded. "For the evening."

Alasdair snorted. "It's well past evening."

"All is quiet," Bowen said as if he hadn't spoken.

"After seeing you at supper, Leargan all but commanded us to take you rutting." Dallon looked as if was fighting a smile.

"I doubt that."

"'Tis true." Bowen nodded.

"Then why didn't the captain himself tell me I'm relieved for the night?"

"I suppose he didn't think you'd need such *persuading*." Dallon winked.

Alasdair sighed and slid onto the seat he'd been occupying by the hearth before his brothers' disturbance. The fire had burned down, losing its glow as the embers winked in and out. But the room was still warm. More so than his quarters in the solider wing.

"To your feet, Sir Alasdair Kearney. We're going to *The White Sage*. Betha is waiting for you."

"How do you know?" He glared at Dallon.

"I made sure of it. I sent a message. She's eager to see you."

Lady Elissa's face, kiss-swollen rosy lips, heavy-lidded hazel eyes, and pink cheeks flashed into his mind. Her hair, mussed from his hands, had floated around her. She'd been radiant.

"Hardly innocent," she'd said.

She hadn't looked innocent.

Alasdair pushed off the arms of the chair so hard it creaked as he straightened. "Fine."

Bowen chuckled. "Don't sound grateful or anything."

"You're welcome, anyway." Dallon grinned.

He tumbled out of the guest suite, both fellow knights on his heels. Alasdair looked next door and paused. "Wait. I need to check on her."

His brothers exchanged another look he chose not to interpret.

Alasdair grumbled to himself and ignored them. He pushed the door open, half-surprised she didn't have it barred.

She should.

To keep the likes of him out.

He wanted to yell at her to do so. Perhaps he would, even though it'd just add more guilt for speaking to her with such disrespect, on what—three occasions now?

The room was dim, but not wholly dark. Two of Lucan's magic lights hovered on either side of the bed, lit at the lowest setting.

"Lady Elissa?" He called, but kept it low. His stomach quivered when he glanced at the sleeping fur-covered form in the huge bed. She didn't have the curtains drawn.

She's sleeping.

Alasdair's feet carried him to the head of the bed, to the side she was sleeping on.

Leave.

But he didn't.

Lady Elissa lay on her side, facing him. The glorious length of her long flaxen locks was spread over the pillow. Her eyelashes, darker than her hair, looked impossibly long against her cheekbones.

The sleeping furs were pulled up to her shoulder, but she had one arm resting on top of the blankets, the other in a small fist tucked next to her cheek on her pillow. The fluffy sleeve of her sleeping gown went all the way to her wrist, complete with feminine lace around the cuff. It was pale pink and somehow made her seem younger.

He watched the rise and fall of her breathing. She was deeply asleep, her expression serene. Her fair skin glowed in the soft magic light.

She looked radiant. Beautiful.

"So damn innocent." His whisper made his heart skip.

It didn't matter if she'd had a lover — though his gut clenched at the thought. She was so gorgeous, so pure he couldn't breathe.

She doesn't belong to you. She will never belong to you.

His throat tightened and his stomach flip-flopped as if he was a lad of five and ten gazing upon his first naked women.

She's not even naked.

It didn't matter. Lady Elissa was so lovely it hurt to look at her.

He didn't say her name again. Not that he could speak even if he tried.

Alasdair turned on his heel and strode silently from her rooms. He closed the door soundlessly and met two curious pairs of eyes. "Let's go."

"All is well?" Bowen asked.

"Aye. Let's go if we're going." *So I can get back.*

Although he left the latter part unsaid, he didn't miss Dallon muttering that something was wrong with him indeed.

He'd never wanted to hurry *away* from rutting before.

Betha threw herself into his arms. Instead of trying to kiss his mouth, she planted a loud *smack* on his stubbled cheek as Alasdair caught up her barely-clad form and held her tight.

She knows me well.

For some reason, that made him feel like a rogue.

He'd not hesitated to kiss Lady Elissa Durroc.

"Sir Alas," she whined. "It has been much too long!"

He plastered on a grin as she slid seductively down his chest to her feet.

Betha was petite, but she plastered herself to him as soon as her slippers hit the tavern floor, wrapping her arms around his torso, pressing her full breasts into him. She tilted her hips in a bump-and-rub for good measure.

His cock didn't even stir. Which was odd, considering Betha's skill in rotating her pelvis—he had a fantastic memory after all. She'd ridden him more times than he could count.

He pushed away any minute worry. It'd be different when they were naked in her room.

Alasdair would make her scream his name.

Like always.

He met sky blue eyes so different from the hazel ones that'd been haunting him from the moment he'd mounted Tess to accompany his brothers through Greenwald Main, and to *The White Sage Pub.*

Guilt.

It churned in his gut, making his mouth taste sour, his tongue heavy.

Why?

He owed her nothing.

No loyalty.

No fidelity.

They weren't going to be together. Despite the cock-hardening kiss. Despite how good she'd tasted. Despite the noises she'd uttered and how she'd clung to him...or how she'd felt in his arms, her small perfect breasts flat against his chest. Despite...

Shite.

"Sir Alas?" The barmaid's concern had him refocusing on her face.

Alasdair cupped her cheek and tucked wayward ebony strands of her hair behind her ear. Betha couldn't be more different than Lady Elissa—

Stop. Now.

"I'm sorry my duties have kept me from you, lass."

She smirked. "And here I thought you'd just been visiting another tavern."

Alasdair leaned back and gave her an affronted expression. He clutched his chest. "You wound me, lass. You know you're my favorite."

She giggled and beamed. "I bet you say that to all the lasses." Betha winked. Even if she knew he did, she wasn't offended. Wasn't attached to him.

Betha enjoyed their time together. He pleased her physically; she enjoyed sex. If she didn't assure him of that in words, her body always did. They found mutual pleasure in each other's arms, even if coin was involved.

He released a breath and let go of some tension. He needed this. Alasdair needed to feel normal again. Needed Betha.

To wash a certain lass and nonsensical ideas from his head.

And his....heart?

Banishing the last word that had the audacity to pop into his mind, he mock-growled at his familiar lover and swung her up over his shoulder. He pushed her thin skirts away and smacked her bare, delectable bottom.

Betha yelped, but it was delight, not fright or pain. She held on tight and dared him to take her upstairs.

So he did.

Chapter Sixteen

etha made quick work of her skimpy corset and thin skirts, sashaying toward him completely naked, hands on her rounded hips and *come hither* in those blue eyes.

Alasdair's gaze tracked her movements, trailing up and down her bare form. Ebony hair hung to her hips, loose and swaying as she walked. She smelled good, too; like roses.

Betha was a beautiful lass, with ample breasts and curves in all the right places. Normally, just a look at her rosy nipples, already peaking at him, and her trimmed tight triangle of dark curls would have him granite in his breeches.

Nary was a tingle going on below his belt.

She helped herself to the ties on his tunic, then slipped beneath it, dragging her soft hands down his chest.

He sucked in air; her touch was nice. Familiar. But didn't stir him just yet.

Alarm started to wash over him, but Alasdair banished it. Panic wouldn't cause arousal, for certain.

She pulled his shirt up. He obliged and lifted his arms, allowing her to continue pushing it up. He helped her get it the rest of the way off. Then watched the dark green fabric fall to the wood floor.

Betha continued her exploration of his chest, adding kisses and nips as she went. Alasdair closed his eyes and tilted his head back, tugging her closer. He rubbed her back in long strokes as she teased him. Normally, his cock would be straining toward her by now, urging him to take her.

The lass rubbed her breasts against his abdominal muscles, moaning as she traced his defined lines with her tongue. "Hmmm, Sir Alas, I missed you." Betha's mumble was lost against his skin.

He muttered an appropriate response and caressed her bottom, squeezing and kneading encouragement until she squirmed and started to rock her pelvis against his.

Alasdair didn't stop her when she opened his belt and loosened the ties on his breeches. Greedy blue eyes devoured his manhood when he was bared.

He'd never been shy. Had always been satisfied to be desired and visually pleasing to the women he'd lain with.

Not tonight.

His stomach quivered; he wanted to cup and cover himself.

She released him long enough for Alasdair to step out of his breeches and boots, but when Betha met his gaze, hers was confused. She'd noticed he wasn't hard for her like normal. "Sir Alas, is something wrong?"

"Nay, lass. Come here."

Without hesitation, she obeyed, wrapping her body around his. He lifted and carried her to the soft bed he'd been in dozens of times. Alasdair laid her down, following to nestle into the cradle of her body.

Betha nibbled his chin.

He flashed a grin. "I missed you, too, Betha-lass."

She smiled and buried her hands in his hair when he drew one of her already-taut nipples into his mouth.

Alasdair laved her, cupping and kneading as he suckled, then continued down to the soft part of her belly, showering kisses and dragging his tongue over her pale skin he continued.

Betha arched and called his name, tugging his hair now. He slid a hand between her legs. She was wet, ready for him. Wanted him.

His cock stirred and jumped, but didn't make a real effort to harden. Alasdair tried not to gulp, and prayed she hadn't noticed his manhood's continued disinterest.

Growling, he buried his hand in her heat, teasing the tight bundle of nerves at the top of her sex until Betha was writhing and rocking her hips. She panted his name over and over, wetting his whole hand with her excitement. The scent of her arousal was sweet, should spurn him on.

It isn't.

Alasdair's body wasn't on board. With one hand, he fisted himself, tugging with too much vigor as he begged his cock for an erection. With the other hand, he continued to pleasure his favorite tavern girl. His manhood teased *him* as much as he was teasing her.

He would start to stiffen, then soften in stages.

Get hard, dammit.

When had he *ever* been with a beautiful naked woman and not been able to tup her?

Never.

Not even when he'd over imbibed.

What's wrong with me?

His mental want of the lass spread out before him wasn't translating to the physical. Stroking himself wasn't pleasurable, either. Jolts of something that felt good would hit him, then recede. Nothing was sticking with him, to make him hard and wanting.

Alasdair's heart pounded and his forehead was damp as he continued ministrations on himself and Betha.

He made her come twice before collapsing to the bed and fighting the urge to cover his face in shame.

Betha shivered against him. She panted as she calmed. He slid his arm around her and hauled her closer, holding her as the last remnants of her orgasm faded. She nestled into him, her large breasts against his side, giving a sated sigh.

Alasdair rubbed her back automatically, but couldn't look her in the eye.

"That was wonderful, Sir Alas. But...don't you want to take me?" Betha's query was steady.

When he finally had the nerve to meet her gaze, her blue eyes had cleared of the hazy desire he'd seen. "I..."

They both looked at his flaccid member at the same time.

"Shall I try?" Betha reached for his cock.

He blocked her hand. The idea of her touch there turned his stomach for some reason, though she'd stroked him dozens of times, not to mention sucked him, but tonight he didn't want her hands or mouth on him.

Alasdair couldn't explore that particular *why*, either.

When their eyes met, hers were wide. "Sir Alas?"

Heat crept up the back of his neck, stinging, and he rubbed the spot. "I'm sorry, lass." Embarrassment kissed his cheeks, too. They seared, and he broke eye contact again. He hadn't blushed—ever. Then again, he'd never failed to perform in bed, either.

It wasn't that his cock was broken. He just...

I don't want Betha.

Confirmation in his head made him shudder. Alasdair couldn't have who he wanted.

Small hands on his cheeks tugged his face back to hers. Her thumbs caressed his stubble, making a scratching noise. There was no censure in her sky blue eyes. Betha smiled. It was sweet, held no pity. She genuinely liked him. Which made him feel worse. "No worries, Sir Alas. Will you tell me what's wrong?"

I'm in the wrong bed. "Nothing, lass."

"You've never—"

He leaned forward, pressing his lips to hers. Betha yelped, which gave him the opportunity to invade her mouth. Alasdair had never kissed her before.

It didn't take the tavern girl long to respond. Betha kissed him back enthusiastically, skillfully. She wrapped her tongue around his and slipped her hand to the back of his neck, tangling fingers in his hair.

His cock didn't even twitch.

They were naked, her breasts flattened to his chest. Her arms held him tight, her supple flesh hot against his. Her tongue coaxed, danced, teased. She moaned into his mouth.

Didn't matter. Nothing was happening to his body from her kiss.

Without breaking the seal of their mouths, Betha slid her leg over his middle, straddling him. Her wet sex ground into his as she started to rock in his lap.

Still nothing from below more than a twinge. A tingle of awareness, but no heat. No hardness.

Wrong.

It's wrong.

This is wrong.

The words roared in his head. His gut clenched and bile rose in his throat. Alasdair yanked his mouth from hers.

Wide blue eyes met his gaze. Passion faded quickly and her hands slipped from his hair.

Please don't be hurt.

"I'm sorry," he croaked.

Confusion, not pain, darted across her pretty face. Betha looked away, shoved her black locks from her flushed cheeks, but when she looked back at him, she'd composed herself. She wore a smile. Offered a nod and lifted herself off him. She patted his bare chest as she settled beside him. "You never kiss me. This is more than mere distraction. Your mind is with another woman, in a bed other than my own." Delivered without a missed breath, without hurt. Just fact, as she saw it.

He crushed his eyes shut as she hit the nail on the head. "I cannot have her."

They both froze with his unwanted candor. Alasdair couldn't look in her direction for the tenth time of the night.

Silence blanketed them.

Warm, comforting hands rested over his, though Betha's were too small to cover his completely. "Why not?"

Alasdair's breath stalled. His pulse pounded in his temples. He didn't know what to tell her. Reasons—some of them his own, not King Nathal's—piled against his lips and pushed. He swallowed instead of speaking. If he tried, everything would come out in a jumble that made little sense. Besides, he couldn't talk to Betha. Not about Lady Elissa.

"You can confide in me, Sir Alas. I shall not tell a soul."

He'd never really confided in anyone. Perhaps Leargan, but not many times, though they'd known each other for turns. His brothers usually came to him for such things. He was the eldest of the personal guard, and a good listener. Could even be serious when necessary, though they teased him relentlessly for it.

"Sometimes the body is guided by the heart," Betha whispered.

"What d'you mean?"

She smiled, looking younger. And much more innocent than a lass in her profession should. Betha had a gentle soul. In that, she wasn't so different than Lady Elissa. "You can't...you know...because your mind, perhaps your heart, is with her."

Alasdair frowned. He flipped their hands over and grabbed hers. "Betha, look at me."

She did.

"I wasn't thinking of her. Not when I was touching you."
Truth. He'd been distracted, but he wasn't thinking of—or wishing—the naked lass with him was any other than Betha. Not consciously anyway. A voice whispered he'd just been concentrating on the wrong woman, but he ignored it.

He couldn't read anything in her serene expression. He didn't see hurt in her eyes, or sadness. Could she truly be so placid about everything? She was human, after all. Didn't seem resigned, either. Just normal. Like the Betha he'd always known.

"I have enjoyed our many times together, Sir Alas."

Alasdair studied her blue eyes. "Why do you say it like that? As if our time has come to an end."

She laughed and patted his chest. "Tonight does not prove that to you, my fine knight?"

He wanted to squeeze his eyes shut as heat suffused his face again. Embarrassment was not something he would *ever* get used to.

Betha must've read it in his expression. She leaned up and kissed his cheek. "I don't refer to what happened tonight. I refer to how you feel here," she rested her hand over his heart. "For another lass. You never have before, so I'm happy for you." She winked. "And I don't believe I'll be the only tavern girl mourning your loss."

He blinked. "I don't."

"Don't what?"

"Feel...like that. For her."

She smiled instead of contradicting him. But her eyes called him a liar.

Alasdair's heart skipped. "She is to be married," he blurted.

"To you?"

"Nay."

Betha was crestfallen. "I'm sorry, Sir Alas."

He shook his head as unwanted—and unfamiliar—emotion caught in his throat. Alasdair ignored it all, shoving it away and reaching for a smile. "All is well, worry not, Betha-lass. I don't like you looking so sad."

Her next smile was kind, and she rested her hand against the side of his face. "Would that all my visitors were like you, Sir Alasdair Kearney."

By *visitors*, she meant the men she laid with, but Alasdair had never held her profession against her. Or asked if rutting for coin was a choice she'd made. Part of him didn't want to know, because he liked her too much. Even if what'd been between them had always been hot, sometimes sweet, and definitely consensual, he paid Betha to give herself to him. As did every man she was with.

He'd no illusions about that. He cringed. What a time to have a touch of conscience.

Is she happy?

Why had he never thought to ask?

Alasdair was the worst kind of rogue.

He forced a laugh and tried to reach for the humor he was known for. "Ah, lass, there is no other like me."

Betha giggled. "I believe you're right."

Chapter Seventeen

Three days had passed since they'd brought the water mage to Drayton from Terraquist Main. The lad was barely a man, but had put up a quite a fight when Bracken had grabbed him from behind and slapped a meaty palm over his mouth. Charis had stunned him with a spell and they'd hied back to Drayton's cave within a few hours of grabbing him from the market.

They'd left him with the old mage.

Charis and his lads had resumed their search for the powerful female elemental, but they hadn't gone far from the old mage's cave. This morning, they'd been magically summoned back.

Drayton had ordered him to dispose of a body.

What'd happened in that cave had obviously led to the water mage's demise, but what exactly Drayton had done to the lad was the mystery. The body was a shriveled husk that weighed nothing when Charis had retrieved it.

He'd probed for magic as soon as he'd gotten the lad's remains to the woods where Bracken and Nason awaited him.

And found *nothing*.

When they'd taken the lad from the market, his aura had burned brightly, blue in color—denoting his water magic—and surrounding his form so brightly Charis had had to avert his gaze until the mage had been unconscious on the back of Bracken's horse.

Even in death, magic should've been there. A slight trail his own magic could've sensed.

What had Drayton done to the lad before he'd killed him?

Unease settled over Charis.

Bracken and Nason hadn't much magic—just a weak ability or two—so they didn't share his concerns. Probably couldn't tell something was wrong with the body.

Charis had thought it was his imagination that Drayton had appear younger before his eyes when he'd bowed to the old elemental and then gathered the body up.

What if…

He swallowed and looked at the hole his companions had dug. Stories about old Aramourian blood magic stirred in the back of his head.

Dark things.

Evil things elfin parents warned their children against in the earliest stages of training. Stealing another's magic, another's life, did things to a mage he or she couldn't come back from.

Rumors of that kind of thing had been around for centuries. Secret elfin sects that'd wreaked havoc on their own clans for turns. It'd gotten so bad at one point that all the clan chiefs had come together and appointed a council of their most powerful mages to hunt down the sects and destroy them.

They had…and discovered a natural element that sucked all magic away in the process. No one with powers could be around it, as the tale went. One particular sect had worshipped the rock like a deity, and had stolen numerous human children to sacrifice to it.

Now, hundreds of turns later, Dimithian was a myth in Aramour, and most humans in the Provinces had never heard of it—even humans with powers. The Elves of Aramour were different. They never forgot, so they could prevent the horrors from repeating.

Charis shuddered.

If the old codger had performed blood magic… No wonder Drayton's aura had a black ring around it.

It wasn't his power in and of itself, it was taint. Evidence of stolen magic. Magic that'd been melded with Drayton's, but didn't belong there.

"Why are you so quiet?" Bracken asked as he tossed the lad's body in the hole like a sack of pebbles.

Nason started shoveling dirt on top without hesitation, or paying them any attention.

"I think I know why Drayton wants the lass."

"Does it matter?"

Charis met the big man's dark eyes. "It doesn't." *Or, it shouldn't.* "We'll find her, give her to him and collect our coin."

"Like always," Nason agreed, proving he was more observant than he looked.

"You look as if somethin' is wrong." Bracken studied him, and Charis wanted to shift in his boots.

He schooled his expression and squared his shoulders. "Nay. Just strategizing. I don't think she's in Terraquist at all." He tucked a strand of long hair that'd worked its way lose from his tie behind a pointed ear. As always, he'd made sure his ears were bare for his audience with Drayton.

"I don't disagree." Bracken cocked his head to one side. The wind caught his short shaggy locks and tossed them as if he'd run his hand through. The brown mass was a mess on top of his hatless head.

"We need to go to Greenwald."

"Greenwald?" Nason straightened, jabbing his shovel into the dirt and leaning on it. "Sense something?"

"My gut says that's the right direction."

Bracken narrowed his eyes. "We've been ta Greenwald."

"Aye, but perhaps we should inspect the holding where this all started."

"It was a lord's holding. With a castle. It'll be guarded. Perhaps occupied," Bracken said.

"We'll be careful."

Bracken grunted.

Nason scanned the horizon. "'Twill be dark soon."

"We can leave on the morn." Something nudged his senses and Charis froze, his conversation with his lads falling away.

Bracken—always the keener of the two—shot him a sharp look. "What is it?"

Charis gestured for silence and turned away. He concentrated, sniffed the air, and closed his eyes, sending his magical senses out wide.

A marker he'd left had been tripped.

He'd left pockets of magic everywhere they'd been. The markers could be anything, a rock, a tree, and were undetectable to most mages. He'd left them tuned to elemental magic specifically. If any elemental powers were used within range, he'd sense it.

Like he had now.

Problem was, they were too far away from this particular marker for him to tap in to it. To see exactly *what* had caused the surge. Or know exactly *when* it'd been tripped. The magical signal could've taken a day or two to get to him from where they were in Terraquist, even though they weren't far from the Greenwald border.

Simple concentration told him exactly where this marker was.

Greenwald.

Charis smiled and brandished a fist. "Elemental magic. One of my markers was tripped."

"Where?" Bracken demanded.

"Greenwald."

Nason whistled. "'Tis as if you have the gift of foresight."

Charis laughed. "I wish, my friend. It'd make our task much easier. This was just my gut...and a little luck."

⋆   ⋆   ⋆   ⋆

Not hide, nor hair. Charis made a fist and cursed. Savagely.

Drayton was on his arse, too. He should've never told the old mage about the marker being tripped. Excitement had lit the old man's usually cloudy eyes. Now, the magical check-ins were bordering on obsessive and Charis had nothing to share.

The damn ancient fool knew a spell that could show him where they were at all times. If there was a flat surface around, his face would appear, and they could see each other. Hear each other. Talk to each other.

Damn trick was as good as tracking magic, and Charis *hated* it. He didn't need a supervisor.

He had bigger problems than his annoying employer.

His magic was failing him. For the first time in his life.

He was going to have to tell the old codger he had no idea where the elemental was. He'd not sensed her—if *she* was the cause of the magic—anywhere near where his marker had been set off.

Somehow, his leeriness of Drayton had increased tenfold since he'd seen the water mage's brittle remains and suspected what the old mage had planned for the coveted elemental lass.

Charis was worried even more about being the bearer of bad news. The old man was powerful, and not to be trifled with. His wrath lay in wait, highlighted by Drayton's black-ringed aura.

"Nothin'?" Bracken's harsh face settled into even more terrifying lines at Charis' headshake.

"Are we fooked?" Nason wanted to know. He sported soot on both cheeks from the fire he was minding.

Charis frowned. "Not if I can help it."

"Aye, that's worked well so far." Bracken snorted.

He glared. If he wasn't so desperate for a magical solution, he'd cross the distance between them and put his fist in the big man's face. Maybe he could improve the bastard's many-times-broken nose. They hadn't had a good fight in months. It'd probably make them both feel better.

Charis and his lads had only been in Greenwald two nights, southeast of where they'd been on the border of Terraquist. He wasn't looking forward to the trek back to Drayton's cave if they decided to give up and report in. He wasn't ready to call it quits just yet.

The marker had revealed the remnants of a magic-induced thunderstorm a few days ago at best guess—but when he'd tried to track it, he got a big fat *nothing* to latch on to—with tracking spells *or* good-old-fashioned mercenary skills.

There was nothing in the area he suspected the storm had been. The signal was concentrated in a wooded area right off the main road, as if it'd had no purpose. As if the mage had lost control.

The trace was slight too, with most of the power fading at the end of the short burst of magic—that told him it'd been a short-lived storm.

Charis' marker had recorded a seriously powerful elemental. Since it was a thunderstorm, he could only assume he or she was a water mage, but the magic was much more powerful than the mage they'd brought Drayton from the Terraquist market. Thicker, inferring there might be more than just water magic there.

But was it Drayton's mage?

If so, what the hell happened to her?

The magic had just *poofed.* There was no trail to follow.

That just *didn't happen* to Charis. His tracking magic was the best. He was no egotist to ponder on his powers, either. All his elfin teachers had boasted on what he could do. Before he'd left Aramour for bigger and better things—more gold, of course—he'd been sought out by all the clans when a tracker was needed for a difficult task.

Like he'd told Drayton, if he couldn't find her, she was dead. Or…covered in more powerful magic than his own.

But there's no such thing as undetectable protection magic, is there?

Magic wasn't working, so they'd gone back to the holding of the first lass Drayton had charged them with checking for identity. The site had been stripped of magic and bodies, evidence.

Charis and his men had kept their distance because knights wearing Greenwald armor had been all over the place.

His ears made him memorable. There weren't that many half-elves running around the Provinces, so it was imperative he hide his heritage as best he could. He'd stick out even more in a Province where the duke happened to be half-elfin like him, too.

They *had* to blend in. He and his lads were just three men traveling. They always had a cover story in case they were stopped. This time, they were on their way home to Aramour. All three of their far Northern accents were authentic. It was best to stick to simple truths and build on them.

"We need ta move on." Bracken's gravelly voice broke into his desperate musings.

"Nay." He shook his head. Instinct warred with good sense. Or maybe it was denial that his magic was failing him. Either way, Charis always listened to his gut. "We need to stay here."

"Why? We've got nothin', according ta you."

"I can't explain it." He stood to his full height and squared his shoulders. Maybe he'd get that fight after all, if the expression on the big man's face was any indication.

"Try." Bracken's meaty hands were tight at his sides, as if he was restraining himself.

Charis narrowed his eyes. "Watch your tone."

Since when does Bracken command me?

His companion was getting too big for his breeches.

Bracken strode forward, closing the distance between them. "I don't have a problem wit' your leadin'. I have a problem wit' wastin' time and coin. And that's all we're doin'."

"Nay. We're doing what needs to be done. Sorry you can't understand the hows."

Growling again, this time deeper in his throat, Bracken towered over Charis. "You should watch *your* tone wit' *me*."

Nason said nothing. Just watched them, pitched on the edge of his log seat, fists clenched in front of him. He'd abandoned his fire-tending. The embers crackled as if protesting. The little blond man was never one to step between them anyway. Charis and Bracken both outweighed and outmuscled him.

"My gut says we stay in Greenwald. So we stay."

"Your gut or your magic?"

"Both." Charis pushed the word out with more confidence than he felt. He straightened and sucked in a breath.

Bracken's huge shoulders finally loosened, but his expression didn't soften one iota. "Get tha shite worked out so we can find the lass."

"I'm working on it. I don't like to be thwarted any more than you. Something's not right here. My magic *doesn't* fail." Both his lads knew that from their turns together.

That seemed to relax the oversized oaf even more. After a few paces back and forth of their campsite, Bracken grunted and sat on a wide log Nason had dragged over from the woods when they'd stopped for the night.

Charis released the air he'd trapped in his lungs as silently as possible. He hated the idea of weakness. Holding his breath to see what Bracken would do? *Unheard of.* He didn't fear the big man.

Maybe his powers had abandoned him for being a coward. He fought a shudder and planted his arse on a log next to Nason.

"What's next then?" Nason asked.

"Greenwald Main. First thing in the morning."

Bracken arched a dark brow. "Why?"

"Something's telling me we need to go to market." Charis didn't dare question the urge now.

"Another mage for Drayton?" Nason asked.

"*The* mage, I hope."

Chapter Eighteen

Confusion and misery were her constant companions as the next few days passed. Too bad they had little to do with her purpose in Greenwald; meeting her suitors.

To make Sir-Alasdair-matters worse, Elissa felt an irrational abandonment since the king and queen had departed. Especially since the goodbye with her cousin had been teary-eyed. She'd never seen Queen Morghyn cry. Of course she'd lost control of her own emotions then, too, squeezing her cousin in a tight hug when the queen had reached for her.

"Be happy," Queen Morghyn had whispered in her ear.

Elissa's eyes had darted to a visibly uncomfortable Sir Alasdair. Pain had really taken a bite out of her then, and not because the only family she had was leaving Greenwald.

The knight still wouldn't look her in the eye.

She'd called herself a fool—then and now—and forced her attention on King Nathal and Sir Murdoch when both men wished her farewell. It was hard to see the man she'd considered father go, and even more so when the king enclosed her in a hug.

Her unsaid anger had dissipated, but she hadn't forgiven him for keeping her past from her—not by a long shot. She couldn't hold on to her anger right then. Desperation and loneliness had threatened to swallow her whole.

Elissa wasn't alone. She shouldn't feel as if she was, but a part of her did. Somehow, even though she'd made friends with the ladies of Greenwald, including the very shy newlywed, Mistress Avril, the fact things were not right with Sir Alasdair made her feel worse.

She'd cried herself to sleep after the argument in the corridor. After that horrid dinner, when he'd refused to talk to her about their kiss.

Elissa had woken up after dark, her torso sore from the rust gown's tight bodice, combined with the position she'd been lying in. She'd scrambled to her feet, dressed for bed, and tried to forget about him.

Reading one of her favorite books by the light from Sir Lucan's glowing orbs had only made her feel worse; the story was a romance. A handsome knight pursued his true love, tearing her away from an unwanted arranged marriage.

Of course.

For some reason, she'd always loved that story. Now she couldn't even look at it. Buried the small leather-bound volume at the bottom of her trunk.

She'd crushed her eyes shut afterward, praying to the Blessed Spirit for sleep. And Peace.

Unfortunately, she'd dreamt of *him*; his kiss, his taste. His arms around her.

She'd fantasized that things had gone further when he'd had her back against the wall in the room that had once belonged to her parents. Her knight had taken her breeches down and touched her where only her own hands had been, and *only* during a bath.

Elissa had even imagined he'd come back to her in the guest suite that night. In the dream, Sir Alasdair had stood by her bed, softly calling her name and reaching for her.

She'd woken with a start—to a very empty bedroom and an aching chest.

Sleep had eluded her the rest of the night.

Which only made the next morning even tougher. Elissa had met the next of her suitors, the lord from a large holding in the south of Tarvis, Lord Audon Croly.

She supposed he was nice, but he hadn't stayed at the castle very long. He'd said all the right things, and he was certainly handsome with cropped sandy hair and light brown eyes, but they'd only shared two meals and a walk in the gardens—a location that was becoming tiresome, truth be told.

Lord Audon hadn't asked anything about her magic like Lord Avery had. He'd mentioned that he didn't have any magic of his own to speak of. He'd seemed indifferent about—well, everything.

How was one supposed to decide the suitability of a marriage partner from *one* afternoon and evening?

Perhaps he didn't like her? Had Lord Audon run from her? He'd said he had to take care of some urgent business in Greenwald Main for his father, and he'd come back if she wished.

Elissa didn't know *what* she wished.

He'd even assured her that he wouldn't be far, but Lord Audon hadn't expressed that he'd *wanted* to see her again. To be fair, she hadn't responded when he'd told her he could come back to spend more time with her.

Had he been expecting her to say *aye*?

Sir Alasdair had hovered, glowering the whole time, anyway. His presence had made her feel awkward with Lord Audon, something she hadn't felt with Lord Avery.

She was so confused when she looked at her knight. *Hurt. Longing.* It'd all hit her at once, swirling in her head and heart, then she'd remind herself it didn't matter.

He's not one of my suitors had become her mantra, but it didn't relieve the tightness in her chest.

Lady Aimil's cousin, Lord Lakyn, was next to arrive at Castle Aldern. He'd been the handsomest of her suitors thus far, flashing charming dimples when he smiled. As was typical for people from Ascova, Lord Lakyn had ebony hair and deep brown eyes, as well as an olive complexion that enhanced his looks. His hair was cropped short, which made him even more appealing.

He was almost as tall as Sir Roduch—who stood at about six and a half feet—and just as broad, but his personality made him a gentle giant. Lord Lakyn made Elissa feel elfin, but it wasn't as bad—comical—as seeing him next to his cousin. Lady Aimil was exactly five feet tall.

She'd thrown herself into her cousin's arms when he'd arrived. That'd been quite a sight, too, but all the surrounding witnesses, Lord Jorrin and Lady Cera included, had worn silly grins.

Lord Lakyn had spent three days with her in Greenwald and Elissa had quickly grown fond of his jovial personality. She did worry that she would have to stand on a step stool to kiss him, but thinking of kissing had just made her obsess about her knight, so she'd shut down that trail of thought.

Unfortunately, as lovely as Lord Lakyn was, the man had talked of little else than horse breeding. She'd had to swallow yawn after yawn. Smiling and nodding had made her head spin and her mouth hurt.

She'd tried not to watch her chaperone, but of course her uncooperative gaze wandered, as if drawn to him. Even Sir Alasdair seemed to have trouble not being bored by Lord Lakyn's one-track-conversations.

Her gentle-giant-suitor had asked after her knight's red roan mare. The man had insisted on seeing Contessa as well. Evidently, Sir Alasdair had purchased her from Lord Lakyn's father. She was *fine Ascovan stock,* a phrase Lord Lakyn was overly fond of.

She'd gone to the stables with the men, taking a moment to visit with the gray mare King Nathal had given her. The lass still needed a name, but Elissa had yet to come up with one. She could've asked her horse-loving suitor, but she'd been afraid Lord Lakyn would've turned a simple question into a soliloquy about how important a horse's name was, so she'd refrained.

The mare's leg was better after their wild ride, and for that, Elissa was grateful. Guilt swirled in her stomach for the whole incident. Her gray must have forgiven her, though. The horse had neighed a greeting and sought Elissa's touch with her soft muzzle. She'd rested her forehead against the mare's much wider one, whispering nonsense to the beast and wishing for simpler times.

Elissa had tried not to stare at Sir Alasdair while he'd been conversing with Lord Lakyn by his red roan's stall, but it'd been the first time she'd seen a smile on her chaperone's face since he'd kissed her.

No matter which of her suitors stood next to Sir Alasdair Kearney, Elissa couldn't stop comparing them. Her preferences were with her knight every time, despite his sour disposition since *the incident*—what she'd taken to calling the day at Castle Durroc and their kiss.

Lord Audon was kind and reserved.

Lord Lakyn was fun-loving and upbeat.

Both were handsome. Both were wealthy and suitable matches, as the king intended. Neither of the men offered her a spark of attraction.

There was only one more suitor.

Lord Camden Malloch—the Duke of Dalunas.

What if I don't like him?

Sir Alasdair's kiss had scrambled her brains and her fantasies. What if she couldn't see the appeal of any other man?

She and Sir Alasdair were of a rank. He was an elevated knight—one of the personal guard to a duke. She was a minor lady. There was nothing stopping them from a match. The king was fond of Sir Alasdair. He was wealthy in his own right. Could provide for her. Besides, she had her own land. Her own coin.

Would King Nathal object to her knight as her match?

Elissa's heart sped up.

Don't be a fool.

Sir Alasdair regretted their kiss. His apology had spoken of as much, after all.

Not to mention his refusal to discuss *the incident* and the indifference with which he regarded her now.

Elissa felt like a duty he'd rather not have. He was maintaining his lack of decorum as far as proper escorts, too. If they touched at all, even by accident, a small brush of her fingers against his, or if he thought she walked too close, he'd scoot away, or yank away, unless they were with other people. If he *had* to touch her, it was hesitant, as if her skin burned his. And never for any length of time.

A canyon as big as the Netian Valley was between them.

Elissa *hated* it.

The knight still seated her properly at meals in the great hall, but he wouldn't dance with her if the bards sang after evening meal, even if other couples were dancing. Her knight didn't address her unless absolutely necessary. Sir Alasdair wouldn't blatantly ignore her, but his speech was curt and unnatural. Gone was their easy conversation and friendly company as before he'd kissed her.

It stung. *More* than stung, no matter how many times she called herself a fool for it.

Elissa shook her head and shook *herself*.

She had a free day.

Her final suitor wasn't arriving until the morrow, and Lady Cera had asked her to spend the morning in the duchess solar with her and the other ladies. She was excited to have female companionship—and perhaps even some time *away* from Sir Alasdair. Maybe she could even breathe a little.

She'd told him she'd go herself, and he'd agreed, explaining he had a private lesson to teach swordplay to whom he called *the lads* – Sir Lucan, and squires to two of the knights of the personal guard. Elissa thought their names were Brodic and Alaric. She'd seen the lads with the young knighted mage. Lord Tristan, the healer and Lord Jorrin's Second, had teased that the three lads were rarely apart.

Sir Alasdair hadn't told her when he'd collect her, if at all.

Elissa had tried not to let that hurt, but it did. She rounded the corner of the wide corridor, chiding herself for dwelling on things that didn't matter.

A whining noise had her glance up.

Startled, she locked eyes with an ice blue set that was becoming familiar. But the silver wolfling only regarded her for a second. He scratched at a door; his muzzle, as well as his pale chest, was covered in something dark and thick. Caked onto his coat, like mud.

Mischief was begging entry into Elissa's destination. The duchess solar.

"Where are you, you scoundrel?" Someone – female – yelled.

Elissa jumped when the Headwoman appeared at the end of the hallway, brandishing a wooden spoon like it was a knight's broadsword.

The wolf whimpered, spared Elissa one more look, and dashed away in the opposite direction of Morag, running by Elissa close enough to touch.

Whatever he was covered in had to be food. The scent teased her nose, and it smelled delicious.

"Oh you! Come back here, *Mischief!*" The headwoman muttered a few phrases that made Elissa blush, then seemed to notice her for the first time. "Ah, my lady, good day." Morag bowed, looking a bit awkward with the spoon still firmly in her grip.

"Hello, Headwoman." Elissa opened her mouth to ask what'd happened, when the door swung open.

"What did he do now?" Lady Cera stood half in the room, half in the corridor. Her question was steady, but her expression was chagrined, and her cheeks were pink.

Two dark heads popped out of the door behind the duchess. Lady Aimil's dark eyes went wide with one look at the headwoman, and Mistress Avril retreated back in the solar without a word.

"My lady, I'm at my wits end!" Morag's words were as rushed as her bow to Lady Cera. "That beast spilled a *whole* kettle of stew I had simmering in the kitchen."

"You ran all the way here from the kitchens?" Mistress Ansley wanted to know. She slid into the corridor between Lady Aimil and the duchess, a redheaded baby on her hip.

Morag frowned. She looked at the duchess. "My lady, the beast has *got* to go. I put up with rest of the pack; they are quite well behaved in comparison, but Mischief—" She threw her hands up in exasperation and sputtered, as if her anger had seared her tongue away.

Lady Cera cast her eyes to the ceiling and a toddler, also a redhead, snuck out of the solar. His hair was curly in the back, and his ears were tapered. He had to be the duchess' son. Little Lord Fallon grinned, oblivious of the adult tension, and pointed to Elissa. "Lady," he said.

Five sets of eyes regarded Elissa.

"Elissa! Good morning, we've been waiting for you!" Lady Cera was over-bright.

She smiled, not minding in the least that she was a distraction the duchess seemed to need.

Lady Cera hugged her, and swept her son into her arms. She looked back at the woman in charge of all her staff. "Morag, I'm sorry he was troublesome this morning. I promise I'll find him a bondmate soon. And I'll call Trik. I don't know why they aren't together."

Morag frowned and brandished her spoon to the corridor in general. "I'm sure his sire is as tired of his antics as I am. Begging your pardon, my lady, but you've been looking for months for someone to saddle the wretch with."

The duchess sighed. "He's not a wretch. He needs guidance. A bondmate will get him—and keep him—in line."

The headwoman scoffed. "It has been almost six months, my lady."

"I know, Morag. I'm sorry about your stew."

"You'd be sorrier if you went hungry."

Elissa gasped. She'd never heard someone address a duchess like that.

Lady Cera rolled her eyes. "Don't be overdramatic, Morag."

Someone muffled a giggle. Surprise washed over Elissa. Perhaps they had an informal relationship. She'd liked the somewhat stiff headwoman when they'd met, and she'd never spoken to Elissa with anything but respect.

"Elissa, join us. Morag, I'm sure the kitchen staff requires your supervision." The duchess' gray eyes narrowed.

The Headwoman huffed, but bowed at her dismissal and stomped away, as no fine lady ever should—or would.

Mistress Ansley started laughing first. Then Lady Aimil. Lady Cera mock-glared, but couldn't swallow a smile when little Lord Fallon giggled.

Elissa found herself laughing as well, the little lad's giggle was infectious, though he probably had no idea what he was laughing about.

"What a morning," Lady Cera breathed.

"Thank you for the invitation this morning, my lady." Elissa curtseyed.

"Cera. As I have told you before." The duchess shook her finger at Elissa, and they all laughed again when little Lord Fallon imitated his mother.

"Are you going to stand in the doorway all morning, or come inside?" Mistress Avril called, a cheeky grin on her pretty face.

The duchess put her son to his feet, and he dashed over to a rug by the large hearth, where Mistress Avril sat with two little girls. The smaller of the two was in the lass's arms, and had to be Mistress Ansley's daughter, twin to the baby she was holding.

The other was closer to Lord Fallon's age. She was walking and babbling, and held out a toy to the little lord when he joined her.

"Elissa, have you met everyone?" Lady Cera asked, as if reading her mind.

"The ladies, aye."

"This is Brogan," Mistress Ansley said, grinning and bouncing the redheaded laddie on her hip. "Avril is holding Brynn. My twins. They're nine months old."

"My daughter is Aislinn." Lady Aimil smiled. "She's one turn and two months."

"And last but not least, my son is Fallon. He's one and a half."

"As if anyone could mistake the pointed ears," Lady Aimil teased.

"They're all beautiful." Elissa meant it. The children were adorable. "So close in age; it'll be great for them to grow up together."

The ladies nodded and beamed.

"Cera's got them all but married off to each other, of course." Mistress Ansley flashed a grin when the duchess mock-glared.

Mistress Avril and Lady Aimil giggled at the same time.

"Sit, sit, relax! There's no need for us to stand around all morning." Lady Cera led by example, smoothing her simple blue gown and taking a seat on the plush sofa closest to the hearth.

Elissa took a seat across from her in padded chair. The room was open and welcoming, light streaming in from all the windows. It was warm too, both from sun and the huge fire in the hearth. Overstuffed chairs of various styles were arranged loosely, set up for comfort and conversation around the hearth. There was a pale colored wood oversized desk and matching carved chair in one corner by the window, too. As well as a door in the far corner she assumed was a privy.

"What are you going to do about Mischief?" Mistress Ansley asked.

The duchess groaned. "Don't remind me."

"You have Morag at her wits' end. She might up and quit on you."

"No she wouldn't. Then she wouldn't have anyone to boss around." Lady Cera waggled her eyebrows and Mistress Ansley shook her head.

Lady Aimil smirked and looked at Elissa. "There's cheese, fruit, and bread on the tray, if you're hungry."

"No, thank you, I broke my fast in my room this morning."

"It's nice to have a private meal once in a while, away from the formality of the great hall, isn't it?" Lady Aimil smiled.

Elissa forced a nod, not wanting to think how her first meal could've been better if shared with Sir Alasdair. Her belly flipped.

"How is married life, Avril?" Lady Cera asked.

"It's wonderful. I've a good man. I hope to be with child soon," Mistress Avril said, though she blushed and looked down at the cooing baby girl in her arms.

"That you do. Your children will grow up with ours, too." Then Lady Cera's gray gaze zoned in on Elissa. "Speaking of marriage, how's the hunt for a husband going?"

"Way to be subtle, Cera." Mistress Ansley's unusual teal eyes danced. She gently removed her long red plait from her son's chubby hands and tossed it over her shoulder.

Elissa cleared her throat. "As well as can be expected, I suppose. I've liked them all so far."

Lady Aimil leaned on the edge of her seat. "What about my cousin?"

"I like Lord Lakyn very much."

"He bored you to death with talk of horses, didn't he?" The lady grimaced. "I told him not to do that!"

Elissa winced and then nodded. Everyone laughed.

"Please don't hold it against him, he's a good man, I promise," Lady Aimil pleaded.

"I won't. But I don't think I'll make a decision until I've met the last suitor."

"Lord Cam. I can't wait to see him again, it's been too long." Lady Cera grinned, then her expression sobered. "Jorrin told me you've declined my cousin's suit, though?"

Heat licked her cheeks and Elissa nodded. "Aye, my lady." Her heart thumped. Was the duchess going to demand an explanation?

"Cera."

"Cera," Elissa repeated.

"Don't worry about Avery. I didn't think you'd pick him. My cousin's too young for marriage, and too shy. I doubt he's even kissed a girl. Unless—"

"Cera!" Mistress Ansley exclaimed at the same time Elissa affirmed Lord Avery hadn't kissed her.

"What?" The duchess shrugged, wearing a lopsided grin.

"A lady does not kiss and tell," Lady Aimil said.

Elissa giggled. So did Mistress Avril, from her place on the rug with the children.

Then four sets of eyes silently regarded her.

"Any kisses you want to confess?" Lady Cera winked.

"You are not proper at all, *my lady*." Lady Aimil grinned at the duchess.

Lady Cera shrugged as if her friend had stated the obvious, and she was unrepentant.

Elissa's heart skipped. Nay, she couldn't tell them about kissing Sir Alasdair, and she had nothing to gossip about regarding the other two suitors.

"How could she kiss anyone? With Alas there the whole time?" Mistress Ansley said; Elissa wanted to hug her.

The duchess frowned in her friend's direction. "True." She looked back at Elissa. "Well, if the time comes when you *do* want to kiss one of your suitors, just tell Alasdair to go away."

"Aye, like that'd work." Laughter wrapped Mistress Ansley's words. "He's supposed to keep them *from* accosting her."

"Accosting?" Lady Aimil giggled. "They are all decent young men, I don't think she's in danger of that."

Elissa watched the ladies in more wonder than the night of the wedding feast. These ladies were like sisters. She wanted to be close to them like that.

"The only one that might accost her would be Alas, no?" The duchess' tease had Elissa freezing in her seat as the other ladies laughed again—even Mistress Avril.

"Nay." She cleared her throat when Lady Cera's keen gaze landed on her. "Sir Alasdair has been nothing but kind to me."

Silence fell and she wanted to squirm. They all watched her.

"I'd expect him to be," the duchess finally spoke.

Elissa forced a nod and plastered on a smile, praying her face wasn't red. *He's not one of my suitors* played in a loop in her head. "I like him very much." Something in the back of her mind teased it was more than that, but she didn't dare think it—let alone say it.

"Oh, we do, as well," Mistress Ansley said. "We only tease because he's got quite the reputation with the lasses."

"Ah." Elissa hadn't heard that, but how could she? She'd only been in Greenwald a sevenday. Her gut burned. Did he often kiss lasses he barely knew? Maybe that was why he'd reacted as he had. To him, she wasn't anything special at all.

"Elissa, are you all right?" Lady Aimil asked.

"Oh, aye. I'm fine." She straightened her shoulders.

"You look a bit pale," Lady Cera said. The duchess popped up and poured mead into a goblet. "Are you cold? Here, this'll warm your belly a bit."

"I'm fine…"

"Don't argue with her, you won't win," Mistress Ansley put in.

The duchess' eyes glinted with satisfaction when Elissa accepted the glass and sipped. Lady Cera returned to her seat on the fluffy sofa.

"Thank you," she whispered. "It's good."

"Suitors aside, how's your stay been?" Lady Aimil asked. She tucked a strand of her raven hair behind her ear and smiled. It was kind and genuine and eased Elissa's internal tension. The lady's gown was dark red, and elaborately embroidered on the bodice. She was the most feminine of the four friends, as well as the most petite. The two redheads were much taller, at probably nine or ten inches past five feet. Even Mistress Avril was several inches taller than Lady Aimil.

"Wonderful. I very much like Greenwald."

"Oh, good, I'm glad," Lady Cera said.

A wuffing sound and series of scratches at the door had Mistress Ansley on her feet. "I'll let them in, will you hold him?" She handed her son to Elissa without waiting for an answer.

Elissa scrambled to right the baby boy, and was rewarded with a three-toothed grin by the laddie. She smiled back. He cooed and stuck his small fist in his mouth, starting to gnaw. Drool slid down his little chin.

"All he does is drool. Here." The duchess tossed her a scrap of linen and made a face. "Teething will do that. Not the most fun stage of development."

"At least he's not squalling," Mistress Ansley called, her hand on the door handle.

"He's fine," Elissa assured them, and whispered to the tiny lad as she wiped his mouth.

Brogan grinned, then giggled.

"Oh, you're a natural."

She tried to smile at the duchess, but for some reason her chest was tight.

Did she want this? Children?

Aye. Problem was, she only imagined having children with one man.

Stop being ridiculous. One kiss doesn't mean forever...it didn't mean anything...to him.

Mischief rushed into the solar, rescuing her from forbidden thoughts—thank the Blessed Spirit.

The huge white wolf, Trikser, was close behind—nipping at his heels was more accurate. Two more wolves, one pure black and the other a mixture of red, brown and gray weren't far behind, either.

"Oh, geesh." Lady Cera covered her face.

"What's wrong?" Elissa asked, sitting the baby up against her chest.

"Trik's thoughts are dark. Mischief was up to no good."

"The stew is gone from his coat," Lady Aimil said.

The huge black wolf rushed to Elissa, who froze in the chair, a tremor shimmying down her spine. The beast's yellow eyes were huge as she surveyed them, only a few feet from Elissa's gown.

"Ali, easy," Mistress Ansley said. "It's all right, Elissa. She's protective of the twins. She'll sniff you and move on. I've told her there's no danger."

A growl filled the room.

All eyes shot to Mischief. His hackles were raised, his body stiff.

"Mischief?" Lady Cera said.

Ali and the wolfling locked eyes. The huge black she-wolf's hackles rose before Elissa's eyes, and she returned Mischief's growl.

"Don't move, Elissa."

She wasn't planning on it, so the duchess didn't have to worry. Her heart thundered. Elissa clutched the baby close, though Brogan was cooing, waving his tiny arm as if to reach for his mother's bondmate.

Trikser wuffed and Ali backed away from the chair, her wide shoulders loosening as she moved gracefully for a beast her size.

Elissa concentrated and exhaled. Her eyes tracked the she-wolf as she greeted Brynn. Ali wagged her tail for the baby, and lay next to Mistress Avril.

Mistress Avril stroked her hand down the wolf's back. Ali swished her tail again, as if she hadn't been a fierce beast just moments ago.

"What was that about?" Lady Aimil asked.

"I don't know. I've never heard him growl before, let alone have his hackles raised. At Ali nevertheless." Lady Cera blew out a breath as if she'd been holding it.

"I've—" Elissa faltered when all eyes settled on her. "Run into him in the corridors a few times."

"Mischief?" Lady Cera asked.

The young wolf darted to her side as if beckoned.

"Aye. He's never approached me, but I'm not scared of him."

"Well, you don't have to fear any of them," Mistress Ansley said.

"Interesting." Lady Cera tapped her cheek with a long, slender finger. She failed to expand on what was interesting, and as the children laughed and played, the semi-scare faded.

Elissa relaxed into the chair and back into the easy conversation with the ladies, enjoying herself as she continued to hold little Brogan. She even took a turn at holding Lord Fallon when he wanted up on her lap.

The duchess explained the ladies often spent mornings in the solar with their children before seeing to duties. She loved the idea and hoped to do the same when she was married and had her own. Her heart thumped at the thought—and the simultaneous knock at the door.

Sir Alasdair bowed as he entered the solar, and his sapphire gaze zoned in on Elissa, who was still holding the heir to Greenwald on her lap.

Lord Fallon scrambled down and dashed to the knight. Sir Alasdair squatted down to greet the tiny lord, and she couldn't tear her eyes away from the sight of him and the child.

Lady Cera said something teasing, and they all laughed.

Elissa's chest tightened and she swallowed against a lump in her throat when he avoided her gaze, but continued pleasant interactions with the ladies. She rose to her feet and bowed to the duchess, almost regretting her knight's interruption.

Things still weren't—and wouldn't be—right between them. It hurt to see him speak as his normal self to others.

"Have a good day, Elissa," Lady Cera said, squeezing her hand fondly.

She wanted to cry.

When they were alone in the corridor, she intended to ask him how the swordplay lesson went, but he looked away as soon as the door was closed, and her heart slid to her toes.

Elissa only had one more day of Sir Alasdair's company alone.

Problem was, it was going to be an arduous one.

Chapter Nineteen

"Do you need to go back to *The White Sage*, brother?" Sir Bowen knocked her knight on the back of his shoulder outside the great hall.

Sir Alasdair glared.

"What? Did you not get enough of Betha the other night?" Sir Dallon winked.

The other night?

Elissa's heart plummeted, and she flushed to her toes. Her magic responded, warming her limbs, but it didn't make breathing any easier.

The two knights chuckled and continued to pass ribald remarks. Obviously they hadn't noticed her approach, but this was one time she *wasn't* grateful for the soft sole and soundless footsteps of ladies' slippers.

Her gut churned.

"The lass certainly looked well pleased when we left." Sir Bowen laughed.

She swallowed against the lump in her throat. Betrayal threatened to take her over, even though she had no hold over him.

"Don't you two have duties?" Sir Alasdair's voice was a growl, but he glanced over his shoulder. His eyes widened.

Of course he hadn't expected to see her standing there.

Elissa hadn't told him she'd make it to the formal sitting room outside great hall on her own. He'd probably been planning to get her from her rooms momentarily. He'd left her there after midday meal to change gowns.

An unnamed emotion passed over his face. Was it guilt?

Nay. Stop seeing what you want.

Another day of misery had passed.

After spending time with the ladies in the duchess solar the morning before, she and the knight had shared an awkward midday meal with barely a word. She'd spent the evening alone in her rooms, reading. Or more accurately, pretending to read.

Sir Alasdair hadn't collected her for evening meal, and she'd been relieved. Hadn't wanted to seek him — or any other company — out. The young maid she'd been assigned, a pretty fair-haired lass named Jonah, had offered to get him and she'd declined.

Elissa had asked if Jonah would get her meal, and the maid had agreed. She'd seemed to sense Elissa's need to be alone after that, and had excused herself for the night.

After eating, Elissa had laid out a lavish teal gown to wear for the Duke of Dalunas herself, since she'd refused Jonah's offer to help her prepare for bed or the morrow, as well as declined a hot bath.

Teal and yellow were the colors of Lord Camden's Province, and the queen had made sure she had a gown especially for him. The dress was exquisite, billowy and full of lace embroidery and details that must've taken the seamstresses sevendays to finish. The fabric was rich and the bodice low-cut enough to make her blush; not that she had a much of a bust to show off anyway, not like Lady Cera or Mistress Ansley.

She'd twirled in the mirror when she'd put it on, but the man to impress in her mind hadn't been the duke. Now, she regretted that she'd hoped her knight liked the gown, because he'd just crushed her yet again.

Elissa didn't want to think about him kissing another woman. Touching another woman. Doing more than merely *touching* her. A tavern lass, nonetheless.

Did he pay her, too?

Her heart thundered, stabbing at her with each beat, but she schooled her expression fast. Sir Alasdair couldn't have a clue anything his fellow knights had said had any impact on her.

She was about to meet her final suitor, and she looked fantastic. Even Jonah had agreed. The maid had helped twist her hair up in an elaborate design reminiscent of her cousin. Braids and flowers overflowed and free curls intentionally framed her face.

So...damn Sir Alasdair Kearney.

Lord Camden was a duke. A good man, by all accounts from those around her.

I'll make sure he's the man of my dreams.

"Good day, my lady." Sir Dallon bowed deeply to her, but Elissa couldn't muster a smile for the handsome knight.

She inclined her head and tried to convince herself what she'd just decided about the Duke of Dalunas was true.

Sir Bowen bowed as well from where he stood next to her chaperone. "You look radiant, Lady Elissa. Truly magnificent. Lord Cam won't be able to resist you."

She allowed him to take her hand and press a kiss to her knuckles, ignoring the heat that burned her neck and cheeks. He spoke the truth; there was no reason to feel shy or embarrassed.

Sir Alasdair fidgeted, his face marred with a frown, but she ignored him.

"Thank you, Sir Bowen." Elissa looked into the sandy-haired knight's unusual golden eyes. She smiled for him, keenly aware her chaperone was staring at her.

Sir Bowen beamed. He was handsome, especially with his one-dimpled cheek. But he didn't stir her. Neither did Sir Dallon, who was equally appealing, with dark hair and eyes and a cleft in his chin. Tall and broad, as if all of the above was a requirement to be a member of the Aldern personal guard.

No, she was drawn to the broody man next to them.

Who wants nothing to do with me.

Sir Alasdair cleared his throat as Sir Bowen released her hand. "The duke should be here shortly. I've been told the room is ready for us, with a light repast already set out."

Elissa squared her shoulders and reached for a regal expression. She wished she was taller, so she could look down her nose at him. "Very well. I'm ready."

She whirled away from the three men, crossing the distance to the wide doorway of the nearby sitting room without a backward glance. Elissa heard someone whistle, then the low rumble of a laugh and a male voice—either Sir Bowen or Sir Dallon, because the responding growl was definitely her knight.

Unfortunately, that sound from Sir Alasdair was all too familiar as of late.

Elissa didn't let allow what was behind her to force her step to falter.

If Sir Alasdair chose to follow, very well; if he didn't, that was fine, too.

I'm done with him.

She ignored the inner voice that called her a liar.

☆   ☆   ☆   ☆

Alasdair had never felt murderous toward men he considered brothers before. Today made it official—and tempting. Instead of bashing Bowen's face in for laughing at Dallon's whistle, he bowed to his two fellow knights and clenched his jaw. Forcing a smile was too much to ask for, so he didn't try.

"The lady is irked with you, Alas." Bowen had the bollocks to wink.

"Aye, I'd noticed." Dallon beamed.

"I wonder what he did, Dallon."

"Hmmm, as do I, Bowen." Dallon framed his chin with his thumb and index finger, cocking his head to one side. Then they both looked back at Alasdair.

He swallowed a snarl. "Good day, my *brothers*." He pushed the pleasantry out, not responding to Dallon's smirk or Bowen's raised brow. Alasdair bowed again.

He tried not to stalk to the doorway. The urge only deepened when one of them laughed. *Again.* Visions of violence danced into his head, so Alasdair quickened his pace, blocking out his brothers and taking his first step in to the lavish sitting room where they were to meet Lord Cam.

Guilt hit him in the gut, almost doubling him over before he'd made it very far and glanced over at the lass he couldn't have.

He had no intention of mentioning the trip to *The White Sage* or asking her to clarify exactly how much she'd heard of his brothers' reprobate teases. Alasdair wasn't keen on remembering his failure to perform, let alone relate it to the person who was the *cause* of said failure.

Who he chose to tup was none of Lady Elissa Durroc's damn business anyway.

However, he wanted to shout, "Nothing happened!"

Apologize to her if something his brothers had said had hurt her feelings. Which was ridiculous.

She stood by the fireplace, her back to him, staring at the painting that hung above the mantel. It was a wildlife scene, complete with a white wolf and a lush forest at the edge of a huge lake.

A real place, it wasn't far from Greenwald Main. There was a large field of long grass behind it, and a small profile that only hinted at the village in the distance across the water, both reflected true-to-life in the painting.

The wolf was posted high on a ridge like a king, but the beast was gazing out of the painting as if he could see the whole world—in and out of the scene. Something made him want to avoid the wolf's painted amber eyes as much as the hazel ones that'd held so much pain when he'd ignored her request to speak about what'd happened between them.

What could he say, anyway? He'd already lied his way through multiple apologies.

"Is this Trikser?" Lady Elissa asked, turning to him.

Alasdair's breath caught when he allowed himself to look at her—*really* look at her—in the teal gown. It had to be the finest he'd seen her in, with its detailed stitching and swirls of embroidery and lace. The bodice was low, the corset tight and snug all the way to her hips, before the fabric billowed.

For some reason, he wanted to grab a shawl and wrap her in it. Her breasts were on display for another man.

He swallowed and suppressed the urge to growl. Tried not to think about how what he was trying *not* to stare at had felt up against his chest.

Her expression fell and he mentally kicked himself. She'd asked an innocent question, and his delay had probably made her think he had no intention of answering. Or speaking to her.

Alasdair had acted like the worst cad the past few days. He'd not directly ignored her, but he'd kept their conversations abrupt—at best. Talking to her made him crave her even more.

Every time her eyes flashed with disappointment because he'd snapped at her, or been too curt, had been like a kick in the stomach. However, he still couldn't convince himself to be at ease with like he had before he'd kissed her. To be at her side, to talk to her, touch her, felt right somehow.

But it isn't right.

His chest burned.

Treating her like he had been made him a feel like selfish bastard, but the illusion of being with her, but not really *with* her was even worse.

The lass would get over whatever tender feelings she thought she had for him. As soon as she was good and married.

Alasdair wanted to rub his chest.

Lady Elissa turned away, looking back up at the painting and Alasdair closed his eyes.

He sucked in a breath and planted his feet to where he stood so he wouldn't rush to her side. An apology and reassurance teetered on the tip of his tongue. He held back. "I don't think so," he said finally.

"What?" She spared him a glance over one bare shoulder.

Damn the teal gown.

"I don't—" He had to clear his throat and try again. "I don't think the wolf in the painting is actually Lady Cera's bondmate."

"Oh." Lady Elissa didn't look at him again. "It's beautiful, at any rate."

You're beautiful.

Alasdair didn't realize he'd spoke aloud until she whirled on him, her hazel eyes huge and her delectable mouth parted on a gasp. They stared at each other until he ran out of curses in his head. His pulse thundered in his temples. His cock twitched when her tongue darted out to moisten her bottom lip.

Stop looking at her mouth. He couldn't. Nor could he banish the vivid memory of her innocent taste.

"Who, in all the lands, is this vision?" The male voice made them both jump.

She pinkened—across exposed upper chest and those bare shoulders, too—and touched her cheek as her gaze darted to the doorway. The curls above her ears bobbed. Lady Elissa looked pure—and adorable.

Lord Cam filled the doorway, dressed finely in yellow and teal, his Province's colors. Somehow, the outfit didn't look anything but masculine, despite the loudness in hue. The duke was impeccable, as always, not a lock out of place on his blond head. He was clean-shaven, and his hair was trimmed shorter than even Dallon's. He wore a wide belt and decorative sword with a gold-plated, jeweled hilt.

Alasdair wanted to growl and dart in front of Lady Elissa, hiding her from the lord's view. He stayed where he stood instead, plastering on a smile for a man he'd always genuinely liked but suddenly loathed.

"My lord." Lady Elissa curtseyed deeply, lowering her lashes as any fine lady of her station would.

Lord Cam crossed the room in two strides. He gathered her hands and kissed her knuckles. "My lady, I'm overjoyed to finally meet you. King Nathal has told me much about the queen's cousin."

She murmured something appropriate but her statement was lost as Alasdair tried to talk himself out of the red haze that clouded his vision.

"You are *lovely*. And you resemble Queen Morghyn so." The duke openly admired Lady Elissa until her cheeks shone an even deeper crimson.

"Thank you, Lord Camden."

Somehow, it irked Alasdair that the man hadn't introduced himself, but she'd said his name almost breathlessly. As if she'd been waiting all her life to meet the Duke of Dalunas.

"Lord Cam. Actually, just Cam." The man beamed.

Alasdair sucked back a growl.

The lord's eyes shot to him. "Alas, it's good to see you, old friend."

He forced a nod and consciously schooled his expression as Lord Cam slid forward and gripped his forearm in a familiarity that stirred his guilt—but only a little.

"It's good to see you too, my lord."

"You've been doing well in Greenwald?"

"Aye, my lord." Alasdair made himself relax and look into the man's pale blue eyes. "Quite well indeed."

The smile he received was easy and genuine. More guilt bit at him. "Glad to hear it. You've been taking good care of my intended?"

Guilt shot into rage—and jealousy. Alasdair spared her a glance as he nodded for Lord Cam. Lady Elissa's gorgeous hazel eyes were wide—and wary. She looked at them both, saying nothing.

His stomach started at a slow churn that did nothing but raise the bile up to his throat. Alasdair wanted to spirit her away. Hide her. Hold her. Kiss her.

The Duke of Dalunas was the first of her suitors that worried him. Word was, Lord Camden Malloch was playing for keeps.

He should be overjoyed. The duke would take her off his hands. The man was charming and handsome. Surely, she'd be infatuated with him in hours.

Pain bit at him, clenching his roiling gut.

Alasdair straightened his shoulders and let his arm sweep the room. "Why don't you sit? The journey from Dalunas is long. Are you interested in the light repast, my lord?"

The look Lord Cam flashed was grateful. He didn't disagree as he gently took Lady Elissa's arm and seated her on a plush gold sofa before taking a seat across from her.

The lass stared at Lord Cam as he talked and ate. Lady Elissa declined the offer for food, but she accepted the goblet of mead the duke himself poured for her.

Alasdair backed up to the hearth, forcing himself to remain on his feet instead of resting his back against the warm brick as he was inclined. He propped his elbow on the mantle and told himself not to watch them. Or listen to their conversation.

He failed.

His eyes darted back and forth from the lady to the duke. Over and over.

She seemed to relax more and more as Lord Cam spoke. Lady Elissa reclined into her seat and her conversation took on a normal edge. She even laughed.

Somehow, although they spoke of nonessential things, consisting mostly of questions to get to know one another, Alasdair hung on every word, as if they were speaking to him.

His chest burned again, and this time, he did rub the spot. It hurt to watch them together.

This is only day one.

Alasdair shook his head and turned his body, making himself look into the bright fire and blocking out the conversation behind him.

Lord Camden Malloch and Lady Elissa Durroc together was…right.

Sir Alasdair Kearney and Lady Elissa Durroc was not.

Chapter Twenty

Charis circled the busiest market street for the hundredth time.

Bracken and Nason were both cursing behind him, but he ignored them, probing for magic as inconspicuously as he could. He was agitated and frustrated, so he had trouble focusing specifically on elemental magic.

Powers of all kinds kept bouncing off his probing spell. He tried to block them out, wade through what was coming back at him, but it was difficult.

"If we walk past tha square once more, one of tha marshals is bound to stop and question us. We haven't stopped at any of tha stalls. We carry no purchases." Bracken had an irritated edge that rose Charis' hackles even more.

"Shut up. I need to concentrate."

"Bracken's right. There're too many eyes on us," Nason complained. "We don' look like we're shoppin'."

"Then go to a tavern. I'll meet you later," Charis said.

His two companions exchanged a glance.

"I'm on to something."

Bracken snorted. "Doesn' look like it."

Charis scowled and marched forward. "I need to concentrate." Repetition was lost on his foolish lads. He wanted to strike them both, but that'd surely attract the attention of one—or more—of the many Greenwald marshals on patrol in the busy market.

Word on the street was that the provost was good at his job and rarely had empty cells in the large jail. The Duke of Greenwald required order in his Province, and even Charis wanted to avoid Dread Valley at all costs.

"Good. Shall we book a room for tha night?" Bracken crossed his arms over his broad chest.

"Want ta waste coin on tha'?" Nason asked.

"Coin is the last thing I'm worried about." Charis scowled.

Nason's face lit up. "Lasses. I can 'ave a lass. Maybe two. I don' have ta sleep alone."

Rare amusement darted across Bracken's face. "You always have ta pay fer it."

Charis didn't have time for a chuckle, although the indignation on Nason's countenance *was* laughable. "Pick an inn, but make sure it's worth the coin. I'll meet you at the stables before sundown." They'd boarded their mounts in the public stables near the city center. Unfortunately, it'd been unavoidable. They would've been obviously out of place on horseback at the market. "Stick to Greenwald Main. I'd not want to venture to Lower Greenwald."

Although the less reputable part of the city would help their anonymity, Charis wasn't in the mood to slum it. He could benefit from time between a lass' legs, too. He'd rather she be employed by a higher quality tavern than not. One got what one paid for, after all, even where whores were concerned.

Bracken nodded, and soon his lads disappeared from sight, heading toward the public stables. There were a few taverns near there that'd fit the bill. Being close to their mounts would provide accessibility for a fast getaway if need be.

Charis tugged his hat down when his gaze brushed one of the marshals. The man was tall and broad, with fair hair that danced in the slight breeze. His silver shoulder epaulette denoted he was a captain, but his pale green doublet matched all the rest of the Greenwald marshals. His helm was under his arm, but the other hand was poised on his sword's hilt. His posture suggested relaxation, but Charis knew better. The marshal could strike when necessary.

The man offered a nod, so Charis returned it and went about his way.

Bracken had been right; they'd spent too much time in the square, walking past the big fountains too many times. Even in the places where people tended to loiter, they could be noticed as someone who didn't quite belong. They weren't shopping, or sharing a meal on the fine fall day.

There was a bite to the breeze, hinting at the winter that was right around the corner, but it didn't deter families from stopping to eat. There was even a covered pavilion to encourage such behavior, and many merchants who sold hot, ready-to-eat foods.

Marshals were everywhere, with keen eyes scanning for disorder in the busy chaos of shoppers.

Charis forced himself to relax and turned down a street with permanent shops instead of the stalls on the square that merchants set up and broke down daily. He stopped between two buildings and leaned on the wall. A quick scan to the alleyway told him he was alone. There wasn't much traffic on the street, either.

Perfect spot.

Taking a deep breath, he ordered his heart to calm so he could send out his magic again.

Young voices caught his attention, and he glanced to the paved road. Three wee lads kicked a leather ball back and forth, laughing as they played. An older woman with white hair in a bun on top of her head swept the wide porch of a dress shop. She hollered at them to get away from the street, but the lads ignored her and moved on, chasing the ball as one of them kicked it long and high. They shrieked and yelled to one another as they pursued.

The dressmaker *tsked* and kept up her sweeping, shaking her head. He wasn't so far away that he couldn't see the smile on her wrinkled face.

Charis closed his eyes and flattened his shoulders to the wall behind him. Something told him he was close. Greenwald Main was where he needed to be.

The *clop-clop* of hooves as well as the creak of a cart's wheels echoed in and out of his hearing range. Voices and footsteps were the same; coming and going as people went about their tasks. Everything sounded close-but-far, giving him a sense of security.

He sent his magic out, breathing deeply and concentrating on anything elemental.

Charis waited. And waited, covering most of Greenwald Main as he probed.

A burst of heat pinged off his probing spell and he startled, pushing off the wall behind him. He swallowed and concentrated on the spot of warmth.

A fire mage?

The more he concentrated, the more the magical trail became clearer—and it was moving toward him. His heart skipped and he peeked his head around the side of the building he was nearest.

The dressmaker was still on her covered porch, but she was waving wildly to the cart moving down the street—right to the shop.

The wagon was well-made and appeared either new or of the highest quality. The dark wood had sheen to it. The two horses that pulled it weren't the average cart nags, either. They were chestnut mares—a matched pair, with healthy, shiny coats.

A man—barely so, though—with shaggy brown curls drove the cart. He pulled the horses stop with a deep, "Whoa," that didn't seem to fit his youthful appearance.

"Thank you, my lad." A portly woman with her silvering dark hair in a thick plait down her back patted his shoulder, then jumped down from the cart without assistance.

Two lasses from the bed of the wagon did the same. They wore matching outfits, a brown skirt with a white apron and matching hair kerchief on top of their heads.

Uniforms?

The dressmaker bowed deeply, like one would to honor nobility, and Charis blinked.

He scooted closer to the edge of the building, so he could hear the conversation.

"The Headwoman and Steward of Castle Aldern themselves? To what do I owe this honor?" The older woman bowed again, posture and expression a mix of awe and sincerity.

"Oh hush, Melenia." The woman who'd been riding up front in the cart spoke first. She stepped forward and embraced the dressmaker while the only male dismounted from the cart and landed beside the two lasses.

"I wanted to thank you personally for my wife's new dress," the lad spoke, bowing to the merchant woman.

"It was an honor to make a fine gown for the Steward's wife. I'm delighted she liked it." The dressmaker nodded, touching her cheek as if she was nervous.

He's the Steward of Greenwald? He's naught but a child.

The lad beamed and patted her hand.

"I want to put in an order for twenty more maid uniforms myself. Were you able to mend the ones I sent back last time, or were they too far gone?" the woman who was the logical choice for headwoman spoke.

"I mended what I could. Twenty more? When do you need them by? I have ten ready today."

"A fortnight, if possible. I'll have all my lasses presentable, with spare outfits." She spared a glance to the two maids with their party.

Both young, one was blonde and one a redhead. They inclined their heads simultaneously to the dressmaker.

All five of them stepped into the shop, but the double doors of the building were open for the business day, so Charis could still hear them without straining. The two maids did the headwoman's bidding, and came out of the shop with two large bundles they flopped in to the back of the cart.

He scanned the wagon and the horses. If they were from Castle Aldern, the quality of what was before him made sense.

But where had the magic come from?

He sent out his senses as the four women and the steward-lad came out of the dress shop. Power bounced back at him.

The fire mage was the headwoman.

Charis concentrated so he could see her aura. She was the only one of the party who had magic. The light surrounding her glowed pale red, but its heat suggested she wasn't a powerful fire mage. As he probed further, he didn't sense any other elements. His stomach jumped.

She definitely wasn't Drayton's lass, but something made him watch her. She moved with grace as she climbed back up into the bench seat of the front of the cart.

Follow them, his gut said.

He didn't question his gut—ever. So when the steward turned the horses back toward the market center, Charis followed.

Although they were in a cart and he was on foot, it wasn't hard to weave in and out of market-goers and keep up with them. Charis tried to stay away from the patrolling marshals, and he avoided tracking and masking spells alike—as there was a good chance a marshal or two had talents similar to his own.

The party from Castle Aldern made a few more stops—purchasing twenty prize hens from a vendor in the square, as well as three whole pigs from the most expensive butcher, and four huge sacks of flour. The vendors scrambled to fill the orders, and he was close enough to hear the headwoman's specifics for the delivery of her purchases that didn't fit on the wagon.

He watched from a safe distance, but made sure not to lose sight of the cart. When they concluded their shopping and went toward the road that led to Castle Aldern, he hung back, but didn't cease trailing them. Getting close to the castle was dangerous, but he needed to risk it.

He'd figure out the *why* later.

Multiple armed guards were posted at the wide gates. More men wearing armor and padded doublets with the Greenwald seal patrolled atop the walls that concealed the castle from the public eye.

Charis had never been inside, but if it was like most castles, it was heavily fortified, and had several sets of gates inside the main protective wall around the center. The walls before him were perhaps thirty feet high, and so thick a whole army could line the top of the embattlement.

Definitely just the outer gates.

Castle soldiers weren't the only thing that caught his attention.

His magic surged when he only probed a bit. Blinking to clear his vision, as well as the magical buzz in his head, Charis gasped. His temples throbbed, but he didn't stop to rub them.

Castle Aldern was covered in a protection spell so thick it manifested as a visible bubbled around the whole area.

"What the hell?"

That kind of power would take multiple mages. Mages who had tons of their own *strong* power. He'd never seen the like, not even in Aramour.

He clenched his jaw and straightened his shoulders, studying the gleaming magic before him. The bubble reflected the sunlight, making him squint.

Movement caught his peripheral vision, and Charis lowered his gaze to the wide entrance of the open outer gates. He watched the guards stop the cart, but they didn't inspect people or contents after seeing who drove it.

The protection spell didn't seem to interfere with anyone coming and going through the castle gates.

That puzzled Charis even more. Couldn't they feel the magic? There was no way something that thickly woven wouldn't trip even the lowliest mage's senses. Hell, probably even Bracken and Nason could feel it.

But…if it was this strong, why hadn't he felt the protection spell when they'd ridden into Greenwald Main?

He shook his head. *Nothing* made sense.

The mages who'd laid the groundwork of that spell were strong. No one to tangle with.

Charis stared at the castle gates, wishing he could move closer to peer inside. It was too dangerous.

He was on to something.

They needed to stay in Greenwald.

He didn't know the why or how, but his elemental quarry was close.

The protection spell around Castle Aldern was the first piece of the puzzle.

Charis would just have to figure out the rest.

Chapter Twenty-one

The shout went up, but Elissa didn't even get the chance to glance over her shoulder to see what all the fuss was about. Her legs were swept out from under her, the fluffy underskirt of her purple gown flying up, blocking her vision as the corridor floor rushed up and grabbed her bottom. She yelped. Her right hip hit hard and smarted. Pain shot into her thigh and she whimpered.

Elissa couldn't move.

Something soft—furry—and *heavy* had planted itself atop her.

Sir Alasdair cursed.

Lord Camden exclaimed concern.

A wet tongue started to bathe her face, and she squeezed her eyes shut and tried to fend off the beast. Air swooshed over her legs.

Mischief?

Although she'd seen him several times since the morning she'd spent in the duchess solar, the wolf had never come directly up to her or sought her touch, even when Elissa had tentatively petted him the other day with Lady Cera.

He was wagging his tail.

She was glad for the fullness of her gown, complete with petticoats and underskirts. *Hopefully* even though she was disheveled and her legs were now bare, the wolf was blocking her body from view with his own.

"Mischief, get off of her this *instant*." The feminine command did nothing to move the young wolf.

Elissa pried one eye open, then the other, only to meet the now-familiar pair of ice-blue eyes.

The wolfling wagged his tail harder.

She tried to be cross with him, tried to frown. She really did. The lolling tongue and pretty eyes focused on her destroyed Elissa's ire. A smile played at her lips. He pawed her bodice and whined.

Lady Cera commanded the cub again to no avail.

A pair of boots came into her line of sight.

Mischief gave a low rumble.

"My lord, best back up," Sir Alasdair warned.

"Aye, 'tis for the best," Lord Camden whispered.

"Mischief, that's not nice, my lad," Elissa said, looking the wolfling in the eye. The possessive word should have jolted her, but it didn't. Calling Mischief hers…felt right.

He whined again.

She placed her hand on his silver chest and urged him backwards.

Soft. He was so soft she wanted to stroke him, bury her fingers in his warm coat. Because Mischief might mistake the touch for praise, Elissa did not. It wasn't all right that he'd knocked her over in the first place.

The wolf obeyed, but bumped her hand for further contact when she planted her palms to the stone floor to right herself. Her hip smarted, reminding her of the impact.

Lord Camden immediately offered his hand.

Mischief growled.

For some reason, Elissa's eyes landed on Sir Alasdair. He squared his shoulders and an unnamed emotion darted across his face. The apple of his throat bobbed. He stared. As if *he'd* wanted to be the one to help her to her feet.

Her chest tightened and she tore her gaze away, meeting her suitor's. Eyes that were also blue—yet so different than the knight's—were bathed in concern for her.

Elissa cleared her throat. "My lord, I think I should stand on my own. I don't think he likes anyone's hands on me."

The duke nodded.

She couldn't stop herself from looking at Sir Alasdair again. It seemed as if *he* didn't like the idea of Lord Camden's hands on her, either.

That's stupid...considering.

Heat crept up her neck and kissed her cheeks.

Her chaperone still hadn't spoken much—to her anyway—over the past few days. He seemed to converse with the duke just fine, as if Elissa was the intruder on *their* time together.

She liked Lord Cam, too. Spending time with him wasn't a chore. Even if she couldn't stop watching a certain knight—and prayed every moment the duke wouldn't notice.

Lord Cam was pleasant and funny. She enjoyed talking to him, and looking at him. Tall and broad shouldered, he was built just as well as Sir Alasdair, although he was more streamlined, leaner. She was still waiting for the spark of attraction that only one glance at the knight made her feel.

Sir Alasdair had called her beautiful the other day in the sitting room. Her suitor had broken in before she'd been able to muster an answer. It wasn't like it mattered. She had no clue what she would've said to the knight, anyway.

Elissa had to repeatedly shut down all thoughts about why Sir Alasdair would say such a thing, considering their awkward circumstances. If the man thought her beautiful, why had he rejected her?

"I'm so sorry, Elissa." Lady Cera bowed in a manner not befitting Elissa's rank.

She sputtered. "Please, my lady—"

Lady Cera looked at the duke. "He's not bonded yet, so he doesn't obey me much at all, unless his sire, my Trik, is involved. I was on my own with him this morning, and...well, I'm so very sorry." The duchess' cheeks were red when she looked back at Elissa. "I was trying to get him out into the courtyard."

To hear the Duchess of Greenwald stumble and rush over her words made Elissa feel about two inches tall. "Lady Cera, really—"

"You're not hurt, are you?" The duchess was dressed in brown breeches and a tunic, instead of a gown. Her garments were still fine, though, and she wore a dark brown leather jerkin over her shirt, a sword sheathed at her waist. Her curves, as well as how the breeches hugged rounded hips and thighs, would ensure she wasn't mistaken for a man, but somehow, the outfit was fitting.

"It's fine. I promise you. He's no trouble." Elisa looked down at the young wolf. She stroked his head and Mischief's tail beat the corridor floor. She smiled into his ice blue eyes.

"He's nothing *but* trouble." Lady Cera sighed. "I think he's trying to kill me. I introduced him to a Journeywoman Rider this morning, and he rejected her—along with every bondmate presented to him. She would've been a good match; her older brother is a Senior Rider, and a friend of mine. But he wouldn't hear of it. I'm at my wits end."

Elissa frowned, and her stomach roiled. Jealousy bit at her. She didn't want Mischief bonded to someone else. To belong to someone else. Her heart thundered and she looked down at the silver wolfling again.

The wag of his tail increasing speed made her decision, but before she could open her mouth to tell the duchess what she wanted, a male throat cleared. Elissa's gaze shot to her intended.

Lord Camden smiled, and she couldn't help but return it. "Are you sure you're not injured, my lady?"

She nodded. Her hip smarted and her bottom was sore. However, it was nothing serious, and she wasn't about to volunteer that information.

"I'll call Tristan," Lady Cera said.

"I've no need to inconvenience Lord Dagget. I'm well, I promise."

Sir Alasdair, forever in her periphery, caught her eye again. His arms were behind him, making his impossibly broad shoulders look even broader. His dark blue doublet with the seal of Greenwald sewn into it did nothing to hide his defined chest, and brought out the color of his eyes. He was so handsome. His long dark hair was bound today at the back of his neck, and Elissa couldn't help but wish it was free, swaying about his shoulders. Begging to be smoothed with her hands.

She chided herself and met the gaze of her suitor. The Duke of Dalunas was devilishly handsome, light to Sir Alasdair's dark, with his short flaxen locks and pale blue eyes. Much lighter than the knight's sapphire ones. She preferred Alasdair's.

Damn it all, Elissa Elise Durroc. Stop comparing them. And by the Blessed Spirit, stop looking at him.

Sir Alasdair was her chaperone. Nothing more. He'd *never* be anything more to her.

"Then, shall we continue to the gardens?" Lord Camden inclined his head and offered his arm.

"Are you sure you've no need for Tristan?" Lady Cera's concern was obvious.

"I'm sure."

The wolfling at Elissa's side wuffed and cocked his head to one side.

"Nay, lad." Sir Alasdair spoke directly to the wolf.

Not to be deterred, Mischief fairly glued himself to Elissa's leg. Tromping on the bottom of her gown.

Lady Cera uttered an un-duchess-like curse and muttered the wolf's name, one hand to her forehead. Her embarrassment shone brightly, but Elissa wasn't upset in the least.

She tried not to grin, then couldn't help it. Mischief was making Elissa's wishes known, in his own way.

Could he want me *for a bondmate?*

Triumph—and a little shock that it could be *that* easy—rolled over Elissa, but when her gaze rested on Sir Alasdair, his eyes were dancing. She cleared her throat and glanced at the duchess. "Lady Cera, what if... Mischief and I were to bond?"

Lady Cera blinked. Then a slow smile spread across her full mouth, working its way into a lopsided grin, full of—well, mischief. "I would adore that. And from the looks of things, so would Mischief."

Her heart pounded, but a sense of rightness washed over her. Elissa lowered her hand. The wolf didn't hesitate to push into her touch.

"Lady Elissa—" Lord Camden said.

"Would it bother you if I had a bondmate, my lord?" She should've been mortified to interrupt a duke, but she had to press.

His answer might determine *hers* to his suit. She'd enjoyed the time they'd spent together, aye, but if Lord Camden wouldn't consider Mischief...

Everyone froze, but Mischief wagged his tail, as if he'd understood her question.

She'd had magic all her life, but she'd never considered a bondmate. It wasn't widely accepted as very ladylike. Certainly not for a duchess, despite the one before her that was bonded to a wolf.

And if she married Lord Cam, she would be the instant Duchess of Dalunas.

The duke looked at the cub, then back at Elissa. He cocked his head to one side as the young beast had before. "I suppose 'twould be all right, if he doesn't growl at me."

Elissa grinned.

Lady Cera blew out a breath.

Sir Alasdair narrowed his eyes at the duke, but when he looked at Elissa, the knight schooled his expression. "Lass, bonding is nothing to be taken lightly." It was the first time he'd spoken directly to her in days, other than polite greetings.

Lord Camden shot the knight a look—no doubt for his casual address.

Elissa ignored them both and looked at Lady Cera. "I feel as if Mischief has chosen me. Here." She pressed her hand over her heart. "Is that possible, my lady?"

Dark red curls shifted with Lady Cera's nod. "Aye. Was the way with his sire for me. Trikser chose me." Her expression was thoughtful. "Perhaps that was why I failed to match him. He was waiting for you."

Pleasure melted over her and Elissa smiled. "I love it." She looked down at her soon-to-be-bondmate, then squatted in front of him, despite the definite unladylike posture and her already disturbed gown. She ignored the twitch of protest from her hip.

Mischief sat as if commanded, his tail swishing back and forth as she cupped his muzzle.

"Do you want to bond with me?" Elissa whispered.

He wuffed and licked her cheek.

Lady Cera laughed. "I would consider that an *aye*."

"As would I," Sir Alasdair said.

Yet again, the knight drew her gaze. Elissa swallowed.

Now he's pleased with me?

Her stomach dipped.

She hated that she was so drawn to him. The tremor that always shot down her spine when their gazes collided. The way her heart sped up when he smiled. The way her stomach flipped and her skin tingled if their hands brushed. Or the way her body warmed when he'd guided her with a big hand to the small of her back, though he hadn't touched her like that since they'd kissed.

Elissa straightened and forced her eyes away for the hundredth time that morning. She was supposed to be spending time with Lord Cam.

Getting to know *Lord Cam*.

She fought the urge to close her eyes when guilt assaulted her. She wasn't supposed to be attracted to her chaperone. She was *supposed* to be attracted to the duke who'd traveled a fortnight to meet her.

"My lady?" Lord Camden's baritone dragged her from her tortured thoughts — thank the Blessed Spirit.

"Aye, my lord?" She stood, but didn't take her hand off the wolfling.

The duke stepped closer and cupped her face.

Mischief tensed under Elissa's touch, but didn't growl. Nor did he move from her side. If anything, he leaned in to her harder. His body's warmth seeped through the fine fabric of her gown right above her knee.

Lord Cam's pale eyes bored into her hers. "This is something you want?"

"Aye, my lord."

"Cam," he chided gently, a smile playing at his lips. "If bonding is something you want, then you shall have it." He nodded at Lady Cera.

The duchess clapped, grinning even wider than before. "Excellent! I'll have to speak to Lucan to make sure he knows what's required. So, let's say, after first meal tomorrow?"

Elissa's heart fluttered.

Her suitor studied her for one last moment, then nodded. He leaned forward and brushed a kiss onto her forehead.

Mischief snarled.

Lady Cera and Elissa chided him at the same time.

Lord Cam's expression was sheepish when Elissa glanced at him, but she had no objection to the chaste touch of his mouth.

It hadn't warmed her or given her the spark of attraction she longed for as far he was concerned, but it hadn't been unpleasant. She offered him a smile while she scratched her wolfling behind one ear.

Mischief groaned and pushed further into her.

"After you're bonded, he'll mind you. Thank the Blessed Spirit." Lady Cera's generous bosom heaved as she blew out a breath. "He seems to have already started, and for that, I'm grateful." Her relief was palpable.

Elissa grinned, at the duchess, then at her soon-to-be-bondmate. "Morag will be relieved."

Lady Cera beamed back, but her cheeks were again crimson.

"I was starting to think Ansley might be right, and I'd need a new headwoman."

Sir Alasdair chuckled, the deep sound drawing Elissa's eye to him. Again.

She swallowed and forced her eyes on the duchess. "I'm glad to have helped avert that tragedy."

Lady Cera laughed, as did the knight. Even Lord Cam joined in.

Joy bubbled up from her tummy, and Elissa felt lighter than she had in days. Perhaps she could even endure another turn in the gardens.

☆   ☆   ☆   ☆

"Where is Sir Alasdair?" Elissa looked up into the duke's face.

Lord Cam was so handsome. His hair—like his eyes—couldn't be more opposite than her chaperone, lying on top of his head in groomed golden layers. It was short, stopping at the back of his neck, and not reaching his ears on the sides.

The way he carried himself didn't scream *warrior* like her knight, but it did shout *noble*.

However, he wasn't shallow. He was genuine. Which made the awful comparisons she couldn't help even worse. Settled her with more guilt, too, because comparing them wasn't fair to either man.

Did she want to spend the rest of her life with the Duke of Dalunas?

Lord Cam smiled and lifted her hand to his lips. "I'm sure he's not far behind us."

"He's probably bored out of his mind, following me—us—everywhere."

Mischief hadn't left her side since knocking her over in the corridor that morning. However, Trikser had halted the silver wolfing's exit after evening meal before they were out of the great hall. With a wuff, the cub had shot away from Elissa at the beckoning, without so much as a glance over his shoulder.

Lady Cera had explained the pack was gathering to hunt.

Elissa wasn't saddened—much. They'd be bonded on the morrow, then he'd be hers truly.

"I doubt spending time with you is a trial for him, even in the role of chaperone," Lord Cam said.

She paused. Did the duke mean something by that?

No. He couldn't have.

Lord Cam kissed her knuckles and winked.

Elissa laughed and hoped it didn't sound like the nervous titter she suspected. She allowed the small intimacy from her suitor. He was charming, and in a way, sweet. But not a lad, like Lord Avery. The Duke of Dalunas was all man. And the look in his eyes told her he wanted her.

His desire for her did nothing *to her*. Still. No matter how much she craved the opposite.

After addressing her regarding Mischief, Sir Alasdair had resumed his distance. Their kiss had been over a sevenday ago now, yet his harshness had no end.

As if the whole thing had been *her* fault.

She hadn't done anything wrong. Didn't regret what they'd shared—even if *he* did.

Her first kiss had been perfect.

Stop it.

"I'm sure he'd rather be fighting. Or at least training." The words were automatic. She had to say something, after all.

"Sir Alas is a good man. I've known him for some time."

She nodded for the duke's benefit and ignored how her heart sped up. Elissa didn't disagree with Lord Cam, even with how things were currently between her and the knight.

"My lady?"

"Aye, my lord?" She made herself meet his pale blue eyes.

Lord Cam smiled and cupped her cheek. Elissa tried not to jump.

"I've enjoyed our time together."

"Aye, so have I." Not a lie, but the look on his face made her shift from foot to foot.

"If it's not too bold of me to say, I've become very fond of you, Elissa."

"I'm fond of you, too, Lord Cam." The response was out of her mouth before she could stop it. It was true, though, wasn't it?

Not in the way he means.

She chided herself and maintained their eye-contact. Elissa didn't have to try with him. He was funny. Kind. Regal. Not messy, like Sir Alasdair. Didn't make her feel like a wreck inside and out.

That's good, isn't it?

The smile he presented was genuine and wide. "I'm so glad to hear you say that."

Elissa told herself to relax. There was tenderness in his eyes. He meant her no harm.

"May I kiss you, Elissa?"

She blinked. Her gut told her to refuse him. Lord Cam would respect her answer. She knew it in her heart. Elissa might not feel passion for him, but didn't want to hurt his feelings, either.

The man wanted to marry her. That wasn't a secret—to either of them. Shouldn't she *want* to kiss him?

Lord Cam took a step toward her, even though she'd yet to answer him. His eyes darkened a little. The heat in his pale blue orbs still did nothing to rouse her. Her cheeks didn't warm, her body didn't overheat. Not like when—

Sir Alasdair didn't want her. There was nothing there for her. No matter how much she desired *him.*

He wasn't one of her suitors, at any rate. Shouldn't be on the list of men she was considering marrying.

Definitely shouldn't be the only one she'd pictured as husband.

Foolish lass.

Elissa smiled and sucked in a breath she hoped the duke wouldn't notice. "Aye, my lord. You may."

"I need to make one thing clear, my lady." Lord Cam brushed two fingers down her cheek.

Her heart skipped. "Aye?"

"I am presenting my suit."

She nodded. "I know."

"Nay. Don't mistake me. What I mean is, I want the other suitors eliminated from your consideration."

"My lord—"

Lord Cam's gaze softened. "Don't be alarmed, Elissa. You and I will take things as slowly as you want. As slowly as you need. I just want to make things clear. I don't want to compete with another for your heart."

Sir Alasdair's blue eyes flashed into her mind and she bit her bottom lip. "All right."

The assertive side of him was new, and Elissa understood now why her knight had called Lord Cam cunning, even in jest. However, she didn't sense malice. He was a good man. The duke was just making plain what he wanted.

Me. He wants me.

Elissa's heart rebounded off her ribs. She didn't know what—
how—to feel. Her other suitors had been polite. Handsome and
reserved. None of them had asked to kiss her.

She'd been foolish to fantasize about Sir Alasdair Kearney.
It didn't matter that their ranks wouldn't keep them from being
together.

He didn't want her.

Lord Cam did.

"You'll tell Lord Aldern you reject the other suits, so he can
get word to the king?" Lord Cam asked.

"Aye."

His eyes lit up and her stomach churned. Lord Cam was
genuinely interested in her. He'd said he cared for her. "Cam,
Elissa. Please call me Cam."

He'd asked a hundred times. She'd never acquiesced. If they
moved forward, if they married—Elissa swallowed a gulp—he
would care for her. Perhaps love her one day.

What if she couldn't love him? Would *his* love be enough?

The king had said he wouldn't force her into a marriage
without love. What if the love was one-sided?

For some reason, she wanted to cry.

"Elissa?"

She forced a shaky smile. "Aye?"

"About that kiss…" Lord Cam pulled her to him and warm
lips settled over hers.

Chapter Twenty-two

h e rounded the corner and his heart stopped.

Lord Camden Malloch was kissing Lady Elissa.

Kissing my lass.

Alasdair's hand shot to the hilt of his sword; he jolted when he realized he what he was about to do. He couldn't pull his weapon on the Duke of Dalunas. He flexed his fingers on the grip and took a breath, forcing himself to calm. Had no other choice. Whether he liked it or not, the duke wasn't doing anything wrong. It didn't appear that the man was touching Lady Elissa against her will, either.

His gut twisted.

They hadn't noticed him yet.

Lord Cam had his arms around her, but his hold was loose. Nothing like when Alasdair had held her, kissed her.

The couple broke apart and the duke bowed deeply to Lady Elissa. "Until the morn, Elissa. I had a lovely day, and an even lovelier evening. Thank you."

She smiled and touched her cheek like she always did when she was nervous. Maybe she hadn't enjoyed the duke's mouth on hers.

She better have hated *it.*

He was so mired in jealousy and rage, Alasdair didn't bother trying to convince himself she wasn't his like he normally did.

Nothing he could chide himself with or repeat would get the unwanted vision of Lady Elissa in Lord Cam's arms out of his head.

It's wrong. She's mine.

"Good evening, my lord. My lady." He projected louder than necessary as he closed the distance between them.

Lady Elissa jumped. The duke did not.

"Hello, Alas." The bastard had the nerve to smile as Alasdair approached. "Something wrong?" Lord Cam's fair brow furrowed.

Alasdair forced a tense smile. "Nay, my lord. All is well with you?" He glanced at Lady Elissa when the duke nodded. She wouldn't meet his eyes.

He studied her. The lass's lips weren't swollen, moist, or infused with red like they'd been when *he'd* kissed her. Nor was her beautiful face flushed.

Good.

Alasdair remembered how she'd clung to him. How she'd kissed him back. She'd tentatively touched her tongue to his at first, then rubbed, exploring his mouth with more courage, kissing him deeply, as fervently as he'd kissed her. He'd plastered her to his chest. His cock had been so hard he'd ached.

Lady Elissa still wouldn't look at him.

Was that guilt in her expression?

He narrowed his eyes, watching her. Conscious that he wasn't acknowledging the duke at all.

It should bother him—or worry him—that Lord Cam might notice Alasdair's interest in his potential betrothed. But it didn't. Hell, half of him wanted to grab her up right then and kiss her properly. Show the duke she belonged to *him*.

You're a fool.

Alasdair didn't care about that, either.

"Well, Elissa, I'll leave you to retire. Shall we meet to break our fast in the morn?" Lord Cam asked.

Alasdair wanted to bark at the duke to not address her so casually.

"Aye, my lord." She looked at him. "I'm not meeting Lady Cera until midmorning."

"Ah, yes. To get your new bondmate."

When the lass smiled, it was broad, genuine, and she finally spared Alasdair a glance. Her cheeks flared pink up to her ears and she averted her gaze as quickly as it'd rested on him.

Alasdair clenched his fists at his sides. The condition didn't leave him even as the duke disappeared around the corner after another bow to the lady and a goodnight for him, too. He wanted to punch the smile off the man's face. Odd, considering he'd always liked Lord Cam.

Lady Elissa wouldn't look at him—again.

He threw open the door to her guest suite. Without a pause, he gripped her upper arm and half-shoved, half-dragged her into the room.

She gasped.

It took all he was made of not to slam the door.

"You let him kiss you!"

Her pretty hazel eyes widened, but at least she'd finally looked at him.

Alasdair growled.

Lady Elissa narrowed her eyes, her face darkening. "What business is it of yours?"

He stalked toward her. Instead of cowering, she squared her shoulders and stood taller. Like she had the other time they'd argued. Her demand sunk in and Alasdair froze.

She's right. It's none of my damn business.

He bit down until his teeth smarted. "It's not proper."

The little vixen had the nerve to smirk. She perched her hands on her hips. "No more improper than you being alone with me in my rooms at the moment."

"I'm your chaperone."

"Aye. Where was my *chaperone* when the duke kissed me?"

Alasdair's blood boiled when she arched a fair brow and one corner of her mouth shot up. He intentionally towered over her, but his lass just gazed up at him. As if bored.

"Besides, why is it wrong for the man I'll marry to kiss me?"

Shock stole his breath and made him stumble. "The man you'll marry?" He cleared his throat.

"Lord Cam is my suitor." Lady Elissa spoke slowly, dragging out the words, as if he were daft.

"You've not chosen." More commandment than statement. He didn't care.

"What if I have?"

Rage and jealousy slammed into Alasdair. Pain, too. His chest burned and his head spun. Was she trying to dare him? Hurt him on purpose?

Then again, he'd known her purpose for being in Greenwald, and the king's wishes. He'd seen her with all four of the men King Nathal had selected. Why was it such a shock that she might've selected one of them?

And why the *hell* did the idea make him feel like he'd been run through with a poison-tipped sword?

Silence fell. They stared at each other.

For the first time, he couldn't read Lady Elissa's expression.

"He asked to kiss me. I said aye. It's really not your concern." Her tone was light, as if they discussed the weather.

That hurt even more.

"You want to marry him?" Alasdair cringed at his thick demand.

"What if I do?"

He snatched her waist. The fabric of the purple gown rustled.

Fine tremors shook Lady Elissa's slender frame but she didn't fight him as Alasdair pinned her to his chest and took her mouth. He shoved his tongue between her lips, but he didn't have to force her to open. She did that on her own, kissing him back hard and hungry, just how he devoured her.

She moaned; he groaned.

When she slid her arms around his neck, Alasdair hauled her closer still. He was granite in his breeches, and her hips pressed into his. There was no way she couldn't feel him. Lady Elissa would know how much he wanted her.

She started to rock against him, and his cock threatened to blow like an untried virgin. Alasdair kissed her harder, caressing her back, following the curve of her perfect bottom, squeezing, kneading. Lifting her, rocking into her.

His lass gasped into his mouth, twining her tongue around his.

He wanted to banish the picture of Lord Cam's mouth moving over hers. He wanted—no, *needed*—her to forget the duke. She needed to only see Alasdair. Only want him.

Marry *him*.

Marriage?

The thought jarred him back into his head.

No.

Alasdair ended the kiss, tugging away from her grip. Lady Elissa's mewling protest was almost his undoing.

"Lord Cam didn't kiss me like that," she blurted.

The other man's name on her lips had him taking a step back, even though all he wanted to do was sweep her up into his arms and toss her on the bed that was too close for comfort.

They made eye contact and she blushed to the tips of her ears again. Her breasts heaved in her low-cut bodice as she tried to catch her breath. Her bottom lip was plump and shiny. Lady's Elissa's little pink tongue darted out, tracing it, as if she sought his taste.

Damn, he wanted her. More than he'd ever wanted a woman. Would she say no?

His sense of right and wrong warred with his throbbing cock. *"I'm not innocent,"* played on a loop in his head.

Again, he doubted the meaning of what she'd said that day in Castle Durroc. She didn't kiss like a woman of experience, despite the fervor. The shared hunger threatened to consume him—throwing Alasdair into deeper chaos.

He rammed his hand through his hair. He'd done it again. Taken what he wanted—though one kiss wouldn't slake his desire for her one iota.

It's still wrong.

He thought about Betha and the failed attempt to take her in the room at *The White Sage* after the first time he'd kissed Lady Elissa.

No other woman would do.

And he couldn't—shouldn't—have the one before him.

Alasdair needed to leave, *now*. Before he explored that doubt in the back of his head and did something that couldn't be reversed. "I have to go."

She blinked, and hurt darted across her gorgeous face. "But—"

"I shouldn't have done that." He averted his gaze from the sudden shine of her hazel eyes.

Then he fled the room like the coward he was.

☆   ☆   ☆   ☆

Elissa watched the door close and a mixture of shock and hurt burst in her chest. Magic skittered down her body and she fought it. She had to. Or she'd give in to the urge to fling water at the door. Even worse, she wanted to chase him down and drown him.

Sir Alasdair.

The object of her confusion and pain.

Stupid. Man.

"What is wrong with *me*?" What'd she done wrong?

Had she done anything wrong?

He'd done it again. Melted her with his mouth, with his hands on her body. He'd touched her with sure, but tender ministrations. She'd felt his arousal pushing into her belly. Elissa hadn't been scared. Perhaps nervous, but her core had throbbed. Her legs had gone wobbly.

She'd moved into Sir Alasdair instead of away, like her head had shouted at her to do. She'd told logic to go away and listened to her heart. Held on to him as hard has he'd held her. Kissed him just as hard, too.

As she'd blurted — *nothing* like the duke's kiss had made her feel.

Neither heart, nor body.

I would've done it. I would've…given myself to him.

Handed her innocence to a man who kept hammering her with hurt. Shudders racked her frame, magic following, but it didn't chase away her waves of pain. Tears rolled down her cheeks against her will.

She'd promised the duke she'd see Lord Jorrin. Tell him she wasn't considering the other three men. That equated to her agreeing to marry Lord Camden Malloch.

Elissa hadn't said the words. Lord Cam hadn't either. It mattered not.

Her agreement to reject the other suits was as good as an, '*Aye, I'll marry you.*'

"Blessed Spirit…"

What have I done?

A sob worked its way up and out. Elissa collapsed on her bed, her chest so tight every forced breath was a slicing dagger. Her heart thundered as if it was storming. Her temples throbbed. She rolled to her side and clutched her stomach, but she couldn't get a hold of herself.

Magic pulsed beneath the surface of her skin. Pushing, threatening to spurt out. The water in her washing basin danced, but didn't spill — yet. It would if she couldn't catch her breath, regain her composure.

Elissa rolled to her back on the bed. Her corset cut into her, and her purple skirts rustled, but she spread her arms and legs, staring at the carved ceiling of her guest suite.

Breathe. Calm. She chanted over and over until her powers stepped back, but the tears didn't stop. They were going to soak her pillow at this rate.

Her mouth had run away with her when Sir Alasdair had shoved her into her rooms. She'd been bold with him. Daring. Saying things she hadn't meant, just to get a reaction out of him.

Half-truths, weren't they?

She *might* marry Lord Cam.

His sapphire eyes had flashed with anger. So much rage it'd taken her aback. But there'd been something more, too.

Hurt?

Then he'd grabbed her up and kissed her. Something she wanted with her whole being.

Her knight's *second* rejection hurt worse than the first.

She'd already known he didn't want her. Elissa had refused to accept it, because it seared her from the inside out. Her feelings for her chaperone swirled around in her head.

She cared for him. *More* than cared for him.

Elissa's gasp echoed in her rooms. "I love him."

Agony bit deep at the stupid revelation. She sat up in her bed, crushing her legs into her chest and hugging them tight. Elissa started to rock as more tears blurred the pretty décor in the room.

Sir Alasdair Kearney certainly didn't love her back.

The king said he wouldn't force her to have a marriage without love. She hadn't counted on loving a man who didn't want to marry her.

Now she'd given her word to the Duke of Dalunas that he'd be the only man she considered. Lord Cam was a good man. He *would* care for her. Care *about* her.

"Will that be enough?"

Nay.

Her heart answered and Elissa crushed her eyes shut, shaking her head. She had to push her feelings away. Steel herself against the onslaught or she'd lose control of her magic again.

Lord Cam had told her they could take things as slowly as she needed. She'd just have to give him a real chance. He could make her happy.

Sir Alasdair's blue eyes danced into her head, as always when she lied to herself. She shoved that image away, too. Didn't need his smile, his dark hair, or the memories of his mouth moving over hers to further cloud her mind. "He doesn't want you, Elissa Durroc. Not for keeps."

She'd felt his arousal. He was a man; it was natural, wasn't it?

Elissa couldn't give her innocence to a man who didn't want to marry her. Her virginity was meant for...Lord Cam? She clenched her teeth until her gums ached.

She didn't want Lord Cam physically. Not like she did Sir Alasdair. Her body hadn't responded to the duke's kiss. It had both times with her knight. Her breasts heavy, nipples tingling. Her belly had warmed and between her legs had throbbed.

Elissa had been introduced to desire. Wanted to experience it again. Wanted *more*.

With the knight, not the duke.

Guilt churned her stomach.

Of course, the queen had explained the physical act between a man and a woman when her monthlies had started at age three and ten. She'd been cautioned that lying with a man could lead to a child, so the act was to be reserved for marriage.

Elissa was a born lady, so chastity was even more important for a good match. She'd heard it all her life.

Her cousin had explained it could be pleasurable for the woman if the man was a good lover. With the way Queen Morghyn looked at King Nathal, Elissa had no doubt her cousin was happy with her husband in the marriage bed.

Elissa wanted that, too. Lord Cam looked at her with desire in his eyes. What if she couldn't feel that way for him? What if the knight had ruined her for her husband?

"Stop it!" She cradled her head with both hands.

Elissa stilled on her bed when she thought she heard a scratching noise. She concentrated, waiting to see if it happened again. Hadn't been able to determine *where* the noise had come from.

A low whine accompanied the second, then third, scratch.

She slipped to her shaky feet and looked at the closed door. The next sounds were more frantic as if he'd heard her get up.

"Mischief?" she whispered.

He pushed his head into the door when she opened it only a crack, widening the gap, trying to move past her. The wolfling whined again, until she stepped back so he could enter. Then he wuffed, as if chiding her for being slow about it.

Elissa blinked. She closed the door and turned to her would-be-bondmate. He ran in circles around her, crying and chuffing.

"Mischief."

The silver wolf sat and stared up at her, his tail thumping on the stone floor when they made eye contact.

"How did you...?"

They weren't bonded yet.

How had the wolfling known she needed...something?

"Nay," she whispered. "I didn't need *something*. I needed you." Elissa knelt and buried her hands in the thick silver fur at his neck. He whined and wiggled closer, working his way into a hug. A warm wet tongue caressed her face, up to her ear.

Elissa laughed, she couldn't scold him. Didn't mind the damp cheek. She pulled back and looked into his pale eyes. "How did you know?"

He couldn't answer her. Not like he'd be able to after they bonded. Mischief pawed her knee and nuzzled her shoulder.

She smiled. Relief washed over her and she could breathe easier.

This wolf would become her best friend, her companion, like his sire was to Lady Cera.

"Not *become*," she said lowly. "Already is."

Mischief wuffed, as if he'd understood every word.

Chapter Twenty-three

I'm sorry, Elissa. I didn't anticipate having to leave you so soon." Lord Cam cupped her cheek and she allowed his touch, consciously leaned into him.

I need to try with him.

This man who would become her husband.

After last night and her knight running from her, rejecting her again, Elissa's head knew what she had to do. Too bad her heart disagreed.

"It's all right, my lord. I'll see you soon enough."

"Cam," he chided, but smiled.

Her face warmed. Lady Cera's words all those sevendays ago about him not being a chore to look at teased into her mind. The Duchess of Greenwald was right. "Cam," she whispered.

The duke's—*her duke's*—blue eyes lit up, as if she'd just given him a gift.

"Lady Cera says I must stay here to familiarize myself with being bonded. Training, she called it, but when she feels Mischief and I are strong with each other, I'll come to you in Dalunas."

Her wolf sat at her side, but he was tense. As if he didn't like Lord Cam. He kept glancing over his shoulder toward her chaperone.

The knight hovered not far, pretending to not listen to their conversation. His broad shoulders were tight and he all but paced.

Elissa tried not to notice him. She ignored what her soon-to-be-bondmate kept doing, too.

"Aye. I shall miss being at your side."

She was able to smile genuinely. "I'll miss you too, my lord."

"You should call me Cam," he urged.

Elissa broke their eye-contact. "As you wish, my—I mean, Cam."

"Your Cam is fine, too." He winked.

Her face burned even more and she lowered her lashes.

The duke tugged her chin up gently and their gazes collided, but she was suddenly *very* aware of Sir Alasdair in the periphery. His blue eyes—so different from Lord Cam's—bored into her.

"As I've been calling you by your given name, Elissa." Lord Cam's voice dropped. Thicker. Lower.

She swallowed. His want of her was palpable, swirling around them. All the more off, because she didn't feel that way, didn't echo the same physical draw. Elissa fought the urge to close her eyes. Or at least look away. She forced a smile. "Of course, Cam."

The duke grinned. It lit up his face and made her heart skip.

Maybe trying with him wouldn't be so awful. He radiated happiness—because of *her.*

His large warm hand slipped from her face and he bowed deeply, something that wasn't wholly fitting of his rank.

"Cam—" She reached for him, stepping close. Her hands settled on his forearms. Elissa tugged, then slipped her arms around his middle.

His pale eyes widened, but he allowed her touch, the small embrace. Before she lost her nerve, she sucked in a breath, pushed to her tiptoes, and pressed her lips to his. It didn't take her suitor long to get over his surprise. Instead of rearing back, he pulled her closer, wrapping her in a much tighter embrace than when he'd kissed her the night before.

Lord Cam took the kiss over, running his tongue along the seam of her lips until she opened for him. Elissa did so, returning his gesture by pushing into his mouth.

It was pleasant.

Warm.

But there was no fire.

Her belly didn't flip; her skin didn't tighten and overheat. Her breasts didn't feel heavy. She didn't feel desire settle low.

Disappointment crashed over her, and as he ended the kiss, she tried not to cry. He was so kind, so handsome, so perfect for her.

Why can't I want him?

Elissa tried to smile up at him, banishing tears.

The look in his eyes was so tender. He cupped her cheeks again and pressed a soft kiss to her forehead. "Sweet Elissa, I shall miss you indeed."

A throat cleared and Lord Cam glanced over his shoulder. The captain of his personal guard, Eivan, inclined his head. "I'm sorry, my lord. It's urgent. The horses are ready for us in the bailey."

"Aye. Coming." The duke crossed the distance to Sir Alasdair. "Thank you, Alas, for protecting Elissa. Please continue to do so until you bring her to me. I'll write as soon as I can. I've already explained my situation to Jorrin."

Elissa watched the man she loved nod his dark head and loosen his clenched fists to shake the Duke of Dalunas' hand. He didn't speak but the apple of his throat bobbed. His shoulders were tight, his full mouth a pale bloodless line. Lord Cam seemed oblivious to the tension radiating off the knight's body.

She couldn't stop watching them together. Light and dark. One she wanted, the other wanted her.

"I'll do my duty, as always." The statement was a croak when Sir Alasdair finally spoke, but his jaw was still clenched, barely giving clarity to the words.

Could her knight be upset about the kiss? He had been last night, but this time, *she'd* been the aggressor.

The duke smiled. Nodded. Then he and his captain were gone.

When they were alone, Sir Alasdair wouldn't look at her.

Elissa raised her chin and squared her shoulders. "I have to meet Lady Cera."

Mischief pushed to all fours and wuffed. When he looked at the knight, his tail swooshed.

Sir Alasdair's gaze swept past her. The taut fists he'd had at his sides returned, opening and closing this time. His body was even tighter than moments before. As if he was restraining himself. Anger radiated off him; she didn't have to be an empath like Lord Jorrin to feel it. His handsome face was the harshest she'd ever seen it. Almost as if he was about to go to battle.

Elissa took his nonverbal answer as the only one she'd get, and started off down the corridor. She didn't care if he followed or not—so she told herself. Her chest ached, but she couldn't focus on that now. She had a task.

Why he was so angry, she didn't understand.

He'd run from *her* the night before, reinforcing that he didn't want her. She was doing what she had to do where Lord Cam was concerned.

The Duchess of Greenwald smiled as Elissa opened the door to her solar. The room was bright and welcoming as always. Drapes were tied back on the many windows; fall sunlight streamed in.

Lady Cera stood before the rich brown sofa. She wore soft gray breeches that brought out the color of her eyes, and a puffy-sleeved pale blue tunic with no jerkin or doublet. It was tucked into the breeches, and had lace on the collar—the only feminine touch.

She'd seen the duchess in many gowns since coming to Greenwald, but like the other times she'd seen Lady Cera breech-clad, this outfit wasn't normal ladies' attire.

Elissa's admiration of the woman who'd fast become a friend shot up. Lady Cera was, above all else, herself. No matter her role to her Province. She was half-surprised the duchess didn't have her magic sword at her waist.

"Good morning, my lady." Elissa cursed the shake in her greeting. It had to be nerves about her imminent bond.

"Morning, Issa."

She told herself to relax and widened her smile. Lady Cera had taken to calling her by the childhood nickname. Elissa didn't mind.

"Good, he's with you. I was worried when I couldn't find him this morning after my ride." She gestured for Elissa and Mischief to come closer.

"He's been with me since last night, actually."

"Oh?" Lady Cera cocked her head to one side, her loose auburn curls shifting over her shoulder. Her wolf, Trikser, wuffed from where he lay by the welcoming fire in the hearth.

Her soon-to-be-bondmate returned the noise, but didn't leave Elissa's side.

Heat kissed her neck and she swallowed. She wouldn't tell the duchess everything. Just that her wolfling had scratched on her door. "He came to my room late, whining until I let him in."

The duchess looked at the young wolf. "That's a good sign. Somehow even without magic, you've already formed a bond."

Elissa stroked Mischief's head and the wolf leaned into her touch. "Don't tell the headwoman, but he spent the night in my bed with me."

Lady Cera laughed. "Your secret's safe with me. Come, sit with me." She returned to her seat and patted the cushion beside her. "Lucan's going to bond you two. He should arrive shortly."

The door opened and Elissa's heart sped up, because her body sensed her knight's entry. She didn't need to look his way.

He bowed to the duchess and murmured a morning greeting.

"Hello, Alas, I'd wondered where you were." Lady Cera grinned, but the expression faded fast. "Is something wrong?"

"Nay, my lady."

Elissa still didn't spare him a glance. She couldn't.

The duchess looked at him, then at her. Her expression was thoughtful, but she said nothing. For some reason, that made Elissa want to squirm.

Sir Alasdair perched in the corner against the wall, refusing Lady Cera's invitation to join them in the circle of chairs and sofa by the hearth.

Neomi, Lady Cera's handmaiden, presented Elissa with a tray.

Her stomach gurgled with nerves, so she politely refused cheese and fruit, but thanked the lass for a mug of warm mead.

The maid nodded and offered her wares to the duchess.

"Is Fallon napping?" Lady Cera asked.

Neomi nodded, her brown eyes twinkling. "I got him down without much of a fight, my lady. He wore himself out playing with the duke."

"Good! I hated to miss out on our morning routine, but Ash needed a run as much as Trik and I." She spoke of her black stallion. "Jorrin was late to join the men, then?" Lady Cera grinned when the maid winked.

Elissa watched them interact and relaxed into the plush pillow of the sofa's back. Lady Cera was friends with her handmaiden. That made Elissa like her even more.

"I suspect Captain Leargan suffered the same fate. Mistress Ansley told me the twins are trying to walk," Neomi said.

The duchess giggled. "Don't let it get out that our big tough men are so enamored with their children."

The maid bowed, but she was grinning. She left the room shortly, her blonde curls bobbing as she went. She was married to Gamel, the Head Steward of Greenwald. Elissa had seen the couple together and had been envious of their obvious love for each other.

Yet the same could be said of the other couples of Greenwald. Castle Aldern was saturated in love. Nothing more than she wanted for herself.

Can I have that with Lord Cam?

"I heard Lord Cam had to head back to Dalunas. Something urgent?" The duchess' gray eyes were concerned as she sipped mead.

Elissa tried not to jump.

It was as if Lady Cera had sensed she's been thinking about him. "Aye, my lady. I shall meet him there when he's taken care the problem. He didn't say what."

"Oh? So, you've chosen then?" Lady Cera grinned.

She forced a nod, feeling Sir Alasdair's eyes on her. *Again.* As if daring her to look his way. "Aye, my lady."

The duchess beamed and reached for her hands, squeezing. "Lord Cam is a good man. I like him very much. I'm so happy for you!"

Elissa's gut churned and she bit her bottom lip to keep from giving into a sudden wave of emotion. Her magic skittered down her spine and she forced herself to sit taller and push it back. She couldn't lose control in front of the duchess.

Mischief whined and leaned into her leg.

"Are you all right?" Lady Cera whispered.

She forced a nod. "Aye. It's just happening so fast."

Lady Cera patted her hand. "Oh, don't worry. Lord Cam will take care of you, Issa."

"I know, my lady." Elissa wanted to wince at the strain in her voice, but she didn't.

"Cera, like I have told you so many times," the duchess chided gently, but she flashed a charming, lopsided grin.

Elissa gave a sheepish smile. For some reason, she wanted to spill everything to the woman before her. She wanted to cling to the duchess' hands, meet her eyes, and admit she was scared to death.

She wanted to tell Lady Cera she loved a knight, not a duke. Elissa wanted to ask what she should do. Wanted relief from the confusion. From the pain.

From the rejection of the man who held her heart.

The young knighted mage, Sir Lucan, took that moment to scramble into the room, and relief washed over her. The distraction was needed. Before she confessed things she couldn't take back.

Sir Alasdair is here, for Blessed Spirit's sake.

Elissa straightened and tugged free of Lady Cera's grip.

The mage bowed, his face crimson. "I'm sorry I'm late, my ladies." He bowed again, first to the duchess then to Elissa.

"No worries, Lucan." Lady Cera smiled at the obviously nervous lad. "Issa and I were just chatting."

Elissa swallowed — twice. And told herself the butterflies in her tummy were due to the impending bond. She met the lad's striking green eyes. "Thank you for doing this."

He reddened to the tips of his ears, but nodded.

She felt his nerves, as clear as hers, and smoothed the front of her dark green gown, though the fabric didn't require flattening. Her stomach rolled, and Elissa wished she'd eaten. Perhaps food would've settled her. Her gaze sought the knight that'd been her only constant since coming to Greenwald.

Sir Alasdair was looking her way, but his expression was implacable, betraying none of the anger he'd shown in the corridor when she'd said goodbye to Lord Cam. It hurt that he'd composed himself. Locked his emotions away, because she could not do the same.

Elissa jumped when the duchess called her name. She murmured apologies and looked at the young mage. "What do you need me to do?"

He shoved his dark hair from his eyes and squared his shoulders as he took a seat. Sir Lucan sat across from her, close enough to touch. Magic poured off him.

She wasn't trying to sense it, but he was so powerful she could see his aura without concentrating — something she'd always struggled to do turns ago when she'd trained with the king's mages.

Lady Cera had told her the lad was only five and ten.

So young; so much magic.

It didn't matter. Elissa had never seen a more magical person.

He was handsome for one so young, with ebony hair that kissed his collar and pale green eyes almost unnatural in their hue. High cheekbones gave his face a regal look, and Sir Lucan was tall—six feet already. He'd be broad-shouldered with age, when his lean muscled frame filled out. Surely lasses would be chasing him from all over the Province when he was grown.

Sir Lucan pitched his body forward and offered his hand. "I need you to put one hand in mine and the other on your bondmate. No matter what, don't let go of either until we're done."

"Alas, can you please bar the door?" Lady Cera asked.

"Shall I go?"

"Stay. Please stay." The frantic plea was out of her mouth unbidden and Elissa breathed through her sudden, irrational panic.

Mischief whined.

"All right." Sir Alasdair nodded, and their gazes collided for a few heartbeats.

She watched him walk to the door when he broke their eye contact, and heard the click of the lock. Elissa couldn't take her eyes off him even as he returned to the corner, but this time, her knight took a seat in the nearest chair.

He was still too far away.

"Take a breath," Lady Cera whispered, patting her arm. "You need to be calm before we start. So does he." The duchess stroked her other hand over Mischief's silver head.

Trikser made a barking-growling noise from the hearth, and the wolfling looked toward his sire, swishing his tail. The larger wolf rose from the fireplace, only to cross the room to his mistress and sit next to her, resting his large head on her lap.

Elissa tried not to stare into his amber eyes; she didn't want him to think she was trying to be dominant. He was magnificent, graceful in a way Mischief wasn't yet. He was also *huge*. "Will... Mischief grow as large as...your bondmate, my lady?"

Lady Cera smiled and buried her hand in the thick snowy fur at the back of Trikser's neck. "I don't know, as your wolfling was the runt. But his dam, Isair, is of good size as well. We can hope."

"Are we ready?" the mage asked, his body giving off a calm that made Elissa's respect of him shoot up a notch. He might be young, but he was in total control.

"Aye."

"Get comfortable," Lady Cera advised. She scooted away, breaking physical contact of Elissa as well as her wolf cub.

Elissa settled into the sofa, one hand at the back of Mischief's neck, her fingers spread wide in the soft fur there, much the same as the way the duchess stroked her own bondmate.

Sir Lucan threaded his fingers with her other hand and took a deep breath. His chest rose and fell as he steadied his respiration. Trance settled over him and he closed his eyes.

Her own felt heavy as she felt the effects of the newborn spell. Elissa didn't fight the urge to shut her lids. She squared her shoulders and flexed her fingers against her wolf's warmth. Mischief leaned into her leg as the mage began a chant she didn't understand.

She listened hard, but didn't recognize the language at all. It wasn't her dialect and it didn't have the lilt of Aramourian, though many spells were in the language of the elves.

Magic hit her chest and started to spread out, moving down her arms and tingling her spine, her hips, her thighs. It was hot, searing from the inside out, but it didn't hurt. It burned of power, opening her in a way that felt different than her elemental powers.

This was heavy, where her magic was light, enveloping her, but it didn't constrict. It made Elissa want more. Her breath rushed faster, and she heard Mischief pant, but the wolf moved into her, not away.

She cracked her eyes open and had to squint against Sir Lucan's radiance. His skin was glowing; the more he chanted, the more he brightened.

Elissa gasped as her body reclined of its own accord. She pressed into the cushion at her back, as if it was the only thing catching her. Her ears popped and prickled.

Something felt as if it encircled her. Entwined with her, body and mind. She blinked but the sensation didn't lessen. It... deepened.

Then...

Two heartbeats echoed.

One hers...one...her bondmate's?

Elissa wasn't alone in her own head.

Visceral, primitive thoughts, made themselves concrete. Need. Hunger, thirst. Survival. That soon faded and she was washed with joy.

Love.

Mischief *loved* her.

Tears were born and spilled. Elissa's body shook. She didn't calm until the mage released her hand, a wide smile on his face.

Mischief made a sound that was almost a squeal and Elissa opened her arms. He didn't hesitate to throw his bulk into her chest, and she didn't care, even though it stole her breath. She buried her face in his warmth, his fur tickling her cheeks. She breathed deeply of his scent, somehow clean and woodsy, yet animal, too. Elissa wound her arms around him, holding him tight against her chest.

He was hers.

She was his.

Mischief liked the notion, infusing love into her mind. His thoughts were moving pictures in her head.

His tail wagged so hard it was like a fan over her overheated skin.

She threw her head back and laughed, feeling light in a way she hadn't in days...sevendays, maybe. Confusion regarding the knight and the duke faded into the recesses of her mind, taking her pain with it.

Right now, there was only her newborn bond with the beast on her lap.

Elissa needed that more than she needed to breathe.

Chapter Twenty-four

She's lost to me.

His heart had plummeted to his boots the very moment she'd reached for Lord Cam. She'd kissed the duke, and Alasdair had seen red. But he was overcome with grief, too. And loss so powerful it seized his lungs and made his head spin.

Alasdair had struggled to not show a reaction. To hold onto the appearance of indifference.

I will never have her.

Lady Elissa Durroc would marry Lord Camden Malloch. She'd chosen the Duke of Dalunas.

It's as it should be.

No matter how many times he'd repeated that, his gut never loosened. His heart never beat normally. His head wouldn't stop spiraling. Blessed Spirit, his…*everything*…burned.

The rest of the day was a blur. He'd not even allowed himself to be fascinated by the magic of her bonding with the young wolf, though he'd never been personal witness to anything like that.

Alasdair had shut down the short-lived elation that Lady Elissa had seemed panicked at the thought of him leaving the duchess solar, as well as the retort that'd been on his tongue. He'd wanted to snap, *'Perhaps you should call for your betrothed.'*

He couldn't have run his mouth anyway. The duchess had noticed something was wrong. Alasdair had schooled his expression and squared his shoulders—commanded himself to hold onto that notion for the rest of the damn day.

Lord Cam might be on the road to his home Province, but *he* was trapped with Lady Elissa. Until Lady Cera released her.

Let it be soon.

Then he could get over her.

Move on with his *regular* duties. And with his life.

He'd not stayed for her first bondmate lesson, and neither had Lucan. Alasdair had gone to the fighting yard with the lad, and had a quick—much needed—swordplay lesson with all three of his young trainees.

Alaric had asked to see some of the new techniques, so Alasdair had challenged his co-instructor to a little demonstration. He'd come at Roduch hard, working off some aggression.

His brother had been up for his level of intensity, and now they were on their third round. He'd bested the big blond knight two times, but not by much. They were both too good.

Roduch circled him, sword ready, sweat sheening on his brow in the late-autumn sunlight.

The breeze was chilly, but it felt good as it caressed Alasdair's overheated skin. He'd tossed his doublet and tunic to the ground after their first round.

The men—as well as the three lads—watched raptly. Men-at-arms and personal guardsmen alike not sparring lined the fence surrounding the large training area, including their captain and Lord Jorrin. If he had to guess, wagers were going back and forth amongst their brothers and the newest group of castle men-at-arms.

Alasdair flashed a feral grin, daring his fellow knight. "Come at me, brother. Or has marriage made you soft?"

Roduch hunkered his huge frame down and feigned right, letting loose a deep chuckle. "Nay, brother. Marriage could never make me soft. Now I have something to protect. Something that's mine forever."

Even across the yard, he could see the man's eyes shine with love for his lass.

Alasdair dodged, but his stomach clenched. His friend hadn't meant to fling a barb, but one lodged deep anyway. He rushed the knight.

Their swords crashed together with a *clang*. His arms wobbled when Roduch shoved him back. Alasdair scrambled and jumped to the left in lieu of falling on his arse in the dirt. His brother wasn't the biggest member of the guard for nothing. He was *strong,* damn strong. But Alasdair was faster.

"Get him, already!" Lord Jorrin called from the sidelines.

Leargan shook his fist high, and Lord Tristan leaned in on the top rung of the fence, wringing his hands together eagerly.

"Oh I will!" Alasdair and Roduch called at the same time, eliciting rumbles of laughter and chuckles from their watchers.

They rounded each other, parrying, avoiding and coming together with *clang* after *clang, clash* after *clash.* Everyone watched, frozen; their own weapons resting against thighs, or laying on the browning grass. No one except him and his brother moved.

Horses neighed and shifted in the periphery, as if they too felt the tension of the match rising.

Alasdair felt his own power and aggression steadily rise every passing moment Roduch avoided his attack. His shoulders screamed, he held them so tightly. The fine tremor in his arms and legs was becoming more pronounced. He opened and closed his fingers on the hilt of his sword. Couldn't afford to let his grip slip, even though this was practice.

He wasn't fighting for his life.

His brother arched a straw-colored eyebrow. "Alas, are you all right?" He didn't lessen his hold on his huge weapon, or back away from their spar.

"Be better when you're on your arse."

One corner of Roduch's mouth shot up before he bared his teeth. "Come at me, then." He put his palm up, gesturing. "I know you're not a coward."

Alasdair lunged.

They came together, sword to sword, but Alasdair pushed, until they were almost chest-to-chest and Roduch had to struggle to keep him at bay.

"Relax, you're losing control," Roduch bit at him through clenched teeth. "Wasn't your point to the lads to never lose control? Breathe. Back up and come at me without being reckless."

Reckless?

Alasdair's vision clouded. *Red.* All he could see was crimson. Anger surged up from some place deep down. He growled low. "I. Never. Lose. Control."

His longtime friend's crystal blue eyes widened as he scrambled to fend him off. Locked his arms higher.

Metal slid down metal and screeched.

Alasdair plunged even closer, pushing harder and letting out a bellow so loud his throat scorched and his temples throbbed. He knocked the bigger man down, onto his back, raking his sword down Roduch's chest.

The ties on his friend's tunic were decimated and the tan fabric split in two down to his navel. Revealing a broad defined chest sprinkled with sparse fair hair.

Blood bloomed from an angry slash. The cut was shallow, but more than a mere scratch. And it was long, almost to Roduch's waist.

His brother stared up at him, eyes even wider than before, mouth half-agape. His sword fell limply to his side and the knight made no effort to hide shock or gain his feet to attack.

The crowd gasped. Someone cursed.

Boots rushing toward them took Alasdair's attention. His shoulders slumped, his head woozy, but he avoided anyone's direct gaze as best he could.

Lord Tristan knelt at Roduch's side, laying a hand on the big man's chest despite Roduch's protests that he was fine.

"You cut him?" Leargan shouted. "What the hell's wrong with you?"

"Sheathe your sword," Lord Jorrin ordered. He was much calmer than the captain.

Alasdair swallowed. Did as he was told. His heart thundered and his head spun even more, stealing his breath. He sucked in air, but it didn't help. Numbness washed over him and his legs refused to hold his weight. His knees buckled, and he hit the ground so hard dust floated up. Pain shot into his thighs.

"Alasdair?" Now Leargan's expression held concern. His captain squeezed his shoulder.

They made eye-contact. "I'm sorry," Alasdair croaked.

Leargan spat a curse word or two.

"It's fine. *I'm* fine. Cuts and bruises are the reality of sparring." Roduch's dusty brown breeches filled his vision, quickly replaced by a huge calloused hand as his friend offered to help him to his feet.

Alasdair was grateful the blond giant had spoken before Leargan could command an explanation. He let Roduch pull him up, but he had to lock his knees so he wouldn't slip back into the dirt. He wobbled in his boots, dizzy physically and mentally.

Niall, the second-in-command of the personal guard quickly dispersed the rest of the gawking men-at-arms and whatever knights of the guard were there. He organized sparring matches and shouted orders.

"I need to get back to my lesson with the lads," Alasdair said quietly.

"Nay, you're done for the day." Leargan crossed his arms over his chest.

Alasdair clenched his jaw and avoided the dark eyes of his captain. Somehow his gaze landed on Roduch but his stomach flipped at the concern—and sympathy—his brother regarded him with.

Roduch couldn't know what was…wrong.

Could he? When he finally had the bollocks to look at Leargan, his captain's expression dared him to argue. Lord Jorrin stood next to the captain, silently staring at Alasdair.

Chills raced down his spine and his heart stuttered.

The duke was an empath.

He'd have little choice in the matter if the half-elfin lord saw right through him.

Dammit.

"I'm sorry, Roduch." His lips moved in a jumble. After he'd spoken, he registered that he'd already apologized, but his cowardice in how he'd ended their match deserved two apologizes anyway. Maybe three or four.

All he received from his brother was a curt nod, but it was enough.

The knight hadn't deserved his anger. Roduch stating he'd lost control wasn't a jibe; it'd been fact as the man had seen it. It hadn't been meant like a gut shot, no matter how Alasdair had felt.

He was right, at any rate. You're weak.

Alasdair bit down hard. Until his teeth smarted.

Fleeing the training grounds was new desire, but he wanted nothing more at the moment.

Roduch stepped forward and gripped his forearm. He wanted to yank away from the show of forgiveness and solidarity, but he couldn't insult his friend more than he already had. However, he couldn't look at the big knight.

"Take a breather. You fought hard." Leave it to Roduch to be the one praising when Alasdair had been in the wrong.

He studied his dirty boots, feeling about two inches tall.

"Why don't you return to the castle and check on your charge?" Lord Jorrin asked, but it wasn't a true suggestion.

Alasdair swallowed and forced a breath before he could answer his liege lord. He fought the urge to close his eyes. He'd just been dismissed.

Like a lad.

"Aye, my lord." He couldn't manage more of an agreement. Because checking on his *charge* was the last thing he needed.

His charge, after all, was the *problem*.

☆   ☆   ☆   ☆

They'd fought their way through two meals together, but this one was worse than midday meal that afternoon.

She'd glowed, her new bondmate at her side. And ignored Alasdair for much of the time today.

He admittedly deserved that, after the way he'd been treating her over the last two sevendays. Not to mention the way he'd left things—left *her*—in her rooms the night before.

He'd fled.

Alasdair grimaced and shoved his piece of roast around on his plate. It smelled delicious and was juicy, just like he liked it, but he had no desire to eat. The meat, along with potatoes and spiced greens, had long since gone cold.

"Alas, is something wrong?" Lord Tristan Dagget's soft question made Alasdair stiffen.

Lady Elissa froze at his side. She didn't look at him.

"Nay." He forced a smile and met the younger man's hazel eyes. They were different from Lady Elissa's, despite the similar hue. He preferred the lass', with her gold flecks.

Conversation at the head table died down, and he *felt* the stares of the lords and ladies—as well as his captain. Alasdair prayed none of the men would mention what'd happened on the training grounds today.

The healer accepted his one word answer with a slight nod, but the duke studied him with what appeared to be interest—and concern?

Damn empathic magic.

He made sure not to meet Lord Jorrin's deep blue eyes, but Alasdair couldn't sit still.

"Lord Aldern."

Lady Elissa's voice made him want to sit taller.

"Aye, my lady?" The duke smiled for her.

She cleared her throat. "Do you have time for me in the morning? I must discuss something with you."

Lord Jorrin exchanged a look with his wife before he looked back at Lady Elissa.

Alasdair clenched his fists on his lap. There was no doubt what the *something* was. More than likely, Lord Jorrin knew of Lady Elissa's plans. The duke and duchess probably shared everything. It was no secret the couple adored each other, not that Alasdair was envious.

"Aye, Lady Elissa." The half-elfin duke nodded, shifting his shaggy black hair past a long tapered ear. "Come to my ledger room after you break your fast."

"Thank you, my lord." Her words shook, but it didn't give Alasdair any satisfaction.

His heart sank with the finality.

She'd chosen another man.

She *wanted* to wed the Duke of Dalunas.

Alasdair swallowed as anguish consumed his chest. He straightened his shoulders and pushed into the back of the ornately carved chair. The solid wood supporting him didn't make him feel stable—or any better. He wanted to stab something—or someone. A certain *someone* with fair hair and more status than himself.

"Then to the duchess solar for a bondmate lesson?" Lady Cera asked Lady Elissa.

The lass' face lit up. "Aye, my lady, I look forward to it." Lady Elissa looked down at the wolf cub who'd not left her side.

Mischief scooted closer, resting his head on her lap.

She didn't chide him, despite the headwoman's dislike of beasts in the great hall, let alone on the dais. Lady Elissa stroked his silver head, regarding her new bond with a tenderness Alasdair would've given his left arm—no, his whole body—to have turned in his direction.

He wanted to leave the table, the dais, the great hall. Immediately.

Coward didn't leave a good taste in his mouth, but that didn't alter his urge to flee.

The duchess laughed and the other ladies joined in conversation about bonding, bondmates, and shared stories of their own experiences.

Their voices faded in and out as Alasdair watched Lady Elissa soak everything in with obvious eagerness. The lass balanced on the edge of her chair, leaning into the table, and firing off questions whenever she could.

Soon the bards mounted the stage and started singing. People floated to the dancing area, moving to lively tunes and slow ballads alike.

Alasdair escaped to the personal guard's table as soon as it was socially acceptable. He sat on the tabletop itself, watching his brothers laugh and listening to them throw quips at each other. It was foreign not to be leading the charge in that regard, for his jesting and witty barbs were usually the first slung back and forth.

Bowen teased Teagan—one of the youngest of his brothers—about a tavern lass. The lad's face went red, but he grinned from ear to ear and jested right back. Padraig grunted something about not being proper as there were lasses at the table, but his wife soon dragged him to the dance floor, her cheeks as pink as Teagan's. The roundness of her belly didn't hamper her movements.

Alasdair watched Laith dip his wife, Meara, in a dance, and tried not to frown at her resounding giggle of delight. Roduch held Avril close as they swayed to a slow song. Dallon was charming a lass at a nearby table, and Niall danced with his wife, Lyde.

Even the reclusive Artan—who'd been burned very badly as a lad by his own fire magic—danced with a pretty blonde lass.

His brothers were *happy*—married or not.

Alasdair's stomach turned, threatening to revolt and toss what little he'd managed to eat for supper.

Lady Elissa laughed, and his eyes found her against his will. He knew her laugh, whether near or far. She danced with Lucan, and the lad held her loosely as they moved together to a slow love ballad.

Her wolf was close, staring as if he wanted to be a part of the dance. Her face held the same radiance it had all day, and it just made him feel worse.

Why wasn't she miserable like him?

"You're looking at her as if you'll devour her." Leargan intentionally bumped shoulders with him and Alasdair cursed, barely suppressing the urge to jump.

His captain had surprised him. He'd not heard or sensed Leargan's approach. Not something that happened often. Alasdair didn't want to show it.

When he had the bollocks to look at his longtime friend, Leargan had an eyebrow arched and his arms crossed over his chest. His posture was relaxed as he leaned against the table next to Alasdair. But that dark gaze was keen, belying his nonchalance.

"What?" Alasdair cleared his throat.

"Lady Elissa."

Instead of disagreeing, he averted his eyes.

"After what happened today, I knew something was up. But never in a million turns did I think it was that." Leargan's tone was conversational.

"I don't know what you're talking about."

The bark of laughter had Alasdair glaring toward his brother.

Disbelief reflected in his eyes now. Leargan tipped his head, a smile playing at his lips. "All right."

Alasdair frowned. Didn't know what to say, so he didn't say anything.

"I never thought I'd see it, that's for sure."

"See what?" he barked.

Leargan chuckled and shook his head, making his ebony hair dance across his shoulders. "You have feelings for her."

His gut told him to issue a quick denial. That'd only make it worse. He cleared his throat, but he couldn't look at the captain—again. "She's a fine lass."

"Aye, that she is." Leargan paused, then narrowed his eyes. "What're you going to do?"

"About what?"

"Lady Elissa."

"She's to marry Lord Cam. Did you not know?" He couldn't look toward the dance floor. Didn't want to see her laugh as another male twirled her around, even if it was just Lucan. It was a good thing the Duke of Dalunas was already on his way to his home Province. If he'd been dancing with her right then, Alasdair might've run him through. He met Leargan's gaze again, even though he didn't want to do that, either. "She chose him," he spat, then fought a cringe.

Leargan stared.

Alasdair shifted on the table top.

"You know the king well, do you not?"

He startled. That was the last thing he'd expected his captain to say. "Aye."

"Then you know that King Nathal wants her to marry for love."

"And?"

"No one is blind to the way she looks at you, Alas. She's chosen the duke because she thinks she *has* to. You are of a rank with her. There's no reason you cannot be her match. And if she resides in Greenwald, she can still be safe from those who mean her harm. Along with your protection, Lucan is here. King Nathal won't oppose it, if it's what you both want."

"You're wrong."

Leargan sighed. "For someone who gives such great advice, you're a fool, my friend."

Alasdair didn't answer. He slid to his feet and growled, leaning into the shorter man. "I'm not a fool. And I won't discuss this any further." He made a fist and whirled away from Leargan.

He took one step, then another. Before he'd realized it, Alasdair had stalked across the hall and out into the corridor.

People stared.

He didn't give a shite.

Chapter Twenty-five

It was taking too long.

Despite absorbing the water mage's powers, Drayton's strength wasn't going to last as long as he'd like — as long as he *needed*, not if he kept using his magic like he was. Although he was likely to drive himself crazy for worrying about it.

The filthy half-breed watched the castle in Greenwald, but was it the *right* castle? Could his lass really be ensconced inside?

It made sense, in a way.

He'd known the castle where he'd first encountered the child was one of a lord.

Drayton just hadn't confirmed if the lass was noble or servant. Where he'd found her in the castle suggested either. Her clothing hadn't lent clues either — she'd been a toddler and dressed in a simple ivory sleeping gown — which had ripped when they'd attacked each other. The fabric hadn't been particularly rich or obviously poor.

He'd killed anyone he'd come into contact with, servants and nobles alike, so it wasn't as if he'd stopped to ask questions.

Perhaps he should have. Then he'd have her name, at least. But surely who'd ever rescued her would've changed it. They'd hidden her all these turns.

Who had hidden her away was unknown, as well.

To think she might've been in Greenwald all this time. At Castle Aldern? Why would the duke have taken responsibility for her? It wasn't required for a liege lord to take in orphans, even if the lass was noble. Was she blood kin perhaps?

If she'd been there all this time, she'd survived the decimation a few turns ago by the former archduke who had wiped out the Ryhans—the former duke, his wife and daughter.

One daughter survived, the current duchess.

"Could it be?"

Nay. Drayton shook his head. The Duchess of Greenwald was a redhead—and renowned for such, as well as her toughness. She wasn't his elemental, even if females could change their appearance.

The tiny lass he remembered was blonde. So pale in color it was more white than yellow.

So was the half-breed wrong?

Drayton paced on his dais, fingertips pressed into his bottom lip.

What could he do?

He'd extended his life by taking the young water mage's, but he needed to conserve energy. He couldn't rush to Greenwald and see for himself what Charis suspected. He'd have to wait for his hirelings to come to him. As much as he hated that. He'd never been skilled at giving up control. Needed to maintain his strength so he could father a child when Charis and his men brought his lass to him. His plan would work. He'd be set for several lifetimes.

Drayton stilled and stretched his shoulders. Rested his hands on his hips and rotated. Leaned side to side. His body gave no major protests.

"It's about damn time."

Perhaps the water mage had been more powerful than he'd thought. Or felt.

He looked around his cave home, burning to do something other than pace. Drayton slipped from his dais and glanced toward the large mirror on the natural wall above his sleeping area. The magic flame above it caused shadows to dance in the far-off reflection.

Snapping his fingers, he hurried to the ornately framed mirror. He could call the half-breed and demand a report.

The view of his face stopped him cold, before he could say the spell connected to Charis' mirror. Drayton's hands shook when he raised them to his cheeks. They were no longer sallow. Only one or two age lines, instead of too-many-to-count. Not as full as when he was younger—or had more power coursing through his veins—but he looked as if he was recovered from a disease. He had normal color.

He ran his fingers through his hair, which was no longer white. It wasn't the brown of his youth, but it would be after he got his lass. Salt and pepper waves were soft to the touch, too. No visible bald-spot as before the water mage.

Drayton smiled as elation rolled over him. He was starting to feel...normal.

If he weren't alone, he'd holler for joy. Needed to hold onto this feeling. Because when the half-breed and his men brought him the lost elemental and his plan was underway, Drayton would feel *better* than he did now. He couldn't wait until her power poured through him. Her water magic would only make his own stronger, as had the recent water mage.

Drayton extended his arm and called to the water, grinning when it didn't take much effort. Power shot down his forearm into his fingers. A small wave was born. He didn't want to flood his cave's floor, so he bid it to dissipate instead of infusing more power into it. The fact he could've made it larger without losing precious strength made his body lighter.

"Everything is going to be fine. Everything will go as planned."

Drayton waved his fingers around and forced a warm gust of wind to caress him. It parted his hair and rustled his clothing. Next, he snapped his fingers and gave birth to a warm fire in the ring for that purpose next to his dais. He infused more magic, making it brighter and warmer.

Lastly, he gestured wildly; the loose pebbles rolled away as if he'd swept the natural floor with a broom.

He threw his head back and a laugh broke from his lips.

Gone were the worries of moments past.

He wouldn't run out of magic. He couldn't.

Drayton felt better than he had in months.

Rubbing his hands together, he schooled his expression and said the spellword that would connect his mirror to the half-breed's.

When the haze cleared and he met Charis' eyes, Drayton squared his shoulders. "Report."

⋆   ⋆   ⋆   ⋆

Charis sat watching Castle Aldern's gates. He couldn't answer the consistently demanded, "Why?" from his lads. He just *knew* he had to stay where he was.

No matter how long it took.

Despite the fact it'd been two days of nothing much. Watching people come and go, seeing carts inspected and nobles depart. Word was a Knight of Greenwald was newly married and the king himself had been in attendance.

They'd missed King Nathal's departure by days, according to gossip he'd overheard in the square.

Which was perfectly fine with Charis. He had no problem with the king, he just didn't have any desire to risk being known by the man, either. There was no doubt the multiple murders he and his lads had committed were being investigated.

King Nathal's sense of justice equaled his prowess in battle. Something to be feared.

It was well known to those of Aramour, as well as the people of the Provinces that fell into his kingdom. King Nathal had worked hard for peace with the chiefs of the elf clans early in his reign, as the story went.

Were it to come to light the lasses and their families were killed by them, they'd be destined for the penal colony of the continent, in the far southeastern Province of Dalunas. It'd been nicknamed Dread Valley.

Charis had never been there, but he didn't intend find out why men feared it so, either.

"What're ya doing?" Bracken roared.

"Will you keep your voice down?" he snapped, pushing off the fountain he was sitting on the base of. His eyes darted around the public area.

Marshals patrolled in pairs of two. He'd spotted the captain he'd seen the other day not long ago, though the man had been walking by himself.

Families laughed, ate at tables and strolled through the square, and all over the market in general. It was a rest day, so there were more food vendors with hot and cold ready-to-eat goods than during the working days.

No one was in a hurry today.

The crowd was as large as normal—if not larger—but they

still couldn't afford to be noticed or remembered. Evening approached, yet people lingered.

Unrepentant, Bracken closed the distance between them. Stopped himself short of grabbing Charis' tunic in tight fists, by the looks of it.

Damn good thing, too. Or they'd likely both end up in the provost's holding cells. He drew the line at letting Bracken manhandle him with no physical response.

"I'm doing what I need to do. Like I've told you a hundred times."

Bracken shook his head. "You're wastin' our time."

"You don't have to understand it. Just have to respect it. We need to stay here."

Doubt darted across the oaf's broad face.

Charis narrowed his eyes. "Are you questioning my orders? My magic?"

"Nay."

He didn't let his body loosen until Bracken's big shoulders relaxed.

"For turns we've been in this together. I don't want tha' ta change because of impatience."

Charis leaned back, appraising his companion. That was as close to an apology as he'd ever get, but he was half-surprised. Bracken didn't often show weakness—or let on that he actually had faith in Charis. "Good. Neither do I." He took a breath. "I can't explain it. I just know. We need to stay here."

Giving a curt nod, Bracken's chest heaved as if he, too, had released a breath. "Just get out of tha open. We're in public, but you've not moved from this spot for hours. It's suspicious."

"I don't disagree." Charis looked around. He wanted to run his hands through his hair, but he couldn't afford someone seeing his ears if he took off his hat. "Where's Nason?"

"Buying supplies."

"Ah. Very well. Let's find a less conspicuous spot where we can still see the castle gates."

"Aye, let's."

They turned together, but a howl stopped Charis in his tracks. He glanced over his shoulder when movement right outside Castle Aldern's gates caught his eye.

He and Bracken exchanged a glance, then the big man followed his gaze.

Four wolves—actual wild beasts—moved away from the castle walls. Without challenge from the posted guards.

"Did they just come from inside?"

"Aye, I should think so."

"Aye?" Charis arched an eyebrow, but he couldn't tear his eyes away from the wolves. One was pure white and huge. Another had a full coat of ebony and was even larger than the white wolf. The third was a smattering of grays and browns, with a hint of red on its back.

"'Tis spoken of a great deal. The ladies of Greenwald have bondmates. A proper wolf pack lives inside the castle. The duchess herself is bonded to the white one, just like the wolf on the seal of Greenwald."

He threw his lad a glance. Hadn't given Bracken enough credit for his listening skills. Perhaps Charis had heard the Duchess of Greenwald had a wolf, but nothing of the other three.

His gaze narrowed, scanning for the fourth wolf, since he'd not gotten an adequate look at it. It was smaller than the other three, and moving faster, in front of the pack.

It had a coat of several shades of gray, making it appear almost silver in the waning sunlight. The beast's youth was obvious. It nipped at the haunches of the others and darted back and forth around the pack, until the large white wolf seemed to reprimand it and it settled at the large beast's side.

With the barest probing, Charis sensed the magic all over the animals.

Bonding spells were strong, and carried the signature of the human bondmate's magic. The magic itself appeared as a golden rope if the partners were both in sight. They'd look physically tethered, with thick ropes wrapping around their auras and sometimes looking as it disappeared inside the body.

It'd fascinated him for turns, but he'd never wanted to bond himself. There was too much danger in it. If the beast was killed, the human died, or vice versa. The advantage for the animal was life extension. Bondmates lived the same lifespan.

In Aramour, humans and elves alike sometimes bonded with dragons. In those cases, the human's lifespan would equal three—if not four—times normal. Elves lived longer than humans, so if they gained turns because of a dragon bondmate, it was minimal.

Since he only saw one half of the pairs before him, Charis needed to concentrate a bit harder to sense the magic. He sensed a protection spell covering the wolves, just like the one over the castle.

He probed deeper, trying to move quickly, because the wolves would soon be out of sight.

Elemental magic smacked into his powers, and he staggered with its intensity. "Blessed Spirit," he whispered, shaking Bracken's hand off his upper arm, even though his friend had just been trying to keep him from tumbling to his arse.

"What is it?" The big man asked.

He ignored him and probed deeper.

The silver wolf.

Charis started to run so he wouldn't lose his magical connection to the wolves. He heard Bracken curse and the clunk of his boots as Bracken's longer stride only had to jog to keep up with him.

He sent his senses out wider as he went, trying to focus on the smallest wolf. He needed to absorb everything he could about the beast's bondmate.

Female.

The silver wolf was bonded to a *female* elemental mage.

His heart galloped as fast as his feet. He turned behind the pack as they moved out of Greenwald Main.

"Charis!" Bracken called.

Charis ignored him and kept moving. Studying, sending more strength into his magic, until the wolves faded from view, breaking out into a full run as people and buildings thinned. He panted, bending at the waist and planting his hands on his knees as he caught his breath and willed his heart to slow.

His gut shouted at him. He'd found Drayton's elemental lass.

"What the hell, man? What's got inta ya?" Bracken demanded, breathing just heavily as Charis needed to. "Chasing beasts that could rip out your throat withou' effort? What were ya gonna do if you caught up ta them?"

"I didn't want to catch them."

Bracken ran his hand through his wind-mussed dark hair. His mouth was a hard line and annoyance rolled off him in waves. "What then?"

Charis straightened and took two deep breaths. He grinned. Now his lad regarded him as if he'd gone daft.

"Our search is over."

"For the lass?"

"Aye. I know where she is."

Chapter Twenty-Six

She turned back the thick sleeping furs and swallowed a yawn. Tonight had been lovely. Despite the fact her chaperone wouldn't even look at her.

Elissa had put all dark thoughts aside and danced. Just like the night of the wedding, except she hadn't gotten to dance with Sir Alasdair.

As matter fact, she'd been dancing with Lucan and seen her knight perched on a tabletop one moment and gone the next. She hadn't seen him again. Sir Bowen had escorted her back to her rooms.

"Oh well. I'm not going to think about it now." Another yawn threatened and she failed to stave it off. Her eyes watered. Elissa had wanted to wait for Mischief to return from hunting, but she was too tired. She'd sleep now, and wake when he scratched at the door—she hoped.

He hadn't been gone long, but after they'd been together all day, she missed him. The young beast was already a part of Elissa's *normal*.

Getting used to having him—his thoughts and primal feelings—in her mind was new, and would take a while, but it was more healing to her than a burden. Her bondmate was the bright spot in her despair. Mischief wiped the hurt away—almost.

She rolled her eyes at herself and reached to fluff her pillow, sparing a glance at the dying fire. The embers still had a nice glow and radiated heat she could feel from where she stood, but she needed to get into bed before the temperature dropped too much.

Elissa reached for Mischief through her thoughts. She could sense his elation. He was running with his sire, dam, and the black she-wolf, Ali. He felt free, in his element, and she suspected he didn't sense her because he was so worked up.

She sent him love and smiled when her wolfling returned it without delay.

"So he wasn't so mired down with the hunt after all." She glanced around the large room again, then pictured Mischief lying by the hearth. More likely, he'd get into bed with her. Morag would not be pleased.

Elissa laughed, then felt silly since she was alone.

The door to her rooms was wrenched open so hard the thick wood crashed into the wall. She shrieked and jumped, clutching the closest pillow to her chest.

Her wolf wasn't the one who'd just burst in.

She locked eyes with her knight. Tremors that had nothing to do with the worry of a cold room chased each other down her spine. He stepped into the room and slammed the door shut without looking away from her. Sir Alasdair strode to her, but then glanced at the bed. As if jolted, he stilled about five feet away.

"What are you doing?" Elissa's intended demand came out more like a cracked blurt. Her heart picked up speed.

His powerful chest heaved. Aggression poured off him. Her knight was silent and broody and so handsome it stole her breath. "You intend to tell Lord Aldern you've chosen Lord Cam?" His voice was thick.

Pained?

Nay. He doesn't care.

Elissa nodded, because she couldn't push anything out of her mouth.

"You *want* to marry the Duke of Dalunas?" His brow furrowed, and he looked away.

"Aye," she whispered. Her belly fluttered. She dropped the pillow to the bed, then regretted it. Elissa clutched her sleeping gown at the neckline. It was a thin fabric, and she was suddenly aware that she wore nothing beneath it. Her fingertips shook as they brushed the buttons at the top.

"Aye?" Sir Alasdair echoed. An emotion she was afraid to name darted across his face, and his frown deepened. "Why?"

Elissa startled.

Why? That was a good question, considering she loved the man before her, not the duke. However, she'd never thought in a million turns Sir Alasdair would ask. "Alasdair—" His name slipped from her lips without his honorific.

Those blue eyes flared and settled on her mouth.

Elissa took two steps toward him, but her knight slid away.

"Answer me." A demand that came with a clenched fist. But he didn't look away.

Her blood—and magic—pounded along her arms and legs, in her temples, making her head spin. "He...is...a good man."

"Undoubtedly. But that's not why you want to wed him, lass."

Elissa swallowed and lowered her lashes. Could she be honest with him?

Tell him what—*who*—she really wanted?

He'd likely run from her, like last night.

If so, she could flush her desires away as far as he was concerned, and marry Lord Cam knowing it was her only option, because Sir Alasdair Kearney *really* didn't want her.

Right?

It's now or never.

She sucked in a breath and shoved her magic back. Elissa squared her shoulders and met his sapphire eyes. "Because he is my suitor. Because he cares about me. Because he...wants me."

The knight's shoulders slumped and the apple of his throat bobbed as he swallowed, but her heart's desire didn't break their eye contact.

It gave her the courage to finish her thought. "Because I cannot have who I really want."

His lips parted. Air whooshed out. His hands opened and closed, as if he didn't know what to do with them.

They stared at each other in silence.

Finally, he moved. But Alasdair didn't come to her. He locked his fists at his sides and moved back another step. "It's...wrong."

"Why?" She forced strength behind her question. Stood taller.

He shifted his feet and averted his beautiful eyes. "It's wrong." The repetition was barely a whisper.

Elissa gathered all the courage she had and wrapped it around herself. She approached him. Pled with him silently to look at her again. "Why is it wrong?"

When he finally turned to her, he shook his head, shifting his long dark locks. He backed up two more steps, putting his palms flat behind him, as if feeling for the door. He was still far from it, but if she moved closer, Alasdair would move away.

Elissa stood where she was instead, forcing deep, even breaths and praying she had the strength to show him what she wanted, since telling him wasn't working.

Maybe he wouldn't leave her.

Maybe he would want her back.

"Alasdair…"

His eyes widened at her second use of his name with no honorific.

"Lass—"

"I want you."

Her knight sputtered. Shook his head again. "You don't know what you're saying."

"I do. I'm not innocent, remember?" She wasn't naïve. Wanted—*needed*—him to see that. See her as a woman, not a lass.

"Lady Elissa—"

"Do you want me, Alasdair? You've kissed me twice. So, I think you do."

"What I *want* doesn't matter." Alasdair looked anywhere but *at* her, but Elissa's heart sang with hope.

He didn't deny it. He does *want me.*

She thought of the bold heroines of her favorite stories. Elissa could be like them, couldn't she? If he wouldn't come to her, she *would* go to him. *Show* him.

Guilt tickled the back of her mind. She'd agreed to marry Lord Cam. She'd told him she wouldn't consider any other suitor. If she pushed Alasdair, if he gave into what they both wanted, Elissa would be giving her innocence away. She'd no longer be a virgin…pure for marriage.

She pushed all thoughts, reservations away.

I love Alasdair. It can only be him.

She'd worry about Lord Cam in the morning.

"A real man would come take what he wants." Elissa played with the top button of her sleeping gown.

He was on her in less than a second.

She probably shouldn't have goaded him, but all thought fled as his mouth crushed hers and she was melded against his hard body. She was getting what she wanted, after all.

Alasdair invaded her mouth, plundering more than exploring. Elissa didn't fight him.

She melted against him, legs weak. Desire pooled low in her belly and she slid her hands down the back of his neck, over his shoulders, and squeezed his biceps. She clung to him, glad he was holding her so tightly. She would've landed at his feet otherwise.

He ripped away on a gasp. "This...isn't right. I need...to go."

She looked up into his eyes. Desire reflected in the blue depths, but he was too conflicted. She swallowed and reached for his belt.

Desire would win out. She'd have him. Elissa couldn't let it matter that he didn't love her. She loved him enough for them both. "Nay."

Alasdair groaned and backed up. Her fingers were separated from his buckle before she could finish the task. "I shouldn't do this."

Elissa stepped toward him, unbuttoning her sleeping gown as she went. "Why not? You burst into my room. It's late. Why not make the best of it?" She parted the soft linen down to her navel.

His eyes widened as she bared her naked breasts, but he looked away. Alasdair dragged a hand through his hair. Her stomach roiled. Hadn't she convinced him yet? He couldn't leave now. Elissa was throwing herself at him. Her bottom lip wobbled.

Maybe I was wrong.

But then he yanked her into his arms again and kissed her. She got as close to him as she could, feeling evidence that he *did* want her—at least physically—against her belly.

Thought fled as Alasdair kissed her harder, rubbing his tongue against hers.

He was so warm; Elissa could feel the heat of his chest even through his tunic. The sandalwood of his soap mixed with scents of the forest, and something clean, masculine. It hit her nose and her body hummed, throbbing and warming even more.

Her knight crushed her against him but she only wanted more.

His kiss seared her, heart, body and soul. It went on until she barely remembered how to breathe.

Fingers fumbling, they ripped at each other's clothing. She got his belt open and tugged at the soft leather ties of his pants. He ripped her gown the rest of the way down, buttons flying. Elissa didn't care. He pushed it off one shoulder as she made a move to tug his breeches off his hips.

He pulled away, his chest heaving. The top of his tunic was open, the ties listing to the side, offering a deep vee. The sparse dark fuzz on his chest caught her eye.

She buried her fingertips in it without thought. "Please don't leave me tonight." The whisper tumbled out of her mouth and her cheeks heated.

Begging? Aye.

One corner of his mouth lifted. "Oh, it's too late for that, lass." His eyes trailed her bared breasts as Elissa shrugged out of her ruined sleeping gown.

She shivered as it pooled at her feet, but not from the temperature in the room. Alasdair's gaze devoured her.

She needed his hands on her. All over her. *Inside* her.

Elissa stood naked before him and this time, she wasn't going to let him reject her.

"Lass…" he whispered. Her knight closed his eyes and swayed. Alasdair gestured, as if daring her. His breathing was uneven and his chest moved up and down, beckoning as much as his hand.

She moved closer, until their bodies were almost touching. Elissa reached for his breeches and their gazes collided. The deep blue orbs captivated her, like always. "Elissa," she told him.

Her steady hands belied her thundering heart and she slowly pushed the leather off his hips. He did nothing to stop her. "Say my name."

Elissa lifted his shirt to his shoulders and he shrugged out of it, not acknowledging its landing place next to her ruined sleeping chemise on the floor.

"Elissa," Alasdair whispered.

She let him divest himself of his boots and breeches.

Biting back a gasp, she took in his full nakedness. He was more magnificent than she imagined. His muscles were defined, overwhelming. His trim waist led to the proud erection jutting out toward her. He was large, but he wouldn't hurt her. Ever.

Alasdair protected. She'd only known that side of him.

Elissa wanted to know him differently, as a lover.

It wasn't polite to stare, but she couldn't help it. The man she loved was beautiful. Standing before her as if on display at market.

He stared right back, but the heat in her form was of anticipation, not embarrassment.

Her eyes traced his powerful thighs and she imagined their bodies entwined. Her hands ached to touch him. Caress every line with her fingertips, and then her lips. She wanted to taste every inch of him.

Never being naked before a man should've registered, but it didn't. Elissa was all want and need.

"If you don't stop looking at me like that, this will be over before it starts." Alasdair reached for her.

They both gasped when their naked skin came together. He hauled her closer, flattening her breasts against his chest. Elissa buried her face against him, letting her eyes slip closed. His scent enveloped her, but she needed more.

"I want to make love to you."

Alasdair's eyes flared at her confession, and his lips parted as he leaned down. Warm breath caressed her face before he took her mouth.

The kiss was just as potent as the others but this time, he was gentler in the way he explored her. She kissed him back with all she was, slipping her hands down his powerful back, following the curve of his buttocks. Elissa pulled him closer, gripping him with both hands, rocking her pelvis into his.

He ended their kiss, chuckling. "Eager?"

The teasing she always associated with Alasdair was back and her heart skipped. He was finally at ease with what would happen between them. She managed a nod and her cheeks warmed all over again. There was tenderness in his eyes as she met his gaze. Perhaps he cared for her after all.

Elissa ignored the way her stomach fluttered. She shouldn't read into anything. "For you, aye," she whispered.

He swung her up into his arms without a word and deposited her on the middle of the bed she'd slept in since coming to Castle Aldern.

Alasdair lowered himself over her. However, instead of placing his body on top of hers, he settled beside her and propped himself above her on one elbow.

Elissa reached to caress his cheek, smiling as stubble scraped her palm.

"You're so beautiful." He dragged his hand between her breasts, his fingertips teasing the underside of one, then the other.

Her nipples tingled and she gasped.

He traced her birthmark and she shivered. "This is the only mark on your skin."

"My half-moon. I was born with it."

"It's perfect. Like you." His gaze was intense. "Touching you this way…I've imagined it dozens of times."

Her brain was too muddled to focus on his admission. "More," she breathed.

Alasdair smiled, slow and sexy. "Lass, we're only getting started." He cupped her breasts fully, brushing her nipples with his thumbs.

She gasped, thought dissolving as his hand trailed downward. He touched the soft part of her belly, teasingly circling her navel and continuing on, brushing the soft golden curls that guarded her sex. He didn't linger and chuckled at her whimpered protest. Alasdair caressed her inner thighs, never touching her where she needed him to.

She throbbed at her core, writhing beside him. "Alas…"

Their eyes met as she whispered the nickname his fellow knights always called him. He leaned down and claimed her mouth without a word. Her arms shot around his neck and she arched into his hard chest. She deepened the kiss, needing more of him, needing him on top of her, inside her. Elissa rubbed her breasts against him.

He groaned into her mouth and shifted, his body coming into the cradle of hers as if it belonged. As if things had never been complete until they touched in this manner.

His hard arousal lay against her, burning her thigh. She shivered, and her sex throbbed. Her knight wasn't in the right place.

Alasdair pulled back, staring down into her face.

"I need you," she whispered.

His answer was another groan and his mouth slanted over hers again. His hands moved as his mouth did, shooting between their bodies. Alasdair's fingers pushed into her and Elissa gasped.

"Blessed Spirit, you're already wet for me," he breathed.

Heat burned her face and she glanced away.

"Elissa."

"Aye?"

"I'll take care of you." Her heart stuttered.

"I never doubted that."

He smiled and she had to bite back the sudden urge to cry. Why couldn't he mean that in more than a physical sense?

Alasdair's lips came down on hers again, but didn't remain. He burned a trail of wet kisses down her neck and across her collar bone, stopping to nip and lick between her breasts.

She cried out when he enclosed a nipple in his mouth and began to suckle, massaging the other breast before turning his attention to it. Elissa writhed and her knight continued downward, lathering kisses along her belly. She lifted her hips and called his name when he separated her knees and ran his tongue down her inner thigh.

When he kissed her between the legs she clutched at him, gasping.

"Relax." Alasdair pressed her back into the bed with gentle hands. "Let me love you, lass." His eyes were tender, sincere.

She gulped and nodded, laying back, her eyes never leaving his.

He trailed his fingertips against her sex.

Elissa bit her lip to keep from crying out at the mixture of nerves and longing.

Alasdair spread her open again, staring down before lowering his shoulders between her legs. He leaned into her, kissing below her belly button and continuing downward, nipping and licking his way to her most sensitive skin.

His tongue drove her wild, and she arched off the bed until he pinned her hips with both hands. Pleasure rushed her body as never before.

She screamed as he drew her sensitive nub into her mouth and began to suck. Elissa buried her hands in his hair, holding him in place. She threw her head back and rode the unfamiliar pleasure, rocking her pelvis, begging for more. It was almost too much.

Tension built, her muscles tightened and strained.

Elissa needed… Something…

What's happening?

She wiggled under his hold. Alasdair looked up, meeting her eyes and slipping a finger inside her. Elissa cried out as he eased slowly in and out.

"Let it come, lass. Don't fight it. Shatter for me."

Elissa didn't have a chance to ask him what he meant. Ecstasy charged her. Her muscles clenched and released of their own accord. Her inner thighs shook and she could feel Alasdair's finger inside her being gripped by muscles she didn't even know could grip.

He shot up her body and took her mouth. She shook in his arms with another wave of passion, but she kissed him back.

Alasdair parted her thighs with his knee and pressed his hips to hers. His hand disappeared between them and then his erection was there, hot and hard, and filled her with one jolt forward.

Sharp pain made her freeze in his arms. Elissa cried out against his mouth, ending their kiss. Tears blurred her vision. Her cousin had told her the first time would hurt, but after what she'd just experienced with him, worry about her virginity hadn't even entered her mind.

He pulled back, sapphire eyes wide. His body poised above hers, Alasdair remained still, his expression confused…and strained. His gaze raked her face, his brow furrowing. "You've never done this before."

Not a question. "Nay," she whispered.

"Elissa." Her name was all warning.

She wrapped her legs around his waist before he could move away or pull out of her. Wasn't about to let him leave her now. The movement shifted their bodies and Alasdair groaned.

Elissa shivered. Pain faded, but she was still throbbing for him. "You're not leaving me now, Alasdair. I still want you." She wiggled beneath him and they both moaned.

"This is wrong," he whispered. However, her knight moved toward her instead of away.

"It is not." She closed the distance between their mouths.

He took control of the kiss and in seconds all remnants of pain faded. Alasdair kissed her harder, rocking his hips, but didn't start to thrust. Elissa broke the seal of their mouths and looked into his intense blue eyes. She tilted her hips, taking him deeper with a whimper.

"Shhh, lass. Give it a moment. I don't want to hurt you." His sincerity flipped her heart.

"You won't leave me?"

One corner of his mouth shot up. "Nay, I won't leave you. I'm sorry I took you so roughly."

"You didn't hurt me," she whispered, shoving her hips against his again.

Alasdair grunted and thrust forward. Conversation slipped away as he led their bodies to a natural rhythm.

Elissa moved under him, with him, against him, their legs and arms entwined. She returned his every touch and every kiss. Couldn't get close enough to him.

Pressure like earlier started to build and she thrashed under him. Her head rolled back and forth on her pillow, until he took her mouth in a heated kiss and drove in and out even harder.

The feelings were more intense than before. She lifted her hips as her whole body tightened, and Elissa screamed his name.

Climax hit him at the same time, his shoulders and spine stiffening. He grunted and stilled above her. His erection jerked inside her. The warm, wet rush of his release caused them both to shudder. Alasdair dipped down, fusing their mouths until she couldn't breathe.

Her muscles went lax into the bed. Alasdair collapsed on top of her and Elissa held him tight, wrapping her arms and legs around him. She wasn't ready for him to part from her body, now, or ever.

She kissed his rough cheek and forehead. The sweat of their lovemaking was salty on her lips but she didn't care. Elissa loved this man.

When their eyes met, silence reigned.

"Now what?" she whispered when she worked up the courage to speak.

Alasdair grinned. "Now you let me go so I can get something to clean us up."

Heat blanketed her neck and face, creeping all the way to the tips of her ears. She forced her arms and legs to fall from his body.

He gently separated them and caressed her cheek.

"You won't leave me?" She tamped down irrational panic as he slipped from her bed.

Alasdair shook his head. "I'll be right back, Elissa." Her name rolled off his tongue with his northern Terraquist accent. The sound was as appealing as he was.

Considering what they'd shared, she shouldn't have flinched as he tenderly cleansed her with a warm linen square. Her sex throbbed, but the smart felt good. It was a reminder of what she'd given the man she loved.

Elissa bit her lip when she saw the blood on his upper thighs but Alasdair wiped himself without a word. The hard set of his lips made her swallow against a sudden lump in her throat.

She didn't regret giving him her innocence.

If he did, it would break her heart.

Alasdair said nothing. He tossed the cloth in the basket for linens in the corner, and slid back into her bed, tugging her into his arms. She snuggled into him, more content than she'd ever been. He still hadn't spoken. Elissa tried to banish butterflies in her tummy.

Neither grabbed the sleeping furs, but she wasn't cold.

Elissa stared at the contrast of their naked bodies, his skin darker than hers, muscular thighs cradling her pale slender ones. Her femininity was more obvious against his defined physique.

She explored him, dragging her hands through the springy curls on his chest, moving downward, skimming her fingertips across his toned abdominal muscles then returning to trace each line. She told herself not to stare at his manhood, but the more her fingers roamed, the more it jumped. As if it was ready to take her again.

Elissa's body tingled. She wanted him again.

Alasdair's groan caught her attention and their eyes met. His gaze was intense as he studied her. He gripped her wrist, and the apple of his throat bobbed. "Don't fall in love with me, lass."

She sat up, looking him square in those blue eyes.

Tell him the truth.

"It's too late."

"What?"

"I love you, Alasdair."

His expression darkened, brow furrowed, his mouth a hard line. "Don't mistake lust for tender feelings."

"Excuse me?" She straightened, crossing her arms over her breasts. Bile burned the back of her throat. "I believe I know my own heart."

"Then this was an even bigger mistake than I imagined."

"Alasdair..." Her shoulders shook. Next her arms. Anger mixed with crushing pain, her lungs burned with every breath. Magic pushed back, threatening to breech the surface of her skin. She fought it, forcing her eyes to remain on her knight.

Do. Not. Cry.

Elissa couldn't show him that he'd just ripped out her heart and stomped on it. The hole in her chest widened as he pushed past her to leave the bed, keeping their bodies from touching, as if it was offensive.

Alasdair grabbed his breeches and yanked them on. His belt buckle clanged, but he made no effort to fasten it.

Her vision blurred and she looked away.

"Tomorrow I'll inform my captain and the duke you'll need a new chaperone." His even, matter-of-fact tone made Elissa's heart stop.

"What?"

Her knight didn't turn to face her.

Tears spilled over, hot on her cheeks.

"This won't happen again." His voice had bite, an edge she'd never heard before.

Her throat started to close and she sucked back a sob. Power made her chest smolder, her hands shake as water demanded she let it free.

Elissa fought her magic with all she was, because she would likely drown Alasdair. And although the thought had merit, later she'd probably regret harming him.

So she sat still, sucking in her cheeks and begging for strength. When that didn't help, she started to rock, and clutched her bed linens with tight fists.

Mischief howled within her mind, and instinct told her that her bondmate would fight to get back to her side. Sensed him leave his packmates. She could feel him running. No doubt, he'd return to her in minutes.

She said nothing as her knight gathered his tunic and stuffed his feet into his boots with stiff movements. Elissa bit her bottom lip until it bled to hold back every whimper. She *would not* let him see—or hear—what he'd done to her.

Not once did he even look at her.

His tunic was slung over his arm, and he made no move to don it or tie his boot laces. His buckle clanged again with his frantic movements.

To get away from me. He can't go fast enough.

Alasdair paused with his hand on the doorknob. Her heart leapt with a small hope that he crushed as he remained silent.

He's really leaving without another word.

As soon as the door closed, with him on the wrong side, Elissa—and her magic—fell apart.

Chapter Twenty-Seven

Alasdair rushed out of Elissa's rooms and dashed into his own.

I'm too damn close to her.

He tried not to slam the door, but he couldn't help collapsing against the thick carved panel and sliding down until his arse smacked the stone floor. His tailbone smarted, but he could hardly feel it over the pain in his chest.

"Weak coward."

He cradled his head in his hands and barely staved off the urge to weep like a lass. Hell, *his* lass was probably sobbing right this second. Naked. In that huge bed. Where he'd…

Alasdair sucked back air, but couldn't stop panting. Couldn't catch his breath.

He'd taken her innocence.

She loved him.

Which is worse?

His gut churned. Bile rose and scorched his throat. Alasdair swallowed. It didn't help. He took another deep breath, but that didn't clear out the urge to vomit.

Thinking the word acted as a trigger.

He put his hand to his mouth, then wrenched it away just in time to avoid a drenching. Turned his head and bent over to expel the meager contents of his stomach.

Alasdair straightened and slammed his shoulders into the door. He bowed his head and pinched the bridge of his nose, barely resisting the urge to crash his head into the wood, too.

He wanted to get up, move into the room and rinse out the awful taste in his mouth, but his body refused all commands.

'*I love you, Alasdair,*' played in a loop in his head.

Her gaze had been open. Hopeful.

His response had crushed her. Although he'd made himself avoid her gaze, he'd caught more in his peripheral vision than he wanted to face. Those gorgeous hazel eyes had shone not with love, but with unshed tears. The air had rippled around her form; no doubt Elissa's magic.

She should've drowned him.

Put him out of his misery.

He wanted to scream, but that wouldn't fix anything either.

What am I going to do?

He'd taken a lady's innocence. His doubts about what she'd declared hadn't been unfounded after all. Had Elissa lied to him? Nay, he'd misunderstood somehow. Or she had.

"That has to be it." The statement was as scratchy as his charred throat.

Elissa wasn't the type of woman who'd lie to trap a man. She had too much honor.

"Honor? Hah!" Alasdair's eyes burned as he scoffed at himself. Where was *his* honor? "Blessed Spirit save me." His vision blurred, but he swiped the moisture away before it could soak his cheeks. He wouldn't cry. Hadn't done so since he was a lad, and a tiny one at that.

Divine intervention was about the only thing that *could* save him, though.

"Nay." Alasdair shook his head and pushed to his feet. He frowned at his puddle of vomit, and guilt bit at him again. What he'd done couldn't be reversed.

He snatched a bathing linen from the private privy of the guest suite. He surveyed the rooms, so lavish it made his quarters in the soldier wing look like a stall in the stables. Two—if not three—of his room could fit inside the suite before him.

The bed was huge and wide, with finer bedding than he owned. The hearth was twice the size of his. The desk was fine dark wood, and ornately carved. Alasdair preferred his own simple furnishings. He was out of place here. In this room.

With her.

He clenched his jaw until his teeth smarted. Threw the bathing sheet over his mess and patted the spot with the tip of his boot until the whole thing was absorbed.

Alasdair cursed as he gathered the cloth up and dumped it in the basket for the maids. Didn't swear because he'd cleaned up his vomit. He cursed because he was weak.

His heart thumped and his chest seared from the inside out. He rubbed the spot, but touching his bare skin only reminded him of Elissa's naked form in his arms. Her supple flesh against his. Soft. Smooth all over.

Her small breasts had heated his pectoral muscles and hardened his nipples. She'd touched him tentatively at first, then with firm caresses.

Alasdair could see it all as if she was still before him. He didn't even have to close his eyes. The slight roundness of her hips, her slim legs, the curls at her center. They were a darker blonde than the hair on her head.

Her kiss, her tight grip around him as he moved in and out of her. How perfect she'd felt around his cock. Hot, wet and so damn tight every thrust had made his balls burn. His cock jumped and Alasdair yelled a curse so loud the whole wing probably heard. He whipped his breeches down and squeezed himself until the sting was white hot pain that forced his hand to open. He gasped.

Ripping off his manhood wasn't going to solve any problems. His sex alone wasn't the reason he'd acted so rashly. He'd wanted her from the first time he'd seen her, but Alasdair hadn't been driven by lust alone.

It wasn't about the rutting.

He hadn't *rutted* Lady Elissa Durroc. Even putting the word next to her name made him wince. It was *wrong*.

Alasdair's heart had been in that room as much as the physical act. And *that* scared the hell out of him. Perhaps that'd been the reason he couldn't refute her request. *"I want to make love to you,"* she'd said.

He'd kissed her. Over and over. So many times he'd lost count. He'd tasted her mouth *and* her sex. Licked and nipped until her essence had enveloped his senses.

Kissing was as foreign to him as using his mouth on a woman below the waist. Yet, he'd done both to *her*. Alasdair had been moved to do so. To please her. Make her want him. Burn for him. Crave him.

Him alone.

And she had. Shattered in his arms more than once, despite her inexperience.

Alasdair shuddered. He should be in that room right now. Holding her. Kissing her. Taking her again.

I love you, Alasdair.

"Blessed Spirit, stop!" He plopped on the end of his bed, ignoring his open breeches. His belt buckle ended up beneath him and dug into the bottom of his thigh, but the pain was no less than he deserved.

There was only one thing he could do to make this right.

Alasdair gulped and stared at the wall. A painting he'd not noticed before filled the space before his eyes. A fair-haired barefoot lass was running across a meadow, her skirts hiked high in both hands and an expression of utter joy on her face. Her eyes were bright and free.

He couldn't tell what color they were from his distance along with the dimness of the room, but the lass' hair was a close match for Elissa.

Free. Happy.

I'm neither.

Trapped. In agony.

His actions tonight had ruined Elissa's chances at marriage with Lord Cam. Had ruined her for *any* good match. He'd stolen her virtue. But the thought of Lord Cam in bed with Elissa, hovering above her, thrusting into her, made him growl. He inserted himself into the little fantasy, where he slid his sword into the duke's back.

He couldn't kill the man, no matter what happened.

Alasdair didn't want her to marry the Duke of Dalunas, even if the man would accept a debauched bride. Most likely, Lord Cam would set her aside; choose another, if he knew.

Unless…

If he didn't tell anyone, and neither did she…

It wouldn't be obvious until the wedding night, right? Then it'd be too late, after vows were exchanged.

"Coward. Just do the right thing."

The *right thing* would be to offer for her. Wed her because he'd taken what'd been meant for another man.

Wed her because…

I love you, Alasdair.

"Nay!" he shouted to his empty room. Alasdair couldn't—*wouldn't*—put a word to the burn in his chest, especially not *that* word.

He stood on shaky legs, then started to pace so he wouldn't fall on his arse. Alasdair gnawed his thumbnail and tried to convince his heart to calm, his breathing to even out, but his disloyal body refused every order. His stomach roiled.

Doing the right thing wasn't something he was unfamiliar with. He usually managed honor and decorum without struggle or disagreement, but this was…permanent.

"*This* is precisely why I don't touch nobles. Or virgins…" Touch her he had. *More* than touch.

"*I want to make love to you.*" She might've said it, but… Alasdair had…made love…to Elissa.

Made love. He choked and tripped. No matter how he shook his head and tried to deny it, Alasdair had to accept it. He'd made love to someone for the first time in his life.

It'd been…

Perfect.

If he married her, he could touch her like that again. Assuming Elissa would speak to him…eventually. He grimaced. He'd been an arse.

If he walked away, he'd never get the chance to experience being with her again.

He could get her to forgive him for what he'd said, couldn't he? Alasdair crushed his eyes shut. What he'd said had been wrong.

A lass like Elissa deserved someone who could take care of her. Treat her right…return her tender feelings…*not* break her heart. He couldn't do that. Had no experience with such things, nor did he want it.

Do I? "Nay." His whisper was a lie.

He *did* want her like that. To be with her *completely.*

Alasdair had been her first lover. If he married her, he could be—*would be*, dammit—her *last* lover. He couldn't fathom anyone touching her the way he had.

If a man did, he wouldn't survive Alasdair's wrath, anyway.

He blew out a breath and whirled around, starting the pacing routine all over again. He could go to Leargan in the morning. Tell his captain what had happened—what he'd done.

No.

He'd have to go to the duke. Lord Aldern was the one in charge of her marriage contract. Then King Nathal would have to be contacted.

Did the king have to know he'd taken her already?

Alasdair frowned. Admitting Elissa was no longer a virgin was the quickest way to marriage.

Damn. Hope no one — including Lord Cam — wants to run me *through.*

Perhaps it was a boon that the Duke of Dalunas had left Greenwald. He was about to steal the man's betrothed.

Alasdair made a fist, but his stomach somersaulted.

Am I really going to do this?

"I have to." Couldn't see her marry another man. Not when he— "No." He still couldn't put words to the tightness in his gut, to the thunder of his heart. He just refused to lose her.

Alasdair had wanted Lady Elissa Durroc from the moment he'd seen her. Now he'd had her, and he couldn't look back. Wasn't going to let her go.

She would be his wife — whether she wanted to or not.

☆   ☆   ☆   ☆

Her whole body shook as she reached for the decorative handle when Lord Jorrin called for her to enter. Elissa bowed to him and ploughed forward, taking a seat without looking around. Her heart thundered, resounding in her ears.

"Good morning, my lady." His smile was pleasant. His handsome face and tapered ears drew her gaze and she hollered at herself to calm.

"Good morning, my lord."

Lord Jorrin's smile widened and they made their way through more polite conversation. She was more nervous with every word that wasn't about her purpose for meeting with the Duke of Greenwald.

"I've chosen a husband."

"Oh?" Lord Jorrin arched a dark eyebrow, his gaze now piercing more than friendly.

Elissa nodded and launched into her decision. Without giving the duke a chance to answer, she fired off questions about her dowry, the marriage contract, her property of birth, and even the impending journey to her betrothed's home Province.

After answering her barrage of demands, Lord Jorrin was quiet—too quiet. He met her eyes head-on, and she tried to concentrate on anything but his face. "Are you sure about this?"

"Aye, my lord." Elissa tried not to look at the empathic half-elfin duke. He was staring, and she didn't like the look in his deep blue eyes. She could barely meet him in those eyes, anyway. They were too much like Alasdair's.

She had to choke back a sob at the mere thought of his name. Elissa sat taller and looked around the ledger room. The same room from which she'd overheard the devastating news about her family. She tried not to think about that, because then she'd be angry at King Nathal all over again. Then she'd think about running away, and how Alasdair had kissed her for the first time in the castle she'd been born in.

Her stomach clenched and she swallowed.

Elissa studied the map on the wall. It was a replica of the one in the great hall Lady Cera was so proud of, but smaller. She looked at the duke's bookshelves full of castle ledgers, rather than a library of pleasure reading.

"My lady…" His hesitation brought her gaze back to him. He looked concerned, with more than a touch of worry in the tightness of his dark brow.

"I've made my decision, Lord Jorrin." She cursed the shake of her voice and made her mouth curve up in the semblance of a smile.

The Duke of Greenwald sighed and leaned back in his chair. He dropped the feathered pen he'd been writing with. It gave a soft *thump*, landing next to the inkwell on his desk. "You do realize your every word is at odds with your emotions?"

Elissa startled on the edge of the chair. "You do realize it's impolite to use your magic without permission, let alone point out what…I'm feeling."

Lord Aldern smirked. "I figured it'd do no good to censor our conversation. As far as picking up what you feel, I can't help it. Your emotions are…overt."

Heat curled around the back of her neck and took over her cheeks. Elissa looked down and clutched her hands together in her lap. His response had been amused, and preferred to what he could've said to her. She'd been abrupt. Rude. However, she didn't want to apologize.

She cleared her throat and looked back at the duke. "Lord Cam is a good man."

"Yes, he is." Lord Jorrin narrowed his eyes and tilted his chin up.

"I look forward to going to Dalunas."

"Do you?"

"Aye." Elissa forced a nod.

"I'm going to ask you something, my lady, and I urge you to be honest with me."

Her heart stuttered. "Very well."

"Do you *honestly* want to wed Lord Camden Malloch?" His sapphire gaze was keen.

Nay. "Aye."

Disappointment darted across Lord Jorrin's handsome face. His lips parted, but he paused, as if he'd changed his mind about what he'd planned to say.

Elissa sucked in her cheek and bit down. Perhaps even if he hadn't been an empath he would've known she was lying. "I feel this way, because choosing a husband is a difficult task." Another lie.

"It can be." His tone called her the liar she was, even if he was too polite to do so aloud. "I'm sure King Nathal wouldn't have tasked you with the decision if he didn't think you capable."

"Lord Cam is a wonderful man," she repeated, because she didn't know what else to say. Elissa wasn't capable of choosing, because she'd fallen in love with a man who didn't want her. A man who wasn't on her list of choices anyway, so it didn't really matter.

Lord Jorrin nodded, as if he didn't know what to say about her repetition, either. He took a breath. "If you're sure about this, I'll have Gamel draw up the contract and send our resident Senior Rider to inform the king."

King Nathal had posted Senior Riders at all the major holdings in the Provinces for about the last turn. It was at the suggestion of Sir Leargan, and the goal was to keep communication open and prevent tragedy such as what had happened to Lady Cera's family.

As Elissa understood it, the king's messengers rotated out every six months. The current Rider in Greenwald was a stunning blonde lass named Jinala. She was bonded to the biggest bobcat Elissa had ever seen. The Senior Rider went by Jin and got cross with anyone who dared use her full given name. She was petite and full of fire. Elissa had liked her from the moment they'd met.

"I'm sure." She nodded and clenched her hands so tight her nails bit into her palms.

"Very well." Lord Jorrin's tone said it was anything but.

"Why don't you want this for me?" she blurted. Elissa touched her cheek when the duke aimed the full force of his gaze at her.

"Because *you* don't want it."

"I do."

Lord Jorrin cleared his throat and gave a curt nod. "As you wish, my lady." He grabbed his pen, dipped it in the inkwell and started to jot something on the parchment in front of him. "Cera says you and Mischief should only need a few more lessons. She says your bond is surprisingly strong for one so new. Soon you'll be free to go. I'll have you escorted to Dalunas."

Elissa swallowed as mixed emotions churned her stomach. She didn't want to think about leaving Greenwald. Going to live with — and *marry* — Lord Cam.

She scrambled to her feet and curtseyed to the half-elfin duke. "Thank you, my lord. Everyone has been wonderful to me and I've enjoyed my stay." She needed to meet Lady Cera in the duchess solar for her lesson.

Her bondmate had been sent there to wait for her. Mischief had begrudgingly agreed. He'd wanted to be with her for her assignation with the duke. Even after such a short time, it was odd to have him missing from her side. No doubt he'd felt her nerves even if he couldn't understand them.

Again, the duke looked as if he'd say something, but thought better of it. He offered a slight smile and nod. "Good day, Lady Elissa."

"Good day." She inclined her head and turned to go, before she could give in to temptation to spill the truth and reject Lord Cam's suit. But she'd given her word and she'd see it through.

Alasdair had made himself plain with his third and final rejection.

Too bad it'd left her heartbroken.

Chapter Twenty-eight

Three sevendays later, Lord Cam answered her missive with enthusiasm.

"Of course he did," Elissa whispered. She swallowed and read the letter again—she'd lost count of how many times and yet it hadn't made her feel any better. *'You won't regret it,'* and *'I cannot wait to call you wife,'* jumped out at her. Her stomach roiled.

She'd written him with shaky hands the very morning she'd left Lord Jorrin's ledger room after telling him what she'd decided. She didn't even remember what she'd jotted to her future husband, she just remembered the letters didn't look like her own hand when she'd finished.

At evening meal that night, the duke had announced her betrothal to everyone in the great hall. Congratulations, hugs, and clapping had just about killed her. Elissa couldn't look at Alasdair—who'd been true to his word about being replaced. Sir Bowen had sat at her side on the dais, then and now, as her new chaperone. She should've considered it a blessing her knight had been so far away.

Every day of the agonizing last three sevendays he'd done the same. She'd barely been able to lay eyes on him at all.

Mischief whimpered and shot to her side from the hearth. He put his head on her lap without invitation, but she buried her fingers in the soft fur between his ears. Her bondmate was her saving grace right now. If it wasn't for him…well, she would've been mired in *more* despair than what currently weighed her down.

He didn't understand the heartache she was feeling, but in his primal innocence, he loved her. Constantly reinforced that love, wrapping her in comforting thoughts.

Elissa needed it to make it through.

Three long sevendays since she'd given herself to Alasdair, and had her heart crushed…

She was sick of crying. Sick of hugging her pillow and thinking of him. Wishing she could smell him on the bed linens that had been changed out several times.

Elissa had told Jonah, her monthly had started unexpectedly—to explain the blood on the sheets the morning after. Of course, she'd never be questioned, but she didn't need castle staff gossiping, either. She'd played off her reservations, even mentioning that she'd been planning to see Lord Tristan straightway for unbearable feminine cramping. She'd grabbed her middle for good measure. Truth was, her body *had* ached, but it had nothing to do with menstruation.

Thank the Blessed Spirit the lass's expression had softened with sympathy. The maid had confided that she, too, got bad pains every month.

Since then, she'd stayed in her room as much as she could—but she couldn't avoid meals, her new chaperone or her bond lessons with the duchess.

Sir Bowen, the handsome knight with sandy hair and a dimple in one cheek. He was witty, funny and *very* nice to her, but Elissa hadn't felt like talking. He seemed to understand, which just made her feel guilty, instead of comforted.

She didn't feel pressure when they were together, she just missed Alasdair so much she felt as if she was dying. All the time. Then she would get angry at herself—because where was the strength she'd always prided herself on?

Elissa constantly asked herself if she was really so weak.

The knock on the door made her jump. Mischief whined and reared back, but she smoothed his hackles and soothed him mentally, as Lady Cera had taught her.

"I'm sorry I'm such a mess. It's not your fault," she told her bondmate.

Mischief swished his tail once when they made eye-contact. He sent her reassurance and love. Her wolf might not comprehend all her words, but he did her emotions... her wallowing.

"Issa?" A female voice on the other side of the door made her perk up.

She couldn't holler for the Duchess of Greenwald to enter her suite—it wouldn't be proper. Elissa hurried to the door. She bowed to Lady Cera. "My lady?"

"Oh, stop. Say it with me. Cera. Cera. Cera." She spaced out her name, but her expression was amused, not annoyed.

Heat shot into her face. "Cera," she whispered.

The duchess smiled. "See, that wasn't so hard, was it?" Cera took her hand and squeezed. "I'm sorry if I embarrassed you. May I come in?"

"You didn't embarrass me," Elissa muttered. She scooted back in the room so Cera could enter.

"I just assumed by now, after all the shared meals and the bondmate training, that you and I were friends."

She was able to smile genuinely when she met the lady's gray eyes. "We are, of course."

Cera looked around the room with interest, then plopped down on the end of the bed, as if she was a young lass instead of a lady with the power to run a Province. She was clad in tan hide breeches that looked soft to the touch, and an ivory tunic. Her mass of dark red curls was loose down her back. "Good."

Elissa wandered over to the bed, in lieu of pacing or impolitely demanding why Cera had come to her rooms.

Mischief greeted the duchess with enthusiasm, jumping on the bed, and licking her face. Cera laughed and scratched him behind the ear.

Silence fell.

Elissa shifted back and forth in her ladies' slippers while the Duchess of Greenwald couldn't look more relaxed on her bed. Mischief had moved, he lay beside her.

"How are you, Issa?"

She startled.

"Something wrong?" Cera arched an auburn eyebrow.

She shook her head. "Nay." Elissa clutched her hands in front of her, then threw them behind her back.

"Hmm, are you sure? You look nervous. Have a seat. Relax. This is your place, after all."

"As you wish." She gave half-bow and dragged the chair she'd been sitting in moment before away from the desk. Swinging it around, Elissa took a seat across from the duchess. "Did you...need something...from me?"

Cera shook her head. Her curls danced. "Not particularly. Just wanted to chat."

"Ah. We could go to the solar."

"Here is fine."

"All...right."

"Are you ready to depart for Dalunas?" Cera asked, as if Elissa hadn't struggled to speak a moment before.

She sat taller. "I am. Senior Rider Jin brought me Lord Cam's message. All is well, and he awaits me."

The duchess looked down, then stroked her hand along Mischief's back. "Is that what you want?" The question was nonchalant, but when Cera looked up, Elissa was pinned by her gray gaze.

It took everything she was made of to not glance away. "Aye. Of course." She tried to make her lips curve up.

Mouth. Smile. Now. But Elissa couldn't. She swallowed and tried with all her might not to shift in the chair.

The duchess didn't move, nor did she pause in her caresses of Mischief's silver fur. "Are you sure?"

"Aye." She sat taller.

Cera harrumphed.

Elissa's heart sank.

Please, Blessed Spirit, don't mention Alasdair.

The duchess straightened on the bed, pulling her hand away from Elissa's wolfling. Mischief uttered a protest in his throat and stretched, bumping into her, pleading for more attention.

They both admonished him at the same time and then locked eyes. The laugh bubbled up from nowhere, and Cera laughed, too. Elissa blew out a breath and relaxed into the back of the carved chair. The tension snapped, just like that. *Thank you, Mischief.*

Her bondmate sent her a quizzical thought, and she grinned. She'd accidentally thought-sent.

"Sorry, I shouldn't scold him. He's all yours now." Cera flashed a lopsided smile.

"It's perfectly fine, you were his...mother...for longer than I've been."

The duchess looked at the wolfling and he wagged his tail. Her smile slid into a grin. "I was, wasn't I? Well, I'm glad he has you now."

"So am I. I'm more grateful for him than I can put into words."

Cera nodded and slid to her feet. "You don't have to put it into words. I see it when you two are together. I'm glad he rejected all the bondmates I offered before you arrived."

"He was meant to be mine." Elissa sent him love and warmth, which he returned. Her body relaxed even more.

"I agree." Cera paused. "Well, I just wanted to check on you. From what Jorrin told me, you should pack your things. I think your party will pull out of here in a day or two."

"Aye, thank you, my—Cera."

Her mock-glare evaporated when Elissa said her given name. The duchess grinned again and inclined her head. "Dalunas is a hard ride, but with Alasdair leading the charge, you'll be fine."

"A-a-a-lasdair?" Elissa stumbled over his name and braced herself on the chair arms, her feeling of contentment due to her bondmate's love dying as if it'd never been born.

Cera raised an auburn eyebrow. "Aye," she said slowly, but her gaze was keen all over again. "He insisted upon it, though he's not really leading the party. Leargan is going. Along with Lucan, for magical protection."

He...wants to see me off? Why?

Her stomach turned inside and out. She swallowed the bile rising in her throat. Exquisite torture...to have him see her off. She'd walk away from the man she couldn't seem to stop loving, only to marry one she couldn't seem to start.

"Is something wrong, Issa?"

"Nay, my lady." Elissa shook her head, but her denial was automatic. The room started to spin. She flexed her fingers on the chair and begged it to stop.

"Are you sure?"

She was coming to *hate* that phrase. Elissa shook herself and tried to release her death grip. "I'm well."

The look that crossed the duchess' face called her a liar.

Mischief whined, and Cera shot him a look before meeting Elissa's eyes again. "You can talk to me, you know. Friends and all that."

Blessed Spirit, I want to.

Her bottom lip wobbled and she bit it so she wouldn't release the hovering whimper. "I know. Thank you."

Cera stared a moment longer. "There's nothing you want to tell me? Something you need get off your chest?"

She forced a smile she didn't feel. "Nay, but again, I thank you for the offer." Silence fell, so she rose from the chair to distract them both. "I'm feeling a bit woozy, so I think I shall lie down."

"Do you need Tristan?" the duchess asked.

"Nay. Just a lie-down shall fix me up. Then…I have to start packing. I'll see you at evening meal in the great hall." Elissa intentionally let her gaze sweep the room so she could avoid Cera's too-knowing eyes.

"All right. If you need something, please call. I won't send you off if you're under the weather. Tristan will examine you. If you need to rest more after that, we'll postpone things a day or two. Or a sevenday. Whatever might be needed." She brooked no argument, so Elissa just nodded.

The duchess left then and she barred the door as soon as it was closed. She collapsed on the huge bed next to her bondmate, throwing her arms around him and burying her face against his soft fur.

Mischief whined and nuzzled her.

Elissa cried until her mouth and throat were so dry her body begged her to call to the water.

Damn Sir Alasdair Kearney.

☆   ☆   ☆   ☆

"Marry me."

Her heart catapulted against her ribs. Elissa faced the warm fire, spreading her hands before it. She couldn't look at him. If she did, she'd utter the word that wanted to break the seal of her lips. *Aye.* With all her heart—her body, her soul—she wanted to shout she would marry him.

The man I love.

"You don't mean that," she said instead, still unable to turn toward him. "Please leave my rooms."

Why did he wait three sevendays to ask, anyway? If he truly meant it, if he truly wanted her, he would've come back to her much sooner, instead of ignoring her for the last three sevendays.

Not the night before she was leaving to be delivered to the man she'd marry.

He hadn't said a word after dinner, either. Of course, Sir Bowen had sat beside her on the dais, but after their meal, her new chaperone had taken her to the personal guard's table.

She'd spoken to most of the knights of the guard, met the wives of the married ones, and sat talking to lovely Lyde, wife of Sir Niall, second-in-command to Sir Leargan. She'd also chatted with Daicy, who was married to Sir Merrick, Meara, who was married to Sir Laith, Sir Padraig's wife, Briella, and of course, Avril.

The lasses were as much of a group amongst themselves as the knights. Sisters.

It'd been a wonderful, lighthearted evening. She'd even danced a few times with different partners.

Elissa didn't need Alasdair shattering what little joy she'd mustered. He'd burst through her door much like the night they'd made love.

She needed him to leave. Now.

"Elissa."

Her heart stuttered.

"Lass, look at me."

"Nay," she whispered, but against her will, her body pivoted. Her gaze darted to his handsome face, then she lowered her lashes. She couldn't look at him...risk seeing those blue eyes with feeling in them.

It hurt. Everything...hurt.

"Elissa."

Her name on his lips for the second time had her wringing her hands in front of her so she could keep her gaze low.

"I do mean it, lass. Marry me. Not Lord Cam. Me."

She shook her head. Crushed her eyes shut at his sincerity. "Nay. I can't. I gave my word to the duke."

"But you don't love him."

Elissa squared her shoulders. "What I feel for my betrothed is none of your concern, Sir Alasdair."

He winced and she tried to ignore the guilt that roiled her gut.

"My decision has been made. I won't marry you because you say you mean it, when in reality, I'm nothing but an obligation to you."

"It's true I took your innocence and have a duty to—"

"See? You even say it yourself. Obviously you've been wrestling with the decision over the last three sevendays. No worries, Sir Alasdair. I release you from any obligation to me. I'm marrying the Duke of Dalunas."

"And what of your wedding night? When your *husband* realizes he is not the first man between your legs?"

Elissa jolted. He'd been crude, but her belly warmed and memories of them entwined assaulted her. "None of *your* concern."

"You told me you love me."

Shock washed her blood to her toes. She blinked. Felt as if she'd been slapped. Her magic tingled. *How dare he?* "I lied."

Alasdair narrowed his eyes. If the next words out of his mouth were a confession of like feelings, Elissa didn't know what she'd do. She sucked back a whimper.

"You did not."

"Didn't what?" she croaked.

"Lie."

"I did. I don't love you." She had to lock her jaw to keep from taking it back. "It was as you said. I confused lust with tender feelings. I know better now."

Something darted across his face. Something emotional. Something that made her want to declare loud and fast that she was lying *now*.

He stared until she shifted on her feet. The apple of his throat bobbed. "Fine."

Elissa startled. She hadn't expected him to acquiesce.

"We leave in the morning."

"Leave?" She was already packed. She'd known they'd go at first light, but the question had fallen out of her mouth anyway. Because it was a reminder *he* was going, too.

"Aye, I'm taking you to your betrothed." Alasdair whirled around. He disappeared in his rooms, shutting the door with a *thud* that resounded in her head. And her heart.

Elissa's knees buckled and she doubled over with a sob she had no right to.

Marriage.

"He didn't mean it."

And he'd not argued with her…much. Hadn't insisted he wanted her. Made no declaration of love, only accused her of lying about her own feelings.

He hadn't *fought* for her.

Alasdair had left her rooms. Walked away.

Like she'd demanded.

Her vision blurred and Elissa cried as hard as she had the night she'd given herself to him.

If Alasdair was only doing what *she'd* asked, why did it hurt so much?

Chapter Twenty-nine

The next morning arrived much too soon, and she couldn't shake the sense of foreboding that clung to her like the fat gray clouds grouped together above. The unusual warmth of the Greenwald fall had faded. It was chilly; the wind was blowing as if her magic had called to it. The air smelled clean, but with the barest kiss of winter.

Hope it's warmer further south.

That was the only positive thing about their direction of travel. Dalunas was far southeast, and had much milder winters than the northern Provinces.

Elissa's ears stung with the wind's strength as she made her way across the courtyard to where her escort party waited. Knights of the guard and men-at-arms chatted, laughed and threw quips at each other.

They seemed excited as they prepared for the journey, tossing packs back and forth and stacking supplies on the racks of the carriage they were bringing. She'd already told the captain she'd prefer to ride her gray mare than sit inside, so her mount was waiting with the other horses; she could see the horse saddled and ready.

Mischief darted ahead, wuffing a few times as if scolding her to hurry up, but his thoughts and feelings were encouraging. He, too, was looking forward to leaving, seeing the world. He wagged his tail at a few of the men, then proceeded to sniff out a perimeter around their gathering spot.

She swallowed; couldn't even muster a smile for her wolfling's delight. More dread hovered and she shook herself, tightening her mantel around her, squaring her shoulders. She didn't tug her hood up because she didn't want obscured vision but the air was cold enough to merit it.

Her new chaperone bowed deeply and Elissa took his arm when offered. She muttered a polite greeting for him, as well as Sir Leargan when the captain threw her a smile.

Sir Bowen helped her atop the gray mare's back. Although she said nothing, she really didn't need assistance, despite her gowned attire. She ignored his large hands around her waist. His grip wasn't unpleasant or unwelcome, but she couldn't stop thinking about Alasdair touching her in the same way the day she'd run away—what now seemed like ages ago. Then the other times he'd touched her body, clothed or unclothed.

Elissa shivered and pushed away the unwanted memories. She forced a smile and met the knight's unusual whiskey colored eyes. "Thank you."

"Anytime, my lady." He grinned, flashing his single dimple.

She told herself to relax. And failed.

"If you get tired, alert me, and you can get in the carriage. Are you sure you don't want to ride inside? Lord Cam left it especially for you."

She looked at the ornate coach, carved decorative edges all over and painted in Dalunas' bright colors. "I prefer the open air of a ride, but thank you."

He nodded. "Well, it's handy to have for supplies, but it's yours. Remember that. Whatever you want, my lady."

Elissa made herself nod as emotion hit her square in the chest.

I can't have whatever I want.

Her magic tingled and Mischief whimpered from where he stood. He sniffed the air and cocked his head to one side when they made eye contact.

The knight paused, glancing at her wolf, then back at her. "Are you well, my lady?"

She sent a mental calm to her bondmate and forced her lips to curve upward for her chaperone. "Aye, thank you for asking, Sir Bowen."

"You can just call me Bowen, my lady."

"Thank you." Elissa brushed a wisp of her hair away from her face when the wind caused it to tickle her cheek. She wouldn't call the knight by his given name even with permission. It'd only remind her of the knight she'd lost.

Sir Bowen offered another curt nod, then he was gone. She noticed him conversing with his captain and then Sir Dallon. The other men were scattered around the bailey, but she could see that preparations were close to being finished; quite a few men were already on horseback.

What's the delay?

When two men lead their horses from the tied group, she spotted Contessa standing alone. The mare was saddled and ready, but her rider had yet to arrive.

Her heart skipped. She didn't want to see him.

Sir Lucan sidled up to her on the back of a sleek black mare. His horse's closeness forced Mischief to move away. Her wolfling howled a protest. The young mage apologized to the wolf, which made Elissa give a genuine giggle. It surprised her, but was welcome, just like the knighted mage's appearance. Maybe the lad could keep her mind off the man she told herself she wasn't anticipating.

"Good morning, Lady Elissa. Are you well?"

"I am. How are you this morning?" She inclined her head. "What a fine horse you have there."

His cheeks pinkened but he nodded and patted his mare's neck. "I'm well. Thank you. She was a gift from Jorrin and Cera. Her name is Obsidian, but I call her Sid. Her sire is Cera's Ash."

"She's gorgeous." Elissa's mount neighed and shifted. She patted her and whispered calming reassurance.

"Your horse is fine as well, what's her name?"

It was her turn to be embarrassed. She touched her cheek. "I haven't named her yet. The king gave her to me only before we left to come here."

"Ah, well maybe something will come to you."

Elissa thought of the run they'd had, and how her mare had been spooked when Tess and Alasdair had chased them. She'd made it worse when she'd lost control of her magic. "Actually…" She looked down at her mare's gray mane. It was several shades lighter than her dark gray coat. Like Mischief, she was multihued silver.

Sir Lucan grinned. "Did you think of a name?"

"I think so."

"I'm excited to be the first to hear it."

She flashed a grin, feeding off his excitement. "Storm. I'll call her Storm."

"I love it!" The young mage clapped once. His mare whinnied and Storm echoed it, fidgeting again.

"Hush, lass. I mean, Storm. Do you like your name?" Elissa whispered, caressing the supple warm flesh of the mare's neck. The horse calmed and whinnied again, soft this time.

"I think she approves!" Sir Lucan said.

Her smile widened, and some weight lifted from her chest. "I'm glad. I like her very much."

One of the knights hollered.

Sir Lucan looked around. "Looks like we're going to head out."

"Aye." Movement to the right, toward the castle caught her eye, then stole her breath.

Despite the fact he stalked across the bailey with a tight expression she could see even from his current distance, Alasdair was gorgeous.

His long dark hair billowed with his movements and the pack slung over his shoulders made her think of his muscles. Her knight's clothing was a mix of browns and Greenwald colors, complete with an embroidered doublet with the Province's howling white wolf seal on it. The silver roping on his right shoulder indicated his place in the duke's personal guard.

He didn't look her way, but she couldn't stop staring, even as he secured his things and greeted his brothers and the men-at-arms.

Sir Leargan was leading the party, but a mix of men would accompany them. Several knights of the guard, Sir Bowen, Sir Dallon, and Sir Kale, in addition to Alasdair as well as half a dozen other Greenwald soldiers and Sir Lucan, for his magic.

Elissa made her gaze sweep the courtyard—*away* from Alasdair. Her stomach flip-flopped and Mischief whimpered again, but she didn't calm him. She glanced at Castle Aldern—a place she'd come to love, as well as the people who lived there.

I don't want to go.

The realization was like a ton of bricks crushing her. She didn't want to leave this place, where she'd found *her* place. Where she'd made friends who were more like sisters, in a way, closer to her than her cousin or little Princess Mallyn.

Her unease wasn't wholly because of the man who'd smashed her heart.

"Are you ready?" Sir Bowen guided his chestnut stallion close.

Elissa jolted, then forced a nod.

Sir Lucan flashed a grin and a nod for her chaperone.

"We'll ride as far as we can today, but if you need a break for any reason, you let me know." The knight's tone brooked no argument, proving Sir Bowen could be as stubborn, too. "Sometimes a group of men travels hard, and we've far to go. If we need a reminder we travel with a lady, please do so." He smiled, showing his charming dimple.

She relaxed in her saddle. "I will."

A curt nod was all the response she got, and he turned his horse around.

Sir Leargan called out and they moved as one, making their way through the multiple sets of castle gates.

The guards they passed saluted.

When they got out to the road, the carriage lead, with only one rider ahead of it. Elissa looked left and right. The knights surrounded her, riding in a protective formation. They'd take up the entire width of the road this way, but no one seemed to take note or break off to ride in front of her, or behind.

Sir Lucan stayed close, and they exchanged a smile.

Mischief barked and ran ahead, causing a few chuckles from the men.

"He's going to get awfully tired if he plans to do that whole time," Sir Bowen called. His voice was clear, and instinct told her he was right behind her. Close, on Storm's right flank.

Elissa giggled. "He can always ride in the carriage."

Sir Lucan laughed beside her, and so did a few of the knights within hearing range.

She settled in for the long ride and loosened her death-grip on the reins. Needed to relax so her body wouldn't be so stiff.

Alasdair was out of sight, so she could only figure he was bringing up the rear of their party. Elissa needed him to stay where he was. She might not be able to banish him from her thoughts, but at least she didn't have to look at him.

★   ★   ★   ★

He saw the wolf dart from the gates and waited, watching, expecting the other three wolves to be behind the silver beast. They didn't appear.

The thud of horses' hooves — a lot of them — followed instead, as well as the creak of carriage wheels.

The wolf paused, throwing a barking-howl over his shoulder as he waited for whatever was behind him to catch up.

Charis perked up when the large party came into view, exiting the castle's gates.

Bracken nudged him, but he hadn't missed miss a thing. "Noble carriage."

"I agree. Dalunas colors." Charis didn't tear his eyes away from the group, even when he heard Bracken's grunt in answer.

Nason didn't comment, but he shifted his feet beside them.

They watched Castle Aldern's gates from a safe distance, but where they could still the comings and goings. Perched behind an abandoned shop barely on the crest of the square. Many people trudged by, but no one seemed to give the place a second look. No wonder the former business — whatever it'd been — had failed. The building was small and invisible out in the open. And falling apart. The former sign hung by one nail, and the words were so faded they were unreadable.

Charis hadn't asked questions, just darted behind it the first chance he'd been out of keen marshal purview. Bracken and Nason had followed.

It'd been two whole sevendays since he'd seen the wolf for the first time and his gut had shouted what he sought was *inside* Castle Aldern. He'd been contemplating *how* they'd get within since then.

Charis had charged Nason and Bracken with observing as much as they could and not get caught. They'd followed knights and men-at-arms to many taverns, watched them ascend countless sets of stairs with willing lasses.

Nothing had come of it.

Even the whores that lay with the personal guard were loyal to the men. No amount of coin promised had loosened feminine lips.

There was nothing of consequence in the conversations they'd overheard, either.

He was beyond frustrated, and Drayton's patience was tried. He'd told the old mage what he thought about where the lass was, but the codger was as skeptical as his lads.

They'd seen the wolves come and go several times as a pack. Each time, Charis studied the bond to the extent he was capable. He was sure the silver wolf was bonded to the elemental mage Drayton was paying him to find.

"Look. A lass. On that gray horse," Bracken said.

One look in her direction went from glance to stare.

A lass indeed.

Charis stared. Wanted to rub his eyes.

Magic blinded him. Had him doubting what he could see. What he *was* seeing.

She had to be *the lass.*

Everything hit at once, he didn't need to probe or use his powers. He understood why magic—his own and Drayton's—had failed to find her.

The protection spell covering the petite form on horseback was woven as tightly as the one covering Castle Aldern. And had the same magical trail. Both had been cast by the same mage. But her tie to the wolf was thick, brighter, as the beast made its way to her side, so Charis hadn't been wrong. The wolf was covered in elemental magic, and he was bonded to the lass protected by a spell that made her magically invisible.

The source of both rode next to her, on a black horse. A lad, not quite a man, if his frame was any indication. His magical aura was so radiant Charis had to look away. "It *has* to be her."

"Let's get her then." Bracken stepped forward, but Charis grabbed his thick forearm.

"Don't be a fool." He looked back at the party. "There are knights there. Four...no, five, not to mention other soldiers."

"I'm no' afraid of a good fight."

"Neither am I." Nason flexed his skinny hand on the hilt of his sword, but he didn't draw it.

"And neither am I. But we have to be smart about this. You want to get paid, don't you?"

Both his companions nodded.

"They'll stick to the main roads, no doubt. We get the horses. Catch up. Then we wait. We watch. Attack when they're vulnerable. Away from reinforcements." He thumbed toward the castle.

Again, Nason and Bracken nodded. Almost made him want to remark on their rare agreement.

Charis glanced over his shoulder toward the party of knights, then back at his lads. "The dark-haired lad worries me," he admitted.

"The skinny one riding next to the lass?" Bracken cocked a dark brow.

"Aye, it's as if he's made of magic." What he left unsaid was the lad was the source of the protection spells. Charis couldn't wrap his head around how one lad had done both acts of such power, all on his own. "I need to consult with Drayton."

Nason made a face. "If that's her, we can't afford ta miss 'em. Need ta go now."

"I agree."

Narrow shoulders relaxed. "Good."

"You two get your horses and go. I'll consult Drayton and catch up."

Bracken paused and studied him. "You need to tell 'im now?"

"Aye, and not much time for it, either. If the colors on that carriage mean they're headed to Dalunas, we need to catch them before they get too far."

Nason shuddered; the apple of his throat bobbed. "I've no need ta get near Dread Valley."

"Dalunas is a fortnight's ride, or more." Bracken smirked.

"But still—"

"Just go. Before they get too far." Charis had no use for Nason and Bracken bickering. Time was of the essence, *finally*. "Bracken," he called when the big oaf's back and shoulders faced him.

"Aye?"

"Don't do anything stupid. I'll catch up. Only observe until I arrive."

Narrowed eyes presented the only answer he got, but it was acquiescence enough. Bracken wouldn't jeopardize the potential coin purse for getting the lass to Drayton alive.

He forced a breath and closed his eyes. Didn't want to contact the old codger. His gut told him the lass was destined for blood magic. Which would make Drayton infinitely powerful.

Why do you care? Charis didn't.

With a curse, he pushed off the side of the decrepit building and dug in his pocket for the small mirror he'd been communicating with Drayton through. He'd stolen it from his last whore at a tavern in Greenwald Main, and it fit nicely in his palm. A little large for his pocket, but he made it work. Besides, the smaller the better; that meant less of Drayton's ugly face he had space to see.

He whispered the spellwords and waited.

The mirror started to glow, then the portal opened. Magic, appearing as an opaque cloud, slowly started to clear, revealing the dimness of Drayton's cave. Charis couldn't see much; the mirror he'd called to was perched high on the wall above the old mage's sleeping pallet. That he knew from memory of the layout. It was much larger than his own mirror. A magic torch was above it, but it didn't illuminate more than the reflection of the opposite wall. At this distance, it was just bumpy-looking and brown; undefined.

"My lord?" he called. When he didn't receive an answer, he cleared his throat and tried again, this time louder. Impatience got the best of him, and Charis started pacing behind the small building, clutching his small mirror high and tight, until sharp edges bit his fingers.

"Half-breed."

He glared on instinct. Sucked back a curse and schooled his expression fast, Drayton could see him, after all.

They made eye contact and Drayton arched a busy eyebrow. It wasn't as gray as it had been. "What news have you?"

"I've found her."

Delight took over the old mage's lined face. Charis could feel his excitement, even though he wasn't an empath, and even though they only spoke face-to-face via a spell. "Where?"

"She was in Castle Aldern after all. Until this morning."

"Tell me."

The order should've irritated; he launched into what he knew instead, revealing his worries about the lad that'd performed the protection spells. Charis told Drayton how his aura had glowed and how much power had radiated from his thin frame.

"He is Sir Lucan, the only Mage of Greenwald."

Only mage?

Most noble households employed as many mages as they could get—if they didn't have magic of their own. Charis wasn't about to ask questions, though. "You know him?"

"Only *of* him, and rumors of great power. You're right to be concerned."

"Then—?" He didn't want to voice his whole thought—*then how am I supposed to get the lass?* Couldn't afford to look weak in front of Drayton.

"Stand back, I have something for you. Something that can help."

He frowned. "Stand back? Wha—?"

"Just do as I say," Drayton commanded.

Charis growled low, then belatedly hoped the codger hadn't heard it. Both of them had kissed their patience goodbye.

Now it was different. She was so close. Everything had more urgency.

He did as the old mage had instructed, but Charis could still see him on the surface of the small mirror. "What are you going to do?" He cleared his throat and reminded himself to appear respectful. "If I may ask, my lord."

Drayton didn't spare him a glance, but he did answer. "A reverse retrieval spell. To send you something."

"Send me what?"

"Something I've been keeping as a secret weapon."

Charis wanted to roll his eyes. Why was the old mage being anticlimactic? He changed his mind when he took another look at his employer. Drayton's expression was tight and there was a tremor to his jaw.

Whatever the codger had—

Is he afraid?

He narrowed his eyes and concentrated until he could see Drayton's black ringed aura. Yellow wariness was all over it. Sometimes colors varied in people—bright white could be extreme fear or joy, but Charis' gut told him he was seeing a negative emotion. As if Drayton didn't trust what he was about to 'gift.'

Great.

Drayton started to chant, panting harder with each word of the spell. Even so, the air in front of Charis didn't start to ripple until he'd been at it a good ten minutes.

Soon, a small buzz sounded, causing Charis' to wince. His ears were more sensitive than a full-blooded human. The buzz whistled until it was so high pitched any dog within hearing range would probably start to howl.

Attention he didn't need.

He didn't dare interrupt his employer, though.

Something hit the ground with a *thud* and Charis stepped forward to lean over the small object. He coughed, and his stomach coiled from the inside out. He fought not to liberate his last meal.

Drayton's chuckle had him glaring. Shouldn't the old arse be taxed after such a spell? He'd just sent something from Terraquist to Greenwald. Charis didn't calculate the distance. Trying not to be openly offensive to the old mage was an afterthought. "What the hell is that?"

"Dimithian."

His heart dropped to his stomach. "Nay..." Childhood horror stories churned in his head, memories of an animated old elf wizard scaring children by firelight under the guise of magic lessons hit him in the chest like a brick wall.

Breathe. In. Out. Repeat.

He cleared his throat and tried again. "Dimithian isn't real."

For the second time, a cackle was the first response he got. "That's what the great elfin clan chiefs in all their wisdom want you to believe."

Charis swallowed—two or three times. Avoided looking at the little black menace, though it had to be a dud. It wasn't taking his magic away. He was just repulsed. He slid back two more steps, evidently to Drayton's delight, because the old mage laughed again.

"In its current state, my Dimithian can't hurt you. It's covered in a protection shield."

Since when can Drayton read minds?

Fear skittered down his spine, as much as he hated to admit it. "Ah." He let his gaze dart to the dark stone and back to his employer—whose eyes still danced at him in the mirror. Charis had never seen the codger so upbeat. He sucked back a growl, since it was at his own expense.

Although it'd always been his policy to never ask questions, a plethora swirled around about the supposed-mythical element in front of his eyes. Maybe Drayton really was from Aramour originally, despite his odd accent.

"Keep the shield in place at all times, unless you're using the rock's powers. Do not touch it with your bare hands even then. It will take your magic, too."

"How?" Charis croaked.

"It works like a storage device, but only for a time. If the magic is not transferred or claimed, one of two things can happen."

"What?" His fascination and revulsion were equal, and he couldn't stop staring at what was no doubt, many a mages' demise.

"The magic dissipates and returns to its natural possessor on its own, if not taken with the right spell by another. Or—" Drayton paused.

"Or, what?" Charis barked.

Annoyance glittered in the codger's eyes. Evidently he didn't like his storytelling rushed. "It explodes. Of course the damage scale of such a thing would depend on what kind of magic it holds at the time."

"How do you know the difference in what it will do?"

"You don't. That's why it's so feared. So dangerous. It can be very unstable."

"Yet you want me to use it?"

Drayton laughed again. Charis' anger rolled over into a slow boil.

"Calm, half-breed. I've had this chunk for many turns. Keeping it shielded has altered the stability. No harm will come to you or your magic."

Again, inquires he never gave swirled around in his the back of his mouth. *Why do you need me if you had Dimithian all this time?* led the charge, but he held his tongue.

"What do I do if I need to use it?" Charis gulped, trying not to look at what he'd eventually have to pick up.

With a patience that surprised him, Drayton explained what the rock did, and how to remove—and replace—the magic shield. It didn't make Charis feel any better.

"Whatever you do, don't try to use your magic when the Dimithian is unshielded," the codger cautioned.

"What happens?"

"It'll harm you. If it takes enough of your magic beforehand, it can kill."

Charis cursed, whipped the offending chunk up from the dirt and ending his mirror's spell. Drayton laughed again, instead of the anger he'd expected.

He shook his head and shoved the Dimithian in his pocket. His stomach churned and his spine burned. Instinct throbbed, his magic shouting at him to get rid of it.

I hope for the Blessed Spirit's sake that's not a damn omen.

Chapter Thirty

They'd followed for most of the day, and it would be dark soon. They couldn't wait much longer to take her; they were getting farther and farther from Terraquist. The large party was making excellent time.

Now that Charis had the Dimithian, there wasn't really a reason to wait.

"They have to stop soon. They didn't break for a meal yet," Bracken said.

"I'm sicka waitin'," Nason mumbled as he gnawed on a piece of dried meat from his pack.

"It won't be much longer." Charis tried not to bark.

"Perhaps the lass isna' a delicate flower." Bracken smirked.

He doubted she was. She was bonded to a wolf, after all. "Nay, but they all have to eat. And I'm sure they'd not force a lass—a *lady*—to travel all night, even with a carriage."

"Aye, you're probably right. So when do we make our move?" Bracken's tone suggested Charis' answer had better be satisfactory.

"Soon," he forced out through clenched teeth.

"Look, they're stopping!"

Bracken and Charis exchanged a look, but Nason was right. The party had slowed their grueling pace, and the men were looking around. One called orders and they turned off the road into the least densely wooded area of the forest that lined the road.

"Smart to stop before reaching Beret," Bracken said.

"Never mind tha', the trees are thin here. We need cover," Nason complained.

"We'll be fine. We've a secret weapon, remember?" Charis said.

They'd taken the news of Drayton's *gift* with wide eyes and a hundred questions Charis didn't know the answers to. Although neither had elfin blood, they'd known each other for turns, and like him, had grown up in Aramour.

Nason's family had served Charis' father's elfin household for generations. Bracken descended from a long line of blacksmiths. He'd walked away from his family's trade for reasons unknown. His policy of no questions extended to his lads, too. As long as they got the job done, he didn't care.

"There's likely a clearing that way." Charis pointed to the right. "We'll let them set up camp. Relax. Disarm. Then we attack."

"Before it gets dark?" Nason asked.

Charis shrugged. "It matters not. With the Dimithian, it'll be quick."

"Then we hie to Drayton? Tonight?" Bracken crossed his arms over his chest.

"Aye. Under the cover of night will be best, before they can recoup."

Bracken gave a grunt and nod.

Nason licked his lips, drawing attention to his pocked face.

"Let's get as close as we can and remain undetected. We need to know the layout if they pitch tents."

"We need ta keep the lass in sight," Bracken said.

"Aye, agreed."

Nason rubbed his hands together. "I can taste tha' coin."

Bracken snorted. "Put your tongue in your head and draw your damn sword."

The smallest man of their group glared up at Bracken.

"Hush, both of you, and pay attention. We have to get the lass before we get any gold." Charis scowled.

Both his lads snapped their mouths shut and nodded.

Nason tied their horses and they hunkered down together, crossing the empty road as soundlessly and as stealthy as they could.

Charis was tempted to cover them in a masking spell, then quashed the idea. If that lad, *the* Mage of Greenwald was as powerful as suspected, he'd sense *any* magic. There were knights in the group, too. Smart men who'd lay out a perimeter and have the lad probe for danger.

"Shite," Charis whispered as they paused behind a close copse of fat trees. They could hear conversation, but didn't risk peeking around to see just yet.

"What?" Bracken's gaze snapped to him.

"If the lad covers their camp in a protection spell, we'll have to use the Dimithian earlier than planned." He quickly briefed them on what he'd sensed about their prey, as well as Castle Aldern.

Bracken shook his head. "We'll just hafta be fast."

"Aye," Nason agreed.

"You're right. We'll do what we need to do."

"For the coin," Nason whispered.

Bracken grunted, but didn't look at blond man. "At any rate, watch now, worry when we have ta."

"You're right." Charis nodded.

In unison, they moved as close as they dared, using a huge fallen tree as cover, right outside the clearing. All three drew their swords, but rested them at their sides.

From their view, they could see everything, but the overhanging foliage from the felled tree, as well as the low hanging canopy above would hide them from being easily spotted.

Men laughed, talked and tossed supplies back and forth. They were efficient. A large bonfire already burned at the center of the camp, a neatly stacked pile of wood ready to reenergize it as needed, and one tent was already pitched, flying the flag of Greenwald atop its triangular peak.

The carriage was off to the left side of the clearing, and their more than a dozen horses, including the lass' gray, stood side-by-side, two troughs in front of them. Some munched from feedbags that'd already been set up.

"How did they—"

Charis ignored Bracken's rare wonder and sent out a quick magical probe. "Magic. They used magic with the horses' tethers, water and food. Probably the big tent, too."

"Ah," Nason said.

Two men were putting a second tent up, but this one was

smaller. Made of a finer material, too, because it had a sheen in the firelight.

"For the lass," Bracken said, as if he'd read his mind. "She's a lady, after all."

"Where is she, anyway?" Nason asked.

Charis scanned the area. He only spotted three of the five knights he'd seen outside the castle gates. "There's another—smaller—clearing, to the right. See how the trees thin again?" he gestured. "And I smell water." His tracking magic confirmed when he sent his senses forward.

"She'd want privacy, and a bath, if there's a creek." Bracken nodded toward where Charis had indicated.

"With guards," Nason said.

"Thirteen in sight," Bracken said.

Charis' headcount came to the same number. "Fifteen in all, not including the lass and the wolf."

"We can't kill it," Bracken boomed.

"Nay. They're bonded, it'd kill her. We have to take it out, though. Get her away from it. Magic'll do it."

"Good."

Silence fell as they watched. One of them men started cooking in a large pot over the fire. Both tents were up now, and more men came and went in and out, preparing to bed down for the night.

"What now?" Nason whispered.

"We wait."

"Until the right moment." Bracken finished Charis' statement.

"False sense of security." Nason flashed a toothy grin and raised his sword.

"When they least expect it," Charis said, ignoring how his heart skipped and his stomach churned because of the so-called-mythical rock in his pocket.

★   ★   ★   ★

"Where's Elis—the lady?" Alasdair demanded of Bowen, then winced.

His brother arched an eyebrow. "*Lady* Elissa is bathing."

The emphasis on the honorific he'd forgotten made his wince slide into a scowl. The last thing he needed was for his fellow knight to comment. He'd obviously—unfortunately—noticed Alasdair's mistake.

Bowen crossed his arms over his chest and cocked his head to one side. "I'm her chaperone now. I have things handled."

He narrowed his eyes at the dismissal and tried to ignore the ripple of Bowen's lips as the knight fought a smile.

"You can go back to camp," Alasdair said.

Bowen shook his head, scattering his sandy locks about his shoulders. "Nay. 'Tis my duty to keep her safe."

"Which is why you're yards from her."

His brother laughed, which made his blood boil. "Aye, I'm sure *you'd* want me closer when she's unclothed. Her bondmate is with her. She knows to holler if there's trouble. Besides, she has more magic than half the people I know."

Unclothed. Right. Of course, that's what you focus most on.

Alasdair cleared his throat. "Well, at any rate, you can go. I need a word with her."

Bowen smirked. "It's not proper for me to leave her unchaperoned. Especially with the likes of *you*." His brother's humor didn't damper his rage.

He grabbed the knight by his collar. "Go. Back. To. Camp."

Instead of fighting him, Bowen chuckled again and tugged out of his grip. He threw his palms up. "Fine. Fine." Then his expression sobered. "Don't hurt her again, Alas."

Shock rolled over him and he backed up; stumbled. "Hurt her?" The question was cracked, telling Alasdair he couldn't fake innocence.

If Bowen had noticed, his lass didn't hide her pain...maybe she *couldn't.*

Alasdair clenched his jaw and fought the urge to crush his eyes shut. His emotions teetered back and forth from agony and shame.

The look on his brother's face was a mix of sympathy, and something else. Was Bowen angry at him, too? "I don't know what happened between you two, but I can guess. You don't have to say anything, but *none* of us are daft. Keep that in mind."

Alasdair studied his boots.

Bowen sighed and walked past him, then paused. "Keep something else in mind, too, Alas."

He glanced over his shoulder, then jarred when his gaze collided with his brother's serious amber one—something that was unusual for his fellow jester. "What?"

"We're on a journey to deliver her to her *betrothed*. He's a good man, and a duke. Don't ruin that for her."

His tongue was thick in his mouth. Alasdair could only stare at his brother and reject his statements. Especially, the word *betrothed*.

Bowen shook his head. "Go back to camp. I'll stay here."

"I can't."

His brother sighed again. "Be quick about it. Do not. Hurt. Her. Again. She's a sweet lass, and she deserves better than that."

Better than me.

Alasdair nodded, because it was all he could manage. Hell, he agreed with Bowen.

He could hear the knight cursing as he walked away. Hesitation in his broad shoulders told him Bowen wouldn't give them long.

What are you doing?

Bowen was right. He should go back to camp. His intention to call his brother back dissolved before it could be born. He wanted to see her.

Nay, I need to see her.

Alasdair's boots carried him forward, closer to the small burn.

Mischief saw him first, rising to all fours and wagging his tail. Well, at least the lass' bondmate didn't want to rip his throat out.

A series of splashes caught his attention and his eyes glued to her. She was naked, standing in the water up to her thighs. Her slender back and the perfect curve of her bottom caught— and held—his eye. Her supple skin was shiny from the water.

The birthmark high on her side, tucked neatly under her right breast, was only partly visible from the angle she was standing. He remembered tracing the half-moon shape the night they'd made love.

When Elissa glanced over her shoulder, she gasped. Her lips parted.

Alasdair wanted to go to her, tug her to him and kiss her.

He didn't.

Their eyes locked. His heart sped up. "Aren't you cold?" Words tumbled from his mouth.

"Nay. I warmed the water."

Idiot. She's an elemental mage.

Hearing her voice made his stomach flutter. She'd answered him normally, as if everything between them wasn't a torn mess.

She turned toward him, but didn't exit the small creek. Elissa made no efforts to cover her nudity, and it took all he was made of to keep his eyes on hers. "What do you want, Alasdair?" This was harder. Her mouth set in a hard line and her eyes flashed.

Mischief didn't approach him, but the wolf's head lowered, his tail stilled and his shoulders pitched as if he might pounce.

"For him not to attack me, for one."

Elissa arched a pale eyebrow, but moments later, her bondmate lay on the bank again. His body relaxed, but his icy blue gaze was keen.

"I've told him you mean me no harm." She lifted her chin and perched her hands on her shapely—perfect—hips. "Do you?"

"Never." Against his will, his eyes trailed her body. Alasdair took in her high breasts. Her nipples were hard, probably from the cool air. He remembered the taste of her skin, especially there, and his mouth went dry. Her flat stomach with its rounded edge at the right spot beckoned to him, her lithe skin glossy from the water. The curls between her legs were golden, also from her bath. Darker in color than when dry.

He burned for her. Like he had for no other woman.

Elissa laughed. It was bitter, and nothing like he'd ever heard from her before. But it jolted him from the arousal clouding his brain.

"Right. That's all you want. That's all you came for. I understand." She narrowed her eyes, daring him.

"Nay. You don't understand anything. I just want to talk." Frustration had him pacing.

Mischief growled. Alasdair froze but Elissa admonished her wolf and he quieted.

"I don't believe you."

His gut clenched. "I know. Can you please put some clothes on so we can talk?"

"Why? You can't talk now?"

"Nay. Not with you...like that..." Alasdair gestured to her bare form.

Triumph glittered in her hazel eyes but it didn't feel right. Nor did the hard expression on her beautiful face.

She exited the water, but the short distance to the folded pile of garments wasn't hurried. Elissa's actions were on purpose. She held her body open, making sure he could see every naked inch. She knew Alasdair didn't have the willpower to look away.

The little tease.

His anger rose hotter the slower she went, especially when she made sure he was looking at her before she picked up her chemise.

"Just hurry and dress."

Elissa smirked. "Why?"

"Aren't you cold?"

"Nay." She smiled and slid one arm into the fine dressing gown.

"Stop daring me."

"Daring you to what? You've made it plain you don't want me." Her eyes were wide, and the innocence of her expression might've been something he'd fall for—had he not known her.

"If you won't dress yourself, I'll do it. You won't like it."

"Relax, Alasdair. I thought you were a big, strong, knight. Always in control."

Who is this lass? This woman so blatantly daring him?

Where was Elissa, the sweet, shy lass who'd laughed at his stupid jests and listened to his stories?

This lass before him was an experienced seductress. He didn't know which Elissa he preferred more.

Alasdair wanted them both.

"I'll wait for you in the clearing." He stormed off, because if he didn't, he'd rip her chemise right back off and show her what happened when a woman goaded a man who wanted her.

Elissa's laugh was his only parting gift. Too bad it had that same bitter edge.

He paced next to a big tree until she came into view, her wolf on her heels. Her front-laced gown was simple and dark brown, much less flashy than other he'd seen her in, but her appeal was no less for him.

She'd braided her wet hair, but must've used magic to dry most of it, because pale little wisps escaped, framing her face and making him want her even more.

Alasdair swallowed and let her approach him. If he didn't, he'd grab her up and kiss her.

"Sir Alasdair." Elissa inclined her head.

"My lady." Perhaps decorum could convince him to keep his hands to himself.

"I don't want to argue with you." She stopped a few feet away, and the cool breeze washed her clean scent over him. Teasing. Tempting.

He closed his eyes and breathed her in. "I don't want to argue. Just want to talk."

"What's there to talk about?"

Alasdair sighed and met her hazel eyes. He'd proposed. She'd rejected him. That wasn't what he wanted. "I...don't know."

Her face softened for the first time since he'd approached. "There's nothing left to be said."

"Aye, there is."

Elissa shook her head and stepped closer. She reached out, as if she'd grab his arm, but then pulled her hand back.

He didn't protest. It was a bad idea for them to touch.

"Just...let me go." Her eyes implored when their gazes met again.

I can't. He couldn't say it aloud, either.

Alasdair tugged her to him, wishing he'd not demanded she get dressed moments before. He took her mouth brutally, making her open for him and shoving his tongue against hers. He whirled them around and walked her backwards until her shoulders bumped the tree. He pressed into her hard, kissing her with everything he was.

Elissa fought him at first, but then she gave a little whimper and started to kiss him back. Her mouth just as hungry as his.

She lifted her palms, resting them on his chest. But she didn't wind her arms around his neck. Elissa shoved backwards with surprising strength. Glared up at him, both hands on her hips. "Nay."

"Nay?" Alasdair whispered, his head spinning.

"You're not going to do this to me again. I won't let you." She raised her chin and squared her shoulders. "I won't let you tie me in knots and rip my heart in half."

He said nothing. Didn't know *what* to say.

"Besides, it isn't as if you *really* want me. More than my body."

"What'd you mean? I made myself clear when I asked for your hand."

"What about *The White Sage*?"

Alasdair blanched. Tried to hold onto his anger and not gulp like a caught lad. "What?" he sputtered.

"I'm sure you've made another trip since you *fled* my bed." Elissa glared.

"Nay." Alasdair rammed his hand through his long hair and looked away. Then he grasped onto courage like he'd never had to do *ever*, and met her beautiful eyes. "I've not touched another lass since you."

"Since me? But I heard—"

"I know what you heard. Nothing happened when I went to the tavern. I let Bowen and Dallon think what they would."

Pain darted across her face, despite what he'd just confessed. "But you went anyway."

"I thought of nothing but you." Alasdair wanted to reach for her, but didn't. He contemplated telling her about Betha, but it'd only hurt her more. Guilt bit at him, because he hadn't been completely chaste that night, even if he'd not rutted Betha.

Elissa gasped and blinked. Her lips parted and he took a step closer, but she threw her palm up. "Nay. It's too late."

"Why?" Pain rose slowly from his gut, consuming every inch of his being, constricting his chest, his breathing.

"I can't do this with you again."

"Elissa—" He wanted—*needed*—to fight, but didn't know how. What to do, what to say was beyond him.

I've already lost her.

He fought the urge to double over and pant for breath. His lungs burned.

She slid back when he reached for her, shaking her head hard. Her shoulders bumped the tree again. "I'm betrothed. I gave my word. I'm marrying Lord Cam, Sir Alasdair. Just accept it."

Chapter Thirty-one

Mischief growled low in his throat, his hackles raised all the way to his tail. It took her a moment to realize her bondmate wasn't growling at the man who'd broken her heart. His pale blue gaze was focused on something behind them, toward their camp.

She heard a yell of something unintelligible, but it was definitely an alarm.

The shouting drew Alasdair's attention as well, and he frowned, throwing a glance over his shoulder.

Elissa tried to look around his body, since she wasn't tall enough to peer over his shoulder, but her knight shoved his palm in her face.

"Stay here." Gone was the man with pain in his blue eyes. He was all knight again, a man of protection and action. He whirled around and drew his sword even before he was two steps away from her.

Lucan dove toward them from the other side of the clearing, his young face pale, his eyes wide. He too, had a sword in his hands.

Elissa's stomach somersaulted. She'd watched Alasdair and Sir Roduch training with the three lads on the Greenwald fighting yard, so she'd seen firsthand the knighted mage using the weapon, but he looked so scared.

"We're being attacked!" Lucan shouted. "Leargan told me to find you two."

"Protect Elissa at all costs," Alasdair ordered. He looked back at her.

Their eyes locked.

Panic inched up from her belly. She splayed her hands on the tree behind her, pressing in, letting the rough bark bite her palms.

Mischief glued himself to her side, but she took no comfort from her bondmate.

"Elissa." His voice was deep and smooth, despite their argument moments before and his white-knuckled grip on his sword. "It'll be all right, lass. Lucan and Mischief will keep you safe."

Gone was her anger with him. The hurt, the pain. He'd kissed her and she'd kissed him back like there was no tomorrow. Denying him, hurting him was the hardest thing Elissa had ever done in her life.

She wanted *him*. Couldn't bear him leaving her, even if it was to fight *for* her.

Don't leave me. I want you to keep me safe. She didn't realize she'd spoke aloud until his face softened.

"Lucan has more magic than anyone I've ever met. I'll come back to you."

The lad circled the tree she was against, throwing a nod to Alasdair. Though he didn't speak, Elissa recognized Lucan telling Alasdair he was ready for anything.

Her knight gave a curt nod back, then he was gone.

Without another word. Without….a touch. A kiss…

Anything.

Mischief darted across the clearing, patrolling the edge of the woods.

The clash of swords was closer now, as well as the yelling. Metal on metal made her wince, and her gut jump.

Elissa's panic was a living thing. Her temples throbbed, heart beat so hard it stole her breath. Her magic tingled under the surface of her skin, making her hot all over.

Wind was born of terror, whipping her hair around, in her face. Leaves rustled, then tree limbs creaked as they waved high above. Overhead, thunder pounded and a streak of lighting parted the sky.

She was going to start a storm. Again.

"My lady." Lucan's intense green gaze collided with hers. "Breathe. Please. Alas is right. We'll be fine. I'll protect you."

Elissa forced a breath, grateful for his presence. Having to answer him helped her regain control. "I know. I trust you." She did, even as she screamed inside her head to get a hold of herself.

Fear wouldn't solve anything, and she was only upsetting her bond. Mischief whined and whimpered, staring her down, but he didn't come to her, as if he couldn't return to her side without putting her in jeopardy. He too, had to be ready for anything.

The mage threw her another nod, and one corner of his mouth lifted, as if he was thanking her.

The wind let go, dissipating; the trees stopping their movement as if they'd never started.

Mischief paced the tree line of the clearing, growling from time to time as he studied whatever was ahead of him — the sounds of what they couldn't yet see. He dared someone to come closer. He might not have reached adulthood just yet, but his instincts were locked in place. Her wolf was ready to strike. Maim and kill to protect her.

Logically, she knew Lucan's magic and her bondmate's physical strength would keep anything bad from happening to her. It didn't make her stop wanting Alasdair to be the one in front of her brandishing his sword, vanquishing the enemy.

"If anyone breaks through those trees, you throw magic at them. You're more powerful with the elements than I could ever be. Do what you need to do. Drown them, my lady."

"Aye. I will."

He didn't answer but the glance he gave her was approval enough. Lucan circled, looking ready for anything.

Blessed Spirit, I hope he is.

Two men burst into the clearing from through the same spot Lucan had moments earlier.

Her bondmate jumped at the one on the right, but the villain was ready. The man raised his arm and threw a spell at Mischief.

The young wolf yelped and collapsed in a pile at his feet.

Elissa screamed, frantically thought-sending to him. If he was dead, she would die, too.

Mischief didn't answer her call, but his mind, his being, was still present, entwined with hers, so she tried to push her fright away and concentrate on the danger. Her bondmate was stunned, but they'd both live — for now. She implored him to wake up, but he didn't move. She didn't know the spell, so she couldn't counter it.

Lucan hollered a spellword and the bigger of the two men flew across the clearing.

He hit a tree and grunted as he tumbled to the ground, but gained his feet much too soon. He advanced on the young mage. The man was huge, his shoulders seemingly as broad as the trees that surrounded them.

Her mage protector made eye contact with Elissa for a split second, then pointed at her. Lucan shouted a spellword. She didn't understand it, but it sounded Aramourian.

The area before Elissa went hazy, and all the sound was sucked away. She blinked to clear her vision and shook her head, because it went fuzzy, too. To no avail, because all sounds were still gone.

She could see the clearing, and her wolf lying in the long grass to her right, but it was as if a veil had been draped over her.

Lucan had enclosed her in a bubble.

So much for his order to attack.

The other man rushed toward her only to skitter to a stop a few feet from Lucan's bubble, his face contorted in pain. He reached out, then yanked his hand back before making contact with the magic wall.

His mouth moved, but she couldn't hear what he said. Didn't know if he spoke to her or his companion.

When he looked away, she saw a long, tapered ear, like Lord Aldern. His hair was long, lose and dark, but he, like the duke, was too tall to be a full-blooded elf.

He rushed away from her as quickly as he'd tried to touch the bubble. In moments, he'd disappeared back the way he'd come, into the trees.

The big man circled Lucan, but the mage kept him away with a visible shield in front of his lean body. He brandished his sword and tightened his stance when the attacker drew his own weapon, which was much larger than Lucan's sword.

Elissa swallowed and helplessness rolled over her. She touched the bubble with both hands. It didn't hurt her as it appeared to have done to her half-elfin enemy.

She was torn between wanting to see if she could help Lucan, help Mischief, and sinking to the bottom of the bubble and wrapping her arms around herself.

I'm not a coward.

Like the lad had pointed out, she had great magic in her own right.

Should I try to break free?

And if the two men had made it through the line of knights, did that mean...something had happened to them all?

Is Alasdair all right?

Elissa ignored the pain in her chest and leaned into Lucan's magic bubble, pushing harder every inch she went. The magic was pliable, shaped itself around her hand, but shoved back at her, as if chiding her.

Movement to the left drew her eye. The half-elf was back, with a smaller, blond man on his heels. Her heart stopped when she saw the dark red dripping from the short sword in his hand.

Alasdair...Sir Dallon, Sir Leargan...Sir Bowen...Sir Kale. The other men of their party... Were they alive?

Lucan's mouth moved, but she still couldn't hear. Elissa guessed he'd shouted something at the big man trying to get close enough to fight, but the enemy's gaze was on his two companions instead of the knighted mage.

The half-elf had an odd look on his face. Not exactly as if he was in pain, but features contorted, as if he was very uncomfortable. He wore dark gloves that extended to his biceps and his hands were clutched together high, away from his body.

He carried something. There was a glow around his joined fists.

A force shield of some sort? What on earth does he have?

Elissa's stomach fluttered. Instinct told her it couldn't be good. Her insides recoiled. She shifted her feet, squinting so she could see better through the hazy magic of the protection bubble.

The half-elf appeared to yell something, and the huge man left Lucan's side. He, along with the smaller blond man flanked the half-elf.

He must be their leader.

Lucan readied himself for another attack. Elissa did, too, tensing. It didn't come in the way she expected.

The half-elf threw something at Lucan. It was small and held its glow as it sailed through the air.

The young mage's magic body shield *poofed* from sight.

Even at the distance she was, Elissa saw the shock on the lad's face. His back bowed and his arms extended, his face red and tight, as if in agony. She gasped when Lucan collapsed.

He didn't move.

"Nay!" Her shout bounced off the bubble, resounding in her ears. Tremors started in her hands, working their way up her arms, into her shoulders, then shimmying down her back, down to her thighs. Elissa's knees knocked together and her teeth chattered.

Lucan was the most powerful magical being she'd ever met. What could have taken him out? Was he dead?

Blessed Spirit, no. Please. Have mercy.

Her bottom lip wobbled and she fought tears, then lost the battle. Elissa's vision blurred even as the half-elf darted to Lucan's crumpled body and grabbed whatever he'd thrown at the lad.

The look on his face was the same discomfort as before. He threw at her and the bubble disappeared. An iridescent piece of something—maybe a rock—landed at her feet.

Elissa looked down at the same time her knees buckled. Pressure compressed her chest, making it hard to breathe. She panted, not sure whether to grab her bodice and pull it loose, or try to push herself off the ground.

Everything…hurt.

She tried to move, but her limbs weighed a ton. She tried to call to her magic, but the response was agony that doubled her over and scorched her skin from the inside out.

Nothing magical happened.

A whimper slipped from her lips.

Her whole body was on fire, as if her bones were melting. She didn't have the strength to try to call water to her again, which had always required the smallest efforts.

"What's…hap…pening?"

Her shoulders hit the ground because her torso couldn't hold her up any longer. Then, Elissa couldn't move. Numbness poured upward from her toes, but it was blessed relief from the pain as it spread over her whole form.

Six booted feet came into her blurry line of vision.

"My lady, meet Dimithian. It sucks your powers away. But no worries, it's not forever."

Dimithian? It's not supposed to be real.

Elissa met a pair of very blue eyes. He smiled.

Her eyes were too heavy to look anywhere but at his face. Even holding her lids open pained her. She tried to open her mouth, tried to say something—*anything*—but her lips refused to part.

The half-elf touched her forehead with his gloved hand.

Everything went black.

☆   ☆   ☆   ☆

He kept her asleep with a spell so she wouldn't get hurt fighting him—or kick their arses with her magic. Charis kept her with him on Barley's back, too. He didn't trust Bracken or Nason with her. Not after they'd worked so hard to get her away from the knights with magic and brute strength.

Thank the Blessed Spirit for the Dimithian. Drayton had been right. They'd needed it. It was currently locked away in his saddle bags, and his magic had returned to him, and the lass' to her.

Even unconscious, her power radiated around her, her aura throbbing so brightly that if he sought it out directly he had to squint. Now that the protection spell around her was gone, Charis could feel the strength of the elements beneath the surface of her skin.

She had more magic than any other elemental he'd ever encountered.

Like that lad, though the young mage's powers weren't elemental. That lad could do...anything, Charis suspected. He almost regretted having to leave him. With the power of Dimithian perhaps the lad could've been controlled. They could've explored his magic.

The lass moaned and started to stir against his chest.

Charis cursed and cupped the back of her head, saying the spellword to keep her asleep. They had two days' hard ride— if they really pushed their horses—back to Drayton's cave, and he needed to be careful with his sleep spell. It was intended for short periods. Using it over and over could damage the lass long term. She was so powerful the spell burned out even more quickly than with someone with no—or less—magic.

He could use the rock, but then his powers would be taken down, too, since he needed to keep the lass close physically. She had to remain asleep, or she could—and *would*—free herself.

Charis knew a spell that *should* damper her powers, but since she had so much magic, he didn't have faith that it'd work. Or, it might for a little while, like his sleep spell. Either way, he didn't want to chance her getting away.

If she did, Drayton would probably kill him—them. Unless they went on the run. There was too much opportunity for coin in the Provinces. He'd be as careful as required to deliver his charge.

They wouldn't stop to make camp tonight—they couldn't afford it. Whatever guards weren't dead would come after them. And her bondmate. They needed to get far enough away so the wolf wouldn't be able to locate her through their shared magic. It'd be a challenge, because Charis didn't know just how far they had to be before she'd lose the ability to thought-send to the beast.

He'd put his greatest masking spell in play to cover their trail, but that lad would no doubt sniff it out in seconds. Someone that powerful was feared, and rightly so.

Charis had thought about fleeing with no magic at all, but that'd leave them to detection even faster. Being at top speed didn't allow for careful coverage of what they'd left behind, no matter how much other traffic marred their trail on the roads.

"Ride hard and fast, lads. We can't stop. Get as far away from here as we can."

A grunt was all he got from Bracken, and Nason didn't say anything, just leaned in hard and pushed his horse harder.

Charis clutched the lass closer and kicked Barley.

Chapter Thirty-two

It was dark, it wasn't just his imagination.

Alasdair's temples pounded as he sat up, and he gripped his head with both hands. Couldn't help but hunch his back. His leg smarted when he bent it, and his side throbbed, which turned to white-hot pain shooting into his chest when he explored the tear in his tunic and came away with blood-tipped fingers.

He hissed, then swore.

Around him, other men were moaning as they came to. Some had gained their feet, others were still on the ground, like him. Everyone seemed groggy; one of the men-at-arms wandered between the tents like a drunkard.

The bonfire at the center of their camp was burning, lighting up the surrounding area, but no one tended it, which told him they hadn't been out so long.

What the hell?

Last thing he remembered, it hadn't been quite twilight, and they'd made camp to eat, right? Rest for the night before continuing on at dawn.

His gaze darted around the large clearing, and it all smacked into his mind, memories of the fight, men screaming, swords clashing, colored flashes of magic.

Alasdair scrambled to his feet and found his sword. His last conversation danced into his thoughts. Then the kiss. "Elissa!" he gasped.

Lucan had been with her, so she was fine.

She has to be.

His side screamed when he broke into a run and his leg protested, but he ignored his body, as well as whoever had just called his name.

He saw Mischief first. The wolf lay unmoving, and his gut seized. If her bondmate was dead—

"Nay!" His shout was greeted by nothing. "Elissa?" He rushed to the tree where he'd kissed her. She didn't lie beneath it, or further into the woods. Alasdair darted to the burn where she'd bathed. Murky water flickered in the moonlight, but his lass wasn't there, either.

His heart slid to his stomach when realization settled over him.

They'd come for her. The protection spell must've failed, because somehow the men who'd killed the look-alike lasses and their families had found Elissa and...

Taken her.

Anger boiled up, washing the agony away. Alasdair clung to it. Needed it.

You left her, taunted, but he pushed it all away.

He was going to find them.

Get her back, and tear the bastards from limb to limb for taking what was his.

He stomped to the clearing. Needed to find his brothers and formulate a plan.

Lucan's still form caught his attention and his stomach jolted.

Alasdair went to the lad, skidding in the dirt as he hit his knees beside him. Relief washed over him when he saw the rise and fall of the lad's thin chest. His side and leg protested at the same time, but he focused on Lucan. He shook his shoulder. "Lad. Wake."

Thundering footfalls sounded, but he didn't look up from the mage who was like a younger brother to him, as much as the knights of the guard. Not to mention the most powerful magical being he'd ever encountered.

What the *hell* was powerful enough to take Lucan out?

"Blessed Spirit," Leargan muttered, appearing beside them. "Is he alive?"

"Aye." Alasdair met his captain's dark eyes and saw the apple of his throat bob. No doubt Leargan was thinking the same thing.

"Mischief's all right, coming around now."

Alasdair glanced over his shoulder to see Bowen kneeling next to the wolfling, tentatively stroking his head and neck, whispering to him. "Careful, Bowen; he's a wolf, after all."

Bowen nodded his sandy head, but didn't take his eyes—or hands—off Mischief.

"Lucan, lad, please wake up." Leargan patted Lucan's chest, then gave it a hard thump.

A long groan sounded, even more relief for Alasdair. Lucan came around, blinking and panting to catch his breath. Alasdair helped the lad sit up and couldn't hold in a smirk when Lucan cradled his head first thing, much like he had.

"Lucan," Leargan said.

Dallon and Kale rushed the clearing, swords drawn.

"All's well, you can breathe," Bowen called.

Their brothers sheathed their weapons, but neither appeared relaxed. "We've three dead, and three more injured. One badly. Are you all well?" Kale asked.

"Lucan's coming around—"

"I'm well," the lad croaked, interrupting the captain. "Lady Elissa?" His green eyes widened when no one answered right away.

Alasdair exchanged a look with Leargan. Evidently his brother had come to the correct conclusion that she was gone.

Bowen had Mischief to all fours, but the young wolf looked like he'd broken into the ale, wobbling on his legs. He shook his great head and made a beeline for Lucan, practically bowling the lad back over.

The knighted mage wrapped his arms around him—as if he had a choice. Mischief nuzzled Lucan's chest over and over, his whining gaining an octave with each rub.

"What's wrong with him?" Bowen asked.

"Other than the obvious? She's missing," Alasdair barked.

Bowen's expression went sheepish, then angry.

The lad put his cheek on the wolf's head, and they both closed their eyes.

Alasdair's brothers all gathered around, watching intently. No one moved, they just stood or kneeled and stared as Lucan did something magical to Mischief. Both glowed briefly. Alasdair squinted, but didn't bother shielding his eyes. He was the first person Lucan looked at, but then the lad rested his gaze on Leargan.

"My magic's back." The words dripped relief, and the lad released a long breath.

Alasdair didn't have time to puzzle over that.

"News of our lady isn't good. She's out of thought-send range. I can't sense her, even through her bond with Mischief." Lucan's expression was grave.

There were a few curses, but Alasdair had to tamp down the panic inching up from his gut. They knew next to nothing about her captors. They assumed she'd been stolen by the men who'd been after her, but where would they take her?

How could they find her without her bondmate's assistance?

"What'd you mean, your magic's *back*?" Kale asked, yanking Alasdair from his brewing torture.

"They had Dimithian. It took my magic; Lady Elissa's, too." Lucan's young face was absent of color again.

Mischief whimpered when the lad's grip on him tightened, but the wolf burrowed closer, instead of trying to pull away. As if the beast knew Lucan was the best chance to magically communicate with Elissa.

"Dimithian?" Bowen and Dallon asked at the same time.

"I thought it wasn't real," Leargan said.

Alasdair didn't have time for a lesson on some supposed-mythical magic-sucking element from deep in the mountains of the elves' territory. He needed to find Elissa *now*. But his brothers' attention was raptly on the lad as he spoke of all he knew about Dimithian. He couldn't stand still while the mage talked, so Alasdair paced, ignoring Leargan's attempt to calm him.

Kale and Bowen helped the lad to his feet when the recital ended, brushing him off and making sure he was in one piece.

Mischief clung to his side, almost impeding Lucan's footsteps he was so close.

Leargan was talking to the lad, but Alasdair tuned it all out. He continued pacing. His side hurt. He ignored it. Chaos enveloped his mind, visions of all the horrible things that could be happening to her marching around on an endless loop. He saw her bloodied, broken…raped?

Kale and Dallon went with Lucan, while Bowen stayed with him and Leargan in the clearing. The captain called his name, and Alasdair joined his brothers, but his thoughts were still with Elissa.

"We need to find her, now," he bellowed.

"We will, Alas." Leargan's assurance was even.

It did nothing to comfort him.

"Lucan'll look around, and see if he can sense a trail—magical or otherwise. He said he's up to it, so that's what I've sent him to do. Hopefully we can determine what direction they went. Kale is going to tend our men-at-arms and see who we can send home. I've sent Dallon back to Greenwald at top speed. We need help, and we have to inform Lord Jorrin and Lord Cam."

Alasdair fought a wince at the mention of her betrothed. "I'm going ahead. I'll find her."

"Nay. *We'll* find her, Alasdair. Being rash won't solve anything. We have to know where we're going. We have a plan. Let's work together, like always."

"Time is of the essence."

Bowen said nothing, but watched them, amber eyes intent, his sandy hair swinging as he moved his head from Alasdair to their captain and back.

"I agree. Don't fight me on this. Think it through. Let Lucan do what he can. He's the best chance to a quick answer, and you know it. We'll get her back."

Rage boiled up, but Alasdair didn't know who he was angrier at, Leargan for accusing him of being rash or himself.

You left her.

He pinned his white-knuckled fists to his sides.

"Alas…" His name was a warning, but concern darted across his captain's face. Leargan reached for him. "You're hurt."

He shook Leargan's hand off his arm. "I'm fine."

Bowen leaned in to inspect his wound. "Alas, that looks bad. You're bleeding. Your breeches are soaked to your knees."

"You can both sod off. I need to find her."

His brothers exchanged a look.

Leargan tightened his grip. "Alasdair—"

"Now." He tore away from his captain's fingers, growling as he broke their physical contact.

Leargan cursed.

Alasdair whirled in the direction Lucan and Kale had gone. His head spun. He ignored it, as well as the sharp jolt of agony his side gave.

Wind caressed his face and he swayed into it, thinking of her and how she'd warmed him with her magic that day at Castle Durroc. A tremor traveled his frame, and his vision danced.

"Alasdair?" Leargan sounded far away.

"Alas!" Bowen's exclamation did, too.

His legs buckled, and pain shot into his knees as he hit the ground. It didn't last, though, and soon he could see the moon high above.

Why is it blurry?

The sound of his brothers' boots rushing toward him faded as everything went black.

☆　☆　☆　☆

Everything was fuzzy. Elissa tried to sit up, but something was restraining her.

Deep voices went in and out. She blinked, but her vision didn't clear.

Her back brushed harsh roughness.

A tree?

She attempted to pitch her body forward again, using the tree as leverage, but only resulted in sliding sideways, half-slumped. The bark bit into her elbow, scratching through the fabric of her dress' sleeve. Her temples throbbed and her hands weren't even free to rub them or grab her head. A groan broke from her lips.

Conversation ceased, and three sets of boots came into her shadowy line of sight.

"She's awake," a man said.

"Knock her out, so she won't call her magic," another demanded. His voice was deeper than the first one, gruff.

"Does it look like she can use her magic? She's barely awake, at best." This voice was baritone; she'd consider it pleasant, had it not belonged to a kidnapper. Instinct told her the half-elfin man with the very blue eyes had just spoken.

All three had distinctly northern accents, but the lilt wasn't of Terraquist. It was from farther north, suggesting Aramour.

Like Lord Jorrin.

The men sounded like the Duke of Greenwald.

"Maybe Dimithian has long-lasting effects?" the first voice asked.

"Hmmm, maybe," the half-elf said. His long, dark hair was loose and flowing, unlike before when he'd worn a hat. Even with blurry eyes, she could make out long, slender, tapered ears.

"Wh…what…do you want…from me?" Elissa's throat scorched.

Silence fell, as if her kidnappers were surprised she could speak.

"Water, get her some water," the half-elfin one directed. "Then tend that fire. Don't burn our meal, either."

One set of boots disappeared and she heard shuffling as someone did his bidding. Then a drinking skin was pressed to her mouth, but she had trouble opening her cracked lips.

Rough hands gripped her jaw, but the hold didn't hurt. "Open. Drink." Right above her ear was the smooth baritone again.

Cool liquid slid down her throat, lessening the burn to a dull throb. Elissa swallowed twice and he took the water away. She didn't thank him. Wouldn't, no matter how pleasant he was being. They'd still taken her against her will.

She wanted to sit up. Fight. Get back to her—

Blessed Spirit! Mischief!

She was alive, so her bondmate had to be, but what if the magic had injured him permanently?

Elissa sent a frantic thought-send to him, but in her weakened state, she could barely sense their bond. Tears stung her eyes. No doubt her wolfling was frantic. If she couldn't hear him, he likely couldn't hear her. How would he find her?

Alasdair. The other knights...Sir Leargan, Sir Dallon, Sir Bowen...Sir Kale? The Greenwald men-at-arms, too.

Lucan!

He was much more powerful than she. Had the Dimithian killed him?

Her belly fluttered and she sucked back a whimper. There was no use showing her emotions to the men who had her. If they saw her as weak, they might try to hurt her...rape her. She gulped.

"What do you want from me? Where're you taking me?" Elissa cursed the tremble in her query. She tried to shift her body again. Her shoulders burned as she stretched her forearms and bent her wrists. They had her bound from behind, and she was sitting on her hands. Her limbs went back and forth from throbbing for freedom to numbness.

"That's not for us to tell," the one with the deepest voice growled.

The half-elfin man brushed her hair back from her face with surprisingly gentle fingers. "No one'll harm you."

Elissa wanted to yank away from his touch, but her body wouldn't respond to her commands. At least she could see better now. Her vision had finally cleared. She tried to glare. "Let me go and I'll beg them not to kill you when they find me."

A bark of laughter had her glancing up. The man with the deepest voice was *huge*. Probably as tall as Sir Roduch, but not nearly as handsome. He was thickly muscled and had arms crossed over an impossibly broad chest.

She fought tremors and looked back into the deep blue eyes of the half-elf, who was still squatted beside her.

His expression was implacable. "Don't waste threats on us, my lady."

Elissa forced a shuddering breath and made herself look around—as subtly as she could. They were in the woods, but it was nondescript. A warm fire burned at the center of a small camp, and three horses were tied not far away.

The sky was grayish, but she didn't know if dawn crested or if it was past twilight. She had no sense of how much time had passed, either. Panic churned her stomach and she fought it. Sucking in air only helped a little, but she reached for calm with all her might.

The third man rose from tending the fire and rejoined the other two. He was smaller, with fair hair and a slender build. His face was pocked.

Elissa studied all three of them as best she could. She needed to remember *everything* so she could recount it when she broke free. She called to her bondmate, but still got nothing, despite the fact her head wasn't nearly as fuzzy as it'd been when she'd woken.

"This one's much prettier than the others," the blond man said, a grin displaying rotted teeth.

Others?

He reached to touch her cheek, and Elissa gasped, recoiling, but she didn't need to worry.

The half-elf shot to his feet and slapped the man's hand away. "Don't touch her. *No one* touches her."

"Relax. I was jus' sayin'."

"Keep your hands to yourself and your ideas in your head," he barked.

The big one chuckled, but she didn't sense humor in it. "He's right, though. This one's comely. What's tha harm in a little fun?"

The half-elf slid in front of her and gripped the hilt of the sword at his waist. "I said *nay*."

Elissa looked from man to man, feeling the tension rise and thicken.

"If ya want 'er for yourself, all ya 'ave ta do is say so," the blond man muttered.

"I do. I claim her. Here and now."

Her heart dropped to her toes.

Is he going to rape me?

The big one arched a dark eyebrow and cocked his head to one side. "Do ya now?"

"Aye. So back off, both of you."

Two more seconds of silence passed. No one moved. The men stared each other down.

"He always gets tha good ones." The blond man shook his head and shrugged. He looked from man to man, then left to tend whatever was cooking on the fire.

The scent of meat made her tummy growl. They'd taken her before she'd eaten.

The half-elf was still having a stand-off with his other companion, but finally, with a grunt, the large man sent a glare her way and walked away.

Elissa watched him go to the horses and dig for something from a saddlebag before he took a seat next to the blond man by the fire.

Her remaining captor glanced at her, but said nothing. Soon, he too joined the others, only to return shortly with steaming meat on a crude plate. The half-elf whispered some spellword, too low for her to catch.

A cool flush caressed her body and her powers were suddenly inaccessible. Her magic wouldn't respond to any of her calls, even water, which usually came to her without effort. "What did you do to me?" she demanded.

"Just a little dampering spell, so you don't drown me. Water is your strongest element, right?" He had the nerve to smile as he knelt beside her.

She glared.

"Hold onto that. Be strong. You're going to need it."

Elissa finally straightened against the tree. There was a crease to his brow as he spoke. Was that regret?

Can I use it to my advantage?

"What's your name?" Maybe if she was nice to him, he'd be nice back. He'd already asserted that he'd protect her from his companions. Could she talk him in to letting her go?

He laughed, and shook his head. "Nay, my lady. Nothing you need to know."

"Are you an empath?" Elissa blurted.

"Not that it matters, but no." He wore a grin that could pass for charming, and she wanted to kick herself for thinking he was handsome.

She frowned.

"I have a question for you," he said after a moment.

She could sense the slightest hesitation in his low tone. "What?" She let her frown slip into a scowl.

"Do you have a mark, high on your right side?"

Elissa froze. They stared at each other in silence, until she swallowed, shouting at herself to not show any reaction.

Why does he want to know about my birthmark?

"If you don't tell me, my lady, I'm afraid I'll have to look for myself."

She shook her head.

"Nay about the mark? Nay about me looking?" Amusement darted across those blue eyes.

Elissa bit back a growl. He hadn't hurt her, but it didn't mean he wasn't quick to anger. Admitting it would be better for her. She wouldn't want him to rip down her bodice and bare her breasts to the other two. Not after the blond one had already expressed interest in touching her. "I have the mark."

Her captor squared his shoulders and gave a curt nod.

"Why?"

He narrowed his eyes, and she knew he wouldn't tell her. "Enough talking. Eat. We've a long ride ahead."

"To where?"

The half-elf didn't answer, just shoved meat against her lips until she opened. He fed her but didn't release her hands. Elissa wanted to spit the roast rabbit back in his face, but she needed to keep up her strength for her escape, so she ate without complaint as he served her like a babe.

He wouldn't answer her demands between bites, either, so she gave up—for now.

After she'd whispered she was full, he merely nodded and rose, not appearing to expect the *thank you* Elissa failed to utter.

She watched all three of them as closely as she could when he moved toward the fire and joined his companions.

The blond one kept throwing her salacious looks, and only laughed when she scowled or glared. The hum of their speech settled into normal conversation, but she wasn't so far away that she couldn't hear every word. They spoke of mostly inconsequential things, no doubt censoring anything to do with her. When their voices dropped, Elissa listened harder.

They were careful, never once revealing their names, or letting on to where they were taking her.

Her captors did reference another party, but no name was whispered then, either. They just referred to whoever they meant as *him*. The big one even called the man, *Himself*, and he always wore a sneer when he said it.

Not long after they'd all eaten, the half-elf returned to her side, and tugged Elissa to her feet. "We're leaving." He was about as gruff as she'd heard him.

The passing time had told her it was night, not the beginning of a day. It'd only gotten darker, and the moon had risen high in the black sky.

She resisted, dragging her feet until the half-elf pushed her forward. The huge, dark-haired man came quickly to his aid, pulling on her upper arm.

Elissa lost her balance and careened into his hard chest. She sucked back a wince and put on her best regal glare as his large hands swallowed her waist.

He laughed, like he had earlier, throwing his head back. The brute squeezed her sides. "Are you sure I can't 'ave a little taste? This one's feisty like I like 'em."

"Take your hands off her," the half-elf barked. "If I needed your assistance I would've asked." He tried to wedge his torso between them when he wasn't obeyed immediately.

She struggled, but the brute's grip on her only tightened, and lust flashed in his dark eyes. Her stomach turned itself inside out.

"Not a'tall like the others," he whispered.

"Others?" she blurted. That was the second time he'd said that.

The half-elf sent her a warning glance.

"What harm'd one taste be? I won't use her hard, no' one this fine. *Himself* wouldn't even know." He leaned forward and inhaled, then licked his lips.

She recoiled, but his hold was unrelenting. Elissa tried not to whimper as she frantically called to her magic, but the half-elf's spell still held her powers back, as if they'd been locked away. Not even the barest tingle hit her skin.

"Do not make me run you through. *I* claimed her."

Elissa maintained eye-contact with the large man. She prayed to the Blessed Spirit her fear wasn't showing.

"Stick to whores," the blond man said, staring, but not moving closer. "I think he's serious. Should listen to 'im, or we'll need a new partner."

The tension was thick enough to cut with a knife. Finally, the oversized man shoved her away from him.

Elissa screeched as she fell backwards, but she was in the half-elf's arms in seconds.

He righted her against his chest and scowled at his companion. "Try anything like that again, and you won't have the equipment for whores. I'll geld you myself."

In answer, the brute chuckled.

"What did he mean by *'others'*?"

"Rest, lass." The half-elf put a palm to her forehead and said a spellword.

Elissa gasped and thrashed against him, because his spell would make her sleep—whether she wanted to or not. If she was asleep she couldn't see where they were taking her.

She called to her magic again, a sharp command that went unanswered. Her eyes weighed a ton and slammed shut against her will. A heavy shroud of drowsiness enveloped her, and she didn't have a choice but to give in to the blackness.

Chapter Thirty-three

They were finally here. The last three days had been the longest of his life.

He'd only communicated with his hirelings once, and the conversation had been short, as necessary.

Drayton clapped, the loud *slap* of his palms reverberating off the walls of his cave. Delight boiled up and rolled over him. His magic responded, water bubbling, pushing under the surface of his skin in a way it hadn't had in turns.

He felt *strong*. Things were going his way.

He sensed an elemental even before the half-breed was through his protective spell-wall. Straightening his shoulders, Drayton stood at the center of his dais and waited.

The tall, dark-haired half-breed spilled into his living space with a precious bundle in his arms.

The lass appeared to be out cold. Her brown gown had long, full sleeves. A slender hand peeked out as her arm hung in the air. Her hair was fair, so blonde it was almost white, and cascaded in silken waves over the mercenary's arm and shoulder. Her head was tilted back, revealing a delicate jaw and slender neck. She was dainty. Beautiful.

"What's wrong with her?" Drayton snarled.

Charis inclined his head. "Nothing, my lord. She sleeps. But my spell won't last much longer; she's powerful."

"Wake her. Now."

"Aye, my lord. She's got quite the temper, and my dampering spell no longer works, but I know another that should keep her from attacking you."

"No Dimithian; I need to sense her magic." He already could. Even being asleep in the half-breed's arms didn't diminish the radiance of her aura. It didn't speak of water, it *shouted* her main talent. Almost as strong were the other elements, all hovering around the teal tint that meant water. They were all intertwined, hinting at great magic. Drayton licked his lips.

It has to be her.

"Nay, my lord. Not what I had in mind." The half-breed whispered a spellword and squatted low as the lass stirred. He set her to her feet, and helped her stand.

The lass groaned as she came around, rubbing her eyes. As soon as she was fully aware, she glared at his hireling. Gestured, as if she would throw magic, but the half-breed was faster.

He pointed, and shouted a spell. Light exploded, making Drayton squint.

An opaque sphere appeared, enveloping his lass. It was wide, and as the magic cleared, he could see her standing at its center. And none too pleased, if the scowl marring her pretty face was any indication.

Although *pretty* was too weak a word. The lass was breathtaking. It wouldn't be a chore getting a child on her. He wished he could see the color of her eyes from his distance.

"Clever," Drayton gestured to the bubble, and glanced at the half-breed.

He inclined his head. "She can't harm herself or you from in there."

"Good. What is the spell?"

Charis quickly explained the containment spell and confessed he'd not come up with it on his own, but had gotten the idea from the Greenwald mage, Lucan. Drayton didn't care where he'd stolen it from, only that it worked. He circled the bubble several times, but didn't touch the iridescent surface.

It was fantastic, though he hated to give his hireling any credit. He flicked his wrist and whispered the spellword, reducing the size of the bubble. So he could get within a few feet, examine her more closely. Soon enough the bubble wouldn't matter. He'd put his bracelet on her and she wouldn't be able to use her magic at all.

She tensed, but didn't cower. He liked that.

When Drayton leaned in, his lass squared her shoulders and tilted her head up. Narrowed her eyes.

He threw his head back and laughed. "She *is* strong. I'm glad."

The half-breed looked as if he'd thought Drayton had lost his mind when their gazes brushed. He said nothing.

Drayton disregarded his presence and turned back to his lass. She'd be the mother of his child.

She was obviously highborn. Even if her posture didn't tell him, the wealth of her clothing would've. Her brown gown was of quality fabric, even though the design was simple. Most likely for traveling purposes.

He imagined her clad in the finest gowns, shiny, flowing materials that would highlight her beauty and swirl around her when she walked. How she should be dressed.

If she bore him a child with elemental magic, perhaps he'd reward her with a fine gown to wear. He wouldn't be able to take her magic right away. Their child would have to be weaned first.

Drayton rubbed his hands together. "I want to examine her more closely."

"Her magic is powerful, my lord," the half-breed cautioned.

"She was introduced to my Dimithian, was she not?"

"Aye, my lord."

"She knows what happens if she tries to call to her magic?"

"I think so, my lord."

He gave a curt nod, and heard Charis mutter a spellword.

The magic around the lass disappeared.

She tensed immediately and threw out her hands.

Drayton's elemental sensed tingled. "Now, half-breed!"

Charis tossed the hunk of Dimithian at her feet, but it was still held within its force shield.

"If I say the word, my pretty, he'll release my Dimithian and it'll suck your powers away. So I suggest you stand still. You'll come to no harm." *Yet.* He inched closer, silently strengthening the spell around him to stave off Dimithian's effects. It wouldn't work if the shield slipped from the rock, but it would keep other magic from harming him.

His skin crawled when he neared the Dimithian and he resisted the urge to kick it away from the lass. He needed the leverage. He couldn't use the rock to suck her magic away right now. Drayton needed to gauge her powers—and get the bracelet on her. First, he needed to confirm she really was his elemental. "Open your bodice."

The lass startled. "Nay," she whispered.

First sign of fear. Good. "Aye. Now. Or I shall rip it."

Charis cleared his throat, but Drayton didn't spare him a glance.

"What do you want?" The lass's voice shook, but there was control in her tone. She wouldn't be easily cowed.

Drayton liked the idea of a good fight with her. If he could keep up his strength, that is. "Open your bodice, my pretty. Bare your right side. It'll be over quickly, and I shall not touch you." *For now.*

She swallowed, but narrowed her eyes. "Why?"

"Do it." Drayton moved forward, and gestured to her torso. He stopped within touching distance. "Last chance to do it on your own."

Hazel eyes widened, but shaky hands rose to do his bidding. He'd always been partial to blue eyes, but he'd make do with the lass.

The front-side lacing was as simple as the gown itself, and it wasn't long before it hung open and she pulled the ribbons to open her chemise.

He said nothing as she covered her small, high breasts, but she obeyed when he ordered her hands from blocking the right side of her ribcage, just below the flesh she was covering. Drayton wasn't concerned with bare female nipples, at least not at the moment.

His heart thundered when he saw the mark. A dark spot on her otherwise flawless creamy skin. In the shape of a half-moon, almost perfect in formation. "It *is* you." He paid no mind that he'd spoken a breathless whisper.

She said nothing.

"You may dress." Drayton cleared his throat.

The lass scrambled to obey, her fingers shaking even more than before. "What do you want from me?"

He laughed.

She pinned him with a glare just as fierce as the one she'd given before. Now that she was dressed again, of course.

He circled her and she followed his movements with her eyes.

"What do you want from me?" she repeated, this time louder. With more force.

Drayton stilled just short of touching her cheek. Their gazes collided.

"Everything."

★   ★   ★   ★

Chills raced down her spine and it took everything she was made of to stand still. Not react. And not just because of the Dimithian at her feet.

What does that mean?

Why had he wanted to see her birthmark, like the half-elf? As if they'd both had to verify her identity... What the *hell* had he meant by, *'It is you.'*? Did he know her? No matter how she racked her brain, she couldn't remember ever seeing the diminutive older man before.

He was an elemental, but something was...off about him and his powers. His aura was bright and spoke of water, but it had a thick black ring around it. Elissa had never seen anything like it. She didn't have to concentrate to see it, either. It pulsed around him, dense and calling to her. It felt evil and made her insides recoil.

Instinct told her she couldn't show him weakness. Quivers darted up and down her limbs and she fought a full-body shudder. He'd made her disrobe, and while he hadn't regarded her with lust, revealing her bare body to him made her vulnerable in a way she couldn't afford to let herself feel if she was to survive this.

She swallowed and tried to square her shoulders. Elissa had failed to play on the sympathies of her half-elfin captor. Didn't know how much time had passed since they'd taken her, or since that night in the clearing. Just snatches of awareness here and there and then he'd put her asleep again. He'd only woken her once more and fed her, but she'd been so woozy she had no recollection of time of day or location they'd been.

He was still in the room, too, but she didn't spare him a glance. She needed to be ready to defend herself, even if her powers were still ignoring her calls. Frustration welled and she made fists at her sides. If she did anything, either of them could release the Dimithian.

She looked down at the small rock. The force shield around it throbbed as if strained, like it would fail any moment. Elissa remembered the burning all over her body when she'd tried to use her powers near it. Wouldn't want to feel that again; crippling pain wouldn't help her escape.

Elissa wanted to look around, try to figure out where she was, see if she could get out, but she didn't want to look away from the small man in front of her, or the magic-sucking element that was supposed to be a myth.

Her repeated mental calls to her bondmate resulted in nothing, like it had from the start when she'd woken by the tree. Lady Cera said they'd always be limited by distance, but it was unheard of to be far from one's bondmate for an extended period of time. They needed each other.

She spared a subtle glance around the dark place. A cave?

They must be in a cave. The air was humid and dank. It was dim, but the rough rounded walls had magic lighting them, similar to Sir Lucan's globes in Castle Aldern, but they were magic-born colored flames. Natural formations were all over the lighted areas.

In her peripheral vision, she could see a dais of some sort, with a throne-like chair at its center. A pile of blankets in one corner below a large mirror suggested a sleeping pallet.

"I've a gift for you, my pretty." The elemental was honey-sweet and Elissa tried not to flinch when he approached her. "Give me your hand."

"Nay." Their eyes locked. His were dark, and radiated the same evil of his aura. She fought the urge to run as her stomach dived to her toes.

Rage shot across his lined face, and he snatched her wrist away from her body. Nails dug in and tore her skin.

Elissa locked her jaw to avoid a shriek of pain.

"You. Will. Obey. Me," he commanded. His aura rose and radiated a blood-red color.

She swallowed a whimper, but refused to lower her eyes. Elissa had no clue where her courage was coming from, but she held onto it with all her might.

The evil mage slapped something cold on her right wrist. It closed with a *snap* at the same time a jolt of agony shook her arm. As if the metal had bitten her.

She looked down at what resembled a single slender manacle, but it had no chains attached. A dark red stone was embedded flat in its center. It swirled and glowed with magic.

Her head started to spin and she swayed on her feet. Her temples throbbed and her stomach dipped again. Bile cascaded *up* with a speed she couldn't fight.

Elissa grabbed her middle and bent over, losing the meager contents of her stomach.

A chuckle teased her ears and she tried to glare at her captor. "Good, it's already working."

"What…what'd…you do to me?" She panted as she fought to stand up.

"Nothing harmful, my pretty. The bracelet links us with my blood. Your powers to mine. It'll lock your magic away until I'm ready to use it." He sighed, and the sound was almost wistful. "I wish I had one when you were a tiny lassie. You would've been with me turns ago. How does it feel to be a normal human with no magic?"

His words swirled around in her head while they sunk in. "Turns ago?" Elissa whispered.

He smiled, an evil thing that started small and spread slowly until it threatened to split his face. "Aye. You've always been mine."

It hit her then, like a sword lancing her heart.

Elissa's knees wobbled, then buckled. Her gown wasn't enough padding against the harsh cave floor, but she didn't pay attention to the white-hot blow that shot into her thighs, because the agony in her chest was so much worse. "You… You're the one who killed my family." Tears rolled down her cheeks even though she cursed them.

The mage looked at her half-elfin kidnapper instead of her. "Oh, she's clever indeed. We'll have much fun together."

Elissa gasped until an unwanted sob broke from her lips. She collapsed to the harsh floor and rolled to her back. The bracelet was burning the surrounding skin now, as if branding her. Pain worked its way up her arm, into her shoulder and chest.

She tried to blink and clear her vision, but blackness was inching up and she sighed, relaxing her body. Fighting was no use.

Chapter Thirty-four

The arrival of Lord Cam and his men was more hindrance than help, even though the duke had brought his healer. The man had fixed Alasdair's side and leg. Chided him, too, remarking on carelessness and allowing so much blood loss. Said it'd been no wonder he'd passed out.

That still had bite, though none of his brothers had faulted him for it—or ever would. Didn't matter; he still felt weak.

Alasdair didn't want to see Lord Cam, nor recognize his genuine concern and anger that Elissa had been taken. The duke cared for her.

She's going to marry this man.

Lord Cam and his men had ridden their fastest horses to the northern harbor of Dalunas, almost into the Province of Berat. Then they'd taken a ship up the east coast, halving the travel time by a sevenday, if not more.

They'd met at Castle Marlock, a large holding in the northern part of Tarvis. The lord of the manor, Derack Marlock, had offered men and hospitality. His land sat within a few hours' ride northwest of the camp Elissa had been taken from.

Lord Jorrin had sent more men-at-arms and two more of his brothers, Roduch and Artan. The Duke of Tarvis—Lady Cera's uncle—had also offered men and assistance.

Lucan's magic had given them few answers. They knew the direction Elissa's captors had gone—even farther north, and likely west—but the lad couldn't pinpoint the destination, nor were there any clues to lend to it.

The longer they were delayed, the more frantic Alasdair had felt, and the more he couldn't show it.

Especially since Lord Cam had arrived. Although he wasn't doing a good job of masking his emotions. He carried his rage like a dark cloud. Got looks from all the men, especially his brothers.

Alasdair wasn't entitled to his feelings.

She didn't belong to him, and never would. Elissa had made that clear.

She'd been gone five days, and they were no closer to getting her back than the day she'd been stolen. Alasdair would've broken off and gone on his own — Leargan's orders be damned — but he'd never been the best tracker amongst his brothers. Admitting he needed the help, whether magical or otherwise, was killing him.

Mischief was as frantic as Alasdair, but Lucan was having trouble communicating with him. Despite all the lad's magic, his gifts weren't animal-centric.

"We could call Hadrian," Lucan suggested to an audience of Alasdair's brothers, Lord Cam and his men, and a mixture of men Lord Marlock and the Duke of Tarvis had lent to help. The lord of the manor only had two knights in his service, but even they offered assistance.

Alasdair remembered the elf wizard from several turns before when he'd helped defeat Lord Varthan, the man who'd killed Lady Cera's family. The wizard had strong magic, which included being able to communicate with animals. However, time of was of the essence. "We can't wait for anyone else to arrive."

"I agree." Lord Cam was gruff. The duke sat at the head of Lord Marlock's table in what passed for a great hall of the small castle. He was dressed in Dalunas colors, but travel clothing, instead of the lavish garments Alasdair was used to seeing him in. He leaned back in the lord's chair and crossed his arms over his chest.

Maps were spread out before them. Lucan had tried to scry for Elissa, but the lad hadn't gotten anything even with the Durroc family broach from her trunk. He surmised whoever had taken her had her covered in magic, like they had before the Dimithian.

"We don't have to wait." Lucan's answer was clear and even.

The lad squared his shoulders as all eyes regarded him.

"Meaning?" Leargan asked.

"I can cast a spell. See and talk to Hadrian. But if he cannot communicate with Mischief that way, we'll have to reassess." The lad's explanation was acknowledged with a mix of grunts and nods.

Alasdair paused his pacing—his new constant way of passing time—and stared at Lucan. "Is it possible?"

"Aye, I should think so."

He didn't like the hesitation he saw.

"It's worth a try," Leargan said.

"I agree. We're getting nowhere," Lord Cam said. His face was as weary as Alasdair felt.

They agreed Lucan would contact the elf wizard, and the room slowly cleared out as many of the men were sent to handle duties to prepare for their journey northwest. Alasdair wasn't moving, though, and neither was Leargan or Lord Cam.

The lad took a large mirror and propped it up on the table in front of him. Lucan closed his eyes and said a spellword. He breathed deeply and his skin started to glow, but the radiance receded by the time Lucan opened his eyes and returned to his seat.

Alasdair scooted closer, so he could see the surface of the mirror. A bushy white beard appeared first. Then the elf's thin face became visible, with thick snowy eyebrows and only one long tapered ear. The other was obscured by a black conical hat that sat cockeyed on his head. Did nothing to tame wild white locks that surrounded thin shoulders.

"Lucan, lad. It's good to see you! I'm surprised you called." Hadrian's gravelly voice was heavily accented, denoting the far north. The Mountains of Aramour.

Lucan must've called mentally, because other than the magic word, the lad hadn't said anything aloud.

However, Alasdair didn't have time for fascination about magic—or pleasantries. "Get on with it," he muttered.

Leargan, who'd been close enough to hear, shot him a look he chose to ignore.

"Hadrian, I need your help." Lucan explained the problem quickly, efficiently, impressing Alasdair, despite his impatience. The lad seemed older than his five-and-ten turns.

The elf wizard asked a few questions and shook his head. "Without physical contact, I can't do much more than you, lad. I'm too far for thought-sending to be of help, even if he would mind me. Since he's bonded, without touch, I doubt that anyway."

"How long would it take you to get here?" Lucan asked.

Hadrian scratched his beard and blew out a breath. "You're in northern Tarvis?"

Lucan nodded.

"Four days."

"We're not waiting four days!" Alasdair barked.

Lord Cam murmured agreement.

Hadrian's expression was soaked with regret. "Then there's nothing I can do."

Alasdair's gut clenched, and he paced by the table again. He couldn't look at the elf wizard in the mirror anymore.

Nothing was of any use. Magic was failing them.

Hadrian asked what'd happened, as well as questions about Dimithian, but Alasdair tuned them out. He strode the length of the table and back, his boots heavier with each step.

We don't have time for this.

Not knowing what danger she was in was killing him.

He'd never been a man of great faith, but he prayed to the Blessed Spirit she could stay strong. Stay alive.

I'll find you, Elissa. Just hang on.

☆   ☆   ☆   ☆

She was in a small dark corner of the cave, and she hadn't seen anyone but the elemental mage in what seemed forever. In reality, it'd only been a day or two, but she'd never felt more alone. She was desperate to determine how long she'd been gone, but everything was a guess.

Had traveling to the cave been two days? Three?

Elissa called for her bondmate over and over, with no response. Tried to tamp down her rising panic every time she failed to hear from Mischief. Couldn't sense their bond, although that could've been because of the bracelet as much as distance from him.

Her captor had told her his name was Drayton, and he'd given her a pallet to sleep on along with clean blankets, food to eat. The little area was a nook with semi-privacy, too. It didn't fix the fact that she was a prisoner.

Conversations with Drayton grated, but she tried to gain clues to his weakness—anything that could help her escape. He liked to talk, and Elissa listened, trying to learn what she could while she battled with grief.

He'd killed her parents and Emery—and their staff—in order to gain her magic. He'd explained she'd protected herself. She didn't remember anything he was claiming, but she hadn't been able to remember Castle Durroc the day she'd visited, either.

Drayton went on to tell her there were more deaths on her hands, as well. Three young families in three Provinces, because he couldn't find her. He'd said it with a smile, as if he'd not been sharing news of slaughtered children. He blamed her for his *forced* actions.

Her nightmares all those sevendays ago, before she'd left Terraquist for Greenwald made sense now. They'd been some form of visions—something that'd never happened to her before.

She cradled her head in her hands. Grief and blame wouldn't get her out of Drayton's cave. Elissa needed to stay strong and deal with the rest later. Her parents, her brother, they'd want her to survive this. Her gut told her that, even if they'd been dead twenty turns.

As for the lasses and their families, she'd cried for each and every one. Until she'd been sick on the floor beside her pallet the night before. Because she'd been born an elemental mage, they'd died. She didn't know them, but it didn't matter.

After his recital, Drayton had told her she was his *guest*. Of course, he'd not let her out of his sight, but she was free to roam the cave's main space. Elissa couldn't use her magic, but she soon discovered why Drayton wasn't worried she'd stride out his home with ease.

The place was covered in protection spells. They were thick, wall-like, and would alert the mage immediately if someone breached them. And they were visible, writhing dark waves that reminded her of swarming spiders moving as one. Made her skin crawl just looking at them.

Drayton practiced blood magic, so all of his spells had a piece of him in them.

She looked down at the bracelet on her wrist. The red stone pulsed, but it was no ruby. Drayton's blood was inside the stone. It confined her magic within her body, but also allowed *him* to call her powers if he wanted to. She'd tried to pull it off only once. It'd caused crippling pain all over her body, but worse—tampering with the bracelet had brought Drayton running to her. He'd laughed and praised her strength.

They were linked, and it churned her gut.

Access to her magic had given him access to other things, like her name. If he could read her thoughts, he hadn't said, but she tried to remember to build walls in her mind at all times, just in case.

Elissa's stomach roiled and trepidation rolled over her body. She shuddered and hugged her knees to her chest on the small pallet while fighting the urge to rock.

What she'd been taught about blood magic from the king's mages was that it was dangerous and dark. It'd been forbidden by all human and elfin mages alike, ages ago. Evil that couldn't be redeemed.

"Good morning, my pretty."

"Stop calling me that," Elissa barked.

Drayton chuckled. "Stand, and come to me." His expression was pleasant, but he commanded.

She shivered and reluctantly rose. His temper was lightning fast, and she had no ability to protect herself with magic.

"I have news for you."

"You're letting me go?"

He laughed again and flashed an evil smile. "Nay. It's time for my plan to move forward."

"Plan?"

Drayton ignored her and pulled her to him. "Ah, all in due time, my Elissa."

That's not any better than 'my pretty.' But she didn't say it.

He stroked her cheek. Elissa didn't yank away. The last time she had, he'd slapped her hard enough to knock her out.

They were of equal height—which made him short for a man—and he was lean. His salt-and-pepper locks should've confirmed his age, but didn't. His eyes had the same unnatural black ring around brown irises, like his aura. His face was a mix of old and young, lines and smoothness.

She didn't know why, but she could guess it had to do with blood magic. He could control all four elements like her. He was strongest in water, but his power with fire was almost equal. What he hadn't told her, she'd gleaned from watching him.

Drayton leaned in, inhaling right above her ear. "Hmmm, you smell so good, my pretty. This shall not be difficult at all."

"What won't?"

He didn't answer. Just settled his hands on her shoulders and she tried not to wince.

Elissa's stomach pitched, bile burned her throat. She tugged away from the evil mage and bent over to vomit. She panted through waves of nausea and tried not to let her knees buckle. Whatever had been in the food he'd served her had made her sick since the night before. The nausea was intermittent, and she had no desire to eat again.

"Come here," Drayton called.

"What, you're not going to ask me if I'm well?" Her tone wasn't as dry as she would've liked, but Elissa obeyed, wiping her mouth with the back of her hand and wishing for water.

"Hush." His voice dropped and he rested his hands on her shoulders like he had before she'd needed to throw up. The old man closed his eyes and took a deep breath.

A spell swirled around them and Elissa's limbs warmed. The stone on her bracelet shot a column red light. Her magic moved unnaturally beneath the surface of her skin and she trembled. Drayton's magic was there, too, with evil jostling her, and she fought the urge to vomit again.

Moments of silence passed, and finally, Drayton's eyes flew open, his expression severe. His gaze compelled hers to remain locked with his, even though her body fought it, fidgeting in his hold.

"You've had a lover." He narrowed his eyes.

"What business is it of yours?" Elissa wanted to sound just as harsh he had, but failed. She didn't want to think of Alasdair, because then she'd worry about him. Question why he hadn't found her yet.

"Is he a mage?" Drayton demanded.

"Why?"

"Answer me, my pretty. Or I shall get angry."

"No. He has no magic." She wasn't about to admit Alasdair was a knight.

The mage cursed and tightened his grip on her shoulders. Until his long fingertips bit into her flesh through the material of her gown. He shook her, and Elissa winced. She fought him, but Drayton didn't release his hold. "You'd better hope it doesn't matter. That your magic is powerful enough."

"For what?"

He sneered, pushing his face close enough to kiss her.

"Because if the child you carry has no magic, it's of no use to me. You die sooner."

Elissa flushed to her toes. She couldn't focus on his death threat. "Ch-ch-child?" Her heart thundered until her temples throbbed and her head spun.

Drayton whirled away, grumbling. His cape flew up around him and he disappeared around the corner.

She backed up until her heels hit her pallet. Collapsed in a ball, unable to fight tears. Then a sob.

A child?

Alasdair's child.

She plastered her hand to her lower belly.

It hadn't been long enough for her pregnancy to show, but now her queasiness made sense. It'd started on the road, and she'd put it off to not having ridden Storm since she'd run from Castle Aldern.

"So it wasn't Drayton's food, either." Her eyes clouded with tears again, so Elissa crushed them shut and forced deep breaths.

She was trapped in a cave with a mad man who'd murdered her family, and she was carrying a child.

The child of the only man she'd ever loved.

What about Lord Cam? Surely he wouldn't marry her now. She wouldn't be able to hide it, nor would she trick the duke into thinking the child was his after they wed.

What would Alasdair say?

He'd proposed.

I still can't marry him.

He didn't love her.

Elissa swallowed and sat up, rubbing her tears away. She couldn't worry about the duke or her knight. "I have to get out of here." Her whisper echoed off the walls surrounding her, but it didn't lessen her resolve.

She rested both hands over her womb.

I'm not alone.

But her child was in as much danger as she was. Drayton would use blood magic to steal her powers. Elissa knew it in her gut. If he drained her, it'd kill her *and* the baby she carried. Mischief, too.

"I'm not letting that happen."

Now she had something more to fight for.

I will *get out of here.*

chapter Thirty-five

his lass, *his* Elissa was spoiled. Ruined.

She was highborn. Unmarried. A lady.

Drayton had assumed she was pure. But she carried another man's child.

Whore. He made a fist. His pride was stung, when he should be grateful.

He'd planned on using magic to determine when she was fertile, but it hadn't been necessary. Drayton had seen her vomiting the night before, as well as heard her earlier that morning all the way from his pallet.

His probing spell confirmed something already quickened within her womb.

If the child was an elemental, fine. If it wasn't, waiting for the birth was going to be a waste his valuable time. Eating up months he could barely afford. Drayton could forget his plan and take Elissa's magic now, killing her and the child, or wait...and give it a chance. Given the depth of her powers, it was unlikely she would birth a magicless babe.

He paced the cave floor in front of his dais, pivoting around to start over when he ran out of room. Pressing his fingertips to his lips, he forced himself to breathe normally. "This is good." He wouldn't have to impregnate her himself. Wouldn't have to sacrifice valuable energy.

Although, he'd not rutted a woman in a long time. In his younger turns, he'd had a healthy appetite for the lasses. Perhaps he should partake of his Elissa, no matter the child. For his pleasure. Age and weakness had stolen his drive for anything but magic for so long. A change could be good for him.

She'd fight him, no doubt.

Drayton smiled. A good fight wouldn't be such a bad thing, would it? Now he had her magic to help strengthen him, although the bracelet didn't allow for full access.

Nay. Someone else had already had her first.

He scowled. Shouldn't care that she wasn't innocent—after all, his plan always included her death—but the idea of another man moving in and out of her, planting his seed, grated on Drayton's senses.

The half-breed had assured him the lass was brought to him untouched. By him or his associates, of course. It hadn't mattered. He'd wanted Elissa for so long, and now he had her. Charis had told him she'd been with a party of knights and men-at-arms from Greenwald. She'd been headed to Dalunas where she was to marry the duke. Obviously she and the duke hadn't waited to rut.

Details about the journey he'd plucked from her mind when he'd learned her name, but he hadn't gleaned anything else from her. Elissa's mind was strong, and she was stubborn. Kept him out with robust mental shields.

He'd had her for three days.

Strong as she might be, he'd break her down. Soon, he'd know everything about Elissa Durroc—inside and out, if he took her. Besides, intercourse would strengthen his link to her magic. While they had no interruptions, he should do it.

Drayton had half-expected his hirelings to reappear the previous day. Surely the spell he had on the chest had worn off by now. He'd used a great deal of energy to disguise that rubbish.

He chuckled.

The coin he'd paid Charis over the months had been real, but he'd not possessed of the promised price for Elissa—nor would he have parted with that amount of gold if he'd had it in his coffers.

"Ah, well, it matters not."

If—probably *when*—the half-breed returned, Drayton was ready for him. He had protection magic in place, including a scatter spell that'd make Charis and his lads forget where his cave was when they got close enough. The area was riddled with caves, so it would take his former hirelings a while to find him anyway. And, if they did manage it, he now had Elissa's magic to protect himself. The bracelet would allow that much.

Drayton sighed and stepped onto his dais. He adjusted his cape and sat on his throne. "Soon. Soon."

Or would it be? Could he risk waiting for her child to be born?

As the pregnancy advanced, perhaps he could use magic to determine if the child was an elemental. He'd have to research a spell.

Male or female mattered not. Only magic mattered. The right kind of magic, of course.

His Elissa would prove worth the risk.

Perhaps over the following months, she'd gain an appreciation for him. Drayton would properly care for her, after all. If she never came to him willingly, it wouldn't matter. He'd always liked the lasses who'd put up a fight best. His advanced turns hadn't changed that.

He steepled his hands in front of him. Even though the child she carried wasn't his, they could still find pleasure together.

Her magic was already making him stronger.

Drayton smiled.

And started to plan.

☆   ☆   ☆   ☆

The crushing disappointment of Hadrian's inability to help Lucan communicate with Mischief from his home, four days' ride away in Berat, took the wind out of all the men's sails. But Alasdair refused to let it get him down.

He'd find Elissa—with or without his brothers' help. But he wasn't delaying a moment longer.

He stuffed supplies into Tess' saddle bags. He'd only been able to wheedle a day or two of food from Lord Marlock's kitchens, but he'd make due.

Alasdair wasn't alone in the small courtyard of Castle Marlock; it was barely dawn. Mischief had followed him without question. As if the wolf could sense his plans. Elissa's bondmate sat next to Tess outside the stables. The beast would lift his nose and sniff the air from time to time, whining, as if to hurry Alasdair's preparations.

"Not long now, lad," he whispered, tugging his pack shut and giving the wolf a half-smile.

"What're you doing?"

Alasdair had expected Leargan. He'd been bunking with his captain and their brothers in one of the castles' small guest quarters. The rest of their men slept in the hall, and some in the stables.

He closed his eyes and sucked in a breath. The last thing he needed was a confrontation with the Duke of Dalunas. He turned slowly, and met Lord Cam's blue eyes.

The duke was already dressed for travel. The sword at his waist wasn't the decorative variety. He was ready to fight—too bad it was for Elissa.

"Going to find her. I won't wait and debate magic any longer."

"I don't disagree with you, but you can't do it alone," Lord Cam said.

Alasdair clenched his jaw. "Mischief'll sense her when we get close."

Doubt flashed across his expression. "I wish it was that simple." He shook his head. "I believe we need magic. It'd be foolish to leave without young Lucan."

"We?"

Lord Cam narrowed his eyes. "I'm going with you."

Alasdair shut down his quick denial. He had neither rank, nor right, to assert such things. Instead, he swallowed and straightened his shoulders. "I'm leaving now."

A shout caught their collective attention. Lucan was running toward them top-speed, as if he'd known they'd just been discussing him. "Alas!" the lad panted.

"What is it, lad?" Alasdair rested both hands on Lucan's shoulders when he skidded to a stop beside him.

"I couldn't sleep."

"And?" Lord Cam came closer.

"I probed for magic."

Men started to pour out of the oversized castle doors. A few of his brothers jogged toward the stables, men-at-arms from Castle Marlock, as well as Lord Cam's men, on their heels as they all went to get horses. The Duke of Tarvis' knights weren't far behind.

Tess neighed and shifted her hooves behind Alasdair, but he tried to tune out all the distractions and focus on what Lucan was saying.

Lord Cam was firing questions at the lad.

"I thought you'd already done that, lad. Probed for great miles," Alasdair said.

Lucan's green eyes were determined. "Aye, I had. But I did it again. And I found something."

"What? Speak," the duke ordered.

Alasdair wanted to throw him an irritated glare, but didn't take his eyes off Lucan.

Orders were being hollered. Horses and men filled the bailey around them. Eivan, Lord Cam's captain, led the duke's white destrier and stood waiting with his own horse on the other side of them.

Mischief started to pace and whimper.

"As we already know, one of the men who took her has tracking magic. He's good, so it took me a while to locate him from magical trail alone. Until now, when I found more than just the tracker."

"Go on," Alasdair urged, tightening his grip on the knighted mage and shaking Lucan's shoulders.

"There was a vast darkness. A dead spot."

"A dead spot?" Lord Cam asked.

Lucan nodded. "I sensed blood magic."

"Where?" Alasdair's mind spun over all the information Lucan and Hadrian, as well as Lord Cam's mages had shared with the men about magic. And Dimithian. They'd touched on blood magic and its evils. He knew more about magic than he'd ever wanted to know; the information must've sunk in, because panic threatened to claw him from the inside out.

If a mage who practiced blood magic had Elissa, she was in more danger than they could've imagined. The attack when she was a wee lass confirmed the king's suspicions. Someone *was* after her magic. Perhaps they'd get the answers King Nathal had never been able to obtain.

"Northwest. The area is like a beacon to me now."

"Northwest?" Lord Cam breathed.

"Terraquist," Alasdair said at the same time.

Lucan nodded. "The tracker did something."

"Like what?" Lord Cam's brow was furrowed when Alasdair spared the duke a glance.

"I don't know." The lad shook his head. "But it's clear to me. There's nothing shielding it."

"Lucan!" Leargan strode across the courtyard, his squire Brodic on his heels. Both had rolled pieces of parchment in their hands. "Show me on the map. Quickly, lad, so we can go."

Brodic opened and held the map up while Lucan pointed.

"That area is riddled with caves," Leargan said.

"Not far from Terraquist Main," Lord Cam said.

"Aye." Alasdair remembered times of exploration and curious lads. They'd ridden out to the caves during free time over the turns of training to become a knight.

Leargan seemed to notice him for the first time and glared. "You and I will have words later."

Alasdair nodded. His captain was irritated, so his intentions to leave on his own were no secret. It wasn't important now. They needed to go.

Find Elissa.

"Are you sure, Lucan?" Lord Cam asked.

Lucan nodded. "I'm sure, my lord."

"It's a hard ride," Leargan said.

"We don't stop," Alasdair vowed.

Leargan and Lord Cam exchanged a glance Alasdair ignored. He called himself every name in the book.

Over the past few days, he'd done his best to be stoic. Swallow his anger and pack his feelings away. Didn't want the duke to suspect how he felt about Elissa, even if Leargan and his brothers knew.

A word he still hadn't acknowledged swirled around in his head.

When they got her back, she'd go to Dalunas with Lord Cam. Marry Lord Cam.

Alasdair wouldn't know how she was doing after being taken. Wouldn't know if she'd been mistreated...if she'd be all right.

"Let's go," he growled and swung himself onto Tess' wide back.

Chapter Thirty-Six

Charis couldn't stop thinking about her. It'd been days since he'd left her with Drayton, and right after, he'd gone to the closest tavern in Lower Terraquist and gotten piss drunk. Like he couldn't cope with what he'd done.

He'd killed people and not felt as much guilt, for Blessed Spirit's sake.

Not an innocent lass, though. Not even when they'd raided the three holdings for Drayton. Nason and Bracken had taken care of the killing.

It wasn't that he didn't have the stomach for taking lives, but most of the deaths he'd caused had been justified. They died for reasons other than mercenary duties. Or if it was a hired job, the men deserved death for whatever they'd done.

"She's not dead, get over it." *Yet.* For some reason, he couldn't shake that knowledge. The old codger practiced blood magic, and taking the lass to him had signed her death warrant.

Drayton had wanted her so badly because of her strength. He was going to absorb her magic. Take her powers, and her life.

Charis was at fault. Leaving her there was the same as running her through with his sword. He blew out a breath and knocked his head into the tree he sat against. Closed his eyes and dragged a hand down his stubbled cheeks.

They'd left Terraquist's city center and were about a half-day's ride south. They'd head to North Ascova next; there were whispers of work for men like him and his lads.

Charis hadn't even been able to enjoy their time in the tavern in the arms of a lass. He'd been so in his cups, amber liquid was all he'd wanted to see. Ignored all the female attention trying to drape themselves all over him. Unlike like Nason and Bracken, who'd both spent a ridiculous amount of Drayton's coin on whores.

Bracken's yell had him on his feet, and drawing his sword. He ran toward the center of their camp and made eye-contact with Nason, who stopped tending the fire to follow.

The big man was near their horses. Hovered over the chest of gold the old codger had given them to split three ways. Rage rolled off Bracken in waves, and his back visibly seethed, as if he was panting to hold it together. When he exploded—truly exploded—no one wanted to be in his way.

"What's wrong?" Charis snapped.

"This." Bracken flung the lid open so hard it screeched a protest.

Charis cursed.

Instead of gold coins, the chest was full of rubble. Small pieces of wood and metal, debris filling it to the brim.

"What did ya do wit' our gold, ya brute?" Nason asked, but he didn't get near Bracken. He knew better.

"Nothin'" Bracken hollered. His eye ticked as he towered over the blond man.

Charis slapped a hand on Nason's thin wrist before he could do something stupid. "He didn't do anything. We've been tricked."

Bracken cursed in Aramourian—words so foul there wasn't a human equivalent.

"I seen gold in there," Nason protested. He tugged free of Charis' hold and pointed at the contents of the chest.

"I did, too," Bracken said.

"As did I," Charis said.

"Then what—"

"Magic. Are ya daft?" Bracken barked at Nason.

They bickered back and forth, then both pinned Charis with matching glares.

"How did he get away wit' it?" Bracken asked. "Why didn't ya know? *You* carried the chest out of tha cave." The man threw more accusation than anger at him.

"I don't know." Charis ran a palm over the debris filling the chest. He muttered a spellword, but nothing happened. Not a shimmer of magic touched his senses. He shook his head. "It must've been a powerful spell to just wear out with no trace."

Bracken and Nason cursed again, simultaneously.

"I checked it for magic, I swear. Said every revealing spell I know before I left the cave. He fooled me as much as you two."

Bracken studied him with narrowed eyes, before giving a curt nod. The brute believed him.

"I paid the wenches with coin from here," Nason said.

"It's coin no more, then. If the spell wore off for us, no doubt it has for them," Charis said.

Bracken flashed a grin. "Serviced for free."

"We won' be goin' back to tha' tavern." Nason smirked.

"I guess we wouldn't be welcome." Bracken nodded. When Nason echoed his grin, Charis rolled his eyes.

"I don't work for free," he said, deadly.

"Neither do I."

"I don't, either."

The three of them exchanged a glance, then collective growls.

"I'm gonna kill tha' bastard." Bracken brandished a huge fist.

"Not if I get him first," Charis vowed.

"Let's go, now. Get tha lass back 'til he pays up right," Bracken said. "He pays, then he can 'ave her."

The lass.

He had a chance to get her away from Drayton. Especially if he ran the codger through.

Charis' gut clenched.

Why was he worried more about the lass than being tricked?

☆   ☆   ☆   ☆

They'd retraced their ride from the day before, covering the same ground, but it'd seemed to take twice as long to get close to where the old elemental lived. And, it'd taken nearly an hour of roaming the area before Charis realized they weren't *lost*.

Magic was preventing them from locating Drayton's cave.

He sighed and dragged his hand down his face, slumping in Barley's saddle. When he thought of the cave's location, his thoughts darted to something else. "It's got to be a spell." Disorientation clouded his mind and made him dizzy. He shook his head and shoved the magical haze away.

Damn distracting.

Bracken narrowed his eyes. "Aye, you're jus' figurin' tha' out?"

Nason snickered and Charis sent them both black looks.

"Fix it."

"I'll try. I have to figure out what magic he used before I can block it."

Bracken muttered, "A tracker indeed."

Charis let it go. He didn't have time to haul off and punch the big man.

Had the old codger killed the lass already? His heart rate picked up and he chided himself.

This was about being swindled. Had nothing to do with the lass. He teetered back and forth between Bracken's idea of taking the lass until Drayton paid them what he owed, and just killing the bastard outright. The world wouldn't mourn a mage who practiced blood magic.

"I need a moment," he said.

Bracken smirked, but Charis closed his eyes and blocked out everything—his companions, the sounds of nature, rustling wind, even the neigh of one of their horses. He concentrated on breathing deeply and seeking the magic preventing him from his desire.

His heart fell into a calm even rhythm, and he sent his magic out from his body. Charis' limbs warmed and his skin tingled. He located the magic without further effort. It was a dark spot on the horizon, and it throbbed red and black. The two colors writhed and intertwined, as if alive. Charis probed farther, and clarity hit him.

A scatter spell.

A magical, *'Stay away!'* Now the disorientation and memory loss made sense.

He studied the magic for a moment. Was confident in how to destroy it. The only complication was it would unmask the whole area. If anyone else was looking for the cave, they'd be able to locate it without effort.

Charis blasted Drayton's spell with one of his own.

He squinted at the brilliant flare of golden light. Slowly it faded, taking the black and red with it. When he glanced at his lads, Bracken had his eyes shielded and Nason had his closed.

"Is it done?" Bracken asked.

"Aye."

Without Drayton's spell, the path to his home was laid out before them. The area had many caves. It could take hours to explore them all. But only one direction pointed to something sinister. The ground before it was dark, devoid of magic and exuded evil. Darkness spread out from the entrance, like reaching, rotting fingers.

Blood magic.

The surrounding foliage was dead, even the trees shriveled and black. The old codger was killing the forest. From their distance—probably an hour's ride—Charis could sense Drayton's black protection spells. He shuddered.

How have I not noticed that before?

Bracken snapped his fingers. Nason laughed.

"Let's go get the bastard," the big man snarled.

Charis gave a curt nod and kneed Barley.

They didn't talk as they rode, but it was for the best. Charis was stewing and worrying, trying to convince himself this was all about coin, and not the lass. A noble lady, although he'd never gotten her name. She'd demanded his, and he'd not complied. He never did. Had his lads trained well, too. No one was referred to by name when they were completing a job.

He pulled Barley to a stop outside Drayton's cave. Jumped from his horse's back. His boots kicked up black dust and he fought tremors. Even the debris outside the wide mouth of the codger's home seeped evil.

"Coming with?" Charis looked up at Bracken.

Nason shook his head even though he'd not addressed the blond man.

Bracken hedged, even before he spoke. Made a point to reach for Barley's reins. "I'll leave ya to it."

Charis smirked. "Thought you were going to fight me for the honor."

"Nay, 'tis your duty."

"Aye, I'll handle the old codger." Charis' chuckle was whipped away. A cringe took over as he strode through the protection spell-wall, and ignored the sensation of crawling on his back. Pushed forward hard. Needed surprise, or this'd be a very short confrontation.

He drew his sword and had the most powerful stunning spell he knew at-the-ready. Needed to knock Drayton on his arse—and pray it'd work.

His quarry was in the main room, where he'd always received Charis.

The old codger's eyes widened as he threw the stunning spell without warning. A ball of bright white light hit the elemental mage square in the chest. Drayton crumpled in a heap in front of his dais.

Charis rushed forward. Didn't have much time.

Drayton was ready for him and threw a magical sphere of black light at him.

He dodged, barely. It wasn't anything of the elements he could recognize, but looked nasty. Would probably hurt. Sweat broke out on Charis' forehead, but he couldn't afford to get distracted, or Drayton would kill him in less than a heartbeat. He only had the upper hand because he'd taken the man by surprise.

Charis fired three more spells. Drayton answered by throwing up a wall of water that stopped him short when it crackled. If his spells had hit the old elemental, they hadn't any effect.

Dammit.

He circled the water shield. Couldn't get closer. Sparks played on its surface. It was far from harmless. The spell wouldn't just wet him, but burn him. Jolt through him, like lightning. Kill him. "You tricked me!"

Drayton's high-pitched cackle filled the air.

The lass wasn't in sight, but Charis couldn't acknowledge the sinking feeling in his gut.

Was he too late?

"Took you long enough to figure it out, half-breed."

Charis advanced as far as he dared. He glanced around the cave. Needed something. Anything.

Dimithian.

Where could the old mage keep it?

He racked his brain to remember the spell Drayton had used to call it to him. Charis knew the one to remove the force shield around it.

Two little words he needed. *Now.*

The rock would affect his powers if he could find it — use it — but he still had his sword.

Running Drayton through would be more satisfying than killing him with magic, anyway.

He sucked in air and raised his palm flat and high.

Drayton watched him, head cocked to one side. The water

wall wavered, but only for a moment. The codger raised *his* hand and the wall thickened, less transparent. More sparks danced around and through it. Weaving in and out, like snakes.

Charis yelled the spell and prayed the rock would appear in his palm. Revulsion roiled his stomach at the same time Drayton yelled.

"Nay! Nay! 'Tis *mine*!"

"It's mine, now."

"It'll take your magic!" A mixture of satisfaction and fear coated the old mage's voice.

"I don't care. I don't need magic to kill you." Charis yelled the spellword that vanished the protective magic around the Dimithian. He threw it at Drayton.

The old man screamed, and the water wall disappeared. He cowered as Charis approached.

Shudders rolled down his spine and Charis pushed it all away.

No magic. He felt naked.

He'd get his magic back as soon as he had the shield back in place on the rock. He hoped anyway. "Where's the lass?"

"She's mine." Spittle dribbled down the man's chin, but he didn't move a muscle when Charis put his sword to his neck.

"Nay. You didn't pay for her. Which makes her *mine*." He pushed his weapon forward slowly.

Drayton gasped. The apple of his throat bobbed.

Shouted orders and the rushing of thundering boots had Charis pausing, even though the tip of his sword was pressed tight to Drayton's jugular.

That's not Bracken and Nason.

Too many footfalls for it to be his lads alone. Then he heard the clash of swords. No doubt Bracken and Nason challenged whoever was at the mouth of the cave.

Charis' spell had bared the area to whoever sought it.

The lass' knights?

He froze and Drayton's eyes darted toward the now unprotected cave entrance. A streak of silver-white darted into Charis' periphery, but then it was gone.

The wolf.

He needed to get out of here.

Charis slid his blade into Drayton's throat and didn't even wait to watch the gurgling. The codger slumped in front of his dais. He jumped out of the way of the blood starting to pool and darted around the corner to follow the beast, sheathing his bloody sword.

Relief rolled over him when he saw her.

She's alive.

The lass wept, her arms around the silver wolf.

"My lady." Why he'd had to see her with his own eyes, know she was fine, was something he'd examine later.

Her eyes were wide and startled when their gazes locked.

The beast broke away from her, growling, hackles raised down to his stiff tail.

Chapter Thirty-Seven

Elissa had spent the last two days crying on her pallet. Drayton had tried to cajole her into joining him in the main living space of his cave, but she'd had no desire to join her captor, and didn't hide her glares when he brought her food.

He was gentler to her now, since he'd announced her pregnancy. The old mage hadn't lifted a hand to her for disobedience or sharp tongue, either. But she could feel his patience waning through their link.

And she was so weak. Her magic was there, but being denied access to it gave her a constant headache, plus she could feel Drayton drawing on it. Little by little, as much as his bracelet allowed. When he called her powers, Elissa's head would spin and the stone would alight, shooting out a column of red illumination.

Afterward she was always so sleepy she couldn't fight the heaviness of her eyes.

Elissa worried Drayton's actions would harm her baby. Mischief, too. Was her magic hurting their bond? Even though she couldn't feel her bondmate, she didn't stop calling out to him every day. So far, it'd yielded nothing, but she couldn't lose hope. If she sunk into the hovering despair, she'd die. Then her child would die, too.

She thought of Alasdair way too much. Fantasized about being a family with him. Pretended he'd want her, want the child she carried. She closed her eyes, imagining a dark-haired little lad with big blue eyes and her grin.

Smiling, she sighed and put her palm flat to her stomach. Elissa looked down. "I promise we'll get out of here." Her whisper bounced off the curved walls.

A noise caught her attention and her gaze shot to the entrance of her little nook. The outline of a wolf stood in the doorway.

The bracelet on her wrist opened and fell off, hitting the ground with a *thud.* The red stone was black as night.

Elissa blinked. Surely she was dreaming—about both?

Then Mischief barreled into her chest, whining.

Why'd the bracelet fall off?

Her magic rushed to the surface of her skin but exhaustion enveloped her and she reached for Mischief with both hands. She threw her arms around her wolf and buried her face in his neck. "Thank you, thank you, thank you for finding me, Mischief."

She wanted to ask him how, but he couldn't answer how she needed him to. In words.

Why hadn't she sensed his closeness?

He sent her feelings of warmth and love and she sucked in air. Wagged his tail so hard his body shook, but he didn't leave her embrace.

She needed his warmth, his furry muscled form against her torso. Needed to feel his rapidly beating heart and smell his familiar scent. It made her know—really *know*—he was real.

He's here.

Elissa was afraid to look away from him.

Pebbles sliding across the cave floor had her gaze darting up against her will. The frame that filled the space was too tall to be Drayton.

"My lady," he said.

Mischief broke away from her body and whirled. Hackles up all the way to his tail. He hunched, ready to pounce.

"I mean you no harm. Drayton is dead. And the knights have come for you. Listen." The familiar voice jolted her as much as what he'd said.

My half-elfin captor.

"Dead?" Shock about his presence, as much as what he'd said washed over her.

He nodded. "I must go, but you'll be safe. They came for you."

"What's your name?" she blurted.

He flashed a smile and shook his head.

Then he was gone.

Her heart thundered and she clutched her bondmate to her torso in tight arms. Mischief whimpered and licked her cheek.

The pounding of boot steps had her tensing, and kicked her heartbeat up all over again.

Alasdair gasped when he saw her, but he didn't say anything. His eyes darted all over her, although he probably couldn't see much of her, since her bondmate was plastered against her. Her gown was dirty and torn, a mere shadow of the beauty it'd been.

She resisted the urge to tug it straight or brush the sandy dirt from it.

"Alasdair." His name fell from her mouth in a cracked whisper. The first thing out of her mouth should've been that she carried his child, but when Elissa was enveloped by his heat, she forgot she was filthy. Forgot her whole body ached.

When she felt his lips on her gritty forehead, tears leaked from her eyes. She melted into his chest, wrapping her arms around him.

He squeezed her back. Alasdair chanted, "Lass, lass, lass," right above her ear, his warm breath shifting her stringy hair.

Somehow, she wished he'd say her name.

"Alasdair…" There was so much she wanted to say. Nothing would cooperate.

"Don't cry. I'm—we're—here, my lady. There's no more danger." He didn't wipe her tears away as he had in the past, but his gaze didn't waver from her face. "Are you hurt?"

Elissa shook her head. "Did you see him?"

"See who?"

"The half-elfin man?" She quickly launched into her captor's appearance and what she knew of his identity, as well as explaining to her knight of his companions.

Alasdair listened intently but kept repeating she had nothing to worry about. The men who'd had her were dead.

She didn't correct him that it was only one, nor did she ask questions. Fatigue had her melting into his comforting embrace. Elissa couldn't even muster the strength to tell him about the bracelet or Dimithian.

"Let's get you to Lord Cam."

"Lord...Cam?" Her heart plummeted to her knees.

"Your betrothed is anxious to see you, lass."

Elissa swallowed as a new bout of tears threatened and her throat closed up. The man she loved scrambled to his feet with her in his arms, against his hard body. He strode out of the cave, but he didn't have to go far.

To give her to another.

The Duke of Dalunas sheathed his sword when he saw them, his face a mask of concern. "Elissa!" He rushed toward them, and before she could blink, she was transferred to Lord Cam's arms.

"I can walk," she whispered.

"Nonsense," Lord Cam said, about as stern as she'd ever heard him. His lips brushed hers and Elissa tried not to wince.

Their gazes locked and she stared into his crystal blue eyes.

They're the wrong color blue.

"Elissa, are you hurt?"

"Nay, my lord. Sir Alasdair rescued me."

The duke looked at her knight. Something passed over his expression, but what, she couldn't name. "For that, I'll be forever grateful. He brought you back to me."

Alasdair gave a curt nod and muttered something about duty.

Elissa blinked to clear her vision but the tears wouldn't stop. Her magic didn't push back for once; she was too tired.

The only thing she was to him was a duty, like it'd always been.

Foolish lass.

The hope she'd felt after Drayton had told her she was with child dissolved. She'd felt deep down that Alasdair would find her, come back her as promised by the tree all those days ago.

She'd entertained *stupid* ideas of being his wife and raising his child at his side. He'd demanded her hand before, because he'd taken her innocence. He didn't want her. *Still.* The presence of his child would make no difference.

He'd given her to Lord Cam without hesitation.

"Elissa?" Lord Cam whispered. Her name was a question, but she wouldn't explain even if she could.

Not to him.

She shook her head and nestled closer to the duke, sliding her shaking arms around his neck.

He hiked her higher, held her tighter. But so gently, mixed emotions churned her stomach. "I'm so glad I have you back."

"Thank you." She didn't know what else to say.

Mischief circled them, whining.

Elissa thought-sent to her bondmate that she was all right. At least on the outside.

"Is he well?" Lord Cam asked.

"Aye, my lord. Anxious to leave from here, as am I."

A smile played at the duke's full mouth and Elissa forced one in return, albeit the tiniest curve of her lips.

"Let's get you home."

Home?

She whimpered and his step paused.

"Are you sure you're all right?"

"Aye. I'd like a bath."

Lord Cam nodded. "Of course. We'll go to Castle Rowan for the night, we're close. We'll consult the king. You can soak all you want. We'll depart for Dalunas tomorrow. There will be no pressure. Everything'll be at your pace, Elissa."

Her name didn't roll off his tongue with a Terraquist brogue. Somehow the southern lilt didn't sound right. She swallowed again and begged the tears to cease.

The arms that held her were warm. The chest she was against was firm, muscled and protective. The blue eyes that regarded her were kind, caring.

Too bad it was *all wrong*.

Elissa bit down on the sob threatening to escape.

Chapter Thirty-eight

Watching her be carried away in the Duke of Dalunas' arms was the hardest thing he'd ever done.

Stupidest, too.

If Alasdair was having a hard time listening to his head, he was totally ignoring his heart.

No other choice.

Lord Cam was what she wanted. She'd made it clear the day she'd been taken. When he'd kissed her by the tree.

So, he was doing the right thing. Letting her go, like she'd asked.

The way she'd clung to him in the cave hadn't meant anything. He'd just been the first to her side.

The noise of the tavern grated on his senses, and he flexed his fingers around the tankard of ale that was probably warm by now. Then again, he didn't give a shite what the temperature of his drink was, because he'd lost count of how many he'd tossed back.

The ride home had been a blur, and he'd not even made it to Castle Aldern, let alone his rooms. Hadn't said a word when he'd broken off from the group, either. Leargan had looked his way, but thank the Blessed Spirit his captain had let him go.

Another bite out of his pride; Lord Cam had his own men, as well as two mages. They didn't need anyone from Greenwald to accompany them to Dalunas.

Now that everyone but the tracker was dead, there wasn't a real worry the party would be followed to the far southeastern Province.

She's safe with the duke.

Leargan and their brothers would brief Lord Jorrin and regroup. Lucan and Dallon, along with Kale and Bowen, had stayed in Terraquist. They were still scouring for the tracker, with the help of the king's twin mages. No doubt they'd continue until they found him.

Elissa had told them he was half-elfin, and she'd been able to give a decent physical description. Unfortunately, so far they hadn't any clues to where he'd gone.

Alasdair owed him a *thank you* for killing the mage who'd stolen her.

He'd watched her cry in Lord Cam's arms when she'd spoken of the evil elemental confessing to the deaths of her family and that he'd ordered the lasses and their families killed. She hadn't said so, but his gut told him she felt guilty for their demise. He'd ached to be the one to hold her. Dry her tears. Tell her nothing was her fault.

She hadn't looked his way once.

When the duke had released her to comfort her upset bondmate, Alasdair hadn't been able to tear his gaze away. Even after all she'd been through, with tears on her cheeks and rumpled dirty clothing, she was gorgeous. Elissa had sat in the dirt and wrapped her arms around the wolf.

Lord Cam had hovered, and finally coaxed her to her feet and into a thick mantel. Alasdair had given up watching when the duke had gathered her into his arms on the back of his horse. She'd snuggled into him and closed her eyes.

Snow had started to fall, making them look like the perfect couple on the back of the huge white warhorse. As if they were out for an afternoon ride.

The bite in the winter air hadn't stung as much as seeing that.

She hadn't even said goodbye.

Emotion clogged in his throat and he put the wooden mug to his lips. Threw back the warm ale, wincing as it slid down his throat. Cursed himself to hell and back. "I should've said goodbye."

"Pardon?" The barmaid wiping the counter in front of him leaned close, brandishing a low bodice and barely covered breasts. Blonde ringlets framed her face, and her eyes were hazel, her smile sweet.

The hue of her hair and eyes made him ache.

"Nothing, lass. I'll have another."

"Coming right up!" She whirled around, wiggling her hips and winking over her shoulder as she filled a new tankard with frothy cold ale. She put it down in front of him with another wink. "When you're done with that, we could go—"

Alasdair gestured and slid her some coins. More than enough for his ale. "Thank you, lass, but nay. Not interested."

Her smile fell, but she nodded, taking the gold and moving on to the next man who'd hollered for a drink. The big lad snagged her hand and reached to touch her face. She stroked his arm and grinned. If the bar hadn't been between them, no doubt she would've been on his lap.

Alasdair shook his head.

Burying himself between a willing lass' thighs was exactly what he *should* do. He didn't want anyone but Elissa. Wouldn't risk another incident like the one with Betha. He might never rut a woman again.

"Been looking for you." Leargan's voice sounded behind him.

Alasdair didn't answer.

"This is the third tavern."

Still didn't answer, even when his captain slid onto the barstool beside him.

A different lass rushed over, offering Leargan a drink. He waved her off.

Alasdair could feel his stare.

"Since when do you spend time in Lower Greenwald, anyway?"

He shrugged.

"Alas—"

"You might as well go home, Leargan. Leave me be."

"Nay." The word was hard. When they made eye-contact, his captain arched a dark eyebrow. "What's wrong with you?"

Alasdair grunted. Sipped his new cold ale, cradling the stein with both hands. "What's *not* wrong with me?"

Leargan said nothing for a few breaths. Then his warm

calloused hand landed on Alasdair's forearm. "Then fix it."

He closed his eyes and shook his head. His hair, loose because he'd not bothered with it, danced around his shoulders, tickled his neck.

Loud laughter and boisterous conversation surrounded them, but Alasdair had never felt worse. "I can't."

The captain's sigh made him meet Leargan's dark gaze. "Are you willing to let her go because you're a stubborn fool?"

"Nay."

"Then go get her. Before it's too late. Before they wed."

"She doesn't want me. I already asked her to marry me instead."

Leargan reared back, eyes wide, mouth half-agape. "What?"

"I asked for her hand. She declined."

"I don't believe it."

"Believe it." Alasdair stood from the stool, ignoring how his eyes swam and his head spun from those endless tankards of ale. "I'm not letting her go because it's what *I* want, all right?"

"Alas—"

"Leargan. Listen to what I'm saying. She rejected me. She chose Lord Cam. The knight lost to the duke. It's only natural." He whirled away from the bar, even though he had nowhere to go. Alasdair just wanted *away*. Wanted to go somewhere he could mourn in silence. Alone.

Leargan's hand shot out. Landed on his wrist and squeezed. "Ansley rejected me."

"That was different."

"How so?"

"Her words were untrue. She was protecting herself."

His captain snorted. "Exactly." Leargan released him, crossing his arms over his broad chest and leaning back on the stool. His gaze was sharp, and he wore a smirk.

"What?"

"You're right, Alas."

"I'm right?"

"Ansley was protecting herself, because she thought I didn't love her. Same as Lady Elissa."

"Well, I don't lo—" Alasdair's head spun. He couldn't assure Leargan of a…lie? His knees wobbled. He listed to one side, then grabbed the bar with both hands. Planted his arse on the barstool he'd just abandoned so he wouldn't slide to the dirty planked floor.

I love her.

His mouth went dry, his tongue glued to the roof of his mouth.

Leargan's chuckle made him glare. "Light dawns, does it?"

Normally, Alasdair would fire back a quick retort, but he had none. His brain and tongue worked in tandem to fail him. He blinked. Swallowed hard—twice.

"Everyone knows how you feel about her. Just once glance, Alas; it's obvious. Considering I've never seen you like this over a lass, well, that's the amazing thing," Leargan said with a gentle edge. Like he wasn't really calling him the idiot he was.

"I—"

"What's more," his friend continued as if he hadn't tried, "is that she looks at you the same way."

"Nay. She picked Lord Cam." His denial was quick and even. Composure settled back over him, despite the ale *and* the revelation. He'd never felt like this before. And he wasn't going to ever again.

Too bad it doesn't matter.

Leargan gave him a long look. "You hurt her. I don't know how, but I can guess."

Alasdair wasn't about to confirm or explain. "It doesn't matter. It's over. She rode off into the sunset with her duke. They'll live happily ever after. Have a hoard of fair-haired lassies and laddies."

"Alasdair the Bard." One corner of his captain's mouth shot up. Then he sobered. "What about you?"

"What about me? Life goes on. There're other lasses. I was a fool to think I could change my ways." He cursed his almost wistful tone. Emotion caught in his throat and he had to look away.

Leargan's hand squeezing his forearm again brought Alasdair's gaze back. His longtime friend's expression was too serious for a rundown tavern in Lower Greenwald. "You've made up your mind?"

His heart rejected his curt nod. It fought back, making his body tense, shoulders tight, and his stomach roil. All contradictions of how relaxed he should be from so much ale.

Something flashed in Leargan's eyes, but he didn't voice his obvious disagreement.

Alasdair wasn't sure what to say, so he didn't say anything.

Reassurance or denial. Both would've been lies. He simply wanted something he couldn't have. Wasn't the first time in his thirty-one turns; wouldn't be the last.

"Getting gutted by a poisoned-tipped sword hurts less than a broken heart," Leargan whispered.

Alasdair didn't—*couldn't*—refute that. "I'm ready to go home." Other words played at the tip of his tongue. Nothing he wanted to say to his captain, though.

"All right."

He stood, not waiting for Leargan as he turned, wading through male and female bodies to reach the door. Ignored the lass or two that bid him to stay, blowing kisses and rubbing breasts on his biceps, tugging on his hands.

Aye, heartache seared him from the inside out, but it couldn't last forever.

Could it?

★   ★   ★   ★

"Lord Aldern wants to see you."

"Me?" Alasdair looked up from the sword he was sharpening in the armory. Normally it was a squire's duty, but he'd just needed away from everyone. Couldn't stand to be around even his brothers.

Leargan nodded. The captain stepped into the dim room, the door open wide behind him.

Alasdair squinted against the bright winter sunlight behind his brother. He blinked as Lucan's globes dimmed and then returned to their former radiance when Leargan shut the door. "What about?"

"I generally don't question my duke." His dark eyes belied him, dancing with amusement. Lips twitched as if the captain was fighting a smile.

He wanted to snap, *"What the hell's funny?"* Alasdair sighed and ignored his longtime friend, making another pass over his blade with the stone.

"Lucan can do that with magic, you know. Or Brodic would've done it for you with the stone."

He grunted. "It's my sword, I wanted to do it."

"Alasdair." Leargan leaned against the armory wall, between two racks. One held men-at-arms swords, and the other, battle axes.

"What?"

"How're you doing?"

Pausing, Alasdair tried to avoid his captain's gaze. "I'm fine. Why wouldn't I be?"

Leargan arched an eyebrow, but said nothing.

"If you don't watch out, I'll test the sharpness of my blade on you."

His brother pushed off the wall chuckling. "I was serious."

"So was I." He smiled. A little.

"We're all concerned about you."

Alasdair sighed. "Just...leave it. All right?" Pain threatened to cripple him all over again, and he shoved it away, like he had every moment of every day for the last month and a half. She'd been gone for the six longest sevendays of his life.

How could he move on if everyone kept nagging him? His brothers were worse than a group of chattering lasses.

They hadn't caught her half-elfin captor, either. That grated on many a temper, including Lucan's. The young knighted mage was taking it personally. The lad had taken the Dimithian from the cave, too. He studied it non-stop, as if the so-called myth could help.

It was his captain's turn to sigh. "For now." He took a breath. "The duke's in his ledger room waiting for you."

He stood from the long bench and stretched. His lower back gave a protest. Alasdair had lost track of how long he'd been in the armory. "I can't imagine what Lord Jorrin could want with me."

Leargan's face was a mask of innocence he didn't buy for a second. The captain shrugged. "He didn't say. Just bid me to summon you."

"Right." Alasdair wiped his sword down and sheathed it at his waist it. Tossed the blade cloth and Leargan caught it. He walked past his brother without another word, and glared when the captain laughed.

Being alone suited him, but he couldn't avoid returning the greetings of people he encountered on his way to Lord Jorrin's leger room. Wished he had magic and a good invisibility spell. All the forced smiles and lies of *"I'm well, how are you?"* were threatening to kill him.

He was dying without her.

A little more as each day passed.

Alasdair sucked in a breath when he reached the duke's dark-wood door. He made a fist and knocked. Lord Aldern called before he had to knock again. "You wanted to see me, my lord?"

"Aye, come in and shut the door. Have a seat." Although the duke's voice was even, and his smile pleasant, he'd given orders.

Alasdair tried not to shuffle his boots or seem as reluctant as he felt. He swallowed and took a seat across from his liege lord. The man he'd sworn to protect with his life. His eyes darted around the ledger room he'd been in dozens of times. Just rarely one-on-one with Lord Jorrin Aldern.

Bookshelves lined one wall. The Greenwald seal complete with its howling white wolf hung on one wall, and a detailed map of Greenwald on the other. Somehow, even with a quick glance, Castle Durroc was like a beacon he couldn't avoid.

Lord Jorrin cleared his throat to draw Alasdair's gaze.

He dug for propriety to address his duke. "How can I help you, my lord?"

"It's how I can help you, Alas."

"Oh?"

The duke shoved a small roll of parchment across his wide desk. "This came today."

Alasdair made eye-contact with the duke before he accepted the rolled missive. One touch told him the parchment was of the highest quality. Instead of the natural color of cured paper, it was stained teal. The golden wax seal of Dalunas was broken, of course.

His heart lurched, then plummeted to his toes. He fought tremors. Didn't have to unroll the scroll to know what it was. He'd expected to hear about it. Evidently he'd not adequately prepared himself.

Shaking fingertips skimmed the broken wax. Alasdair didn't have the bollocks to open it.

"Read it," Lord Jorrin said, as if he'd read his mind.

The duke was an empath. He didn't have to read minds. He could read Alasdair's feelings. Which was much, *much* worse.

"I know what it is," Alasdair croaked.

"Read it anyway."

He closed his eyes. "I wasn't aware you enjoyed torturing men in your service," flew out of his mouth unguarded.

Lord Jorrin laughed. "I don't."

Alasdair didn't answer. Instead, he slowly unrolled the unwanted missive that hadn't even been meant for his eyes. The parchment was trimmed in gold leaf. His heart rebounded off his ribs as it made a second journey south. His gut was so tight it ached, spreading pain down into his pelvis. His lower back renewed its throb, too.

Perhaps he was fond of self-torture, because he read every painful word slowly — twice. From the greeting addressed to Lord and Lady Aldern to, *"...honored to require your presence..."* and of course, Lord Cam and Elissa's full names and titles.

He winced at, *"...to witness the nuptials of..."*

The date was only a fortnight hence, but it could've been yesterday, or tomorrow for all the helplessness — and hopelessness — that washed over Alasdair.

He couldn't look at the duke. Or speak.

Everything was agony.

It wasn't like it mattered; his empathic liege lord would know exactly what his emotions were.

"Given what you're feeling, I actually have a little hope," Lord Jorrin said, breaking through Alasdair's anguish.

"At least it doesn't say something like, *'to join two hearts.'"*

The duke wore a smirk when Alasdair finally tore his gaze away from the teal parchment. "You're jesting? Perhaps you're not as bad off as I'd thought."

Alasdair sighed. "Why'd you show me this?"

"Leargan said if he couldn't get through to you, I didn't have a shot in hell, but I thought I'd try."

"I don't know what you're talking about."

The duke cocked his head to one side. Didn't call him a liar, but his expression did. "Do I have to order you?"

"Order me to what?" His hand closed around the parchment of its own accord. Alasdair stopped short of crushing it. The scroll didn't belong to him, after all.

Neither does she.

"To go to Dalunas and stop Lady Elissa from making a mistake you'll both regret for the rest of your lives. Marriage is permanent."

"What?" Alasdair croaked.

Lord Jorrin tapped his forehead. "Empath, remember?"

"Don't remind me."

Amusement darted across his face, and he tucked a thick

lock of ebony hair behind a long, tapered ear. "I wrote the king."

Alarm washed over Alasdair. "Wh-wh-what?"

"He's not opposed to a match of you and Lady Elissa, if it's what she wants. What you both want."

"Wh-wh-what?" His stammered repetition was all he could muster.

The ghost of a smile played at the duke's mouth. "Since you seem fond of repeating yourself, I will as well. Empath, remember?"

"What'd you tell the king?" Alasdair blurted. The demand was rude, and not the way he should address his liege lord, but Lord Jorrin didn't seem bothered. As one not born to nobility, he often didn't offend as easily as the naturally highborn.

"Just relayed my observations, of you *both*. Don't worry, he's not going to thunder into Dalunas and break up their wedding. He's leaving it up to her."

"And me."

Lord Jorrin nodded. "And you."

Alasdair startled in the chair. Gripped the armrests tightly, then opened and closed his hands over the carved wood when his fingertips throbbed. His mind spun.

The king had basically given them his blessing.

King Nathal, the man who'd been a father to him when his true father had failed. The man who'd meant the most to him in his life, other than Leargan and their brothers.

"She wants Lord Cam," he said.

The duke's blue eyes were kind. He shook his head, making his shaggy locks dance and drawing attention to his tapered ears again. "She doesn't."

"I...don't...."

"You don't have to say anything, Alas. You're one of my knights. More than that, I consider you a friend. And since you've come home from rescuing Lady Elissa, you've been walking around here half-dead. We're all worried."

"I do my duty."

"Of course you do. That's not in question. But everyone misses your easy smile, your laugh. Even ribald quips."

Alasdair gave a small smile.

"We're all behind you, is my point. *All* of us. You're well-loved in Greenwald. In the short time Lady Elissa was with us, we grew to feel the same way about her. We support you both. Me, Cera, Leargan and Ansley, and all your brothers. Your happiness is worth something. *You* are worth something."

He couldn't speak. The lump in his throat took over and his eyes smarted. "Thank you," he finally whispered.

Lord Jorrin nodded. Then grinned. "Go show Lady Elissa she still has a choice."

Chapter Thirty-nine

Lord Cam had taken the news well, all considering. He hadn't seemed that surprised. Mayhap he'd expected it; despite the fact he'd said he'd be a father to her child.

Their wedding was supposed to take place in the morning.

Since the winter was so much milder in the south, the duke had wished the ceremony to be outside, in his massive, mazelike gardens. Even now, as Elissa peered out the window of the duchess solar, she could see the preparations. Decorations being arranged, the next even more elaborate than the last, especially in the large gazebo. Serving lasses bustled, appearing to laugh as they worked. Enjoying their duties.

Rows of chairs already lined the walkways. A red runner made of lush crushed velvet lay in a roll, ready to be set to rights for them both to walk the aisle.

When would Lord Cam tell everyone all was for naught?

There wouldn't be a wedding on the morn.

She sighed and battled an achy chest against a wobbly stomach. Guilt churned over her, making her feel worse. No matter how many times her logical side called her a fool for her decision; her heart wouldn't allow her to marry the Duke of Dalunas.

Elissa didn't love him.

She'd given her heart a chance, for two months now.

Feeling anything romantic for Lord Camden Malloch had been all for naught, too. She allowed his touch. Caresses on her face, holding her hands. Allowed him to hold her, too. His kisses — whether chaste or not so innocent — did nothing to stoke her desire for more. He'd been respectful, never pushing her.

Of course, he'd also assumed she had her virtue, so being the man of decorum he was, hadn't planned on taking her innocence before they were wed. He'd told her as much, too.

He'd made her cry when she'd told him she was not a virgin, because he'd offered no judgment. Lord Cam had rubbed her back and held her until her tears abated. When she'd confessed she was carrying a child, he didn't even ask after the sire — except to threaten the man's life for hurting her. Perhaps he knew and chose not to say, the duke was not stupid, after all.

Lord Cam had been supportive. Patient. Loving. Told her he'd healed from a broken heart once himself. He'd assured her that her place in Dalunas — as duchess no less — was not in jeopardy.

He still wanted her. Intended to marry her.

The duke cared for her. She could see it every time she looked into his pale blue eyes. He'd not declared love, but it was only a matter of time.

Well, it had been. Not now. Not after she told him she couldn't marry him.

The man was nothing if not tender, gentle, and so kind he made her cry — all the time.

Why couldn't she love him?

Now she was hurting him, too. He'd not told her so, but his expression had been pained for the whole of their conversation that morning. He'd looked resolved from the moment she'd opened her mouth and had been *completely* honest with him. Save for the name of who'd fathered her child. Again, he hadn't even asked.

Renewed guilt warred with her pain.

I'm doing the right thing. But —

Why couldn't she move past Alasdair?

Elissa cringed. Even *thinking* his name made her want to dissolve into a pile of sobs.

She needed to hold herself together. Stay strong. Move on from Dalunas to…her new life.

Lord Cam had deeded the home of her birth back to her. His steward had readied the scrolls and she'd signed in the necessary spots. Another clue that the duke had been expecting her to break their betrothal.

He'd told her that he'd see her safely back to Greenwald as soon as she was ready to go. She had her own coin, and he'd provide it in full, as everything had been given to him from Lord Jorrin. Lord Cam had been stalwart in the fact that he'd see her settled himself, despite her protest.

She'd have a home to raise her child in.

Elissa closed her eyes and sucked in a breath. She rested her hand on her lower belly. She wasn't showing yet, except for a slight roundness noticeable when she was naked. She stared at it every morning in the mirror.

If she hadn't known her body so well, it might just look like she'd been eating too much and had gained a few pounds. But she knew the tiny distention was a hint of what was to come.

She'd become large with the child she carried. Unable to hide her impending motherhood forever.

Her heart skipped.

This morning, Lord Cam had urged her to tell her child's sire, but she couldn't reach out to *him*. Not yet. Everything was too raw. Her conscience kicked at her for that—her knight had a right to know of the child they'd created. But he hadn't wanted her. She didn't want to put her child through the same rejection.

Elissa wanted this baby—a piece of Alasdair—more than anything.

Would the man, Thomad Uncel, who'd run her property for all these turns see her as a harlot? Refuse to remain in her employ?

Elissa had written to him of her homecoming, and asked to see him and his family upon her arrival. The King's Rider posted in Dalunas, a man named Simond, had left with her message that morning.

She had hopes Thomad Uncel would remain as her steward, move into the castle. She intended to offer his wife a position, and any other family who wanted it.

She'd be the lady of her castle.

Alone. With a fatherless child.

Elissa could ask Lady Cera for help, but she didn't want to.

She wanted be alone. Didn't she?

Definitely didn't want to think about King Nathal and Queen Morghyn.

Lord Cam would have to report that they hadn't married,

but he said he'd wait as long as he could—knowing the delay would result in the king's ire.

She wanted to be long gone by then, ensconced in Castle Durroc before the king stormed her home and commanded an in-person explanation. She didn't doubt that he'd do so. Her cousin would likely accompany him.

Elissa didn't know what would happen then...and didn't want to think about it now.

I can't. She had to be strong to get through the next few sevendays.

Mischief whimpered, and she spared him a glance. Her bondmate slept by the warm fire burning in the great hearth of the solar. Elissa studied him for a moment, but he didn't wake. His thoughts and feelings were deeply mired in sleep, so whatever was bothering her wolfling must be in the land of dreams.

She really couldn't call him a *wolfling* anymore. He'd been thriving in Dalunas, even as she'd wilted more and more each passing day. He was huge. Probably close to his sire in size, though he was not yet a full turn old.

"Someone's here to see you, Issa." Lady Aresha's soft voice had Elissa turning away from the window.

Mischief wuffed and stretched by the fireplace, giving a loud yawn that had the lady smiling. The wolf wagged his tail and made a beeline for her.

"Oh?" Elissa smiled at the lass who'd become a fast friend since coming to Castle Malloch. Her bondmate had been quite taken with her from the start, too.

Aresha nodded as she stroked Mischief's silver fur. She leaned down to him, making her long ebony locks sway. She wore them loose today, with only a ribbon across the top of her head to keep them out of her face. Her hair flowed to her hips, surrounding her like an aura. She was clad in a rich green, her gown simple, yet displaying her ample bosom and hinting at her rounded hips.

Her dress brought out the color of her leaf green eyes, and her beauty stunned Elissa, like most times when she gazed upon her new friend.

The lass wore her heart on her sleeve regarding Lord Cam, so Elissa hoped something good could be had from her breaking their betrothal. She prayed the duke could see what was so plainly before him and find happiness with the woman who did love him. Lady Aresha had been a ward of Lord Cam's father as a child; they'd grown up together.

"A knight. From Greenwald." Her gaze was knowing as she straightened.

Elissa's whole body flushed. Her pulse pounded in her temples. She'd not confessed much to Lady Aresha—other than her heart had been bruised by another before coming to Dalunas. The lass had never faulted Elissa even though she'd been betrothed to Lord Cam. In a way, they'd grieved together, although Aresha had never admitted how she felt about the duke.

She'd also not told her she was with child, but Elissa suspected her friend knew. Whether Lord Cam had told her, or she was just intuitive was left to be unsaid. Either way, the lady hadn't judged her—shocking considering she was in love with the man Elissa was supposed to marry.

Elissa hadn't told her of the broken marriage plans, since it'd just happened, but she'd planned to, so she could urge her new friend to bare her heart to Lord Cam.

Aresha could've treated her horribly, but she was a gentle soul who'd embraced Elissa, and for that, she'd always be grateful. She wanted her to be happy, as well as the duke she couldn't marry. Instinct told her the two of them belonged together.

Elissa wasn't ready to see the man who'd put a baby in her belly. The knight who was hovering just inside the door of the solar.

He bowed to her as he stumbled into the room.

Lady Aresha moved out of his way, looking at her, then at Alasdair. "I'll leave you, Issa."

Please don't.

Her friend went anyway, taking her wolf with her. Barred the door, too, with magic, if the glow around the entryway was any indication.

Dammit.

Traitor! she thought-sent to Mischief, but her bondmate didn't send anything back. She planted her fists at her sides as emotions ran all over her body. Her magic tingled and Elissa fought it.

Alasdair bowed again, then shifted from foot to foot. He stared hard, and his sapphire gaze burned. He didn't speak.

Her bottom lip wobbled and she bit down on it, fighting tears. Even looking at him hurt.

Now her wolf thought-sent comfort and love, but it didn't help. He didn't scratch at the door, or try to rush back to her side. It was as if even Mischief wanted her to have this *very* unwanted meeting.

Alasdair looked like hell, even worse than he had when he'd rescued her from Drayton. His dark brown hair lacked its normal rich luster, hanging limply past his shoulders, stringy. His face was layered in thick stubble at least three days old and the black bags under his eyes made his gorgeous deep blue orbs appear sunk in. His normally supple golden skin was sallow.

He swallowed, making the apple of his throat bob.

His clothing was clean but messy, as if he'd not bothered to straighten his appearance after a hard ride. His ivory tunic was wrinkled, and he wore no doublet like normal. His gray breeches hung low on his hips, as if he'd lost weight, even worse on the side that held his heavy sword.

Somehow, even with all that was before her, her Alas was still wickedly handsome.

She damned herself for the thought.

"I need you."

Elissa froze. Of all the things she'd imagined he'd open with, the three words emitted from his cracked lips weren't it.

"I need you," Alasdair repeated with more desperation.

She gulped as the first tear rolled down her cheek. Elissa cursed it—she'd sworn she wouldn't let him see her cry ever again.

When he started to close the distance between them, she whipped her head around the warm inviting room. She wanted—no, *needed*—to flee, but there was nowhere to go. She had to protect herself from him. Couldn't let him hurt her again. Now she had more to think about than just herself.

"Elissa," he breathed. His large hand landed on her wrist and she couldn't pull away even though her mind shouted the command.

Tremors racked her frame as Alasdair pulled her into his arms, but he was shaking as much as she was. Against her will, her traitorous body moved into him instead of away, and a sob broke from her lips as she slipped her arms around his waist.

She could feel his heart hammering against her ear and Elissa crushed her eyes shut as his warmth seeped into her.

Pull away. Shove him away. Tell him to go to hell.

But she couldn't. Nothing had ever felt so right. Elissa *hated* that.

She loved him so much. She hated that, too.

Alasdair was talking, but she couldn't process it as her mind and heart were at odds, screaming opposite orders that did nothing but spin her into chaos.

Tears cascaded and she cursed every one. Again.

"Shhh, please. Don't, cry. Not because of me."

"I'm done crying for *you*." Elissa lifted her head from his chest and tried to glare.

He smirked at her obvious contradiction and it made her blood boil. She tried to tug away, but Alasdair was too quick. Her knight cupped her face and started to thumb her tears away.

Elissa whimpered. Averted her gaze, but he didn't release her.

"Even with puffy eyes and pink cheeks, you're still the most beautiful lass I've ever seen."

Her breath caught and she sucked her bottom lip into her mouth to stave off another sob.

"Please. Can I hold you? I just need to hold you."

She didn't nod, but her body went soft—still against her will—and Alasdair drew her back to him. Elissa didn't want to go. She really didn't. Didn't want to find comfort against his hard chest, in his strong arms.

Not when he was the source of her pain.

More—*stupid*—tears were born when he stroked her back.

"What do you want?" she tried to bark. Instead it came out broken. Stammered. She refused her instinct to wince.

Alasdair pulled back. He set his palms on her upper arms and squeezed. His hold was gentle, but firm, the heat of large calloused hands compelled her to look into his handsome face. "Forgiveness."

Elissa opened her mouth. Nothing came out except a hitched squeal. She cleared her throat and tried again. "Forgiveness?"

He nodded. It was curt, but pain darted across his countenance.

Her heart skipped.

"I was a colossal arse. A wretched fool."

She didn't disagree.

"I let you go. I never should have. I said things I didn't mean." He flinched.

Elissa clenched her jaw and ordered herself not to react to the agony in his gorgeous blue eyes. She planted her feet so she wouldn't keel over. "Is that all?"

"Nay."

"What else?" She arched an eyebrow and tried to look regal.

"I came here to beg forgiveness. To explain how sorry I am, and vow if it takes a lifetime, I'll make it up to you."

"A lifetime?" Elissa could only manage a pained whisper.

"You cannot marry Lord Cam."

"Why not?"

"Because...I want you to marry me. *Need* you to."

Her heart didn't just skip. It stopped, then rebounded off her ribs. This proposal sounded as sincere as the first one. But this time was different, too.

Tears poured all over again. She didn't fight when her knight's hands settled around her, urging her back to his chest.

His mouth fitted over hers naturally, and Elissa met his kiss instead of pulling away.

Her brain nudged her, reminded her that he'd not declared any kind of love, scolded that an apology and another marriage proposal weren't enough. She told all cognizant thought to go to hell and moved closer, molding her body to his, reveling in the feel of him, how much she'd missed him, how perfect he was against her.

He smelled the same, clean, masculine. She scented sandalwood she'd always loved, and forest, too, like the wind was still clinging to him from his ride.

Alasdair slanted for a deeper kiss, burying his hand in the hair at the back of her neck, holding her closer still. His arms were so strong around her, his chest so hard against her breasts.

Perfect. He was perfect.

She loved this man more than her own life.

Elissa met his probing tongue, moaning as warmth spread down her limbs and settled between her legs. Leaving her throbbing with desire for him. Fine tremors slid down her spine, and were only made worse when Alasdair shuddered. He kissed her harder, taking her mouth with desperation she felt, too. She kissed him as fervently, twining her tongue around his, his familiar taste enhanced by longing she felt to her soul. Elissa rocked against him, her pelvis rubbing his, and a thick erection pressed right back.

His arousal reminded her of news he didn't yet know — their child.

Her belly flipped for reasons other than passion. Nerves inched up and paralyzed her. Her magic prickled at the off-kilter opposite emotions, but she gained control before it pushed hard enough to burst out.

"What's wrong?" Alasdair leaned back, his blue eyes heavy-lidded, but concerned as he studied her face.

"I'm with child."

He froze, his kiss-swollen lips parting on a gasp. He panted — she didn't think it was from their kiss.

When his fingers flexed and released her, Elissa frowned. She backed away. "Blessed Spirit help you if you ask me if it's yours. I'll drown you." She brandished her palm.

His eyes widened. "I wasn't—" Alasdair sputtered. Shook his head.

If the circumstances were different, she might've laughed. She'd never seen him so stumped.

Alasdair's dark brows knitted, and he reached for her.

She slid further, avoiding his grasp.

It was his turn to frown. "Lord Cam…didn't…." He waved a white-knuckled fist. "I'll kill him if he touched you." He stalked to her, grabbed her forearm.

Elissa laughed, she couldn't help it. "Funny, he said the same thing about you."

His frown slipped into a scowl. He cupped her face, forcing her to look at him. "He did, did he?"

She grabbed his wrists and squeezed, but didn't pull away. "I didn't tell him it was you. He knows about the child, though. He said he'd marry me anyway."

Agony darted across Alasdair's face.

"I've never been intimate with Lord Cam, Alas. My child is yours."

"I know." He kissed her again, this time something tender that had her heart thundering all over again.

Elissa moved into him, slipping her arms around his neck and kissed him back with all her might. She yelped when he swung her up into his arms. His gaze bored into her.

"You will never be *intimate* with any other man." The growl had her belly flipping. "Where's your room?"

"Alas—"

"I know we're not done talking, Elissa. But I need you."

She stilled in his grip. "Say it again?"

"I need you."

"Not that."

A slow, sexy smile spread over his full mouth. "Elissa."

"Alas." She grinned.

"I love you."

Her heart skipped again, making her doubt it'd ever beat normally again. Tears spilled all over and she nestled into his embrace.

He loves me.

Finally what she needed to hear more than anything. Elissa closed her eyes and smiled again when she felt his lips on her eyelids, then on her nose. He pressed a gentle kiss into her forehead, too, and her breath caught. "Alas," she whispered.

"Aye, lass?"

"I'm not marrying Lord Cam. This morning, I told him I couldn't go through with it."

The apple of his throat bobbed and drew her gaze before she could look into his eyes.

"Elissa." Her name came out a half-gasp. His hold on her tightened as his body stiffened.

"I want to marry you. But—"

"But what?"

"You…haven't said how you feel about…the child."

"Lucky," he croaked.

Her breath caught. "Lucky?"

"I came for you. Now I get you *and* a precious little one. To love. Hold. Always. You're both mine."

Mine. The word reverberated in her head. And in her heart.

Elissa wanted nothing more. His acceptance was hard to believe. Too good to be true. "Even though it wasn't planned?"

He flashed a lopsided grin. "I planned to seduce you. A child could've happened then, too. Blessed Spirit knows I can't be careful with you."

She giggled and felt a chuckle rumble in his chest. "Alas."

"Aye, love?"

The term of endearment stole her focus and made her stomach flutter. She swallowed against the sudden lump in her throat. "I love you, too. And I forgive you."

He kissed her, hard and fast, making Elissa's head spin. "Good. Where's your room?"

Chapter Forty

h e kicked the door Elissa's room shut and set her to her feet impossibly gently. Right next to the bed.

A place he'd join her…as soon as he got his bearings.

Alasdair couldn't even manage to look around the quarters he guessed to be the duchess' rooms, due to their size. Right down the hall from the solar the dark-haired lass had shown him to.

They shouldn't be here right now. He should've taken her right to Lord Cam. Should've paid the duke his due, not stolen his betrothed.

But he'd had to see her first.

He'd almost collapsed when he'd seen Elissa, her expression forlorn, looking as pale as the ivory gown she was wearing.

Alasdair had ridden as hard as he could. He'd been alone, and left Greenwald the very day Lord Jorrin had shown him the wedding invitation. Even with his infrequent stops, it'd still taken him a damn fortnight to get to Castle Malloch. Tess would probably never forgive him for pushing her so.

All is not lost.

His head spun, and his heart galloped.

She'd forgiven him. She still loved him.

She'd agreed to marry him.

She's carrying my child.

He swallowed a gasp and made a grab for the thick post at the head of the bed as wooziness threatened to take him over.

"Are you all right?" Her concern had him meeting her beautiful hazel eyes. Her delicate hand landed on his wrist and squeezed.

"Aye," he croaked. "I...can't believe...my good fortune." Blessed Spirit it was *true*. Alasdair knelt before the love of his life, fumbling for the ring in his pocket and wincing as his knee smacked the stone harder than intended.

"Alas?" Elissa whispered.

Their gazes collided and he reached for her hand. Kissed her knuckles without looking away from her hazel orbs. "Lady Elissa Durroc, will you be my wife?"

She cocked her head to the side, the corner of her mouth twitching as she fought a smile. "I thought we'd already established that. Aye, I'll wed you."

He swallowed. Couldn't help it. "I...failed to give you this." He slid the modest ring on her left hand and held his breath. It was nothing a lady would wear; didn't even have a jewel. Only a simple gold band with double hearts finely etched at its center.

Elissa gasped and examined the ring as he scrambled to his feet.

"I know it's not much..."

"I love it." Her eyes were misty when she looked up at him and his heart stuttered.

"It's..." he had to clear his throat, "the only...thing I have of my mother, and I want you to have it."

"Oh, Alas."

"If you don't like it, I'm sure we can get you something with a diamond, or a sapphire—" Words fell from his mouth, a tripping babble that he cut off because his betrothed glared at him.

"I said I love it. I don't speak untruths."

Alasdair felt the weight float from his chest, even though Elissa was cross with him, both hands perched on her perfect hips. He laughed. Threw his head back and let loose a deep chuckle. He didn't bother calling her on that. She'd lied to him, denied loving him. He could tease her later.

"Alas?"

"I'm sorry, love. It's just..."

She jumped into his arms and Alasdair caught her up so they both wouldn't fall over.

"I love you," Elissa said. "I love you. I love you. I love you. I'm sorry I lied about that before. It's an untruth I take back." She punctuated each repetition with a kiss, first to his bearded cheeks, then his forehead, even the end of his nose before pressing her mouth to his.

"I love you, too," he said into her mouth, pushing her lips wider so he could explore her, taste her. Alasdair groaned when she let him in. He couldn't get enough of her. He'd *never* be able to get enough of her.

He deepened their kiss, willing her to feel all his love. Feel the fact it'd *always* be this way for them, he'd love and cherish her for their rest of their lives.

And the baby she carried.

Alasdair was going to be a father.

One nothing like my own.

She moaned into his mouth, scattering conscious thought as her small warm hands inched their way up inside his tunic. Elissa caressed his stomach, his abdominal muscles jumped with each pass of her fingers. She crept higher, making his nipples taut even before she touched him there.

He groaned, swallowing her whimper as he kissed her harder.

Her hands slid around to his back and down. His little vixen kneaded his arse, making his cock jump and throb. When she tugged him forward and rocked her pelvis into his, Alasdair almost exploded in his breeches.

He broke their kiss and sucked in a breath. Needed a minute—or three.

"Alas?" she whispered, resting her forehead on his chest.

"You're killing me, love. It's been too long." Alasdair cupped her face and tilted up, pressing a fast kiss to the smirk on her delectable mouth.

Elissa's hair was mussed from his fingers, and her cheeks were flushed the most delicious shade of pink. Her lips were parted and thick, well-ravished. Her hazel eyes glowed with green and gold flecks.

Alasdair had never wanted her more than he did at that moment.

"I want you," she breathed.

It was almost his undoing. "Believe me, the feeling is mutual."

"Then take off your clothes."

He chuckled. "You've become a bold little thing, have you?"

She grinned. "I always was, I was waiting for you to notice." Pain darted across her face and guilt bit at him. "I was waiting for you to want me. Waiting for you to love me."

"Oh, lass." Alasdair swallowed against the lump in his throat. "I wanted you from day one. And I've loved you for so long. I…just couldn't see it."

One tear leaked down her cheek and he wiped it away.

"I thought we were done with that." He smiled.

"Your child makes me an emotional wreck." Elissa's returning smile was wobbly.

Alasdair took her mouth in what he'd intended to be a short tender kiss, but Elissa had other ideas. She clung to him, forced their lip-lock deeper, and started tugging at his clothes. His cock threatened to punch through his breeches.

"Love…" he gasped. "Love…" With strength he didn't know he possessed, he pulled away. "Should we not go to Lord Cam and declare our intentions?"

"After." Elissa reached for his belt and had it hanging open before he could protest.

"After?"

"I need you." Her hazel eyes bored into him and an unmanly shiver hit him from head to toe.

"Those are my words." He fought for a serious expression.

"Doesn't make it less true for me." She undid the ties on his breeches and pushed them off one hip, then mock-glared. "I already told you I do not speak untruths."

He chuckled and gripped the waist of his breeches so his sword wouldn't clatter to the stone floor and rip his pants on the way down. "All right, love." Alasdair dragged two fingers down her cheek with his free hand.

She stared up at him with so much love in her eyes his heart—and his stomach—fluttered at the same time. "Get undressed."

Elissa's command had him grinning like an idiot.

He nodded and stepped back, making quick work of his breeches and boots, then tugged his tunic up and off. He was suddenly grateful he'd not bothered with a doublet, though it'd made for a cold ride. His breath caught when he looked at his betrothed.

She was naked from the waist up, but wiggled to rid herself of her shimmery ivory gown and chemise at the same time. They pooled at her feet, and he couldn't tear his eyes away. Her breasts, which had always been small, high and tight, were larger, even more perfectly round. He noticed her birthmark, the half-moon on her right side, but his gaze didn't stay there.

Alasdair's mouth went dry as his eyes traveled downward. There was a definite roundness to her lower belly that hadn't been there before. Although he'd only had her once, and only seen her naked once more than that, he knew her body as well as his own.

My child.

His vision wavered. Blurred.

"Alas?" Elissa crossed the small distance between them, reaching for his face. Her fingertips came away shiny, wet.

Crying?

He couldn't remember the last time he'd cried. Alasdair swallowed. Twice.

"What's wrong, my love?" she whispered, nestling close. Her bare skin heated him and quickened his heart.

Alasdair's hand shook when he covered her belly with a flat palm. Her skin was smooth. Taut and supple.

Her hazel eyes bored into him when their gazes met. She smiled, and laid her hand over his.

He couldn't speak. Couldn't even muster the strength to say there was *nothing* wrong. It'd never been so right for him. For *them*.

So he lifted her, carried her to the bed and followed her down, careful not to crush her—and their child—with his full weight. "Elissa," he breathed against her mouth as he dipped down again to taste her lips again.

She slid her hands into his hair and returned his kiss, moaning as it became heated, hungry and frantic. She widened her thighs and opened for him there, too. Alasdair slid more fully into the cradle of her body, his cock pulsing when the golden curls between her legs caressed his swollen tip. He wanted to slide into her tight heat, claim her. But not yet. He kissed his way down her neck and across her collarbone.

Elissa whimpered and arched into him, requesting more attention to her breasts, which he was happy to give. Alasdair ran the flat of his tongue around the curve of her breast before suckling her nipple and teasing her tight areola, watching her harden even more. She panted his name as he did the same to the other.

He could taste salty sweat on her skin. He couldn't get enough of her. As she writhed beneath him, the candlelight caught the sheen of her skin from the moisture of his licks.

Alasdair continue downward, until he dragged kisses on her lower belly, pausing to lavish caresses and over the place where his child grew. Lying prone, the slight curve couldn't be seen. It didn't matter. He knew what grew inside, a piece of them both he already loved more than his own life.

She whimpered, tilting her hips, begging without words for what he already intended.

He inhaled deeply and honeyed arousal filled his nostrils, his lungs. He couldn't get enough. Alasdair dipped his head down and licked the knot of flesh at the top of her sex.

Elissa screamed and pulled the hair her hands were already buried in. "Alasdair," she breathed, tossing her head back on her pillow.

His cock was so hard it bounced against his thigh as he adjusted his position so he could hunker down and really taste her. He'd make her come a few times before he joined their bodies. Then, when he was deep inside her, making her his again, he'd make her come again.

Alasdair's scalp stung as she tugged his hair when he sucked her into his mouth, but he didn't care if she yanked him bald. Not as her essence coated his tongue and he savored her.

Her hips lifted from the bed, her back curved, and Elissa clutched his shoulders, but he didn't stop. He needed more. He couldn't stop until he'd devoured all of her.

Moisture flooded his mouth and Elissa screamed. She was close. Oh so close.

Alasdair slid two fingers inside her, swirling his tongue around her swollen nub. Her core clutched at him, soft hot walls pulsing as he moved in and out of her.

His love wiggled and wobbled, rocking back and forth until he had to hold her down.

Orgasm crested when he touched the certain spot deep inside. She shattered and tossed her head back, her glorious flaxen locks spread wide, and her eyes crushed shut.

So beautiful in her passion it stole his breath.

He didn't stop his ministrations until she came in his mouth again. By then, Elissa panted so hard, and grabbed at him until her nails scored his shoulders. Alasdair didn't give a damn if she made him bleed, not when she was looking at him like that.

"Come inside me. I need you," Elissa pleaded, trying to pull him up her splayed body. Her eyes were heavy-lidded, her hands shaky, but he didn't make her wait.

He rose above her, kissing her deeply as he settled his pelvis against hers. Alasdair made him look at her when he parted their mouths. "I love you."

She smiled, her expression hazy and passionate. "I love you, too."

"I'm going to take you. Show you you're mine."

"I've always been yours, Sir Alasdair Kearney."

His heart thundered as he thrust forward, filling her completely with one hard stroke. They both gasped. Their gazes collided. Held. He froze above her, mentally and physically processing how he felt inside her. Loved. Completed. Wet. Hot. Her sex gripped him like his favorite pair of riding gloves.

Emotion drove him forward. So much love it stole his ability to talk, to think, even though he'd wanted to tell her once more how he felt about her.

Elissa tugged him down, snaking her arms around his neck and pressing her lips to his. "You don't have to tell me, Alas. Show me how I belong to you, my love." As if she'd read his mind.

He was lost then, giving her what she'd demanded, heart, body and soul. Alasdair couldn't do anything else. Need took over, propelling him in and out of her again and again. He took her hard, falling deeper into her when Elissa wrapped her legs around his waist.

She matched his every stroke, every kiss, every caress. Their eyes stayed locked the whole time, amplifying the meaning of their lovemaking.

When they cascaded over the edge together, there was no urgency, only intense pleasure for them both, unlike anything he'd ever experienced. It was drawn out, cascading over him in waves. Elissa stiffened beneath him, holding him tight as her core milked him.

Alasdair's whole body quivered. He pulled her closer and buried his face in her damp neck.

She caressed his back as climax receded and his vision cleared. They both panted, her breasts flat against his chest and the ability to think slowly returned.

When he tried to move off her, afraid he'd crush her, Elissa held him hard, fast.

"Don't go," she whispered in his ear.

"I'm not going anywhere, love." He gently pulled from her body and rolled to his side, despite her protests. "I don't want to hurt you." He tucked her into his side. Alasdair stroked her cheeks to reassure her and kissed her tenderly.

She pushed into his mouth, deepening their kiss. It soon melted into something languorous and sweet as Elissa snuggled closer, sliding her leg between his. "I love you," she breathed.

"I love you, too." Alasdair smiled. "That was perfect."

His love smiled back, cupping his face. "You're perfect, but your beard is not. It's scratchy. You should shave." She grabbed fuzz on his cheek and tugged.

Alasdair chuckled. "You seemed to like the roughness against your inner thighs. You wiggled and begged for more."

Elissa blushed to the tips of her ears and mock-glared. "It's improper to speak of such things."

He laughed again. "You're shy, after what we've done?"

She averted her gaze, despite his intended tease.

"Elissa, look at me." Seconds passed before she did so. Alasdair rested his hand against her crimson face, caressing her high cheekbone with his thumb. "Love, I don't want you to be embarrassed with me. About anything."

"I'm not. Really. It's hard to…speak…of such things."

Alasdair winked. "Then we shouldn't do them. If you can't discuss them."

Her beautiful eyes narrowed and she slid her small hand around his wrist and squeezed. "That's not going to work for me."

"Oh?"

"I want you too badly."

He leaned in and kissed her, fighting a teasing grin. "Good. Because I want you as badly."

"Forever," Elissa whispered. Her misty eyes made his heart skip.

"Aye, love. Forever."

Epilogue

A baby's cry made his heart and stomach jump at the same time.

Leargan grinned and slapped him on the back. "Congrats, man, you're a father!"

He'd wanted to stay by her side, but his nerves had affected hers, and her magic had started to react, so Morag had glared him from the large bedchamber that'd once belonged to her parents. Elissa had been able to control her pain and her magic after he'd hit the corridor.

His captain's exclamation sank in, and Alasdair wobbled on his feet.

"Whoa, steady." Amusement rippled through Bowen's voice and a strong hand landed between his shoulder blades, and another seized his right biceps.

Dallon appeared on his left, looking ready to grab him if he did topple on his arse.

"Alas? Are you all right?" Leargan took a step closer, concern in his dark eyes. Lord Jorrin and Roduch stood close behind him, expressions mirroring the captain's. But he couldn't focus on his lord or his brothers.

Elissa.

He needed to see her. Now.

And their child.

He couldn't muster an answer for Leargan, or any of his other fellow knights — or the duke — that'd made the journey to Castle Durroc from Greenwald Main.

Most of the guard was holding up walls in the corridor. He appreciated the support even if he couldn't say so at the moment.

Elissa had insisted his son's birth take place in the castle she'd been born in. Despite his protests of traveling so late in pregnancy.

Lord Tristan had calmed him—but not enough. And with the healer's reassurance that a carriage ride wouldn't harm either wife or child, Alasdair had lost the argument. Besides, the healing lord was at his wife's side with Greenwald's headwoman and the headwoman of Castle Durroc, Phasia Uncel, the wife of the property's longtime caretaker, Thomad.

The duchess had insisted upon coming, but she wasn't in the room. She'd brought the ladies and half a dozen maids. They were all downstairs, organizing a meal for everyone in the great room.

Castle Durroc's small staff hadn't been expecting them, so they'd brought food, too, much to Phasia's embarrassment. Lasses had come and gone from the lord and lady's rooms, staff as well as both headwomen. For hours. The longer it'd taken, the more on edge Alasdair had been.

Mischief had been banned from the room, too, and paced the corridor right beside Alasdair, until he'd managed to coax the wolf to lie down. He'd stroked the silver beast's soft fur. It'd calmed them both, for a time, but the normally happy wolf hadn't wagged his tail once. He whined every time Elissa called out, agitating Alasdair all over.

But now…

His child was here.

The door opened, and he flushed from head to toe.

"You have a daughter, Sir Alasdair. A fine, healthy lass." Morag had a small wiggly bundle tucked in her arms when she appeared under the fancy arched doorway. However, the soft white swaddling obscured his view.

"He's a she?" Words tumbled from his mouth.

Chuckles surrounded him, but he ignored his brothers and rushed to Morag's side. Stared down at the tiny thing against her generous bosom.

His eyes welled with tears and he didn't even give a damn. Alasdair's hands reached out, even though he was scared to death to look at her, let alone touch her. Hold her.

My tiny lass.

The dark blonde tuft of downy hair was what he saw first.

The Blessed Spirit hadn't given her much. What she had was sticking straight up.

He felt a tear roll down his cheek.

Mischief shot into the doorway as soon as the headwoman moved toward Alasdair, and for once, she didn't stop to chide him.

Morag transferred the baby to his arms and took a step back as Alasdair settled her against his chest.

He studied her little face. Rosebud mouth, blinking blue eyes. Her cheeks were round and ruddy, but her skin was so flawless. New, like she was.

Perfect.

His breath caught.

"She's mine."

"I surely hope so." The headwoman laughed and patted his stubbled cheek. "Go to your wife; she's anxious to see you. You lot," Morag addressed his brothers and the duke, "disperse. I'm sure we can find a meal in the hall. No doubt Lady Cera and my lasses have done us well." She kept nagging the knights and Lord Jorrin—as she was prone to do—but her orders faded, male groans and bootsteps following.

The world narrowed as Alasdair couldn't look away from his daughter.

Her expression was tight, as if she was irritated.

He lifted her, pressing a kiss to her tiny forehead and smiling when her little face relaxed. Beauty and innocence stole his heart. Just like her mother had.

Elissa flashed a tired smile when he carried their child to her. "Alas, are you crying, my love?" Her hand was on her bondmate's large head as he sat plastered to the large bedframe, but she must've sent him a mental command, because the wolf soon settled by the hearth on a rug, in front of a warm fire. He didn't look happy about it, though.

"Nay." Alasdair tried to grunt, but couldn't. "Perhaps," he finally whispered.

"Come here." She reached for him.

He took a seat on the bed next to her, but didn't give the baby over just yet.

"My lady, do you need anything else?" Phasia politely interrupted.

"Nay, but thank you, Phasia," Elissa said.

Alasdair inclined his head when she curtseyed, then his gaze found Lord Dagget, who was jotting his daughter's birth record in the Durroc family ledger. "Lord Tristan."

The healer smiled and set down the quill. "Aye?"

"Thank you. So much."

The younger man crossed the room and nodded. "Delivering babes is always a happy part of my duties. You're welcome, Alas."

Alasdair set his daughter in his wife's arms and stood, clasping Lord Tristan's forearm. His throat was thick as the healer returned the gesture.

Everyone at Castle Aldern was as much his family as Elissa and their new daughter. Today—and what they'd all done for him and Elissa proved that. Why it'd taken him so long to realize it made him a fool. Especially after Lord Jorrin's speech before he'd gone to Dalunas.

Lord Tristan's hazel eyes were warm when their gazes locked. As if he could read Alasdair's mind. "Well, I'll leave you three to get acquainted." He looked at Elissa. "You should be completely healed, but let me know if anything hurts. I don't anticipate any issues."

His wife nodded, and the healer slipped from the room. Phasia followed shortly, her arms full of supplies.

When Alasdair sat again, he was closer to his two lasses.

Elissa tilted her face up, asking for a kiss. He obliged, caressing her cheek as they parted.

"I love you," Alasdair whispered.

"I love you, too. And I already love her more than anything."

They looked down at their daughter. Together.

"Me, too."

"All these months, I thought for sure she was a lad."

He chuckled. "You could've let Lord Tristan tell you. I know he offered several times."

She flashed a lopsided grin that washed away the fatigue on her beautiful face. "Nay. I was sure."

"Ah. Now I get to say something I don't often utter about you, love."

Elissa arched an eyebrow. "What's that?"

"You were wrong."

She giggled and looked down at the perfection between them. "I don't care."

"Neither do I." He cupped the baby's head, caressing her downy hair. "She looks so much like you, Elissa."

"I see you in her face."

Emotion caught in his throat. Love enveloped him. "My two lasses."

Her smile was tender when their gazes brushed again, but neither could stop looking at their child. "What shall we call her?" Elissa broke the companionable silence.

"I don't know. We only talked of lad's names."

"Well, we can't call her Emery, as planned."

"Or Exton."

Elissa rolled her eyes. "How long are you going to rub it in?"

Alasdair chuckled. "As long as I can, love." He leaned in and kissed the glare off of her face.

"That makes it better," she whispered.

"Good, because there's more where that came from."

"Focus, Alas. Name your daughter."

"Awfully domineering for someone who's supposed to be exhausted from giving birth."

"Lord Tristan healed me fully."

"Fully, fully. As in…"

She smacked his chest, but giggled. "Of course you're worried about making love already. My body can, aye. But a newborn lass will keep *us* tired, from what I hear."

"As long as we're together, I can handle anything."

Elissa's expression didn't just soften. It melted, and her eyes went misty. Mischief whined but they both ignored him. "I love you, Alas."

Alasdair cupped her face, wiping a tear away as soon as it formed. "I know. Forever."

She grinned and glanced back down at their tiny lass. "Hmmm, my love, what's your name?"

"Kenna. After my mother." His voice cracked but he didn't care. Alasdair looked at the love of his life, then at their daughter. "Her name is Kenna."

"I love it." She had tears streaming down her cheeks when they made eye-contact.

"Why're you crying then?" He went for a tease, but his question was too thick.

"Happy tears." Her magic rippled around them, but it was answered by more magic.

They looked at Kenna together, as a warm wind rippled through the air. "Was that…?"

"I think so." Elissa's tone held wonder.

"She's like you, love."

His wife nodded, her gorgeous hazel eyes wide. "I felt magic as she grew inside me, but she's hours old, Alas. That was…"

"Powerful," they said at the same time.

Elissa's brow furrowed.

"Don't worry, you'll train her and I'll protect her. My brothers and Lucan will protect her, too. No one like Drayton will even get close to her."

Worry still creased her brow. Finally Elissa nodded and their collective gaze regarded tiny Kenna.

Elissa loved him. Trusted him to keep their child safe. Love welled up. "Thank you," Alasdair whispered, cupping her face with one hand.

"For what?" she returned in the same low whisper.

"Everything. Elissa, you've given me everything."

She flashed another smile. "Everything you never knew you wanted."

"Needed, lass. Needed. You and Kenna are everything I never knew I *needed*. When I think of the turns I wasted—"

Elissa rested her fingertip against his lips. "Nay, love. Not wasted. You were waiting for me."

Alasdair grinned and kissed her. "I guess so."

"I know so."

Kenna fussed and their gazes locked.

"She's just hungry." She gave him the baby and opened the ties at the neck of the fresh sleeping gown the headwomen had dressed her in.

Kenna wailed, and the thick drapes rustled with her magic.

He rocked her, but his daughter wouldn't be comforted until Elissa took her back, nestling her close to her bared flesh.

Alasdair watched with fascination as their daughter settled at her breast and latched on. Emotion caught in his throat all over and leaned down, kissing her tiny forehead. Then he slid his arm around Elissa and held her as she nursed their daughter.

His heart was full to bursting, like it would be for the rest of his life.

The End

About the Author

Bestselling, award winning author of romantic suspense and epic fantasy romance, C.A. loves to dabble in different genres. If it's a good story, she'll write it, no matter where it seems to fit!

She's a hopeless romantic and always will be. Risking it all for Happily Ever After is what she lives by!

C.A. is originally from Ohio, but got to Texas as soon as she could. She's happily married and has a bachelor's degree in Criminal Justice.

She works with kids when she's not writing.

WEBSITE: http://www.caszarek.com
BLOG: http://www.caszarekwriter.blogspot.com/
TWITTER: https://twitter.com/caszarek
FACEBOOK: http://www.facebook.com/caszarek
NEWSLETTER SIGNUP: http://blogspot.us7.list-manage.com/subscribe?u=296abc5983ebc51c1d4d0972b&id=fb22ce93be
GOODREADS:https://www.goodreads.com/author/show/5815085.C_A_Szarek
EMAIL: ca@caszarek.com

CPSIA information can be obtained
at www.ICGtesting.com
Printed in the USA
FSOW01n1402150216
16907FS

9 781941 151112